LOVE, FOREVER MORE

"That first time I saw you I knew we would meet again," Lucas whispered huskily.

"But that was a full year ago," Kendra murmured. "If that first time meant so much to you why didn't you search for me? I had dreamed . . . I had hoped . . ."

Unable to hold back any longer, Lucas swept her into his arms and tasted the sweet jasmine of her lips. He knew it was a dangerous thing to do but he had hungered for this beauty for so long.

Kendra laced her arms around Lucas's neck, sighing shakily as she felt his fingers caress her flesh. She leaned her body into his, explored his hard muscles with her delicate hands. And when she sought his mouth, longing for the ecstasy of his fierce, fiery kiss, she knew there was no turning back—she would love him today, tomorrow and forever . . .

BOOK YOUR PLACE ON OUR WEBSITE AND MAKE THE READING CONNECTION!

We've created a customized website just for our very special readers, where you can get the inside scoop on everything that's going on with Zebra, Pinnacle and Kensington books.

When you come online, you'll have the exciting opportunity to:

- View covers of upcoming books
- Read sample chapters
- Learn about our future publishing schedule (listed by publication month *and author*)
- Find out when your favorite authors will be visiting a city near you
- Search for and order backlist books from our online catalog
- Check out author bios and background information
- Send e-mail to your favorite authors
- Meet the Kensington staff online
- Join us in weekly chats with authors, readers and other guests
- Get writing guidelines
- AND MUCH MORE!

**Visit our website at
http://www.zebrabooks.com**

Elusive
Ecstasy

Cassie Edwards

Zebra Books
Kensington Publishing Corp.

http://www.zebrabooks.com

ZEBRA BOOKS are published by

Kensington Publishing Corp.
850 Third Avenue
New York, NY 10022

First Printing: July, 1984
10 9 8 7 6 5 4 3 2

Printed in the United States of America

To Red and Christine Kirtright,
my neighbors and dear friends

Oh lift me from the grass!
  I die, I faint, I fail!
Let thy love in kisses rain
  On my lips and eyelids pale.
My cheek is cold and white, alas!
  My heart beats loud and fast,
Oh! press it close to thine again,
  Where it will break at last.

—Shelley

Chapter One

Nevada . . . 1875

For so long now, all twenty-year-old Kendra Carpenter had seen from the Central Pacific Railway train window had been miles and miles of sunburned nothingness. But things were slowly changing before her eyes as she kept them transfixed on the passing land. Where sagebrush had rolled over the vast, sandy desert like an endless gray sea, flowers of cactus and yucca were now adding splashes of color to the setting. And as she lifted her eyes upward, she took in a sudden breath of air, when, through the haze of noonday heat, she caught sight of a line of snow-capped mountains in the distance.

"We're almost there," she said in a muted whisper. "Surely those are the mountains that Aaron wrote about. I believe he said the Sierras."

She felt her first stirrings of excitement for days. The boredom of the long journey had squelched her first anxious moments on the train. When the landscape had turned scorched and tedious and the heat had diffused

7

through the side walls of the train to engulf Kendra as though she were sitting close to an overheated potbellied stove, she had let misgivings of what lay ahead begin to plague her with sorrowful doubts.

But now her earlier dreams of exciting new adventures on land her brother had purchased and developed were almost a reality. Aaron had promised her her pick of wild mustangs to have tamed for her own personal horse. This promise would open the way for her plans for freedom. A horse . . . a horse that had been free all of its life . . . would carry her to freedom as well.

Kendra had always felt stifled living the life of the elite in Boston. Too much had been demanded of her. The proper attire, the proper walk, the proper everything! On this open range of Nevada she would wear blue jeans . . . she would carry her own six-shooters. . . .

"Good Lord, Kendra, where have your thoughts taken you?" Kendra's nineteen-year-old brother, Seth, spoke suddenly from beside her. "Your face is flushed scarlet."

Blinking her eyes, Kendra glanced downward, seeing the white, lace-trimmed organdy dress, the "proper" attire for a member of the influential Boston Carpenter family. For a moment there she had been on that horse, sitting in a fancy saddle . . . dressed in tight blue jeans . . . feeling the wind against her face and through her long, flowing golden hair.

Kendra realized that most of the men on the train had approved of her beauty and daintiness, seeing her as the picture of womanhood and what all men would want in a wife. Wouldn't they have been shocked to have read her thoughts of only moments ago? In their eyes she was a tall and statuesque woman with blue eyes, soft features, and a voluptuous figure that had embarrassed her to the point of tears when she had been a young, innocent teenager.

"Kendra," Seth demanded. "Is it the heat? Should I get you a glass of water?"

Kendra untied the velvet strings of her straw hat and lifted her hat from her head. She began fanning her face with it, enjoying the breeze she was creating. She gave Seth a quick glance, tilting her chin a bit. "Seth, when Aaron left for Nevada he left you behind to look after me and Holly," she said, now looking opposite her, giving Aaron's wife, Holly, a lingering look. Holly looked too pale. The heat was most certainly getting to her. She even looked as though she might faint. Though Holly was five years older than Kendra, it didn't make her any stronger. But Kendra would worry about her later. She looked back toward Seth.

"As I was saying," she continued. "It wasn't necessary for Aaron to leave you behind to see to me and Holly. I'm quite capable of taking care of myself. But as for Holly . . ."

Seeing the glassiness in Holly's green eyes, Kendra moved quickly to sit beside her. She clasped one of Holly's hands, feeling the clamminess of the palm. "Holly, are you all right?" she asked, now fanning Holly with her hat.

The midnight black of Holly's hair peeped from around and beneath her dainty lace-trimmed bonnet. Her cheeks were a bit hollow, and they became more so as she pursed her red lips. She placed her free hand to her bosom and ran a handkerchief between the cleavage that was partially exposed, edged by a crisp cut of organdy,

9

designed at the bodice and the dress's fully gathered skirt with tiny purple iris and green foliage on a white background.

"How much longer, Kendra?" Holly whispered. "And is Nevada always this hot? What will I do if it is? I can hardly bear this terrible heat."

"It's just the train," Kendra reassured. "It's not a very pleasant ride, and there's no breeze through these tiny windows." She gave Seth a disapproving look. "And Seth, your cigar smoke adds to the discomfort. It's such a nasty habit. Will you please snuff it out?"

Though Kendra disapproved of Seth's cigar, she highly approved of his new outfit—blue jeans, cotton shirt with fancy, red embroidery work gracing its front, and the highly polished cowboy boots on his feet. Soon! Soon *she* would be dressed that way! She would probably have to fight both Seth and Aaron for approval but in the end she would win. She smiled smugly to herself. She always won with them.

"A Cuban cigar and the pleasure I derive from it is never a nasty habit," Seth sighed. He jerked his head in a jovial laugh. "Almost the same as a beautiful woman," he added. His bushy mustache the color of sand twitched as his blue eyes took on a distant stare from the window. "Ah, now there's a subject I am in deep wonder of. I've heard there are some colorful wenches in the dance halls of Reno and Virginia City."

"Seth!" Kendra scolded, yet she was silently amused. She knew that he, like her, carried deep within him the love of adventure and freedom. And he had acquired an early reputation of teasing the girls of Boston. There had even been gossip of girls giving themselves freely to him, lured into his clutches by his stoutness, and the muscles

10

abounding in his shoulders and upper arms. His thick sandy hair and bushy sideburns and his tallness added to his allure. But his jovial manner and sense of humor had always been his finest qualities as far as Kendra was concerned. She had always loved his bear hugs, and, though she would never admit to it, she had depended on him this past year since their mother's death.

"Speaking of Reno and Virginia City," Seth said, flicking ashes from his cigar. "I hear tell of much gambling going on there. I wonder if Father may possibly have heard. Maybe he . . ."

Kendra settled back against the plump cushion of the seat and once more began fanning herself with her hat, noticeably annoyed. "Seth, I do not wish to speak of that man," she murmured. "Why must I keep reminding you that he does not deserve our thoughts? He deserted us all. Many years ago. If not for Mother's inherited wealth, what would have become of us? A woman raising three children without a man?"

She shook her head bitterly. "No. Do not speak of him to me. As far as I'm concerned, we have no father. He was a gambling man, with only one thing on his mind. Must I say any more?"

Seth crossed his thick legs and began tapping his fingers on the leather of a boot. "He just probably didn't like being confined inside the four walls of a building, or being a banker," he argued.

Kendra's eyes flashed in liquid blues. "Ha! That's the worst place for a gambler," she spat. "How tempting it must have been." Her carefully plucked eyebrows narrowed. "Maybe he was even stealing from the bank," she said in a near-whisper. Then she shook her head and fanned herself harder. "I truly don't wish to talk about

11

him, Seth. Please speak of something else."

"All right," Seth said, blowing billows of cigar smoke from between his wide lips. "Let's talk about our big brother Aaron. He seems to have managed well enough since Mother's death. At first, when he mentioned leaving Boston, I was a bit concerned. But when he began telling us what he could accomplish with our inheritance by going to Nevada, I could only see a chance for myself becoming wealthy in my own right."

Stopping the movement of her hat, Kendra leaned a bit forward. "What do you mean? What's swirling around inside that head of yours, Seth?"

Seth uncrossed his legs and placed his hands behind his head to rest against them. "I'm going to work in the silver mines," he said matter-of-factly.

Kendra blanched. "What . . . ?" she gasped. "Seth, you can't be serious. It's too dangerous. And you don't have to do such work. Aaron says he's invested in quite a spread of land. Even on this train there are some purebred dairy cows going to Aaron to put on our land. With all the horses he's already handling, I am sure he will need your help."

"Yeah. The Circle C Ranch," Seth grumbled. "C for Carpenter. But not *this* Carpenter. I've walked in my brother's *and* sister's shadows long enough. I will be working in a mine. Nothing you say will change my mind."

"I know how stubborn you are," Kendra sighed. "And I do understand, Seth. If I were a man I would even be tempted myself."

Holly gasped at Kendra's side and Seth doubled over with laughter at Holly's reaction.

"But you must watch who you associate with, Seth," Kendra quickly added. "I've heard that many Rebels are among the men who have settled in those mining towns. We've been strictly for Lincoln, and with Aaron's having been an officer in the Union Army . . . well, you know, words between the North and South can still cut as sharply as razors."

"Yeah. I know what you mean," Seth growled. "I wonder if feelings will ever ease between the North and South. But at least we have one thing in our favor."

"And what's that, Seth?" Kendra asked, straightening the skirt of her dress as she squirmed to try and circulate the stale air around her.

"Nevada itself," Seth boasted. "It's called the 'battle-born state.' Remember? Aaron wrote all about it in one of his letters. He was proud to have bought land in a state that had worked so hard for the Union cause."

"But he also said that during the war many men were Southern sympathizers and secessionists," Kendra argued.

"But Nevada, out of her tiny population, sent more men to the Union Army than were sent by either California or Oregon, the only states at that time west of Kansas," Seth argued back. "And then, it's because of Lincoln that Nevada got the name the 'battle-born state.' He recognized that Nevada was sending millions in gold and silver to the U.S. Treasury for the support of the Northern cause. He knew this gold and silver could make it possible for the government to maintain sufficient credit to continue the war for the Union, so he moved quickly in passing legislation to form this new state called Nevada."

"I know all of this," Kendra sighed. "I believe you've strayed from the point I was trying to make, little brother."

Seth flipped his cigar butt from the small space of the

13

opened window. "I hear you, Kendra," he laughed. "Loud and clear, *big* sister." He laughed again. "Damn that brother of ours. I don't know how he does it." He clapped a thick hand against a boot as he once more crossed his legs. "In one year he's managed to become president of a score of mining corporations and has started several Nevadan banks and acquired over one hundred thousand acres of land."

Holly, breathing hard, and even paler, spoke her quiet piece. "And he wrote that the ranch house that he had built is something akin to heaven," she said. "Glory be that he wasn't stretching the truth. After this train, I need something akin to heaven to pick my spirits up again. I feel that I shall never feel well again. My insides are quivering so and my head is one mass of throbbing."

"Poor Holly," Kendra said, touching Holly gently on the cheek. "We should be arriving in Reno soon. A short while ago I did see the first signs of the mountains that Aaron wrote of. Aaron said that once we caught sight of them we'd not have too many hours of travel left ahead of us."

"Mount Davidson," Seth said dreamily. "Among those lines of mountains can be found the mountain where it all began . . . where the Comstock Lode was first discovered. Then the rest is history. God, I'd have loved to have been there to have seen those very first rich veins of silver."

"Just don't expect to see anything now to match it," Kendra warned. "Aaron is already worrying about the mines being overworked."

"And, Seth, Aaron even wrote of the dangers of sulphuric hot springs that curse the silver mines," Holly worried aloud. "You surely cannot be serious about working in those hellish pits of underground rivers of heat."

Seth straightened his back and flexed his muscles. "Nothing can hurt me," he boasted. "You'll see. I *will* become rich in my own right. I'm not afraid of a bit of hard work, or the heat I'm going to find underground."

Kendra gave him a worried glance, fearing his smugness this time. In Boston, he didn't have much endangering him when he took off on a round of reckless adventures of the kind that suited his makeup. But the tales Kendra had heard of the wild, woolly West . . . of outlaws, rustlers, wild cowboys and gunfighters . . . made her a bit afraid for her brother. And now, she even had the dangers of the mines to add to her list of worries! Seth *did* believe he was invincible! But didn't all men?

Shrugging, Kendra let her gaze move back to the window, feeling the anxiety building inside her. Surely it wouldn't be much longer now! And thank heavens for trains. How unbearable it would have been to have been forced to make such a journey by stagecoach. Poor Holly. She most surely wouldn't have survived such a trip. Holly was much too delicate. And boredom had set in this past year for her with the absence of her husband. But soon that would be remedied. All of the Carpenters' lives would be set straight again once they reached Reno and the Circle C Ranch!

Silence overcame Kendra, Seth, and Holly as the train rambled on, until the conductor began to make his way down the aisle bellowing: "Reno! Next stop! Reno!"

Kendra's heart began to race. She looked toward the Sierra range towering to the west and the desert on the other three sides. Buttes, mesas, and smaller mountain ranges broke the surface of the region. Then she saw it.

15

The first sight of Reno. She leaned closer to the window, aghast at what she saw. Aaron hadn't prepared her for this! She had expected Reno to be different from Boston from having read so much about western towns in books and magazines, but she hadn't expected that Aaron would settle in a town of this size. Why, it was hardly a town at all.

"Oh, my God," Holly groaned, also catching sight of the town that Aaron had chosen for them to be a part of. "What was Aaron thinking? Why, I refuse to even take one step from this train. We'll die in this isolated sandtrap of a town!"

Seth reached for one of Holly's hands. "Now, Holly," he crooned. "Get ahold of yourself. Do you want Aaron to see you upset the first time he sees you after a full year of separation?"

Holly placed her fingertips to her brow, feigning light-headedness. "Aaron should have known better," she whispered. "I'll never be happy here. Never. If I was bored and frustrated in Boston, what will I be here?"

"You'll be with Aaron," Kendra said flatly. "He should remove all boredom from your life, should he not? Your reason for being bored lately was because of your loneliness for Aaron, was it not?"

Removing her hand slowly from Seth's grasp, Holly reached for her purse to place it on her lap. She evaded Kendra's accusing glance, wondering if Kendra had heard about her one weakness with a man this past year. But surely not. The affair had been very short-lived. "Yes, Kendra," she murmured. "Aaron is what I need. I'm sure I'll be all right."

The screeching of the train's wheels against the tracks and the abruptness of its coming to a stop jolted Kendra almost from the seat, causing her to forget her momentary doubts of Holly. Instead, she secured her hat, retying its green velvet bows beneath her chin. She then reached for her purse, somewhat apprehensive now about her future in this town of false-fronted buildings. Only a few brick buildings broke the monotony of saloons, gambling houses, and various other stores.

"So this is Reno, what is said to be the crossroad, the trading center, the watering hole, the meeting place of the state of Nevada," Kendra sighed, slumping her shoulders a bit.

"Seems that way," Seth said, twisting the tip of his mustache between two fingers. "Interesting, isn't it? Almost as interesting as how the town came by its name. Chosen by lottery, so Aaron says. By slips out of a hat by the first railroad men. They needed a name for this new railroad station. Shorter names were preferred. All short names were placed in a hat and drawn. Chose the name Reno, the name taken from a General Jesse Reno, a Virginia loyalist who fell in the battle of South Mountain."

"They actually named this town Reno to honor the man?" Holly murmured.

"No. No connection with Nevada," Seth said, shaking his head. "This Reno fella was never even in Nevada. The men merely used his name because it was easy for train conductors to call and to spell."

"Makes as much sense as us being here," Holly sighed.

"Whether it makes sense or not we *are* here," Kendra said, holding onto her hat as she rose from the seat. "And since we are, let's hurry outside and see if Aaron is awaiting our arrival. I don't know about you two, but I've missed that brother of mine."

17

Kendra moved out into the aisle. She felt the heat from the people pushing against her as she drew closer to the door. Her heart raced. She had already forgotten her doubts about the town and was now once again remembering what truly awaited her. The open range. Horses. Freedom.

The air that blew against her face when she finally stepped to the door wasn't refreshing but hot and dry, almost stifling. She blew a stray golden curl from her lips as the breeze whipped steadily against her. Then she took her first step from the train and began looking through the mingling crowd, looking for the familiar face of Aaron. She couldn't wait to rush into his arms, to tell him how much she had missed him. But something else grabbed her quick attention. It was a buckboard wagon backed up to a boxcar with a beautiful Indian woman sitting on the seat holding the reins of a horse. Supplies were being loaded from the train onto the buckboard. And sitting tall in a saddle on a magnificent golden-colored mustang next to this buckboard was a man dressed in tight blue jeans fitted with tight-fitting leather chaps. He wore a red plaid cotton shirt, with a red bandana neckerchief at his neck.

Kendra couldn't help but let her gaze wander further over him, seeing his cowhide, high-heeled boots and six-shooters in a fancy holstered gunbelt at his hips, and the wide brim of his sombrero, which was partly shadowing his face. He, for sure, was a true specimen of a cowboy!

But this fact wasn't the reason for her becoming quickly unnerved. It was the commanding force of his eyes. Suddenly they were upon her, appraising her in return. She could feel the heat rise to her cheeks as the steel gray of his eyes roamed slowly down over her and

18

back up again, stopping momentarily where the swell of her bosom rose and fell in unison with her rapid heartbeat.

Then, when his eyes moved steadily on upward and met her wavering stare, she felt something akin to passion sweep through her.

"Kendra!" Seth scolded. "You're blocking the way. What on earth is holding you there? I thought you were the one anxious to see Aaron."

Kendra's fingers went to her throat, embarrassed. She glanced back at Seth and smiled sheepishly. "It was my foot," she lied. "The silly thing. It had fallen asleep from sitting so long. I was hardly able to even get this far on the dead thing. But I think it will be all right now."

"Then get on with you," Seth growled, glancing back across his shoulder at the angry-faced passengers who stood behind them, waiting.

When Kendra turned to look the gray-eyed stranger's way again, his back was to her, and he and his horse were moving away from the train next to the loaded, wobbly buckboard wagon.

Disappointment surged through Kendra, as she feared she'd never see him again. With a sinking heart she stepped down from the train, still not letting her eyes stray from this man. She couldn't help but see how broad-shouldered and thin-flanked he was, and thinking that on foot he would stand quite tall and lithe. Though their glances had in truth been only momentary, she thought she would never forget his face . . . his eyes . . . his sun-bronzed face with its majestic, chiseled features . . . his dark sideburns . . . and the dark arch of his eyebrows. She had never seen such a handsome, virile man! And would she ever again?

"Kendra! Honey! Over here..." Aaron shouted through the crowd.

Kendra stood on tiptoe, now seeing the shine of his bald head towering over everything else around her. "Aaron, oh, Aaron!" she shouted in return. She lifted the skirt of her dress into her arms and made a mad dash for him. But her thoughts wouldn't hold on Aaron. Kendra was again remembering the way the gray-eyed stranger had looked so boldly at her, especially at her voluptuous swell of breasts. A small smile broke out on her face. Yes, he had been as taken by her as she had by him. Surely, they would meet again....

Chapter Two

Reno . . . April, 1876

Breakfast had been served at the crack of dawn and
Kendra was in her bedroom fastening her gunbelt around
her narrow waist. When that chore was completed she
slipped her very own pearl-handled six-shooters into
their separate leather holsters, having finally convinced
Aaron that these were needed for protection against any
wild creature that she might come across while riding
alone on the range. So far her two worst enemies had
been a western diamond back rattler that had spooked her
horse one day, and Zeke, Aaron's chosen head wrangler.
Zeke, as shifty and ugly as he was ornery, had become
trouble for Kendra from the first day she had stepped
from Aaron's fancy carriage on her arrival from Boston
at the Circle C Ranch.

"Oh, how I loathe that low-down critter," she
whispered, then broke into a soft laugh, realizing that she
had picked up some cowboy lingo. That hadn't been hard
to do, with nearly one hundred hands in Aaron's employ.

She lifted her thick mass of golden hair and pinned it into a swirl atop her head, then placed her Stetson hat over it, marveling at her reflection in the mirror. She looked every bit the cowgirl she had dreamed of nightly during the year she had waited for Aaron to send for her. And what a commotion she had made that day she had gone into Reno to purchase her cowgirl attire! She could still see the women's faces now. . . .

When she had asked for a man's blue jeans . . . a pair to fit her . . . the women shopping in the general store had looked at her as though she had been the devil's advocate! Then when she had strutted from the small dressing room in the tight-fitted blue jeans, man's cotton shirt and high-heeled cowboy boots, the women had scurried from the store. Heads held together, they had feverishly gossiped amongst themselves about this new woman in town who was a disgrace because she so boldly had chosen to dress like a man!

Giggling, Kendra had then chosen a pair of pistols and fancy holsters and Stetson hat to complete her new western attire. But not to get the women's dander up any more than it already was, she had not since ventured into town unless she was attired as they were, leaving the open range for her more leisurely and freer mode of dress.

Placing her hands on her pistols and spreading her legs to look as threatening as possible, Kendra laughed. There was no denying that it was a woman dressed in these clothes. There was no way to hide the curves of her body beneath the tight-fitted jeans and the clinging cotton shirt, which she chose to leave unbuttoned halfway to her waist for the breeze to catch when she rode free on her horse. Even her hair hidden beneath the wide-

22

brimmed hat couldn't fool a body that it was a lady on horseback instead of a man. This ploy had been Aaron's idea when he had seen how determined she was to come and go as she pleased. But as much as Aaron had tried, he hadn't succeeded in quelling her independent, fiery spirit.

A knock on the bedroom door drew Kendra around. She grabbed her hat from her head and placed it on her bed.

"Kendra, it's Aaron," he said, his deep voice muted by the closed door. "Hon, are you decent? I'd like to speak with you before I leave for the train depot."

Kendra looked anxiously around the room, seeing her lacy chemise and discarded underthings tossed idly about. She had no real concern about neatness and often worried over any man who might get her as a wife. Would any man put up with her habits? Would ... *could* ... any man have the power to change her?

"I doubt that," she murmured to herself. "I've not yet seen a man I wish to even think of changing myself for."

Yet, somehow, she would suddenly recall, at the oddest times, a pair of commanding gray eyes. . . .

"Kendra!" Aaron persisted impatiently. "Surely you didn't go back to bed after breakfast. I've never known you to do that."

"I'm sorry, Aaron," she finally replied, dashing around the room, rescuing her things. "Give me a minute."

When she had first seen this bedroom, she had felt as though she hadn't left her mansion behind in Boston. Aaron had managed to have the best of their oak furnishings freighted from Boston to Reno, as he had gotten the best of everything for the rest of their spacious

23

ranch house, which lay in a mountain valley watered by melting snow. Over the plate glass of the bedroom windows, lace curtains were draped, and the walls were bedecked with leaf-covered wallpaper with a beige background, matching the carpet and the spread on Kendra's magnificent bed.

Tossing her gathered garments inside her wardrobe, Kendra closed it and leaned against it for a moment to catch her breath, then rushed to her bedroom door and opened it.

Aaron moved past her with wide, heavy strides, filling the room with his overpowering presence. He wore no battle scars from the Civil War, but his bald head suggested that he was aging. But that was a false presumption on most people's part, for, in truth, he was only thirty.

He usually wore a hat, since he was not particularly proud of what he had inherited from his mother's ancestors. His father most surely wasn't bald yet. The last time Aaron had seen his father, Stanford Carpenter, when his father had been forty, he had very proudly displayed a thick stand of blond hair.

When attending to duties besides those of the open range and ranching, as was the case this day, Aaron dressed expensively, in dark suits with silk scarves knotted at his throat. And he always wore high-heeled, highly polished cowboy boots and always carried one heavy pistol holstered at his right hip, hidden beneath his coat.

He towered over Kendra, an imposing figure with thick shoulders and an even thicker waist, and his washed-out-blue eyes traveled disapprovingly over her. He lifted a pudgy hand to his face, to tap his forefinger on the roundness of his cheek.

"Kendra, must I give a formal dinner party to give cause for you to change into something more appetizing?" he growled, setting his lips into a firm, straight line. "Day after day you wear those damned breeches. Soon you will even forget you *are* a lady."

"Please, Aaron," Kendra sighed, placing her fingers over the tops of her jean's rear pockets. "We've been through this before. It gets so tiresome." She heard the sound of carriage wheels at the front of the house and knew that it was Zeke bringing the carriage for Aaron.

"The new schoolteacher should be arriving today," she said. "Are you, alone, going to be the welcoming committee?"

"Yes. Seems that way, Kendra," Aaron said, going to the window. He pulled a curtain back and looked down from the second-story window as Zeke directed the horse and carriage to a hitching post.

Aaron then let the curtain drop back in place and turned to face Kendra. "It's still not too late for you to change your mind," he said. "You could go with me. This young man has the best of credentials. He might even be fit for more than teaching. He *is* single. He *is* a man of breeding. Seems there's not much of that among the cowhands you come in contact with each day around here."

"I'd rather you didn't try to play Cupid," Kendra said flatly. "You failed in Boston. So will you in Reno."

"I only want what's best for you. You know that," Aaron said, hurt swimming in his words and eyes.

"Oh, Aaron," Kendra said softly. She flew to him and reached her arms about his neck and placed a cheek against his shoulder. "I know you do. But, please. Let me take care of myself now. I'm no longer a teenager. I'm a woman. And my heart will warn me when I have found the right man."

She closed her eyes, trying to shut out those haunting gray eyes of the stranger she had seen that one day. But when the moment was upon her to remember, nothing would blot his handsomeness from her mind.

"Please be careful, Kendra," Aaron warned, pushing her gently away. He framed her face between his hands, caressing her chin with both thumbs. "The heart has been known to get many a man *and* many a woman into trouble. Out here, romance can be disguised by sheer loneliness. Remember that, Kendra."

"I will. . . ." she murmured, feeling very close to Aaron at that moment. He was her pillar of strength, as was Seth. But she persisted in not revealing such a weakness to them.

Aaron leaned a soft kiss to the tip of her tiny nose, then swung away from her and walked toward the door.

"Aaron, I thought you came to see me about something specific," Kendra said, rushing to his side. "Surely you didn't come just to warn me again about my clothes and about men. I can't believe you came to ask me to accompany you to the train station, either. What is it? Have you problems with Holly?"

Aaron gave her a sideways glance as he squeezed his fingers around the doorknob and paused before opening the door. His face had suddenly taken on a drawn, shadowy expression. "Holly *has* been behaving a bit strangely these past several months," he said thickly. "But nothing I can't handle."

"Then what, Aaron?" Kendra persisted, looking up into his eyes, reading trouble in their depths.

"It's gossip I've heard from some ranch hands," he

said, shifting his weight from foot to foot and squeezing the doorknob even harder, so much that his knuckles whitened from the grip.

"What sort of gossip?" Kendra asked, eyes wide. "What could upset you so? You know those men. They talk about everything and everybody. They're bored. They don't get into town enough."

"Enough to hear of a new gambler in town . . ."

Kendra's heart palpitated and her face paled. She turned on her heel and sauntered away from Aaron, head bent a bit. "A gambler, you say?" she whispered.

Aaron went to her and gripped her shoulders to move her slowly around to face him. "Yes . . ." he said. "A gambler. He's putting money into a new gaming house. Seems he's planning to stay a spell in this town."

"There are many gamblers," Kendra murmured, but her throat had gone dry with the thought of her father. She hadn't seen him since she was ten. Even then she hadn't seen much of him. Most of his evenings had been spent away from home. It was years later that she had learned where he had spent those times. It hadn't been with women, as she had always suspected . . . but with anyone who would play a game of chance with him. Gambling had been his one . . . and only . . . love.

"I know there are many gamblers," Aaron sighed, dropping his hands to his side. "As there are many towns that attract gambling men. I'm sure he's been to them all."

"So why do you think it can be Father in *this* town? In Reno? Why now?"

"Because of Reno's reputation. *And* because this man fits Father's description."

"He surely has aged. His description would not be

27

what it used to be. Did you ask the hands what this man's name might be?"

"Yes. I did that."

"And . . . ?"

Aaron's voice cracked as he spoke. "Blackie," he mumbled. "Blackie. Some damn name, isn't it?"

"Blackie . . . ?" Kendra said softly. "My God, Aaron. It can't be Father. That isn't his name."

Aaron licked his lips and ran a hand over the shine of his bald head. "Kendra, for Christ's sake, that's this gambler's nickname," he growled. "Short for blackjack, because this gambler's specialty is blackjack. Christ, Kendra, don't you remember?"

Then he shook his head. "No. You wouldn't. You were too small," he murmured. He took one of Kendra's hands in his and squeezed it affectionately. "Our father was known for his game of blackjack."

"Oh, yes . . ." she whispered. "Now I remember your telling me that." She swallowed hard. "So you believe it is Father, do you?"

She had never revealed to Aaron that her father had shown her how to play the game of blackjack when they had been alone. If she had the need, she knew that she could even play the game now!

"When I have the time, I'll check it out," Aaron grumbled.

"Soon?"

"I don't know. . . ." Aaron said thickly. "I'll probably put it off until the curiosity kills me. What in hell would I say to the man if I *did* find he was our father? Say 'Hi, Dad? How are the roulette wheels treating you today?' What else would there be to talk about?"

Kendra went to Aaron and hugged him tightly. "I

28

don't know," she said, sighing. "I know one thing for sure, though. *I'm* not going in search of him. I hate the man. I simply hate him for deserting us."

"Well, for me, I must run into Reno for a much different reason," Aaron said, kissing her nose again. He reached for her Stetson hat and placed it on her head, tipping the front brim of it up. "Don't you get into too much mischief while I'm gone. Do you hear?"

"You talk as though you'll be gone ages," Kendra said, repositioning her hat. "Reno is only an hour's drive away. You should be home in no time flat. Are you bringing this man home for the evening?"

"No. He prefers to get settled in the boardinghouse where I've managed to get him a room."

"And which one is that?"

"Dora Mae's. You know. The best in town."

"Ha!" Kendra retorted. "I've heard a few of those rooms are being used by . . . uh . . . well . . . how would you call those ladies with the scarlet bloomers that drop to the tune of a piece of silver?"

Aaron's face blanched and his eyes widened. "Kendra!" he growled. "Such a thing to say. Dora Mae's is a respected place."

Kendra giggled as she posed before the mirror. "If you say so, big brother," she said. "If you say so."

"Don't wander far today, Kendra."

She swung around. "I'm riding out to the new schoolhouse," she said anxiously. "I'm going to check the supplies. Things like that."

"Don't stay long. That's a pretty good distance from here to that school."

Kendra's white teeth sparkled as she smiled coyly. "I've got these for protection," she said, patting the six-shooters on each hip.

Aaron's eyes rolled upward as he emitted a loud groan. "God . . ." he grumbled and turned and walked from the room.

Kendra knew that he still disapproved of the pistols. She had never so much as even touched a pistol in Boston let alone actually had her own to shoot at her free will. Aaron had worried that she might show up one day with one, maybe two toes missing. But her daily practicing had made her quite skillful and had given her the confidence she needed to not care what Aaron or anyone else thought of her wearing pistols. At least *she* knew that she was prepared to defend herself. She had shot the head from that western diamond back rattlesnake with one careful aim! To her the pistols meant even more freedom. They gave her courage to go where she darn well pleased.

"I may even go in search of my father myself, after all," she whispered. "And when I go into Reno for *that*, I will *not* be wearing a dress. . . ."

Hearing the carriage moving away from the house, Kendra went to the window and watched it, still in awe of the money Aaron had spent on the family carriage and its accessories. It was the finest, with plush leather seats, and both the carriage lamps and the stock of Aaron's whip were encrusted with gold. Not only were the horses shod with silver shoes, but the harness was of silver.

Aaron sat tall and proud on the seat, sporting his fancy Stetson hat and commanding a majestic, soft-colored stallion on its way. And when Aaron was only a speck on the horizon, Kendra seized the opportunity to get her own plans in motion.

The house was quiet as she rushed down the staircase and on into the parlor. She knew that Seth was at the

Con-Virginia mine, having now been underground for two days and nights without seeing daylight. He had quickly learned that the miners were kept underground for days on end, even for a week, near the underground river of heat. This regulation was enforced by the owners so the miners could not tell their relatives or friends if anything rich had been struck. If information reached the surface, it might cause stock to go the wrong way at the wrong time for the "silver kings" on top.

Since Aaron was now such a "king," Kendra had hoped for better conditions in the mines, especially with Seth's determination to keep working there. But one man like Aaron did not have the power to change anything. Kendra had begun to believe that maybe Aaron hadn't even tried to push for any such changes. He was slowly becoming like his father. He was a gambler, but Aaron was gambling with lives . . . not cards or dice.

"Surely Seth will soon give up his dream of becoming rich in his own right," Kendra worried aloud. "Doesn't he now realize that he can't get rich mining someone else's silver?"

She looked slowly around her, seeing the house owned by the wealthy Carpenters. It was all theirs equally, yet Kendra understood Seth's need to have something separately his that he could boast of having labored over and paid for with his own sweat and blood.

The elegantly furnished parlor was always well lighted by the glitter of green, cabbage-leaf wall sconces and a crystal chandelier dripping with pendants, which cast illumination on brocaded gilt chairs and velvet draperies. Gold-framed paintings in shades of the umber and purple and blues of the desert hung on the walls. White marble figures filled occasional niches, and in the library there

31

were leather-bound books, beautifully tooled in red, green, blue, and gold.

The two-story frame house was large and elegant with a fireplace in each room of prominence. A huge hall reached clear to the roof, and between the long hallway and the bedrooms on the second floor was another kind of room, an open space with potted plants and vines climbing up from the main floor below.

In the dining room the long oak table displayed the finest of china and crystal, and each place had a napkin ring that was a carefully crafted silver creature—rabbits, leprechauns, and deer.

"Yes, it is all unique," Kendra said. She grabbed her soft leather gloves from where she had discarded them on a table and began smoothing them on a finger at a time, now moving down a hallway that led past the kitchen. She hoped to find her horse saddled and readied.

"But somehow all this isn't even enough for Holly," she whispered. "She only seems happy when she's shopping in Reno."

Kendra didn't understand this. Reno lacked many shopping facilities. Going there once was surely enough.

The aroma of tea, spices and orange peel met Kendra as she walked past the door that led into the kitchen. Without stopping to look she knew that Hop Sing, the Carpenters' Chinese cook, was already toiling over the woodburning stove, preparing the evening meal. Sam Sing, his brother and the laundry servant, was probably in the laundry room plying his hot iron back and forth like a shuttlecock.

Stepping outside onto a veranda, Kendra spied her horse secured at a hitching rail. Kendra's blood always warmed at the sight of her tamed black and white spotted mustang that at one time had been a wild steed of the prairie. The first time she had seen him fighting for his freedom in the corral, with his flowing mane and eyes of fire, it had been love at first sight.

But though Kendra had wanted him as hers with every rapid beat of her heart, it had saddened her to see the fight leave the horse as the cowhands worked with him for days upon end. The day that Kendra had been able to slip a bridle over the mustang's head, she hadn't felt the victorious one. A part of her ached to see the mustang fight back . . . at least one more time.

"There you are, my lovely Domino," Kendra said, rushing down the steps to her horse's side. She placed a cheek to the horse's mane and rubbed its nose affectionately.

"Domino, are you ready to seek a bit of freedom along with me this morning? Huh? Are you? We will let the wind speak to us today. We will inhale the breath of the mountain streams. You and I, we will be a part of nature, if only for a short while."

"Talkin' to that horse again, I see," Zeke said suddenly from beside Kendra.

Kendra had heard his long Spanish spurs jangling way before he had spoken, knowing he was there, but she had hoped he would pass on by and leave her be. But as always, he persisted in annoying her.

She turned around and glared at him, hating his craggy voice, but, even more, hating his face, which was mostly hidden behind a heavy covering of red whiskers and long, shaggy sideburns. He was tall and stout and wore tight-fitted jeans and a blue flannel shirt and a bandana. A huge bowie knife was thrust into one of his boots, and six-shooters hung from his belt.

"It's none of your concern what I am doing," Kendra hissed, blushing a bit beneath his steady stare. His dark, penetrating eyes were appraising her, especially where her shirt lay half buttoned, exposing too much to this man of no morals.

Kendra's hands automatically went to her shirt and pulled it together in front.

"Saw Aaron leave," Zeke said, smiling crookedly.

"So?" Kendra dared.

"Means we could go somewheres alone," he said, leaning down into her face. "Just placed some mighty soft hay in the barn. We could have us some fun there. It'd be kind a interestin' takin' men's breeches off'n a woman."

Kendra stiffened her back. She raised her hand and slapped him a hard blow across the face. "You keep your filthy mouth closed, do you hear?" she fumed. She swung herself quickly into her saddle and clucked to Domino as she snapped the horse's reins.

"I'll get you for this!" Zeke yelled after her.

Kendra gave him a victorious look over her shoulder, amused at the way he was rubbing his whiskers, as though she had truly inflicted pain there. "Don't threaten me, Zeke," she shouted. "One of these days, you will do that one time too many. Aaron would love to know about your dirty mind. Don't you think so?"

She turned her head forward, laughing. But inside, she was a bit shaky. She knew that if he ever chose to take full advantage of her, he could succeed in doing so. Working with horses both day and night built muscles in a man and Zeke had many years of experience at doing just that already behind him.

"But he wouldn't dare," Kendra whispered to herself.

34

"If I didn't manage to put a bullet in his gut, Aaron would, for sure."

So, feeling more confident, she quickly forgot Zeke and began enjoying her ride on Domino. Beyond her spread the corrals, the barn, the grain shed, the blacksmith shop—all the accessories of a great ranch. The quarters for the cowhands and the mess cabin stood far from the ranch house, and from it extended a line of small bunkhouses, each with fireplaces and two bunks.

The pasture was dotted with horses and colts. Kendra could see a long string of cattle moving up toward the corrals, and she was proud for Aaron. His dream of raising purebred dairy cows had become a reality, though he had been warned against it in this rugged range country.

New calves followed their mothers. It was time for their ears to be cropped or branded with the Circle C Ranch's own special mark—a "C" in a circle.

She moved Domino on at a short, choppy trot. The sky overhead was a vast dome of blue, and the sun was warming with the advance of summer. Snows were still in the upper pockets of the mountains, but the lower, sunburned regions were already waterless and scorched.

But where Kendra rode, there was a grassland of open range, where only a short distance away the only movement was the stirring of the topmost tips of the sagebrush that were tender with the first growth of spring. Larkspur, shooting stars, and white violets dotted the meadows, and lizards with yellow backs slithered beneath plants and rocks. With the wind against her face she put Domino into a lope, stopping only when she caught sight of the newly built one-room schoolhouse. It was right ahead of her, with high stands of aging sagebrush not yet cut close to its front door.

"I never thought much about it before," she murmured. "But the schoolhouse *is* quite isolated."

She became keenly aware of Domino's sudden nervousness in the way he was snorting and jerking his head, appearing to be quite impatient to be gone from this place.

Kendra leaned forward and whispered into Domino's ear. "Domino, what is it?"

She looked cautiously about her, seeing nothing. She patted Domino affectionately, then proceeded on toward the school, now feeling a presence herself. . . .

Chapter Three

Kendra dismounted from Domino, then unbuckled the saddle cinch and lifted the saddle and saddle blanket from Domino's back. "That's the best I can do for you, boy," she said, placing these on the ground. She tied the reins to a hitching rail. "But at least you'll be more comfortable while you wait for me."

She gave Domino one last pat, then strolled up the steps that led directly into the school. The door creaked noisily as she pushed it open, and the smell of fresh lumber filtered upward into her nose. She smiled to herself, a bit proud. She could almost remember when each separate log had been nailed in place. Aaron had let her become involved in the planning of the schoolhouse and then in the actual building of it, since he had overseen its every inch of construction.

To impose even more of his power upon the community, Aaron had managed to be appointed superintendent of public instruction by the State School Board, to act as the executive officer of the board. This title affixed to a person gave him automatic respectability and leverage among the people. He had not only been given free rein to choose the site of the new schoolhouse but also in its construction, *and* in the hiring of the new schoolteacher.

"And he has done all these things well," Kendra whispered. "My older brother does amaze me at times."

Kendra looked toward the rows of benches that faced a podium at the front of the room. Behind the podium hung a huge map of the state of Nevada. The American flag was displayed in one corner of the room and the Nevada state flag in the opposite corner. Bookshelves had been built along one side wall and newly bound textbooks of all sizes and colors were stacked, ready for the first day of school to begin. Though it was spring instead of autumn, school would commence in one week. Too much time had already been lost to those children who had been without a school in this particular, mostly desolate area. Though it would take several hours for many of them to get to the schoolhouse, they would come. Book learning made character, and most children hungered for it, though the young boys would fuss and never admit it.

At the back of the room, close to the door, a potbellied stove had been installed and wood had already been piled next to it for those days when the weather suddenly became cold. Also, to help with the control of the temperature, Aaron had seen to it that many plate glass windows had been installed along both sides of the room. They could be opened or closed at will. It was an innovative convenience that he was really proud of.

Kendra began to move toward the front of the room, then stopped with a start when she heard noises from outside the building. She stiffened inside and turned slowly to face the door, having at first recognized the muffled sound of a horse's hoofbeats. But it was the other, ensuing sound that had given her a true start. It was a thud of sorts, right outside the door.

With hands positioned on her holstered pistols, Kendra moved breathlessly to the door. Aaron had warned her! Hadn't she even felt a presence earlier? Why had she ignored it? Suddenly she felt too alone and very scared. Her knees were weak and her heart was pounding, making her feel even crazily light-headed!

"I've got to get hold of myself," she whispered.

She swallowed hard and held her chin tautly high as she stepped quickly out on the top step to look slowly around her. Her fingers tightened on the handles of her pistols, but she saw nothing but Domino, some tall stands of green grass, and the even taller sagebrush plants dotting the land.

Squinting, Kendra let her gaze travel further, seeing nothing but vast land, occasional valleys, and the ever-present mountains in their magnificent splendor.

"Surely it wasn't my imagination," she whispered.

A low groan from somewhere close by made Kendra's heart skip a beat. With precision, she jerked both her pistols from their holsters, quivering inside for fear of what she might soon come face to face with. Even an injured man could be dangerous . . . especially . . . if he was an outlaw!

Another muffled groan caused Kendra's eyes to narrow and follow the sound. It seemed to be coming from behind a low, spreading stand of sagebrush. The bitter aroma rising from the sagebrush met her as she moved away from the steps. The sun beating down onto the plant caused the aroma of sage to be even stronger, making Kendra's nostrils flare and her throat burn. She stooped the closer she drew to it, and held in her breath a she peeked around a corner.

"My Lord . . ." she gasped, now seeing a small India boy stretched out on the ground, obviously torn wit pain as he held onto his right leg.

Thrusting her pistols back inside her holsters, Kendr hurried to the boy's side and knelt down over him. Tear were streaking his dust-covered, copper-colored face a he silently wept. When his eyes met Kendra's, she coul see a cold fear in their dark depths as he tried to inch bac away from her.

As far as she could guess, she assumed him to be o either the Piute or Washoe tribe, both of which had been victimized by the hordes of white people who ha swarmed over this land to become rich from the silver Most Indians had given in under pressure and ha deserted the only land they had known for generation upon generations, and had slunk away into the hills Kendra silently sympathized with the Indians of th Nevada region, but she had never had cause to hel them . . . until . . . now.

She placed a hand to the young boy's brow and tried t comfort him, all the while letting her gaze study hi injury, slowly realizing just what had to be done.

"I see you've had a bad fall from your horse," she sai softly. "I'm here to help."

Seeing the rapid rising and falling of his chest, Kendr realized that soft words weren't making him any les afraid of her. As his eyes studied her, she studied hin back, taking in his high cheekbones, full lips, square jaw and jet-black, wiry hair that hung long and straight to hi shoulders. The only thing he wore was a breechcloth The rest of him was quite exposed, and Kendra could tel that he was well fed, and she wondered how he had managed so well when other Indians hadn't.

Kendra removed her gloves and lowered her hands to run across the awkwardness of his right leg. She flinched when she felt the break in the bone. Yes, it was broken. Could . . . she . . . actually set it? He was in no condition to be taken anywhere for someone else to care for him.

She forced a smile. "What's your name?" she asked, once more caressing his brow. She had to get his confidence. What she had to do would be quite painful for him. If he hated and mistrusted her now, how might he feel about her once she had caused him the kind of torture that setting his leg would have to put him through?

The boy's eyes lowered and his lips became tight with silence.

"Surely you have a name," Kendra persisted softly. "Mine is Kendra. Please tell me what yours is. I would like to be your friend."

She paused and finally decided that she wasn't going to get one word out of him. What she must do would have to be done without his approval. She felt a sick feeling grab her at the pit of her stomach, never having treated a broken leg before. But she had watched Zeke do it. Many times. When ranch hands had been thrown from the wild mustangs and had busted a leg, Zeke had treated them right on the spot.

"I'm going to help you," Kendra said softly, leaning over him, shading his face from the direct rays of the sun. "I won't mean to, but while I am helping you, I will also be hurting you. But you look like a brave young man. I'm sure you can bear it. And I'll work as quickly as possible."

Again she examined his leg. It was broken above the knee and the lower section extended at an oblique angle. Inwardly trembling, she rose to her feet and went in search of sticks to use as splints. When she had enough she ripped strips of material from the lower half of her shirt and once again knelt down over him.

"It has to be done now," she said quietly. "You must brace yourself on your elbows, young man. And close your eyes, if that will help."

The boy continued to stare silently back at her, bravery showing in the set of his small jaw and the nonwavering of his eyes.

"Now . . ." Kendra said, yanking on his leg. He still made no sound, only gritted his teeth as she worked. She finally managed to see that she had done quite well.

"It's now over," she sighed. "I only have to wrap your leg and tie sticks to it so the ends of the bones won't separate. Then I can carry you into the schoolhouse out of the sun."

Relieved that the worst was over, Kendra acted quickly, worrying now about the welfare of the boy, since he was suddenly so flushed and feverish looking. She quickly tended to the leg, then lifted him into her arms and carried him inside and placed him on the floor.

"Now what?" she whispered to herself, looking at his eyes and the way they were growing heavy. "I must either take him to his village or back to the ranch. And I can do neither on my horse. I must go and get a buggy."

Kendra slumped to the floor and lifted his head onto her lap. "Young man, please talk to me," she encouraged. "You must tell me where your people are. Once I get my buggy, I can take you to them."

The boy still refused to speak. He just closed his eyes

and began lazily dozing.

That answers the question for me, she thought. If he won't tell me where to take him, I *must* take him to my own home.

She rose to her feet, now glancing downward at her shirt, seeing that her bosom was almost exposed because she had ripped her shirt for the bandages. She could just hear Zeke when he saw her. Why, he might even take after her and rape her after his sexual appetite had been aroused by the sight of her bare flesh.

But she would have to take that chance. She had to return home. Now. She couldn't wait for Aaron to return from Reno. She would return home, change shirts, then come back with a buggy and take the child home with her until the Indians missed him and came for him.

Taking one more fast glance downward at the small sleeping figure, she felt that haste was needed. She surely needed to get him settled comfortably back at the ranch before night set in. She wouldn't want to be stranded at the schoolhouse after dark. She knew that the small Indian boy probably wouldn't like that any better than she would. He probably knew more about the dangers of the night than she was aware of herself.

"And I'm afraid that he may have a temperature," she worried aloud.

Swinging around, she rushed back outside. Gathering her gloves up into her hands, she smoothed them onto her fingers, then hurriedly replaced her saddle on Domino, mounted him, and rode away in a hurry.

The distance between the ranch and the schoolhouse seemed twice as far this time. The heat beat down upon her face and the sweat trickled from her brow, dripping onto her shirt like raindrops falling from the sky. The

43

breeze had warmed to an almost unbearable temperature, and the dust swirling from distant sand dunes had managed to find its way to where she traveled, almost choking her with its utter dryness.

But soon the spread of the ranch came into view and the sight of the peaceful grazing cattle and horses gave her back an inner peace she had left behind when she had taken that first glance down at the injured Indian boy and his pitiful expression.

I wonder what the Indians will do when they discover I've brought him home with me, she thought. I only hope they will realize I have helped, not harmed him. . . .

Hoofbeats heading her way drew Kendra's mind alert. She squinted her eyes and cupped a hand over them, groaning when she recognized the grizzly face of Zeke beneath his wide-brimmed sombrero. And as he drew closer, she could even see the look of knowing in his dark, penetrating eyes as he caught sight of her disarray. When he drew rein beside her, Kendra clucked to Domino and thrust her knees into his side.

"Whoa there, Kendra," Zeke shouted, once more moving his horse beside her.

In one swoop he had her reins from her grasp and was urging Domino to stop alongside his own light tan tamed mustang. "What's got you so riled up?" His lips curled into a lewd grin. "I see you ran into some trouble on the trail. You okay?"

"I'm fine," Kendra said from between clenched teeth. She jerked at the reins without success. "Zeke, let go. I've important things to do. Do you hear? Let go."

Zeke looked in all four directions, seeing no one else in sight. Then he looked slowly back toward Kendra, leering after her. "What I've got on my mind is mighty important, too, *Miss* Kendra," he laughed mockingly.

He dismounted and hurriedly stepped beside Domino and grabbed Kendra by the wrist. "Get down here. I see some flesh I want to touch."

Kendra winced, but refused to budge from the saddle. When he gave her one more jerk she felt herself helplessly tumbling sideways, falling into the curve of his arms.

Laughing, Zeke held her to him, carrying her to the shadows of a runty piñon pine tree. He forced her to the ground and stretched out over her, pressing her into the mixture of grass and sand.

Kendra tossed her head and struggled to get free, but she wasn't strong enough to keep his mouth from finding hers in a wet, savage kiss. She gagged on the taste and smell of him. And when his knee spread her legs and his one hand crept to the bare flesh of her abdomen above the waistline of her jeans, she felt desperation rising inside her. She had feared that something like this would happen. But she had never thought him capable of doing it, since he would have to answer to Aaron!

Then to her surprise, Zeke rose quickly from her, laughing boisterously.

"Had you scared, huh?" he taunted. His laughter faded as his eyes captured the full length of her. "Just had to show you how fast it could be done, Miss Prissy. One day I won't stop at just touchin'. When we have the full opportunity of bein' alone, I'll get my rewards. But now ain't the time. The boys could come by any time. I wouldn't want them to get ideas to do the same thing. I want you all to myself."

Kendra slowly pushed herself up from the ground. "You shouldn't have done that, Zeke," she hissed.

"Aaron is going to horsewhip you for sure."

"If you tell Aaron, he won't believe you," Zeke said, casually mounting his horse.

"And why wouldn't he?"

"Because he won't want to," Zeke laughed. "You see, I'm the best hand in these parts. He won't want to take a chance of losin' my skills. He'd rather close his ears to your accusations than toss me out on my ear. Just try it. You'll see."

"You're wrong," Kendra said, brushing dried grass and sand from her jeans. "You'll be gone by sundown. You'll not be laughing then. Aaron'll run you off for sure. Don't be so sure about yourself and your abilities, Zeke."

"You've yet to see the better qualities of my abilities," he snorted, then rode off, laughing hysterically.

Kendra's face was scalding hot from anger. She couldn't stop the thunderous beating of her heart. She hated Zeke. Oh, how she hated him! There was nothing in his kiss but bad, foul taste. His coarse, rough hands had made her insides become cold and the way his knee had parted her legs, oh, so close to doing what men needed a woman for, made fear turn her insides to an almost complete numbness!

Gray, commanding eyes swept through her mind's eye. Funny . . . but when thinking of *that* man . . . she felt so differently!

Shaking her head of all thoughts, she mounted Domino and made her way on to the ranch house, now wondering if she should take the time to change. The sun was fast dipping in the west. Time was against her. No. She didn't have time. Zeke had stolen the precious time that had been allotted her. One day she would make him pay! For *all* his inconveniences to her!

But the time for brewing hatred was for a later date. She had other important things on her mind at this time. She headed on toward the barn where she knew she would find the buggy that had been purchased for her and Holly's use, silently praying that Holly wasn't in another one of her restless moods and already using the buggy.

A line of saddle horses and noisy cowboys all along the front of the bunkhouse distracted Kendra for a moment. She knew that they were assembling for the spring roundup scheduled to begin at sunup the next morning. Some would be driving the cattle north to the rich mountain pastures, to stock the ranges there. Others would be turning the stallions out with the mustangs, to build up their blood, hoping that in a couple of years they would get some fine saddle horses out of them. Other cowhands would be rounding up cows to drive them to the railhead in Reno to be shipped by railway to Chicago meat packing centers. A steer that cost five dollars in Nevada was worth forty or fifty dollars in Chicago.

Yes, the cowboys were the backbone of Aaron's Circle C Ranch, able to perform the most tremendous tasks all in a day's work, never dreaming that they had essentials of greatness.

But to Kendra, they were a never-ending cause for annoyance and uneasiness. Like now—they had spied her disarray and were laughing amongst themselves, with her as the object of their usual filthy jokes. They were without the pleasures of a woman for too long intervals between roundups. This gave them just cause to hunger after Kendra, since she was the one usually on hand for them to mentally undress with their eyes.

Forcing her eyes straight ahead, ignoring the wolf

47

whistles and shouts of "whoopee," she rushed Domino on inside the barn.

"Thank God," she sighed, seeing the fancy buggy standing there, undisturbed. Almost breathless, Kendra removed the saddle from Domino's back and soon had him hitched to the buggy and already back out on the trail. She believed that the buggy would give an easy enough ride for the small Indian boy's return to the ranch with her. Though only two-seated, the padded, black patent leather seats were soft as air, and the long buggy rode like a breeze above its elliptic springs. She would stretch him out between the two seats and cushion his head with her lap.

Four deer broke cover and bounded across Kendra's path. She had been told that when the deer had passed from the desert into the mountains, it was for sure that spring had returned, with summer sliding in quickly behind. The deer were known to seek the nurture of the new green grasses and would nuzzle their dappled fawns into the protection of the deep forests.

She wondered where the Indian boy's parents were, as she urged Domino along the grass-grown trail. It had been dangerous for him to wander off alone. If not for her, a coyote could have even . . .

Then she remembered something else. His horse! She hadn't seen a horse wandering aimlessly about after the boy's fall. But it had probably wandered on back to the Indian village . . . She shrugged.

A tremor rippled through her. When the Indians found the horse without the boy, they would surely come searching for him. How long would it take? Would they come to the ranch?

Seeing the vague outline of the schoolhouse now

ahead, Kendra clucked more loudly to Domino. She glanced upward, seeing a colossal turquoise-tinted sky streaked with glinting threads of silver and orange. The sun had become a mellow red disc, appearing to be resting on the crests of the merging mountain ranges, a warning that the moon would soon take its place.

Kendra sighed with relief when she finally reached the schoolhouse. A cool breeze of evening stroked her flesh as she climbed from the buggy and secured Domino to the hitching rail.

Then in a flurry she rushed up the steps and into the schoolhouse, only to stop short and stare numbly at the spot where she had left the boy to rest.

In jerky motions, her eyes traveled quickly around the room, inspecting all the shadows, corners, and hiding places beneath the long rows of benches. But nothing! The Indian boy wasn't there!

"But how? Where?" she whispered, placing her hands to her cheeks in total dismay. "With such a leg wound he couldn't have left on his own. How . . . ?"

The whinnying of a horse and a horse's hoofbeats stopping outside the schoolhouse made Kendra take a startled step backwards. Had Zeke followed her? He had threatened to get her alone and she couldn't be more alone than she was now.

Drawing her right pistol, she aimed it toward the door, ready. She tensed when she heard the heavy footsteps climbing the wooden steps. She swallowed hard and set her finger against the trigger, waiting to catch a full view of the intruder before filling him full of lead. . . .

Kendra's face paled and her hand dropped her pistol awkwardly to her side when she saw that it wasn't Zeke after all—but the man whom she had spent many nights with in her dreams this past year. It made her heart flutter crazily to remember her fantasies of sensual caresses and kisses with the very man who now stood in front of her.

But now it was *not* a dream, but something very real, feeling the commanding hold of his steel-gray eyes as she stood there, motionless, looking back at him. His face was lined with force and intelligence. And, as she remembered, he was broad-shouldered, thin-flanked, and tall and lean. Dark sideburns rode down the side of his sun-bronzed face beneath his wide-brimmed sombrero, and, as before, he wore a red plaid cotton shirt with a red bandana neckerchief tied about his neck. His hands were resting on the six-shooters at his hip, and his jaw was set, but nothing caused her to lose sight of his handsome, chiseled features.

"You . . ." she finally managed to murmur. "Why are *you* here . . . ?"

Then, like a flash, she remembered the beautiful Indian woman on the buckboard wagon whom he had accompanied to the train depot. Was this Indian woman his wife? Was the boy his son?

Something compelled her to glance at his hands, and she now saw a large silver ring on his left hand with a magnificent round turquoise setting. It was quite obviously Indian made.

"I've come to thank you for helping Quick Deer in his time of need," the stranger said in a smoothly velvet voice.

"Quick Deer . . . ?" Kendra said, pulling her gaze and thoughts from the ring.

"The small Indian boy whose leg you set," he said, moving his gaze down from her face after having surely memorized every inch of it, stopping where her shirt revealed so much of her creamy flesh to his eyes. The sun's rays had dipped lower through a window, and its shadow joined with the shadows where her breasts swelled the shirt away from her, leaving space for his eyes to travel upward to see the bottom curves of her breasts, exposed and pink.

Blushing from the knowing searching of his eyes, Kendra covered herself with her hands. "I was glad to help the Indian boy," she said icily. Her gaze hardened and her back stiffened. "And as you must already know, it took a portion of my clothing to see to it that his leg was properly set."

The stranger laughed softly, lifting his gaze back upward. "Your name . . . ?" he asked, taking a step toward her. He already knew, but he didn't want her to yet be aware of his intense interest in her. It would be hard to explain why he hadn't shown such an interest during the full year between their first meeting and the one now—and chance meetings at that!

"Kendra," she said, tensing. "Kendra Carpenter."

Her eyebrows tilted when she saw something flash in his eyes at the mention of her name. It was as though he had heard the name before. But how?

Once more she remembered the day at the train depot. Had he inquired about her after having stared so openly at her? Had he felt the same as she had . . . as though something magical had traveled between them?

But, no. She knew that she was being foolish. Had he wondered at all about her, a full year would not have passed before this, their second meeting.

"And your name?" she said. "What is your name, sir?"

"Lucas . . ." he said, offering a hand of friendship.

Now feeling awkward with the drawn pistol at her side, Kendra laughed absently and quickly slipped it back into its holster. Then, slowly, feeling a strange rippling at her insides, she lifted her hand to his, hating the fact that her glove was between the contact of his flesh against hers. But still, when he firmly gripped her hand and held it, she could feel the warmth flowing between them and was suddenly awash with that same passion she had felt upon first seeing him . . . the same passion that had pulled them together in her dreams and had sealed their hearts in her fantasies.

When he had stared at her bare flesh moments ago, she had certainly tried to be offended. But in truth she had wanted more than his eyes caressing her breasts. She had wanted his lips. . . .

Kendra, suddenly realizing where her fantasies had taken her, jerked her hand free and swirled around to place her back to him. She wished that her heart would slow a bit. She was afraid that this man . . . this . . . Lucas . . . would realize how he was affecting her. And it was useless for her to let herself behave in such a manner. Surely either way he was married! If not to the Indian woman . . . most surely to the Indian people! It was hard to tell what this man was all about. To her he was like a phantom . . . appearing . . . then disappearing. . . .

"Again, let me thank you," Lucas said, stepping around in front of her. His gray eyes implored her. "You see, the Piute Indians have not had it so good for several years now. And any kindness given to them is always remembered. You will be remembered."

"I only did what most people would do," Kendra said, oh, so wanting to avoid the mystique of his eyes, but unable to.

"Quick Deer had come to see the new schoolhouse," Lucas said. He began moving around the room, touching and exploring everything. "You see, the Indian children aren't allowed in the white man's schools. He was eager to see, firsthand, what this new schoolhouse so close to his village looked like."

"I didn't know . . ." Kendra murmured.

"Most people don't, nor do they care," Lucas growled, now moving back toward her. "Are you the new schoolmarm for the schoolhouse?"

She laughed softly. "No," she said. "The new schoolteacher arrives today. It will be a man. Not a woman."

"Oh, I see," Lucas said. He walked to the door and peered outward at the fading blues and oranges of the sky, then back at Kendra. "Hadn't you best be on your way? You shouldn't be out on the range after dark."

Kendra's eyes widened, not knowing how to take his sudden concern for her welfare. Then she inched her way toward the door. "Yes. You're right," she said. "I must return. I don't care to come face to face with a pack of coyotes."

"And about Quick Deer," Lucas said, very politely helping her down the steps with a strong grip on her elbow.

"Yes . . . ?" she murmured, feeling giddy with him so close to her. He smelled like the mountain air . . . so fresh and clean. She wanted to reach out to him and touch

53

him, to tell him of their many moments together during her long, restless nights.

"He's, I'm sure, settled in with his mother at the Indian village by now," he said, his eyes revealing that he had most surely read her thoughts.

"Who . . . took him there . . . ?"

"His mother."

"How . . . ?"

"When his mother saw him take off alone on his pony this afternoon, she went after him in her wagon," Lucas said. "She was afraid for him. He's a strong-willed, stubborn boy."

"Like father, like son?" Kendra queried, watching his expression for telltale signs of truth.

"Yes. That can be said about most Indian boys, I am sure," Lucas said.

Kendra stepped down onto the ground, feeling a deep disappointment. He hadn't denied he was the father of the Indian boy. She *had* to quit thinking so sensually of him. It was useless.

She let her gaze move to Domino, knowing that soon, when she was out on the range, headed for home, even these moments with this handsome stranger would be like another dream.

Suddenly she felt hands on her arms and felt herself being spun around. Hats collided and then lips as his mouth met hers in a fiery kiss that set her insides to flaming. Lost in the thrill of the moment, Kendra began to loop her arms about his neck, but was abruptly startled when he pulled his lips free and began walking away from her, toward his horse.

"You really must head back," he said from across his shoulder.

Kendra's face flushed crimson, stunned by his change of mood. What kind of man *was* he? Was he playing games with her?

Her gaze once more captured the Indian ring on his left hand, now wondering if somehow she was responsible for making him momentarily turn away from his . . . wife . . . ?

She was confused! But if her heart could speak aloud, oh, the truths it would tell!

Kendra stood as though in a daze as Lucas mounted his horse and wheeled it around to face her. "Would you feel safer if I accompanied you home?" he asked, pushing his sombrero back a bit.

Desire rushed through Kendra, seeing his full features set free from the shadow of the hat. His dark hair was unruly and hung boyishly about his handsome face and his eyes showed a torment of unfulfilled needs. . . .

Kendra grabbed Domino's reins and forced her weak knees to bend so that she could climb onto the buggy seat. She knew that she must get away from this man or all would be lost to her. She knew that if he just asked her, she would stay and share fully in what they had only briefly begun. She no longer cared if he might have a wife . . . even an Indian wife! She only knew that she wanted him.

"I am capable of fending for myself," she forced herself to say.

"Then God speed," Lucas said. He then turned his horse in the direction of the mountains and rode quickly away.

"Goodbye, Lucas," Kendra whispered, tears near. She had to suspect that it might be another year before she saw him again. Why would it be different now

55

than before?

Lifting a gloved forefinger to her lips, she smiled. "But this time I have his kiss to remember," she murmured.

She could still taste him . . . she could still feel the burning passion raging inside her.

"I'll see him again soon," she said aloud, now slapping Domino's reins. "I *know* it. He *must* have the same feelings for me."

She turned her head and gazed at his figure growing smaller in the distance. He was such a man of mystery. Somehow she would find out all about him. She had to! Suddenly he was the force behind her existence.

Chapter Four

Kendra moved down the staircase, almost dreading to meet this Steven Teague, the new schoolteacher of Aaron's choosing. She knew Aaron. He had probably already planted the seed of matrimony inside this most eligible bachelor's mind.

"And even before we have been formally introduced," Kendra fumed to herself.

With her hair free and loose this day, flowing down her back like golden silk, she strutted on down the stairs in her jeans and snug cotton shirt. She was ready to once again show Aaron that he would *not* run her life. She was not one of his ranch hands bowing down to him. No. She was not wearing a dress this day as Aaron had demanded. And she would *not* ride in the buggy at this school-teacher's side. He could travel by buggy alone while she traveled alongside on her horse Domino!

The rich aroma of cigars met Kendra's approach to the library after she moved from the last step and along the hallway. Then, startling her, Holly rushed from the library, almost knocking Kendra from her feet as they clumsily collided. When Kendra regained her balance, she watched as Holly rushed on away from her, sobbing.

Kendra glanced toward the library door, hearing the low mumblings of men in conversation, then back toward Holly, who was ready to ascend the stairs to the second floor. It was obvious that Holly and Aaron had had words. Had it come to this? That they didn't hide their disagreements from strangers? This wasn't like Holly or Aaron.

Rushing to Holly, Kendra placed a hand gently on her arm, stopping her. "Holly, what's going on here?" she murmured.

Holly turned her emerald-colored eyes to Kendra, revealing tear-soaked lashes and cheeks. "It's Aaron," she whispered. "He's going to be gone again. This time for possibly a full week. Kendra, what am I to do with myself? My fingers are already pinpricked from so much embroidery work."

Holly slung her dark coils of curls around and bit down on a knuckle. "I hate this place," she cried. "I want to return to Boston. I've never been so lonely. At least while Aaron was gone in Boston I had my friends to join me for tea and bridge."

Kendra could sympathize with Holly. There were too many miles between neighbors in this desolate area on the range. The Carpenter family hadn't yet become acquainted with any of the neighboring ranch owners. Aaron was too busy and Kendra couldn't have cared less. She didn't need people to make her content. She found enough pleasure in the company of her horse Domino, still practicing and enjoying being free!

And so, though Kendra sympathized with Holly, she still was annoyed. Holly had been warned before

58

marrying Aaron how dedicated he was to business affairs . . . that making more money . . . the "big green," was the major goal in his life. But Holly hadn't listened. Her dreams of what that money could buy for her had blinded her to all other facts of life.

"Holly, you knew Aaron was leaving this morning for the spring roundup," Kendra sighed. "Why give him trouble? And why did you in the presence of a stranger?"

"The spring roundup is only a part of it," Holly sobbed, lowering her lashes. More tears dripped from her eyes, settling on the voluptuous swell of her breasts where they lay only partially exposed at the stylishly gathered bodice of her full-skirted, pale blue silk dress.

"Then what else?" Kendra persisted, dropping her hand from Holly's shoulder. She glanced back toward the library, envisioning Aaron checking the clock on the fireplace mantel, getting impatient for her arrival in the room.

She looked back toward Holly. "Hurry, Holly. I know that the ranch hands are waiting for Aaron at the corrals."

"By all means don't keep Aaron waiting," Holly said mockingly.

"Holly!" Kendra scolded.

"I'm sorry," Holly murmured, wiping more tears from her eyes with the back of her hand. "It's just that Aaron refuses me so much. I can't help but feel bitter toward him."

Kendra looked around her and at the way the ranch house had been furnished, most of it with Holly in mind. She gestured angrily with the sweep of a hand. "How could you say that?" she whispered harshly. "You have everything a woman could ask for. Sometimes you're impossible, Holly."

"I don't have everything," Holly said stiffly.

"What can you possibly be speaking of?"

"A child!" Holly stormed. She lifted the skirt of her dress up into her arms and flew up the stairs, leaving a trail of sobs behind her.

Kendra lifted a silky eyebrow. "A child?" she whispered.

But it did appear to be a logical answer to Holly's loneliness. Now Kendra wondered why Aaron did refuse this to Holly. Or wasn't he capable of fathering a child? Was his refusal to Holly a way of disguising the sad truth that he could never father an heir to the Carpenter fortune? Would that be left to Seth and whomever he chose to wed?

Troubled, Kendra moved on into the library, where two backs were turned to her, both men standing at a window, looking out at the Carpenter family's domain. Both were of the same height but in no way similar in build. Not like Aaron, Steven Teague was extremely thin, as though a sudden puff of wind might even be able to lift him from his feet. His dark hair was trimmed neatly and he had chosen wisely to wear a lightweight broadcloth suit, having surely anticipated the heat of the oncoming summer months. But he was from Missouri and more than likely very accustomed to hot, sultry summers.

Kendra had read reports of the many deaths that the heat spells of summer caused in the city of St. Louis, on the banks of the winding, muddy Mississippi River. Maybe Steven Teague, though painfully thin he was, could survive well enough in this new environment.

Aaron is counting on it . . . she thought further to herself. He's even counting on more than that. Oh, what a disappointment he has coming to him!

"Aaron . . ." she finally said aloud, clasping her hands together behind her, tense, anxious to get this morning ritual behind her.

Aaron and Steven spun around in unison . . . Aaron in his roundup attire of jeans, chaps, and flannel shirt, Steven with appraising eyes set behind gold-framed spectacles perched on a hawklike nose on a hollow-cheeked face.

Steven clumsily mashed out his cigar in an ashtray as Kendra smoothed her way across the room. She extended her hand toward him, forcing a smile.

"You must be Steven Teague," she said. "I'm Kendra." She gave Aaron a haughty look then moved her eyes back to Steven. "But I'm sure I didn't have to tell you that."

Color rose upward into Steven's face. "Yes," he said quietly. "Mr. Carpenter has told me much about you. I'm pleased to make your acquaintance, ma'am."

Aaron took a deep drag from his cigar, giving Kendra a sweeping, disapproving look. "You must forgive my sister's appearance, Mr. Teague," he said dryly. "But it seems the jeans have grown permanently to her person."

Steven wove his fingers through Kendra's and gave her hand a hardy shake. "I think you look just fine, ma'am," he said even more quietly, then gave Aaron a guarded look when Aaron cleared his throat noisily.

Smiling coyly, Kendra gave Aaron a smug look. "Why, thank you, Mr. Teague," she chirped. "I think we're going to get along just fine."

She glanced down at his continued grip and then eased her hand away. She didn't have anything else in mind, and she would most certainly set his mind straight on *that* pretty fast!

"Steven," Steven said, eagerness flashing in his dark eyes. "Please call me Steven, ma'am."

Aaron mashed his own cigar into an ashtray and glanced impatiently toward the clock on the fireplace mantel. "Let's all dispense with the last-name formalities," he said. "Out here in the West, first names are what count. I'm usually in too big a rush to even catch the last name of an acquaintance."

"Aaron, that's not so," Kendra scolded. "Where business is concerned it's always the last name that sticks inside that corporate brain of yours. It's the last name on a loan or deed that matters, isn't that right?"

Aaron walked quickly to a coat tree and lifted his gunbelt from it and secured it around his thick waist, then slipped a revolver into its one holster. "I've no time for such idle talk," he said dryly. "I've got to get out to the men and get this day started."

He covered his shining bald head with his handsome Stetson hat. He looked toward Steven. "Kendra will direct you to the schoolhouse," he said. "Steven, from here on, the job is yours to make things work for the children in our community. I hired you because your credentials read the best. Now don't disappoint me, Steven."

"I'll do the best I can," Steven murmured.

"I can't ask for more than that," Aaron said. He went to Kendra and lifted her chin with a forefinger. "Take the buggy with Steven."

"I've already told you that I prefer to travel on Domino."

"Damn it, Kendra," Aaron said, then walked away in a huff.

Kendra reached to one of her rear pockets and pulled her leather gloves from inside it. "Let's head out," she said.

"Head . . . out . . . ?" Steven said, tilting an eyebrow.

Kendra laughed softly. "Let's go," she said. She reached for her hat and plopped it on.

Steven joined in the laughter and walked hatless with Kendra to the outdoors, where he boarded a buggy and she mounted Domino. "It's not too far," she said. "But the schoolhouse *is* a bit isolated out there on the range."

Steven lifted his eyes to the sky and squinted. "I hope it's not far," he said, running a forefinger around the inside of his heavily starched shirt collar. "The sun seems much closer than in Missouri."

"Yes. I know what you mean," Kendra said. "I'm from Boston originally. I had some adjusting to do out here myself."

She clucked to Domino and snapped her reins and he began a soft trot next to the buggy. There was no breeze. The morning had a sultry, muggy weight to it. It was almost oppressive. Kendra glanced upward and saw some fluffy cumulus clouds contrasting with the ocean blue of the sky. It had been a while since rain had fallen. But once it did, Kendra knew to expect a downpour. It was this way in the spring in this Nevada territory. Steven would get used to the sudden changes of weather. She had.

The snowcapped mountains that lined the horizon offered a panoramic view of color, rimmed by purple, ruby, and blue as their crests fell away and merged almost mystically with the sweeps of the valley land of greens. These valleys then merged with the straight stretches of desert, where sand dunes rose starkly out of an alkali flat that once had been a seabed. The sand dunes' contours were soft and shaped by the desert wind, thrusting razor sharp up a thousand feet above the desert floor. The wind was the sculptor of the desert, creating columns and pillars and spires and skeleton ribs of rocks.

Close by Domino's hoofs, a scaly, dusty rattlesnake glided into the covert of the sage, spooking the horse only slightly. Then the first sight of the schoolhouse gave Kendra reason to reminisce about what had happened the day before. . . .

She lifted a finger to her lips, remembering the fire of his kiss. The steel grip of his arms as he had held her had been too short-lived and had left her unnerved and dissatisfied, as he had left her there alone. . . .

"Looks nice enough," Steven shouted, causing Kendra to draw rein next to his buggy.

"We're quite proud," Kendra said. "It took some time to cut the lumber and bring it down from the mountains. And it took forever to get the plate glass windows from San Francisco."

"Sixteen students will be in my charge—so your brother has told me," Steven said, pulling his buggy to a halt next to the school's hitching rail. "I guess that will be challenge enough for me."

"Well, I'd *hope* so," Kendra laughed, not envying his job of being cooped up all day in one room with rowdy children of various ages and sizes.

She dismounted and together they went inside the one-room building. And once everything was checked and approved of and they were ready to go, Kendra held back a bit.

"You go on without me," she said, avoiding his eyes. She felt a compulsion to once more be alone on this very spot where she had shared a kiss and intimate embrace with Lucas.

Her heart skipped a beat. She suddenly realized that she had not asked his last name. But then she shrugged the thought off, remembering Aaron's words about people of the range very rarely exchanging last names.

Steven stared across the vast, lonely range, then back at Kendra. "You can't mean that you want to be left out here all alone," he said. "Can't that be a bit dangerous for a lady?"

Kendra's hands went to her pistols. "I'm capable of taking care of myself," she said dryly. "After arriving here, I saw the need of learning self-defense . . . not only from the coyotes and rattlers but also from some two-legged creatures I'd hate to meet in the dark."

"Still . . . I . . ." Steven stammered, using a forefinger to push his glasses back on his hawklike nose.

Kendra took him by an elbow and guided him to the buggy. "Now you just go on and don't worry another minute about me," she encouraged him.

"But what will your brother say when he hears that I left you here all alone?"

"He knows to expect it of me."

Color rose to Steven's face. "When will I be seeing you again, Kendra?" he asked guardedly.

"I'll come by occasionally and see how you and the children are getting along."

"Maybe you'd let me see you besides that," Steven said, climbing aboard his buggy. "Maybe you might go into Reno with me some evening and have dinner."

Kendra's white teeth sparkled as she laughed. "You won't have any desire to do that once you've tasted the cooking you'll find in Reno."

"But I will stop by the ranch to see you," Steven said, then quickly added, "that is, if it's all right with you."

"We'll see . . ." Kendra said.

Steven took the reins in one hand and a whip in the other. He once more scanned the land with his eyes. "You be careful," he then said, eyeing her with concern.

"Goodbye, Steven," Kendra said, stepping back as he moved away from her.

Sighing, Kendra lifted her hat from her head and combed her hair with her fingers. She closed her eyes, fantasizing about Lucas being there, ready to pull her into his arms. She even felt the heat of passion rising from her lower abdomen, scorching her insides. Then she let her shoulders sag and went back inside the building to rest and think some more before heading back.

She sat down on the floor and placed her hat next to her, leaning her back against the wall. Slowly removing her gloves, she found her head nodding, having not had one wink of sleep the whole night before for being haunted over and over again by those same gray eyes. . . .

Easing down, to stretch her long, slim body across the floor, Kendra turned on her stomach and rested her head on an arm and slowly drifted into a fitful sleep. In a dream she was being chased on horseback. Suddenly her captor had her and had pulled her from her horse and onto his, where he held her against the steel frame of his chest. His mouth hungrily found hers . . . parting her lips with his tongue. Coarse hands were on her face, framing it. . . .

"Kendra, wake up. It's unwise to fall asleep out here all alone," Kendra heard a voice say. Blinking her eyes, she slowly focused on the face bent down over her, so close she could smell the sweetness of his breath.

With a melting sensation warming her insides, Kendra

swallowed hard, now quite aware of whom it was showing concern for her.

"Lucas . . ." she whispered, turning from her stomach to her side.

"Kendra, you're so beautiful lying there," Lucas said thickly, weaving his fingers through her golden hair. "Any man who might catch you here could . . ."

Tremors of ecstasy rippled across Kendra's flesh. "Could what . . . ?" she said daringly. Her heart beat out the moments before he spoke again.

"Could take advantage of you," Lucas said, lowering his hands away from her.

Kendra raised up on an elbow, blushing, knowing exactly what was on his mind. She wanted to be bold and say "please do," but instead said, "Why are you here?"

"As I told you yesterday, the Indians are grateful to you for helping Quick Deer," he said, rising from his bent knee. "They've sent you a gift."

"A gift?" Kendra said in a near-whisper, now truly aroused in her curiosity about this man and his connection with the Piute Indians. She rose from the floor, shaking her golden streamers of hair to hang gorgeously down her back.

With a thumping heart torturing her insides, she watched as Lucas pulled a necklace free from his shirt pocket. As the sun caught and played on the silver of the necklace, Kendra's breath was captured by a sudden sigh.

Lucas lifted the necklace toward her neck. "May I . . . ?" he queried, smiling.

"Yes. Thank you. I'd love to wear it," Kendra said. "It's absolutely beautiful."

With her gaze held raptly by the command of his gray eyes, she raised her slender fingers to her hair and held it away from her shoulders, trembling inside as his fingers made contact with her flesh while snapping the necklace in place.

"This particular necklace made by the Piute is called a squash blossom necklace," Lucas said. "One day I will tell you the full meaning . . . what the tiny dangling squash blossom replicas represent. Today I will only tell you that the large pendant hanging from the center is shaped to look like the moon in its first or last quarter."

After the necklace was in place and cooling the skin where it lay, Kendra ran her fingers across it, once more admiring it. "Why do you choose to tell me later what the squash blossoms represent?" she asked softly. "Why the big secret?"

"It isn't the time," he said, tenderly cupping her chin with the coarseness of his right hand. "There is a time and place for everything. Today is a time for giving . . . and, tomorrow? Could you meet with me?"

Kendra swallowed hard, utterly enamored of both his touch and his words. Did she dare let her heart lead her into any further bonds with this man? Should she let him be the one to take her innocence? He was still a man of mystery, appearing to be as much Indian as white, yet he had such a distinguished air about him and spoke as one who was highly educated. Generally, Kendra had full control of all her emotions, but with Lucas her whole insides seemed to be rebelling, forcing her stubborn loyalties to herself to go amok.

Dangerously, she let her chin rest against his hand and drunkenly closed her eyes. "I really shouldn't . . ." she whispered. "I don't even know you."

"Destiny has again brought us together," Lucas said. "That first time I saw you I knew we would meet again."

Kendra's eyes moved open, feeling the magnet of his gray eyes upon her. "But that was a full year ago," she murmured. "If that first time meant so much to you, why did you let it take a full year for us to meet again? Surely you could have searched and found me."

"As you could have also found me had you wanted to," Lucas said thickly. "But you must have known, somehow, that the right time would present itself to us."

"I had dreamed . . . I had hoped . . ."

"Kendra, the time is *now*."

Lucas swept her into his arms, unable to hold back any longer. How often he had watched her from afar, hungering for her! But he had realized that too soon he would be battling her brother Aaron for land rights, and he hadn't wanted her caught in the middle. But now was too late to worry about that. Circumstances *had* brought them together and to hell with Aaron Carpenter. His sister most surely would choose her lover over her brother!

Coiling his fingers through Kendra's hair, Lucas drew her mouth to his and tasted the sweet jasmine of her lips. Feeling the painful ache in his loins alerted him to the dangers of the moment, yet he couldn't help but let his free hand move between the unbuttoned spaces of her shirt, to touch the petal-soft swell of a breast. . . .

Kendra laced her arms about Lucas's neck, sighing shakily as she felt his fingers encircle her breast. As his forefinger and thumb squeezed the nipple, delicious spasms of headiness threatened to destroy Kendra's ability to think clearly. And when his tongue parted her lips and began exploring sensuously inside her mouth, she felt as though a volcano was ready to erupt in hot, fiery splashes of ecstasy.

She leaned her body more into his caresses. She joined her own tongue to his, dizzying even more as she felt him fit the steel frame of his body against hers. As he began to move seductively, she could feel the hardness of his manhood swollen beneath his jeans and was suddenly returned to reality and now . . . and the passion that was quickly ensnaring them.

Yes, she wanted him! But, no, it wasn't right! Surely he wasn't free! There was the Indian boy. There was the Indian maiden. There was the Indian ring that he wore that sealed him to a way of life she was not familiar with!

Struggling now, placing her hands to his chest to push him away, she felt his hold loosening and stepped quickly away from him, panting, when he finally set her free.

"Kendra . . ." he said, still reaching a hand to her. "Tomorrow . . . ?"

Still breathless and feeling the heat of flush on her cheeks, Kendra reached for her hat and nervously lifted it to her head. With a trembling in her fingers, she pulled her gloves slowly onto them. Then she squared her shoulders and tilted her chin stubbornly.

"Lucas, for a moment there I lost my head," she said dryly. "I won't again. There can't be any tomorrows for us. There shouldn't have even been a today."

With an ache in her heart, her hand went to her necklace. "Please tell the Piute I appreciate the gift," she murmured, lowering her eyes, feeling her defenses waning under his steady, commanding stare. "And please give Quick Deer my regards. I was glad to be able to help him."

Not willing to give her up so easily now that he had tasted of her, Lucas pushed her hat back a bit and once more drew her into his arms. "There *will* be a tomorrow

70

for us, Kendra," he growled.

He then kissed her demandingly, filled with passion and promise, causing Kendra's knees to weaken and her pulse to race. And, then, suddenly, his sombrero was on his head and he was gone from her again. . . .

Stunned, Kendra listened to the sound of his horse's hoofbeats moving away from the schoolhouse. Panic rose inside her. Now that he was leaving her she was sorry to have sent him away. With her hands to her throat, touching the necklace, her wonder about him and the Indians caused her mind to move in a dangerous direction.

"I must follow him," she whispered. "I *must* see where he goes . . . how he lives."

Rushing outside, Kendra mounted Domino. She paused on horseback long enough to look for Lucas's outline on the horizon, knowing that she was being reckless and foolish. It was growing dusk. She had never been on the trail after dark.

"But I'll stay close behind Lucas," she reassured herself. "If I need help all I will have to do is yell for him."

She placed her hands on her pistols. "And I *can* use these, if necessary."

Clucking to Domino, Kendra began her boldest adventure yet.

Chapter Five

Bored with Reno and its drab, colorless buildings, Holly Carpenter yearned for busier streets and the spirited talk of crowds of people. She had heard that one could find these things in the thriving town of Virginia City. She had even heard that this town, perched on the side of Mount Davidson, had been divided into separate, smaller towns, with the names of Greek Town, Hunky Town, Jap Town, Wop Town and Mid-Town. Mid-town was the middle of town, where all the "white people" lived.

The rest of Virginia City's population included the many who made up the cheap labor for the silver mines, sleeping wherever they could find a spot to drop when they were not in the pits of the mountain, laboring.

Glancing at the red disc of the sun appearing to be resting on the mountains in the distance, Holly had to be quick to make up her mind. Standing on the dust-blown streets of Reno was not the best place to be found when night fell in its utter darkness. Upon first arriving in Reno that day she had thought to make arrangements to stay at Dora Mae's Boardinghouse for the night. But the need for other things was calling her elsewhere. She was lonely and hoped to cast this loneliness aside by seeking the excitement that could be found in Virginia City.

"I must go to Virginia City now," she whispered. "With Aaron gone on the spring roundup, he will never be the wiser."

She wouldn't worry about Kendra's reaction and Seth was surely in the bowels of the earth, digging for silver.

Closing her parasol, Holly glanced toward the private carriage that Aaron had insisted she now travel in, then toward the stiff-backed coachman awaiting her decision as to where he was to deliver her.

Aaron had begun worrying about her welfare since she had insisted on being free to travel to Reno whenever she chose, so a coachman had been hired to accompany her on her restless travels. Holly knew that beneath the coachman's formal black coat could be found a Colt revolver, and in the closed confines of his silk top hat there was a small derringer.

Yes, she was most surely safe with this man with the expressionless face and tightly drawn lips. He wasn't the typical Boston coachman. He was in truth a paid bodyguard.

"Parker, take me to Virginia City," Holly ordered, ignoring the frown suddenly being directed toward her.

"Ma'am, that's not wise," Parker said in a gravelly voice. "Mr. Aaron would not approve."

"Parker, Aaron will never know," she said, warning him with the flashing of her green eyes. "Isn't that right? We will say we've been in Reno the full time, won't we, Parker? You are being paid to travel with me, not to spread gossip to Aaron about where I choose to travel."

"Yes, ma'am," Parker said, lifting his thick shoulders into a shrug. "Whatever you say, ma'am. Virginia City it is."

"Thank you, Parker," Holly said, hiding a sigh of relief behind a gloved hand. Parker took her parasol and purse, then she gave him a hand, letting him assist her up inside the carriage, as she lifted the thick gathers of her light green silk dress up into her arms. With the waning sunlight, the interior of the carriage had lost some of its heat. The heavily cushioned gold velveteen seats afforded Holly a luxurious ride, and the closed-in walls gave her all the privacy she desired.

Settling herself, positioning the fullness of the skirt of her dress all around her, she tried to be comfortable with her decision to wander so freely, unescorted, to the wild city of Virginia City. But thoughts of Aaron and his neglect of her made her know that she was right to seek her own pleasures. Guilt would not dissuade her. In truth, Aaron was at fault here. Had he shown her more consideration, she would have no cause to behave so irrationally.

"Yes, it's Aaron's fault," she whispered, holding her hat securely on her head as the carriage began careening in and out of potholes in the road. "Nobody else's! I shall *not* feel guilty. I will enjoy these moments of freedom . . . to . . . the fullest!"

Holly had parted her long, dark hair and had brought it back in curls that fell to her shoulders from beneath her soft straw hat. Her eyes and lips were bright and her bare shoulders gleaming white where her off-the-shoulder silk dress dipped low to reveal the magnificent swell of her breasts. Though Aaron had warned her against it, she displayed a sparkling necklace at her throat and a tiny circled diamond clipped to each earlobe. White gloves

75

covered the delicate tapers of her fingers, and yards of lace peeped from beneath the hem of her dress.

Pulling a folded rattan fan from her purse, she flipped it open and began fanning herself with it. She kept an eye on the window at her right side, unable to quell her constant fear of outlaws in this wild, desolate country. She knew that the grand, stately carriage in which she traveled reflected the wealth of its owner and could be a temptation for any greedy, evil person who might spy it rambling on down the road.

"But Parker has a reputation for shooting to kill," she murmured, fanning harder. "I surely am safe."

Her thoughts traveled back to the first day of her arrival to Reno. Oh, how she had hated the sight of the ugly town. First she had been inconvenienced by the dusty, hot train, then she had found herself tied to a way of life that was no better than being isolated on an island far out at sea. . . .

"Maybe things will soon change for me," she whispered. "Oh, I pray that they do. . . ."

She leaned her head back against a cushion and dozed lightly until a gunshot rang out, outside the carriage.

"Good Lord . . ." she whispered. "Are we being attacked . . . ?"

Scooting closer to the window, Holly leaned her head out a bit, then felt a true increase in her heartbeat when she discovered that her carriage had arrived in the streets of Virginia City. The gunshot that had awakened her had been fired by a rowdy, drunken cowboy, riding up the street on horseback.

"Well, seems I will no longer be bored," Holly giggled as she let her gaze move slowly around her to capture all the excitement on the street and board sidewalks.

Dusk had just fallen and gas lamps had been lighted along the whole thoroughfare. Holly could see the same types of unpainted stores with false fronts that she had left behind her in Reno. But here there seemed to be many more of them. In one sweep of the eye she could see several general stores, saloons, a barber shop, a livery stable, and a blacksmith shop.

Further down the street some taller brick buildings stood towering over the wooden frame buildings. One was a bank, another was a hotel, and the most impressive of them all was an opera house, with tall white columns in front, and what looked like a red-velvet-covered door that led to the inside.

A sudden tremor of the carriage floor drew Holly's hands to her throat. She gasped. She could still feel it. Now the whole carriage was shaking! Then she suddenly remembered! Seth had spoken of the streets that were becoming increasingly weakened by the tunneling of the mines beneath the ground. The earth had begun shifting and giving in at its weakest points. In some places the board sidewalks had sunk in so deeply they couldn't be dug out. There was a constant fear of the ground's caving in completely at any time, anywhere, swallowing everything and everyone that might be there at the time.

Holly herself swallowed hard now, feeling the same fears that had plagued her in her nightmares about traveling here from Boston when Aaron had first told her that it was his plan to do so. Once more she felt a deep, sad emptiness, hating her new way of life. But this fear . . . this sad emptiness strengthened her need to mingle with people, and this she would do! That was why she had ventured on to Virginia City!

Determination swelled inside her. Her pulse raced.

She didn't wait for Parker to open the carriage door when it pulled to a halt in front of the highly acclaimed International Hotel. Lifting her velvet-embroidered valise from the floor of the carriage and with her purse tucked beneath her arm, she climbed out onto the street.

"Ma'am . . ." Parker said, jumping from the outside carriage seat. "Let me . . ."

Holly turned on her heel, chin tilted haughtily. "Parker, I won't be needing your services until tomorrow," she said dryly. "Please do as you wish until then. I'm sure you can find enough to draw your attention from your duties to me."

"But, ma'am, Mr. Aaron . . ."

"Parker, I am capable of fending for myself," Holly sighed. "I do *not* need you to be constantly at my side."

She nodded her head toward the long row of gambling houses that stretched out at one side of the hotel. "You will find more of interest in those flashy gambling houses, I am sure, Parker," she quickly added.

"You're sure, ma'am?" Parker said, furrowing his eyebrows, an anxious glint in the shadow of his dark, narrow eyes.

Holly laughed softly. "Yes," she said. "I'm sure. Now please. Be on your way. Just be sure to be here shortly after noon tomorrow."

"Yes, ma'am," Parker said, then climbed aboard the carriage and directed it quickly away from Holly.

Holly's heart raced and her insides quivered uneasily. She felt as though she had just been set free on foreign soil, and she wondered momentarily about her sanity. Would she be safe? Was she unwise to be so daring? She was behaving as was expected of Kendra . . . not like the quiet, delicate Holly everyone thought her to be.

78

"Well, this once I shall disprove that myth," she whispered, taking a shallow step toward the magnificent oak door of the hotel.

The front of the building was graced with iron-balustraded balconies, and a large gaslight glowing warmly golden at each side of the door. Rows of windows climbing the brick walls to five stories showed dim lights, appearing to be eyes, watching her . . . accusing her. . . .

Pushing their way through the crowd on all sides of her were miners in blue shirts with unkempt beards, Piute Indians with arrows, gamblers with cards showing from their coat pockets, and women with painted cheeks and gold teeth flashing. Very few respectable-looking women were in sight, making Holly rush on inside the hotel.

The click of dice, chink of coins, and the shuffling of cards drew her quick attention to the left of her. Off the entrance foyer were rows of green-covered gaming tables, surrounded by distinguished-looking gentlemen attired in handsome suits and diamond-studded silk shirts. One in particular drew her attention. Beneath the glittering light of a stately chandelier, this man's hair shone like the gold of a noonday sun, and when he lifted his eyes and met her steady stare, she found herself looking into an ocean of blue.

Something grabbed at Holly's insides. There was something familiar about this man. It was as though she was looking into the face of a slightly older, yet much handsomer Aaron. The difference was the more brilliant blue of his eyes . . . the thick head of hair . . . and the trim, fit figure of the man. . . .

As though a magnet was drawing them together, Holly watched the man rise from the gambling table and move toward her. To break the spell, Holly forced herself to look away from him, to move further into the hotel lobby. Trembling, she focused on the magnificence of the hotel's interior.

Red velvet covered the many gilt-trimmed chairs and crystal chandeliers danced their glittering lights all around the room. Large rooms led from the lobby in all directions, meant to lead one into billiard parlors, dining and smoking rooms, and a sumptuous bar, from where could be heard the throaty voice of a woman singing to the accompaniment of a piano.

Hearing footsteps drawing closer, Holly went to the front desk and tapped lightly on a bell and waited breathlessly for a clerk to appear. Her heart skipped a beat when a male voice spoke from behind her.

"Ma'am, maybe I can be of some service to you," the man said.

Feeling a slow flush rising to her cheeks, Holly turned to meet his appraising eyes. Swallowing hard, she finally managed a nervous smile. "And, sir, are you of this hotel's management? Could you help in acquiring me a room for the night?" she asked softly, again feeling strangely as though she should know this handsome older man.

Yet she knew how foolish she must be. This man, dressed all in black, with a diamond stickpin at his throat, most surely was the only one poured from the mold that had given him his unique, chiseled features. The few lines on his brow and around his mouth were the only clues to his probably being fifty, or possibly a little older.

He bowed at the waist, smiling warmly. "I could offer you *my* room for the night," he said suavely.

Holly blanched. "Sir!" she gasped. With a hammering

heart she had to force her feet to move away from him. Something deep inside her told her that this man was special. She couldn't let him think her to be a gutter tramp . . . a . . . whore . . . !

Relieved to see a clerk step behind the desk, Holly made arrangements for a room. When she began to climb the fancy, thickly carpeted staircase, she felt her valise being lifted from her left hand. Tensing, she tried to grab it back, but when she saw that it was the same man again, she breathed easier and let him have it.

"I'm sorry if I behaved badly a moment ago," he said, climbing the stairs beside her. When he lifted his free hand to her elbow in a gentlemanly manner to assist her on up to the second floor landing, she also let him do this.

"Forgiven?" he asked, leaning his face down closer to hers.

A fragrance mixed with cigar smoke and a rich man's cologne circled up inside Holly's nose, increasing her building euphoric state.

"Well? Am I?" he persisted, wrinkling a heavy, golden brow.

Holly laughed silkily, tilting her eyes to his. "Yes . . ." she murmured. "You are forgiven."

"Ah," he said, sighing. "For a moment there, I didn't think I was. I don't usually approach a woman in such a manner, but you brought out the animal in me."

Holly eyed him questioningly. "I'm not sure how I should take that, sir," she said. "As a compliment, I hope."

"Most certainly."

"Then I will gladly accept it as such."

"And what is the name that goes with such a beautiful lady?" he asked, trying to not feel like a wicked, dirty old

81

man. He knew that she couldn't be much older than his own daughter. But he hadn't felt such an attraction to a woman since the first time he had laid eyes on his wife those many, many years ago. No. He wouldn't let anything stand in the way if she could also become interested in him. Not even age. But was she even free for a relationship? Where had she driven in from? Why was she alone . . . ?

Holly stiffened inside. She realized that Aaron had most surely many business acquaintances in Virginia City, so she had to be careful and not speak the name Carpenter to anyone!

"Holly Klein . . ." she said coyly, blinking her thick veil of lashes up at him as he continued to appraise her with the twinkle of his blue eyes. "And . . . yours . . . ?"

"Jess. Jess Halloran . . ." he said, casting his eyes down, suddenly revealing an uneasiness in his voice, puzzling Holly.

"Well, Mr. Halloran . . ."

"Jess . . ." he interrupted. "Please call me Jess."

Holly smiled warmly. "Jess . . ." she said. "What is your business in Virginia City?"

She stepped up on the second floor landing, hesitating before moving down the long, spacious hallway with numbered doors on each side. What would she do once she reached her door? It wasn't proper to invite a man into one's room. Yet, hadn't Aaron made her feel undesirable? Possibly this man could ease her worries about this. She had the need to feel desirable! She had the need to feel like a woman! And most of all . . . she was tired of being lonely!

"You may not like my answer to that question," Jess said, now urging her by the elbow to proceed on down the hallway.

"And why not?"

"Because, Holly, I am a gambling man," he said. "I own my own gambling house right next door to this hotel. I was only here this evening, checking out their game, comparing . . ."

Once more Holly blanched. Aaron's father had been a gambling man. How strange it was now that she had become attracted to such a man. Was it fate? It *did* seem a bit ironic.

How long had it been since Aaron had even mentioned his father to her? When he discussed Stanford Carpenter, it was always in secret, with Seth and Kendra! This had been another cause of her increasing feelings of loneliness. When they spoke of family, Holly seemed to always be the outsider.

"You're a gambler?" she finally said. Eyes wide, she added: "Why, Jess, that doesn't offend me. I find it even quite exciting."

Jess laughed. "You're a girl after my own heart," he said. When he saw her pause before a door to compare the room number to that on the key, he hesitated, then said, "May I?"

Feeling apprehensions fading, Holly handed him the key. "Yes. Please do," she murmured.

"You're alone in Virginia City?" he asked, fitting the key into the lock.

"Yes. I am," Holly said hesitantly, blushing slightly when the door creaked slowly open.

"You've left your husband home tending the cattle?" he cautiously tested.

Holly turned on a heel and boldly faced him. "And if I said yes?" she murmured.

83

"How should I feel about knowing that you're married?"

"Yes . . ."

"That depends on how *you* feel about the marriage, Holly."

His words triggered a more rapid heartbeat inside her. She stepped on across the threshhold. A lone lighted kerosene lamp flickered softly inside the nicely arranged room. A bed filled most of the space, and there were two gilt-trimmed red velvet chairs arranged beneath a curtained window with a table set between them. Wine sparkled in maroon reds from inside a cut-glass wine decanter on this table, and beside this sat two long-stemmed wineglasses. It was a perfect place for a lovers' rendezvous. It was now hard for Holly to believe that she was here . . . with this man. . . .

"Would you join me in a glass of wine?" she then said softly, her own way of answering his question about her marriage.

"If you will join me later in the dining room," he said, shutting the door behind them. "The cooking is quite gourmet. Just perfect for such a fine lady as you."

Holly frowned. "And you still think of me as a fine lady, though I've invited you into my room for a glass of wine, unchaperoned?"

"Holly, you are old enough to know your own mind," Jess said. "I judge no one, as I wish no one to judge me." His face drew shadows onto it. "But that hasn't always been the case for me. Not everyone thinks of a gambling man as a person of exciting qualities. Some even find it shameful."

Again Holly thought of Aaron and his feelings about gamblers, but just as quickly cast the thought aside when Jess placed her valise on a chair, then reached to untie the bow of her bonnet that was tied neatly beneath her chin. When one of his hands brushed against her cheek, Holly's breath was taken from her. The one other time she had been unfaithful to Aaron she had felt nothing for the man. He had just filled time while Aaron had busied himself in the family banking business.

But now . . . with *this* man . . . there was instant magnetism between them.

This frightened Holly. She did not want to make a commitment. Though highly attracted to this man, she only wanted Aaron in her life. She had enjoyed the respect of the Carpenter name. She had always loved Aaron. It was the bitterness toward him and his feelings about children that had goaded her on, into this type of situation. . . .

"And your gloves, Holly?" Jess said huskily. "While we share a glass of wine surely you would relax better without your gloves on."

Holly began tugging at her gloves, watching as he began pouring the wine. Shame for what she was doing was edging its way inside her brain, yet she wouldn't allow anything to stop her now that she was already entangled in this web of deceit. She tossed the removed gloves on the table, then accepted the tall-stemmed glass into her fingers.

"Thank you," she murmured.

"Shall we drink a toast?" Jess asked, leaning his filled glass toward her.

"Since we've just met, what could we drink to?"

"To . . . us . . ." Jess said thickly, seeing the heaving of her bosom, knowing that she was as excited as he.

Dare he take her to bed so quickly? Might her husband look him up later to fight for her scorned reputation? But the ache for her was leading him on to do whatever she would allow him. . . .

Seeing the passion in his eyes, Holly clinked her glass against his, then began slowly sipping the wine. Its bubbly warmth began washing her insides with desire, and she feared these feelings. Again she had to remind herself of how this had to end. . . .

Jess placed his emptied glass on the table. Cautiously he raised his hand and freed her glass from her circled fingers and placed it on the table next to his. In one fast sweep he had her in his arms and molded her closely to him while his lips sought hers in a frenzied excitement.

Feeling, oh, so alive, having been neglected by Aaron for way too long now, Holly found herself responding with abandonment. She now knew that no matter how much she wanted detached thoughts of this stranger, his hands and lips were telling her just how impossible it was. As his lips warmed hers, then lowered, kissing the hollow of her throat, Holly moaned and closed her eyes to the ecstasy.

"I must have you now," he whispered huskily, already unfastening the buttons at the back of her dress.

"I truly mustn't . . ." she murmured, trembling. "I've never before . . ." She didn't want him to think she was a whore! She didn't!

"I know . . ." he said. "But now you must."

"You will think me a . . ."

"No," he said, then sealed her words with the sweet fullness of his lips.

Again she moaned. She began helping his fingers,

which were busy at work on her clothes. When his lips set her free, she stepped back, flushed, and disrobed completely, almost swallowed up by her anxious heartbeats. She felt wicked . . . but it was a delicious feeling . . . one that she had for too long been a stranger to. . . .

Jess reached and stroked her cheek with his fingertips, then lower, touching the soft flesh of her breasts. He wanted her! Damn how he wanted her. But not only was he old enough to be her father . . . he had even lied about his name. But from state to state, gambling house to gambling house, that had been necessary. Many miles of IOU notes had been left behind him. To protect himself, he had used many aliases. He had to believe that now he was even protecting *her* by not being totally honest about his name.

Closing her eyes, feeling the crazy warmth between her thighs pleasurably paining her, Holly couldn't understand why he was hesitating. Her skin quivered as his lips began to explore her body. Then she sighed when he finally lifted her into his arms and gently placed her on the bed.

Almost blinded with a raging passion for him, she watched through what appeared to be a lazy haze across her eyes as he stepped from all his clothes. And when he climbed atop her and their bare skins made contact, she felt the burning ache inside her rise to an almost bursting. Then he entered her. She cried out with the rapture of the moment. She slung her arms about his neck and her legs about his waist and met his eager thrusts with working, raised hips.

"It's never been so good. . . ." Holly whispered,

feeling the waves of sensuousness enter her brain, dizzying her.

"Baby . . ." Jess groaned, gritting his teeth as his steady rhythm was bringing him closer and closer to the brink. . . .

Holly dug her fingers into his shoulders, then screamed out when the sweet spasms of release engulfed her in fiery splashes. She smiled as she felt him stiffen and cry out his own pleasure. . . .

Jess then relaxed atop her. He burrowed his nose in her neck, breathing hard. "God . . ." he whispered.

"Jess . . ."

He rose a bit from her and raised one of her hands to his lips, kissing each fingertip, one at a time. He watched her intensely, seeing how peacefully calm and beautiful she lay beneath him.

"Honey, I'd rather you call me Blackie," he murmured. "I much prefer my nickname over Jess. . . ."

Holly giggled. "Blackie . . . ?" she whispered. "Why on earth are you called Blackie?"

"For my game of Blackjack," Blackie said matter-of-factly. "For my skills at playing blackjack . . ."

Chapter Six

Wolves cried hungrily in the brush and the trail that led through the break in the cliff lay in deep darkness. The jutting boulders overhead reminded Kendra of outspread wings of birds ready to swoop down to swallow her beneath them. Clutching harder to Domino's reins, she squinted her eyes, no longer able to make out Lucas's outline on the horizon. Maybe the mountain pass had swallowed him up.

Suddenly Kendra was afraid. She had hoped that Lucas would have reached his destination before now. Where was he going? Did he live with the Indians? Or did he make his residence elsewhere?

But, no matter which, Kendra now realized the foolishness of having followed him. If a wolf didn't eat her, most surely some other wild beast would.

The crumbling of falling rocks ahead caused Kendra to stop Domino's further approach. With a pounding heart, she watched the spot from where the noise had come. Moving slowly but deliberately she pulled a pistol from her right holster and cocked it, pointing it straight ahead.

More scattering of rock and the neighing of a horse caused Kendra's breath to catch with a start. But when Lucas moved his horse from behind some tall brush and faced her, she sighed and quickly replaced her pistol in its holster.

"What are you doing here?" Lucas growled, pushing the tip of his hat back a fraction.

The moon had slipped easily from behind a cloud and bathed everything in its reach with its pale, hazy light. Kendra's pulse raced, now that she was able to see how Lucas's dark hair lay boyishly over his forehead in waves, and she didn't need any more light to know the color of those eyes, accusing her in their magnetic grays.

"Well?" Lucas persisted, drawing his horse up next to hers. "Kendra, what the hell do you think you're doing? Have you been on my trail since I left you back at the schoolhouse?"

Kendra was thankful that it was night. It saved her the embarrassment of Lucas's seeing her blushing. But the situation she had now found herself in . . . being off so alone with this man of her dreams . . . was just cause for her face to be the color of a gorgeous sunset and her heart to be all aflutter.

"No. I haven't been following you," she lied. "I just decided to do some exploring here in these mountain passes."

"Why the hell would you do such an asinine thing as that?" he stormed. "Don't you know the dangers lurking out here at night for someone as inexperienced as you?"

Kendra straightened her back and tossed her head angrily. "Lucas . . . whatever your last name is . . ." she stormed right back. "I imagine I can outdraw you and shoot just as straight as you can any day."

Lucas threw his head back with a roar of laughter, then eyed her amusedly. "I'm sure you can," he said, still chuckling. "We'll see one day. But for now I think I'd best escort you back to your ranch."

"If I wanted to return home I could do it without your assistance," she said dryly. "As it is, I much prefer to continue on my journey."

Lucas placed a hand on his right revolver and rested it there. "Where the hell to?" he questioned, lifting an eyebrow.

Kendra rearranged her hat, fidgeting with it. "That's no concern of yours," she stubbornly stated.

"Oh?" Lucas said, then swung his horse around and began moving away from her. "In that case," he said from across his shoulder. "I'll just be on my way."

Kendra's heart palpitated. She reached a hand toward Lucas, then dropped it to her side, hurt and angry. He didn't care enough to truly be worried about her safety. To him, she had only been cause for delay . . . an inconvenience. Nothing else.

"Now what shall I do?" she whispered, now only vaguely able to make him out beneath the dancing shadows of the moon.

She glanced behind her, seeing a vast stretch of nothingness, then straight ahead once more, seeing the dark outline of great, rocky plateaus.

"I have no choice but to continue following him," she whispered. Desperation seized her. Once more he had disappeared from view. Was he playing tricks on her? Would he pounce on her this time and frighten her from her saddle?

"He's heartless," she hissed. "How could I have ever thought him anything but heartless?"

She nudged her knees into Domino's sides and snapped her reins angrily. "Come on, boy," she said. "I've started something. I have no choice but to finish it."

But she now wished to be home, safely in her bed. The thought of sleeping out in the open, alone, was quickly becoming a possibility, and it caused a quick turning of her stomach just thinking of the many ways her life could be brought to a sudden halt. . . .

The canyon suddenly opened to grand proportions and the dark of the night hid the tips of the magnificent mountains. Then just as quickly, she had entered another narrow, rough gulch that grew rapidly deeper and wider. The shadows of the ledges had taken on a purple hue and the trail was full of stones and ruts. And when another wolf cried from somewhere above her, sounding much too close, Kendra tensed and urged Domino even more quickly onward.

Finally, the canyon sloped gradually down to where water ran and fresh green grass grew in abundance. A snapping of twigs behind a piñon pine tree caused Kendra to stop her horse jerkily. Then, seeing Lucas once more urging his horse out into the open, Kendra knew that all along he had been there, knowing that she was close behind him.

"I hope you enjoy playing these sorts of games," Kendra hissed, doubling a hand into a tight fist at her side.

"I could leave again. This time for real," he chuckled. He drew a cigar from inside his shirt pocket and thrust it between his perfectly formed teeth. With a thumbnail he struck a match and set it to his cigar, inhaling deeply on the smooth, sweet taste.

Annoyed at first by her pursuing him, afraid she might cause problems for the Piute, he now was most definitely amused. He hadn't met a woman quite like her before. Though his Indian love, Heart Speak, was as strong as an ox and daring, Kendra was even more so, a definite combination of a lady and a hellion.

Yes, she was the type of woman he could get serious about, but he did have to remember the inevitable and imminent friction between himself and Aaron Carpenter, as soon as the announcement was made of his decision to bring sheep into the community. Just in case gossip of this may already have reached Aaron, Lucas thought it best to not yet reveal his full identity to Kendra. He was afraid of spoiling what time they could share together before she might have reason to hate him.

Not willing to give in to Lucas, Kendra said, "If you wish to go on without me, go ahead."

Lucas flicked ashes from his cigar. "No, Kendra," he sighed. "I won't go on without you. Really. I would enjoy the pleasure of your company. But surely you are through with exploring for the night, aren't you? Or was that what you were really up to? Strange that you'd just happen to be on the same trail I was traveling. Wouldn't you say so?"

"If you must know," Kendra said dryly, "I *was* following you." She relaxed her shoulders, imploring him with the soft blue sparkles of her eyes. "Now you know," she said. "Aren't you proud of yourself for pulling that out of me?"

Lucas clamped his lips tightly onto his cigar, chuckling. "Yeah . . ." he said. "Guess I am. But I have to ask. Why *were* you following me?"

"I wanted to check on Quick Deer," she lied. "To see if

93

he was getting proper care."

"My, oh my, but we have ourselves a devoted nurse here," he chuckled further, patting his horse as his horse began pawing nervously at the ground. "The South could've used you during the war."

Blanching, Kendra tightened her hold on her reins. "What did you say?" she gasped.

"I believe you heard me," he said throatily, realizing her withdrawal. Most surely it had been the mention of the war. Damn. Had her family fought for the Union? If so, there was further reason for possible trouble between them. Had she been as devoted to the Union cause as he had been to the Confederacy?

Then goose pimples rose on his flesh. When the time came to talk with Aaron, would their different alliances during the war cause Aaron to not listen to reason . . . ?

"You were with the Confederacy?" Kendra said in an almost-whisper.

"Does that really matter?"

Kendra thought fast and hard. How could a man who showed such feelings for Indians have fought for the enslaving of the blacks? How could he be sensitive about one group of people and insensitive about another?

Maybe the war had changed him, she thought hopefully to herself.

But then she remembered Aaron and his hatred for the "Johnny Rebs." "Once a Reb, *always* a Reb," Aaron had so often said.

Kendra wheeled Domino around. "Maybe I'd best return home, after all," she said. "I don't like what my exploring has thus far uncovered."

"Kendra . . ." Lucas said, in an almost-shout. "The war has been over for some time now. And if you'll recall, your side won. How is it with you? Must you keep sticking a knife in a man's gut even after he's down?"

Kendra pulled her reins tightly, stopping Domino. Slowly she turned Domino around, seeing Lucas's tall, dark figure in the saddle, wondering how a man like him could have ever lost at anything! There was such command in his eyes and his voice, and in the magnificent way in which he held himself in the saddle!

Suddenly her heart went out to him. There *was* no cause for her to be behaving in such a manner. The war was over! There was no need to revive it between the two of them.

"I'm behaving poorly," she finally said. "You must remember, though, you were the one to make first mention of the war."

"You *would* have been a good nurse for the Confederacy," he teased, hoping she would take it as he meant it.

"Oh, Lucas . . ." she sighed, then laughed silkily as he guided his horse next to hers.

Lucas lifted a hand to her face and traced its outline with his forefinger. "You're so lovely," he murmured. "Even in the moonlight I can see your full loveliness."

Kendra's heart raced and her insides trembled with a creamy sort of warmth. Each spot his fingers touched seemed to sizzle with a searing burning of desire for him. She leaned into his hand as he lay his full palm against her cheek.

"Lucas . . ." she whispered. "Oh, Lucas, you do confuse me so."

Then, just as suddenly, she hated herself for such a confession. The cold of his ring against her flesh reminded her that he was probably not even free to love her in return.

Remembering this, she eased away from him and straightened her hat on her head. "Maybe I should return. . . ." she murmured.

"But surely you'd rather go on to the Indian village with me," he said. "Have you forgotten about Quick Deer? I thought you said that you were concerned for his welfare."

Kendra fluttered her thick lashes nervously, entangled in her innocent web of lies. "Why, yes . . ." she murmured. "I am. He did have a terrible break to his leg."

"Then come. I will take you to him."

"Was that your original destination?"

"Yes . . ." he said, flicking his smoked cigar away from him. "But all along you knew that."

"Yes . . . I . . . did . . ." Kendra murmured. She wanted to come right out and ask him why he had such devotion to the Indians. What had the Indians done for him? If he had fought so diligently for the Confederate cause, most surely he was not from this region. He is such a man of mystery, she thought again.

"How far must we go?" she said aloud, drawing rein next to Lucas as they began to move further down the mountain pass. To her confusion, he seemed to be making one large circle from where they had begun back at the schoolhouse. And if Kendra hadn't known better, she would have guessed she was now pretty close to some of the Carpenters' most fertile grazing land. Where was he taking her?

"Not far now," he said, casting her a fast glance, then a more lingering, appraising one. "I have to ask, Kendra, do you do these sorts of things often?"

"What do you mean?"

"Take off, and I'm sure without alerting your family. Won't you be missed? Won't someone come looking for you?"

"My brother Aaron is on the spring roundup," she replied demurely. "So *he* won't miss me. My brother Seth is in Virginia City, working the silver mines, and my sister-in-law, well, she's too preoccupied with her own little world to even notice my absence."

"All right. That's all well and good," Lucas said. "But you still didn't answer my question."

Kendra's eyes widened. "Question?"

Lucas sighed heavily. "Do you do this often? Stay overnight away from home?"

A slow flush rose on Kendra's face. She avoided his steady stare, now embarrassed. She now understood the implications of his questioning. He thought she might possibly go off with any man at any time and stay the night with him. The thought repulsed even her. What must he be thinking of her? Yet, if she told him this was the first time . . . that he was the first to stir her curiosity so . . . then he would know too much about her feelings for him.

But she could not let him believe she was a loose woman.

"I told you," she murmured, lowering her eyes. "I wanted to check on the small Indian boy, Quick Deer. That's all."

"You still aren't answering my question, Kendra," Lucas growled.

Kendra set her jaw firmly, annoyed, then shouted, "No! I've never done anything like this before!"

She rode quickly away from him, angry that he had

97

such a way with her. Then her breath caught in her throat when he was suddenly beside her again and had Domino's reins freed from her hands, stopping Domino with a start as his horse also stopped.

"What are you doing . . . ?" Kendra gasped. She watched in wide-eyed innocence as he dismounted, then reached and drew her from the saddle and into his arms.

"What do you think?" he said huskily.

He knocked her hat from her head and then his own, then crushed his lips hungrily against hers. Startled by his abruptness, Kendra began struggling. She pushed against his chest. She tried to pull her lips free. But his fingers, coiled through her hair, held her lips in place, while his other arm held her tightly around the waist.

A sweet lethargy began to take over inside Kendra, and she suddenly lost her urge to be released from his hold. A deep moan rose from inside her. She had never felt anything so utterly delicious before. Not even his first kiss had been this heavenly! As though in a spell, she wove her arms about his neck in total surrender and returned his kiss wholly and passionately.

The cry of a wolf in the distance was no longer a threat to Kendra. She was safe in the arms of the man she loved. She knew she had wanted him from that very first day. And she would not let anything stand in the way of this moment of bliss with him. Though the thought that he might be married gave her a slight twinge of guilt, she quickly tossed it aside and relished the touch of his hand inside her shirt, cupping her breast. She was so glad she had chosen to not wear an undergarment beneath her shirt. The clumsiness of removing it could have taken away from this moment. All that lay beneath her shirt, cold on her flesh, was the squash blossom necklace he had given her. She didn't want ever to remove it. It was a part of him. . . .

"Kendra . . ." Lucas whispered, moving his lips to one of her earlobes, kissing her softly there. "Darling . . ."

As his lips traveled across her face, Kendra trembled from the passion rising inside her. "Lucas . . ." she whispered back, gasping as he raised her shirt and found her breast with quick flicks from his hot tongue.

"Remove the shirt, Lucas," Kendra whispered, stepping back away from him. "Undress me and . . . take . . . me."

Her eyes felt hot. Her heart pounded wildly. She had never felt so utterly wicked and daring. She had hungered for freedom in this vast territory of Nevada, but now she was ready to relinquish her newfound freedom to be possessed by a man . . . but not any man . . . only Lucas.

An uneasiness crept through her. She didn't even know his last name. But suddenly that didn't matter. Lucas had slipped her jeans down and off and was now down on his knees before her, kissing her.

"Good Lord . . ." she whispered throatily, apprehensive, yet really not. When his tongue darted and touched the very core of her pleasure, Kendra wove her fingers through his hair and drew him even closer.

She hadn't known that such a thing as he was doing was possible! Yet here she was . . . standing beneath the soft rays of the moon in the shadows of the purplish-colored mountains . . . being made love to by the man of her dreams!

Writhing from the intense pleasure he was bestowing upon her, Kendra loosened her fingers from his hair and instead, tangled them into her own and lifted it from her shoulders as she threw her head back in a long, sensuous sigh.

When Lucas rose to his feet and pulled her sleek, satin figure next to his body of steel, Kendra wrapped a leg around him, a tigress, purring, as he once more crushed his lips against hers. The taste was strange. It was a mixture of both her and him. It was a taste that set her even more aglow inside, and when he released her and stepped away from her, she reached her arms out to him, begging for more.

"Are you sure, Kendra . . . ?" Lucas asked huskily. His eyes were dark with hungry need for her. She could feel the sweet caress of them as he slowly moved his gaze over her.

"Lucas, I'm sure. . . ." she whispered.

With a racing pulse and flaming face, Kendra watched unashamedly as each separate piece of his clothing was discarded. Each new spot of flesh exposed to her fiery eyes flamed her insides even more. And when he was standing totally nude before her, he stood there for a moment, as though he wanted her to first get used to him before proceeding any further.

"Now that you see me, are you still sure you're ready for this?" he queried throatily.

"Even more so . . ." she whispered. "Lucas, you are so beautiful."

Lucas threw his head back in a hearty laugh, then looked at her adoringly. "Darling, a man isn't beautiful," he said. "A man's body is damn ugly."

He took a step toward her and began running both hands across her body, stopping then to cup both breasts. "It is *you* who are beautiful," he murmured. "I've never seen anyone who could match such beauty."

Kendra's thoughts flashed to the Indian woman . . . then back to Lucas. She would *not* let anything spoil this! She would not!

Lucas guided Kendra downward onto the soft, dew-covered grass that was to be the stage on which they were to perform their love. The sequined stars and moon were to be their audience, and the cool breeze whistling through the canyon passes was to be their symphony. It was perfect . . . so perfect that Kendra was not even aware of the growing chill of night. She was too filled with anticipation and too drugged with passion to be aware of anything but Lucas.

"Kendra . . . God, Kendra," Lucas whispered, lowering himself over her.

Kendra swallowed hard and closed her eyes when she felt his flesh touch hers. His curly fronds of dark chest hair tickled her breasts. His breath was hot against her cheek. And his hands! They never stayed still. They continued to travel over her, teasing, tormenting, carrying her higher on this pinnacle of rapture.

His lips quickly took charge. And when Lucas finally possessed a breast and set his teeth gently to its soft, pink tip, Kendra laced her arms about his neck and clung to him.

Then she felt his eyes upon her, studying her as he pushed himself a bit away from her. "You're sure, Kendra?" he asked huskily. "It'd be damned hard to stop now, but if you've reconsidered, I wouldn't hurt you for anything."

Kendra's brows lifted. "Hurt?" she murmured. "You could never hurt me, Lucas. Please. Please do go on. I'm about to burst for want of you."

"That's all I needed to hear," he said. "I will kiss the

moments of pain away."

"Lucas, *what* pai . . ." she began to say, but his lips sealing hers kept further words from flowing.

Her head began a faster spinning as he kissed her hard and long. And as his tongue sought entrance between her lips, so did he enter her from below. First gently, then much harder, causing a moment of sharp pain that quickly blended into a most magical realm of intense pleasure.

With tongues intertwining . . . with Kendra melting slowly inside . . . she wrapped her legs about Lucas's hips and began moving with each of his thrusts inside her. Each time their stomachs hit, Kendra's euphoric state heightened. She clung . . . she moved . . . she sucked on his tongue . . . then something more pleasurable than she had ever imagined suddenly blossomed inside her. It was as though every brilliant color of the rainbow had been ignited inside her head, as she felt her body spasm . . . melt . . . then blend in with his as he also shook and quivered above her.

Their tongues and lips slowly parted. Lucas nestled his nose into the soft silk of her hair and lay there breathing hard. Kendra reached to touch his cheek, loving him deeply.

"Did it hurt much?" Lucas whispered into her ear.

"I told you, Lucas," she whispered back. "You could never hurt me. It was beautiful. Absolutely beautiful."

"You're not sorry?"

"I could never be. . . ."

"Never let another man touch you, Kendra," Lucas growled.

"Never," she purred. "No. Never."

"You love me, Kendra?"

"Yes, Lucas. I do. I do. I *do*. . . ."

"But you've not known me long, darling."

"Long enough, you silly."

Lucas leaned up on an elbow and eyed her questioningly. Then he chuckled amusedly. "You *silly*?" he teased. "That's what you think of me and my lovemaking?"

Kendra curved her body more into the shape of his. She leaned and kissed the hollow of his throat. "Your lovemaking is superb," she whispered.

"Why, thank you, my lovely," he laughed, leaning to breeze a kiss to the soft flesh of her breast, causing Kendra's breath to leave her momentarily. "And if it wasn't so late *and* getting so suddenly cold, I'd want a repeat performance from *you*."

As he rose from atop Kendra, she felt the whipping of the breeze as it picked up its speed. Trembling, she hurried to her feet and began dressing. "The weather here is so temperamental," she said.

"Like most women . . ." Lucas laughed. He hurried into his clothes, secured his guns at his hips, then rescued both their hats from the ground. Brushing Kendra's off, he handed it to her.

Fully dressed now, Kendra gladly accepted the hat and the warmth it was going to give to her. She placed it on her head and walked, clinging to Lucas, toward their horses.

"I'll always remember this night," she said softly.

"Hopefully there'll be many more like this, Kendra."

Pangs of jealousy cut away at Kendra's heart. Now they would be traveling on to the Indian village and to *her*. Would Lucas climb into bed with her . . . make love to her . . . after what they had just shared? The thought made icy goose pimples rise on her flesh, followed by an outward show of chilling.

"We'd best hurry," Lucas said. "You're trembling. I hope you don't catch cold. I should have spread a saddle blanket on the ground."

Kendra leaned into his embrace, cuddling. "That would have been precious time wasted," she said. "Please don't worry about me. I'm strong. I don't catch cold easily."

"I could still escort you back to your ranch, Kendra."

"Lucas, I want to go with *you*," she stubbornly argued. Though they had just shared the ultimate of intimacies, the mystery of him was still threatening Kendra's peace of mind. She *would* get inside this man, get to know more than the passionate side of him. . . .

"Then up you go," Lucas laughed, taking her by the waist to lift her up into the saddle.

Kendra grabbed her reins, then leaned and gave Lucas a sweet kiss. "My, you are such a gentleman," she teased, then watched as he mounted his horse, proud to know him . . . proud to be loved by him.

"Let's be on our way," he said, lifting the corner of his mouth into a half grin. "Seems we somehow got sidetracked."

Kendra laughed softly and followed along beside him, once more silently admiring how tall he sat in the saddle. The sudden shine of the turquoise ring on his left hand caught her eye, causing a slow ache to circle her heart. Her fingers crept up to her neck and touched the cold silver of the squash blossom necklace. Though he had said it had been a gift from the Indians, somehow she knew that this necklace had been given to her out of love . . . *his* love for her.

Had the ring he wore been given to him out of love? Given to him possibly by the waiting Indian maiden . . . ?

A sudden flashing of lightning flared across the dark velvet sky, followed by an echo of rumblings on all sides of them. The wind began to moan through the canyon and peppering raindrops were like ice pellets against Kendra's face.

"Lucas . . ." she said, trembling.

"Damn weather," he growled. "But we're almost there, Kendra."

There was then a sudden, almost drawn silence in the canyon, followed by forked lightning zigzagging across the sky. When another explosion of thunder rumbled through the ground, causing Domino to neigh furiously, Kendra caught her first sight of what she thought had to be the Indian village. She glanced quickly at Lucas, then back ahead.

The Indian camp was on a straight stretch of land, with the mountains at its north side and a stand of tall pine trees to the south. The camp, made in a circular form with a pole and canvas shelter on the outside of the ring, a sort of crude fencing, was fully exposed on both its east and west sides.

Lucas moved on ahead. Kendra silently followed. And, once through the crude fence, they were in an adobe village asleep under the midnight black of night. Kendra saw no stores. Only houses and stables, and a blacksmith shop. A huge well stood in the center of the village, obviously shared by everyone in the community, and horses and mules could be seen grazing at the far end of the camp, where grass seemed to be more in abundance.

"Everyone's asleep," Lucas said, drawing rein at Kendra's side. "Come. I'll take you to my house. You can spend the night there."

Kendra tensed. His house was probably *her* house. . . .

"We'll see Quick Deer in the morning," Lucas added, then gave her an amused look. "He *is* your purpose for being here, isn't he?"

Kendra smiled coyly and didn't answer. She was glad they had finally reached their destination. The rain was coming down harder and small balls of sleet were pelting Domino's mane.

Lucas pointed toward a particular adobe house that stood dark before them. "You go on inside," he said, dismounting. He came to her and helped her from the saddle. "I'll tend to the horses and be right back."

Not waiting to argue, she rushed on toward the house, then cautiously pushed the wooden door open. Barely breathing, she stepped on inside. Feeling around her, she found a table and on it a kerosene lamp. She felt around some more and thankfully found some matches.

With a pounding heart, she lifted the glass chimney from the lamp, screwed the wick up, and placed a struck match to it. And once the room was bathed in a soft, golden glow, Kendra turned and began to look slowly around her, surprised, and yet not. . . .

It was a simple room, with roughly hewn wooden chairs and a table, and shelves filled with dishes, pots and pans, and canned foods. There didn't appear to be a living room . . . only a kitchen . . . with a fireplace at the far end that looked like it was used for both cooking and heating.

The walls of this adobe house were supported by rows of long, slender poles nailed upon heavier uprights at the corners. Between these rows had been poured wet adobe mud that dried as heavy as cement. The floor was of white

106

sand, and footprints in this sand led into one other room, which Kendra feared to enter. If she found *her* there, Kendra felt it most certainly would break her heart!

But having the need to know before Lucas's return, Kendra inched her way on toward the doorway. Holding the lamp up a bit, she let its light enter before her. Then, readying herself for "whatever," she took another cautious step forward.

Seeing the room void of anything but a crude bed covered with bright Indian blankets caused tears of joyous relief to seep from Kendra's eyes. Perhaps she had been wrong all along. Perhaps he wasn't married.

She placed the lamp on the floor beside the bed, ready to stoop to remove her boots. But a stirring behind her drew Kendra around. She was full of smiles, ready to fling herself into Lucas's arms. But, instead, her insides froze, as she saw *her* standing there in a beautifully beaded deerskin dress, with hate in the dark pools of her eyes. . . .

"What are *you* doing here?" Heart Speak asked in perfect English.

Lucas's shadow appeared at the doorway behind Heart Speak.

Kendra felt as though she were in a trap. "Lucas . . . ?" she murmured, trembling inside.

Chapter Seven

Lucas could feel hate heavy in the air and knew that his two women could never be friends. One day soon he would have to speak loudly of his choice. He already knew in his heart who it would be. Telling the one who was not of his choosing would be the hardest job of his life. She was a passionate lover . . . one any man would kill for. But he would not have two women ready to kill over *him*. . . .

"Kendra . . ." he said, now moving to Kendra's side. He put his arm about her waist. "I'd like for you to meet Heart Speak. This is Quick Deer's mother."

Then Lucas reached for one of Heart Speak's hands and drew her closer to him. "And, Heart Speak, this is the woman who set Quick Deer's leg. She has come to check on Quick Deer to see if he's recovering quickly enough."

Heart Speak jerked her hand away. "She didn't have to come clear to Piute village to find that out," she hissed. "You could have told her."

Kendra jerked free from Lucas and placed her hands on her hips. "Why, you ungrateful . . ."

109

"Kendra . . ." Lucas growled, interrupting her, once more placing his arm about her waist.

Heart Speak flashed her dark eyes angrily toward Kendra. "I tell you Quick Deer is all right. I'm his mother. My word should be enough." She leaned into Kendra's face. "Now you can go. We don't need you here."

Heart Speak's gaze fell and captured the squash blossom necklace hanging from around Kendra's neck. Her eyes wavered as her fingers reached toward it, then she thought better of it and withdrew her hand and instead coiled her fingers into a tight fist at her side.

"The necklace," Heart Speak said shakily. "Where did you get . . . that . . . necklace . . . ?"

Kendra could see the disbelief . . . even shock in the petite Indian's eyes. Her own fingers went to the necklace and began tracing the hanging silver squash blossoms with her fingertips. "I thought it was a gift from your people," she stammered. She shot Lucas a questioning glance. For the first time ever she saw a wavering of his usual commanding gray eyes. What was going on here?

Heart Speak squared her shoulders and went and spoke up into Lucas's face. "So this is gift chosen by you to represent our people?" she said, with evident strain. "Lucas, that doesn't represent my people's feelings at all. That particular necklace represents *your* feelings for the blue-eyed white woman. Not ours. You should have given her a simple basket. That's all."

Flipping her long coils of midnight black braids around, Heart Speak ran from the bedroom. Kendra's breath was stolen from her when she read desperation etched across Lucas's face as he raced after Heart Speak.

110

Kendra couldn't help herself. She had to move to the arch of the door to see what Lucas's next move would be, and it tore at her heart when she saw the scene that followed.

Boldly blocking the door that led out into the raging storm, Lucas watched Heart Speak with an ache in his heart. He had forgotten about the necklace. And he understood Heart Speak's feelings about it. The necklace did have a special meaning! Damn! That was the reason he had given it to Kendra. A basket? No. He couldn't have given Kendra just a basket, though most baskets woven by the Piute also had their own symbolic meanings.

"Get out of my way, Lucas," Heart Speak hissed. "You have the white woman to warm your bed this night."

"Heart Speak . . ."

Heart Speak pounced on Lucas and began pounding on his chest with doubled fists. "You heartless . . ." she screamed. "You gave the white woman a special gift . . . you brought her to your house. . . ."

Growling, Lucas grabbed Heart Speak's wrists and wrestled her up against a wall and pinioned her there. "Now you listen to me, damn it," he said from between clenched teeth. "You don't own me, Heart Speak. You never have. I do what I want *when* I want. Savvy?"

Rivers of tears rolled from Heart Speak's eyes. "Lucas . . . I'm sorry . . ." she whispered. "I didn't mean to upset you."

"Oh, Heart Speak, my little Indian," Lucas said, now drawing her gently into his arms. He nestled his nose into her hair as she stood there, only as tall as his chin. "I wouldn't hurt you for the world. You know that."

Heart Speak threw her arms around him. "I'm sorry,

111

Lucas," she whispered. "I'll go . . ."

Lucas withdrew slowly from her and lifted her chin with a forefinger. He bent a soft kiss to her lips. "Yes. Go. Tomorrow we will talk," he said. "Tomorrow Kendra *does* want to see Quick Deer. She *does* care, Heart Speak. She's a good white woman. She's come only because she has a big heart."

Kendra covered her mouth with a hand, feeling tears near. This man she was so desperately in love with obviously loved this Indian woman very much. How had it happened that he was so accepted by the Piute? Why did he love them so much?

Turning, placing her back to the tender scene, Kendra now wished that she hadn't come. The knowing hurt!

"But how much do I truly know?" she whispered.

She glanced around her, seeing the sparse furnishings of the room . . . the roughness of the walls and ceiling and the sandy floor. Was Lucas truly content to live in this way? He had fought for the South. Many from the south had lived in mansions . . . had been bred in the most influential schools. . . . How could he live this way? Was it really because . . . of . . . *her* . . . ?

Kendra knew that love made one do many crazy things. *She* was here, wasn't she? She should have never come.

"Darling."

Lucas's velvet voice speaking from behind her drew Kendra around with a start. It was unbelievable! Only moments ago he had held another woman in his arms, and now he was calling her "darling." She felt furious.

"I'm sorry, Kendra," Lucas said. "Heart Speak is usually not so overcome by emotion. Tomorrow it will be different. I hope you understand."

"Understand?" she said. "I find all of this *very* hard

112

to understand."

Lucas's eyes became cold. "No one forced you to come here, Kendra," he stated flatly. "But now that you are here, you'd best just make the best of it."

"And how am I to do that?"

"I would suggest you first take off your clothes."

"What . . . ?" she gasped.

An amused look gathered onto his face as his eyes once more warmed to her. "Undress," he said, smiling at her continued look of disbelief. Faking a yawn, Lucas began unbuckling his gunbelt.

"Lucas, you are unbelievable," Kendra gasped, taking a step backward. "If you think I'm going to—"

"To what . . . ?" he teased further, draping his gunbelt over a chair, then unbuttoning his shirt. He lifted his lips into a small grin.

"To go to bed with you after . . . after . . . *her* . . . well Lucas, you're *crazy*!"

Kendra watched, dry-mouthed, as he stepped out of his jeans. And when he sat down on the bed, nude except for his boots, she turned her back to him, flushed scarlet. She jumped as she heard the thud of one boot on the sandy floor. She tensed when she heard the second thud and knew that now he was completely nude and waiting for her to join him. He did have some nerve.

"You'll catch your death of cold in those wet things," Lucas said quietly. "You'd best take them off."

Kendra closed her eyes and doubled her fists to her side. She was about to explode inside from mixed emotions! She began to count backwards from ten and when she had whispered the number one she spun around on her heel, ready to tell him to leave the bed . . . to never touch her again!

113

"What . . . ?" she whispered, looking quickly around the room. "Where . . . ?"

Lucas *and* his clothes were neither on the bed nor in the room. Feeling a faint chill of fright pass over her, she tiptoed to the arch of the door and stopped suddenly when she saw that he hadn't actually left the adobe house. Instead, he had pulled wooden chairs up by the fireplace and had draped his wet clothes over the backs of each. Stooping now, he was preparing a fire in the fireplace.

Relieved more than angry, Kendra crept back inside the bedroom, now feeling the dampness of the clothes clinging to her flesh. She hugged herself with her arms, trembling.

"I do need to get out of these clothes," she whispered. "I am freezing. And I don't need a cold to complicate things further."

But neither did she wish to walk around nude in front of Lucas. Their shared embraces were too fresh in her mind. There was no need to tempt him again, especially now that Kendra was convinced that the Indian woman had shared more with him than she wanted to think about. They more than likely had even shared the birth of a son.

The thought stabbed away at her insides. Yet . . . where had the Indian woman gone now? If she was his wife, wouldn't she still be in this house? And where was Quick Deer? If he were Lucas's son, wouldn't he also be sharing this cabin with his father?

But I don't know the customs of the Piute, she thought. Maybe separate houses are required. . . .

"Kendra. Your clothes," Lucas shouted from the outer room. "Bring them to me. We'll dry them by

114

the fire."

A sweet fragrance of wood burning seeped into the bedroom, then the smell of coffee. Kendra's stomach growled and her mouth watered. She had missed the evening meal at the ranch! She hadn't thought of hunger until now.

With trembling fingers, she lifted her hat from her head, then slowly disrobed until she stood shivering even more, completely nude, in the middle of the room. Looking desperately around her, her gaze settled on the striped Indian blanket draped across the bed.

"Ah! At least I'll have something on," she whispered. She jerked the blanket quickly from the bed and wrapped it snugly around her, enjoying the warm feel of the wool next to her body. She flipped her long golden hair to hang down her back and gathered her clothes and hat into her arms.

"If I must, I must," she stubbornly whispered. With a set jaw, she moved barefoot into the outer room. The sand felt strange sifting between her toes. It seemed misplaced, being inside a house. . . .

"So you've decided to join me," Lucas said, rising from a bent knee to meet her approach.

Seeing his manhood so fully exposed unnerved Kendra all over again. She glanced quickly away, but not quickly enough that having seen him there hadn't kept another crimson blush from rising to her cheeks.

Refusing to look at him, she blindly handed her clothes toward him. She cringed when he laughed throatily and relieved her of her wet clothes.

"Lucas . . ." she whispered. "Please cover yourself, uh, you know. Please?"

She clamped her lips tightly together when she heard

115

his low chuckle but eased inside when she heard the rustle of clothes.

"Is this better?" Lucas said, once more chuckling.

Kendra turned slowly around, sighing with relief when she saw that he had stepped back into his jeans. Then her eyes wavered a bit. "But if you wear those wet things *you* might catch cold," she said softly.

She glanced toward the bedroom, suddenly remembering that she had seen no wardrobe. "Don't you have a change of clothes here in your house?" she murmured. Something about the way his eyes drew a sudden coldness into them made her heart skip a beat.

"Come. Sit by the fire," was his only reply. "I've made some coffee. And if you're hungry, I think I can even manage a bite to eat for you."

The crackling lure of the fire drew Kendra toward it, still puzzling over his refusal to answer her question. And now she remembered Heart Speak's reaction to the necklace. The mystery behind this gift was almost as puzzling as the mystery of *him*.

Kendra settled down on the soft sand before the fire, huddling cozily inside the blanket. Out of the corner of her eye she watched Lucas draping her clothes next to his. She couldn't deny the passion welling up inside her as she watched his shoulder and back muscles flex with his every movement.

And when his gray eyes met her steady stare in a quiet knowing, Kendra swallowed hard and forced her eyes away from him. She loved him. Oh, how she loved him! But it was an elusive love . . . a love doomed. He belonged . . . to another.

She listened now as he began rattling dishes from a shelf. "Let's see now . . ." he was mumbling. "A bit of dried apples, beans, and salt pork."

Suddenly a plate of food was there before Kendra's eyes. Slowly she reached her hand to the blue-flower-trimmed dish, flinching when her hand grazed against his.

"Thank you," she murmured. The aroma of coffee was stronger in the air and the sound of rain and thunder had eased somewhat outside the thin walls of the adobe house.

"And now a cup of coffee," Lucas said, offering her a steaming tin cup.

Again she thanked him, refusing to let their eyes meet.

"I hope the storm passes by morning," Lucas said, settling on the floor next to Kendra.

"So you can rid yourself of me? So I can return home?" Kendra said, sarcasm thick in her words. "Lucas, you don't have to worry. I'd be delighted to leave."

"I'd rather you didn't. Not tomorrow."

Kendra's eyes widened. "Lucas, why on earth would you want me here? You know as well as I that I'm not wanted. You saw Heart Speak's reaction to me. Imagine how the entire tribe of the Piute will react to my being here."

She lowered her eyes, picking at the dried apples with her fingers. "I'd best leave at the break of dawn."

"No, Kendra, you're wrong. You *must* stay. I want you to see tomorrow's activities. I'd like you to observe what it is I, personally, am trying to accomplish for these Indians."

"Lucas . . ." Kendra argued.

"You *will* stay, Kendra," he stated flatly. "I won't take no for an answer."

Kendra crashed her plate of food to the floor and then her cup of coffee, rising quickly to her feet. "So!" she said angrily. "I am now a prisoner, am I? We'll see about that!"

She stormed around the room, grabbing her damp clothes. "Damn it, Lucas," she said. "I'm leaving *now*. Don't try to stop me."

Lucas jumped to his feet and jerked the clothes from her arms. "Kendra, you are the most stubborn, bull-headed woman I've ever met," he snarled.

Kendra whirled around, grabbing the blanket back against her as it ebbed downward. "I will *not* curl into your arms and weep like that . . . like that female savage did when she saw that she had angered you," Kendra stated hotly. "You will never get me to whimper after you like a baby needing coddling."

Fire raged in Lucas's eyes as he threw Kendra's clothes across the room. He went to her and grabbed her by the shoulders. "Don't you *ever again* call Heart Speak a savage," he said between clenched teeth. "She . . . like all Piute—is a gentle Indian. If not for them—"

"You'd what?" Kendra said, daring him with a stubborn lift of her chin. As Lucas's fingers lessened their hold on her shoulders, the blanket crumpled away from her and slithered slowly down her body.

A gentle smile curved Lucas's lips upward and his gray eyes darkened in color as he let his gaze move over her. "Damn it," he said thickly. "You're even more beautiful when you're angry."

"Oh, Lucas . . ." Kendra said, disgusted, stooping to rescue the fallen blanket. But Lucas's hands suddenly on her wrists drew her back up, empty-handed, to force her body next to his.

"Lucas, please don't . . ." Kendra whispered, then melted inside when her bare breasts made contact with his bare chest as his lips quickly possessed hers. The same crazy splash of rapture was once more causing Kendra's willpower to weaken. She didn't want to give in to Lucas . . . enjoy his kiss . . . his touch. But her mind and her body were betraying her. It was as though something inside her was handing out orders! "Wrap your arms about his neck, Kendra." "Return his kiss with passion, Kendra." "Enjoy it, Kendra!" "Forget your misgivings . . . forget that beautiful Indian named Heart Speak . . . !"

Heart Speak! she thought, sudden anger scorching her insides.

Renewed fight swelled inside her. With determination, Kendra unlaced her arms from around him and began pushing at his chest, groaning as he held her there, still kissing her. With force she finally was able to set her lips free. "Lucas . . ." she said shakily. "Why are you doing this? Let me leave. Please . . ."

"Like hell," he said thickly. In one sweep he had her in his arms and carried her hurriedly to the bed and placed her there.

"Please, Lucas," she pleaded. "Not like this . . ."

Lucas, heavy-lidded with heated passion, stepped from his jeans. "You know you want this as much as I do," he said huskily.

"Lucas, I'm an outsider here," she said softly. "On the trail I was on neutral ground. It's how *you* may have felt when fighting on Union soil. I can't let you, Lucas. I *can't*."

Kendra began to inch her way across the bed but was soon stopped when Lucas lowered himself down over her

119

and once more had her by the wrists.

"Kendra, darling, I love you," he said, lowering his lips to hers, already being swept away with a wild, exuberant desire for her.

His kiss seared her flesh as his lips lowered to the hollow of her throat. And when he released her wrists she placed her hands to his shoulders and dug her fingernails into him there, writhing with an uncontrollable, urgent need to have him inside her. She hadn't wanted this! She hadn't! But her love for him was too powerful to turn him away.

Kendra's breath caught in her throat as his hands began moving seductively over her body. Her temperature rose to a dangerous peak when he skillfully began to explore and tease her pleasure points, while his tongue circled and flicked from one breast to the other.

"Now tell me you want to leave me," Lucas whispered. "If you can, climb from this bed now. If not, darling, just relax and enjoy."

"Relax?" Kendra sighed. "Lucas, you surely don't know what you're causing inside me."

"Tell me, darling," he said, trailing his fingers softly up and down the full length of her body, setting small fires along the way. "Tell me exactly how you are feeling."

"I'm tingling. . . ." she sighed.

"And . . . ?" he urged, lowering his lips to her navel, circling inside it with his hot tongue, searing her even there.

"I'm soaring," she moaned, opening her legs to him as his tongue lowered, to explore her wetness there.

"And . . . ?"

Kendra moaned with delight as his fingers and tongue

120

continued their love play along her body. "I can't . . ." she whispered.

"Can't what . . . ?"

"Can't say anything else," she sighed.

"And why not?"

"Because nothing I say now could possibly make any sense whatsoever."

Lucas rose over her, nuzzling her neck while he slowly placed his sex inside her. He could feel her trembling from the entrance . . . he could feel her heartbeat against his chest, matching his own racing heart. He closed his eyes and enjoyed the surges of pleasure within him with each stroke inside the warm cavern of her love space. And as he felt her breathing becoming harder and her legs lock around his waist he knew she was close. . . .

The sweet pulsating began in her toes, it seemed, and went higher . . . higher . . . then crashed throughout her in a sweet effervescence, as though she had been bathed in a bath of rare champagne.

Closing her eyes to the continuing rapture of the moment, she waited patiently for his release. He then stiffened momentarily and held still over her, then made another deeper plunge inside her and cried out as though in pain, as his body jerked and spasmed out of control against hers.

Then it was over and his head came to rest against the cushion of one of her breasts. She ran her fingers through his hair, sighing. And when he moved aside and let one of his hands caress the velvet flesh between her legs, she trembled with ecstasy.

"Darling, twice in one night is going to do me in," Lucas chuckled. He raised his head and sweetly kissed a breast.

"To have never been with a man before and now to have been twice in one night is unbelievable to *me*," Kendra whispered. "And, Lucas, I know that I shouldn't have."

"We were meant for each other, Kendra," Lucas said thickly.

Kendra turned her face from him, remembering Heart Speak. "Oh, Lucas . . ." she murmured.

Lucas traced her face with a forefinger, stopping at her chin, to force her eyes around to meet his. "What's this, 'Oh, Lucas' about?" he asked, setting a quick kiss to her lips.

"Nothing," she whispered, drunk with happiness. She would enjoy this time together, for it might be the last. Her fingers went to the necklace. Afraid, yet not, she said, "Lucas, what did Heart Speak mean when she said this necklace was a gift from you . . . not the Piute?"

"One day I'll tell you," he said, rising too suddenly from the bed.

Kendra rose on one elbow. "Why not tell me now, Lucas?"

"Another time will be better," he said, stepping into his jeans.

Confused and a bit hurt, Kendra crept from the bed and on past him, to where the blanket still lay crumpled on the floor. I shouldn't have let him do that again, she thought to herself. I'm weak! I'm weak! Now he's acting as strange as before. I shouldn't have! I shouldn't!

Kendra walked angrily around the room, once more gathering up her clothes that he had thrown across the room in his own rising anger. Again she draped them across the backs of the chairs, then went and cleaned up the mess she had made when she had dropped the dish and tin cup to the floor.

"Let me get you some more food," Lucas said, walking into the room.

Kendra plopped down on the sand in front of the roaring fire on the grate. "I'm not hungry," she pouted.

"Coffee then?"

"I'm not thirsty."

"Then we can talk," Lucas said, stooping beside her to lift another log on the fire.

"I'd rather not even talk," she said stubbornly. "When I ask you a question you won't answer me anyway."

Lucas settled down on the sand beside her, sitting cross-legged. "You mean about the necklace?" he said.

"Exactly."

"Trust me, Kendra," he said. "In my mind I know when I want to tell you about the necklace, and no sooner."

He reached for one of her hands and placed it to his lips. One finger at a time, he kissed her fingertips. "It's important to me," he said. "Timing. Please understand."

His passionate way of kissing her fingers was making the warmth return to Kendra's insides, even causing her to become suddenly giddy. "All right," she finally conceded. "Now what else did you have in mind?"

She giggled. "To talk about, that is," she quickly added.

"Tomorrow," he said flatly. "I want to tell you about tomorrow."

Once again there was that reference to "tomorrow." "What about tomorrow, Lucas?" she asked, glad that when he finished kissing her fingers he didn't release her hand. Instead he was holding it fondly on his lap.

Lucas stared into the dancing flames of the fire, his gray eyes hazy. "I've tried my damnedest to help the Piute," he said. "Before I came along, do you know how these people were living?"

Kendra leaned a bit forward. "No. How?" She strongly suspected that some of the mystery surrounding Lucas was about to be lifted, and this made her feel calmer.

"Many different ways," Lucas mumbled. He picked up a stick and began stirring the shimmering orange coals beneath the grate, causing orange sparks to fly and ignite. "Some had dug deep holes in the sand and had made a roof out of skins."

Kendra paled and gasped. She listened even more intently.

"Some had resorted to living behind the buildings in Reno and Virginia City, to steal what thrown-out garbage they could get their hands on. And some just lay on the streets dying from hunger and thirst. Broken, and with their desert life completely interrupted by the coming of the white man, most turned into scavengers."

"How horrible!" Kendra said, placing her hands to her throat.

"I watched this for a while, helpless as hell. I didn't even think about ways to help them, though, to be truthful. You see, I was too busy digging for silver. My family died during the war and our plantation was burned and ruined. Silver was my only way to rebuild my life."

Lucas stopped and poured two cups of coffee. He handed one to Kendra and began sipping from his own.

"And by God, I *did* strike it rich," he said. "Before those damn corporations seized and began running all the mines."

"So you took the money to help the Piute?" Kendra said, sipping coffee, watching him, loving him even more.

"Not right away," he said. "I turned the silver into cash and placed it safely in banks and kept digging."

"So when *did* you decide to help them?"

"One day, one of those hellish kinds of hot days when the sun's so hot you feel your brains almost scrambling," he began, once more staring into the flames, reliving the day.

"I was tired," he continued. "I was hot. In fact, I was near having a heat stroke. I'm sure of it. Well, this damn rattler catches me off guard and bites me in the leg before I have a chance to blow his damn head off."

"Oh, no," Kendra whispered. "What then?"

"This old Indian, a Piute, so wrinkled and dried up you'd think he would blow away, came along. He doctored my wound, carried me to his people, and took care of me while a temperature tore at my guts. When I woke up and found myself in a hole in the ground, I thought I'd died and had been buried," he said. Then he tore into a fit of laughter. "I can laugh about it now. But then? I was fit to be tied. All I saw was four walls of sand and this strange glowing covering above me. Honey, I thought I was *dead*. Damn dead!"

"And you were only in one of the Piute's makeshift houses dug in the sand?"

"Yes. Exactly."

Kendra giggled, thinking about how funny he must have looked, flailing his arms, yelling, thinking he was dead.

"It's really not funny," he said, sobering. "Imagine my disbelief when I found out where I really was. Up to that point, I didn't know about that particular mode of housing."

"How did you finally realize where you were?"

"Well, when my initial fright wore off and I pinched myself a couple of times, I knew that, yes, I was alive. I looked closer around me and saw the Indian blankets, pottery, and baskets. It was then that this aging Piute crawled into the hole and explained who he was and how I happened to be in his 'house.' Thank God, he had learned to speak English, or my fright would have begun all over again."

"It was *then* that you decided to help them."

"You're damned right. They saved my life. So I withdrew money from the bank, invested in land and began building these adobe houses. Soon after that I directed these people to their new homes, and have since then been fighting for their rights."

"What do you mean, their rights?"

"Indian children aren't allowed school privileges. The Indian adults are not allowed to purchase land. That's what I mean," he growled. "I mean to change all of that. The children, at least, should be taught to read and write and work simple arithmetic problems. They *want* this. That is why Quick Deer was at the schoolhouse that day. He was curious to see what the white children had that *he* couldn't have."

Kendra rose from the floor, hugging the Indian blanket around her. She reached a hand to Lucas. "You are so good," she whispered.

He rose and pulled her into his arms. "I owe them, Kendra," he murmured.

"I wish I could help," she said, leaning her cheek against his chest.

"Maybe you can. . . ."

"How . . . ?"

"Let's wait until tomorrow," he said thickly. "There's something I'd like you to see."

"Tomorrow . . . ?"

"Tomorrow."

Chapter Eight

There was never a change from night into day in the bowels of the earth. It was a land of everlasting darkness, a continuous threat to the living, working miner. Candles in tin sconces threw lurid light on the white, half-naked bodies of the men picking at walls and roof, and miles and miles of dimly lit aisles stretched away in every direction.

Seth wiped his brow with the back of his hand, breathing hard. Every hour he faced the menaces of cave-ins, hot water, noxious gases or fire. Some men had been known to put the point of their pickaxes into a subterranean reservoir and had instantly been seared by scalding water.

But the galleries glittering with silver spun fine as a wire kept Seth going. There were nests of amethyst that glowed with a purple heart; there were clusters of crystal, their prisms flashing like diamonds; there were strips of turquoise and veins of chrysoprase, pale blue and gray with a waxlike luster. Seams of quartz were embedded in dark red porphyry.

It was all these things that kept Seth reentering the

beehive in the bowels of the earth. He was just one of the many bees who had been intoxicated by the sweet pollen of hope.

Seth picked away at the silver streak on the wall, sweat glistening like many sparkles of diamonds along his brow and dust-laden arms. Suddenly the ground beneath him gave way and down he went, caught in a caving mass of splintering wood and rock. His hands and arms were pinned to his body, and only his head and neck projected above the rock. He could feel the dead weight of the earth pressing against his chest, causing his lungs to ache with each breath he took.

"Help me!" he screamed, hoping to have enough air to keep yelling until someone heard him and rescued him. "Please, someone! God, I'm going to die!"

Seth fought angrily with the blanket that had become imprisoned around his arms and legs. He grunted and groaned. He screamed. But gentle, cool hands on his brow awakened him, and he felt foolish, having once again had that same nightmare that had been plaguing him for weeks now.

"Seth, darlin'," Emanuelle crooned as she pulled Seth up into her arms and began to rock with him, back and forth. "It's only a dream. Why on earth do you have to have such a fretful dream when you're with me? Do I cause them? Am I so ugly that I prompt you to dream of . . . death . . . ?"

Seth blinked his eyes and swallowed hard, then composed himself. "It was so real, Emanuelle," he said. "I was in that damn mine again, and the floor just gave way and began swallowing me up."

"Why don't you quit workin' those crazy mines, Seth?" Emanuelle sighed, with a southern drawl. "I've already lost one man there, and I'm only eighteen. I could change my name from Smith to Carpenter, we could settle down in a little house and we could live happily ever after, if you'd steer clear of those ugly mines."

Seth pulled free of her embrace and stretched out on his back on the bed, studying Emanuelle. He didn't understand what someone as pretty as she could see in a man like himself. Compared to her petiteness, he was stout, with wide lips, thick, sandy hair that refused to stay in place, and bushy sideburns. Why, with her hazel eyes, and her blond hair braided and wound neatly around her head, she could get any man her sweet heart desired.

But Seth had always guessed it was the Carpenter name and wealth that had drawn her to him. She had found out in her own way that Seth did not have to work the mines to make him wealthy. He already was, and without ever having lifted a pickax. The wealth had traveled with him from Boston.

"And what would we do to make ends meet?" Seth growled. "Would you rather I become an outlaw, a desperado, working with a gang to steal the gold and silver from the shipments on their way to California? Or maybe stealing my own brother's cattle? You know that a rider can pass through the valley now and count as many as three hundred fifty different brands on horses and cattle stolen from as many ranches."

Emanuelle flashed her eyes angrily back at Seth. She arranged her silk nightgown neatly beneath her and sat on her legs. "Oh, Seth," she said. "You know none of that is necessary. You have money already. You're rich. Why do you refuse to accept that way of life? Do you have a secret death wish, or what?"

Seth jumped from the bed and went to pour himself a shot of whiskey. "I wish you'd preach at me about something else for a change," he growled. He drank the whiskey in one fast gulp, coughing as it scorched his throat.

Turning, he saw her eyes warming to the bare flesh he was exposing to her. "Surely you like something about me besides my money," he said thickly. "Or do you know that you can get that something from any other man on the street? Have you chosen me specifically because I have money in my family? Had you not known that, would you have given me even a second look?"

Emanuelle's lips turned into a pout. "I've my dead husband's silver in the bank vault," she said stubbornly. "It's enough to get me out of this darn boisterous town. But after I met you, I chose to stay a while longer."

"Ha!" Seth said, tipping another glass to his lips, emptying it also of whiskey. He slammed the glass back down on the table. "You *still* haven't denied it's because of the money."

He swung around and moved with his thick legs to the window. Pulling a sheer curtain aside he looked down from the fourth-floor window. He had been paying for Emanuelle's room in this plush International Hotel for many weeks now. He had grown accustomed to having her waiting for him when he came back from the mine. But while he was away from her he had suspected that she entertained other men, if a forgotten cigar stub here and there meant what he thought it did.

"I love you, Seth," Emanuelle purred, slinking up behind him, to fit her now nude body into the curve of his. "Come on. The tub of water awaits our fun. You

132

know that it was poured before you drifted off to sleep."

"I work hard. I was tired," he grumbled, feeling his heart thumping wildly as her breasts pressed into his back.

"Yes. I know," she whispered. She reached around and began running her tapered fingers through his thick mass of chest hair, then caressing his muscles until she felt them relax. "You've never fallen asleep before, before we've made love."

"I *did* need a bath first."

"But instead you flopped down on the bed and fell fast asleep," she sulked. "Now is that the way to treat babykins?"

Sweat glistened on Seth's brow. He stared toward the sky, seeing how the heavens were smutted with smoke, yet the sun was broiling through in its intensity. He gazed downward. Dust drove in clouds through the streets. It was hanging like mist over Virginia City, then fell like ashes as a whirlwind-type wind raced in from the desert. Seth had wondered why the rains seemed to linger in the valley ranges. Why was Virginia City always passed over?

"Seth . . . ?" Emanuelle said, stepping in front of him to block his view. "Where is your mind? Back on that same nightmare?"

Seth moved her aside and walked to the center of the room, where a large wooden tub of water had been placed before his arrival. "Don't talk about the dream," he growled. "Like I said. It was too real. If I experience that too many more times, I expect I *will* seek another profession. You can get swallowed up by the earth in your dreams just so many times. Then you begin to think it's an omen of some sort, warning you."

Shrill laughter rose from Emanuelle. "Sometimes you

are so strange," she said. "A big man like you worryin' about a dream. Seth, I can't believe it."

He turned on his heel and glared toward her. "Believe it," he said. "It has scared the hell out of me."

Emanuelle reached for one of his hands. "Come on, darlin'," she urged. "Climb into the tub with me. I'll soon make you forget all your troubles."

Feeling the ache in his loins, Seth drew her next to him and held her close. His sex throbbed as he pressed it against her. He lifted her upward and positioned himself inside her, gasping as she so magically placed her legs about his waist.

Giggling, she draped her arms about his neck and worked with him. "Step on into the water," she murmured. "Don't worry, hon. I'll hang on."

Awkwardly, Seth managed to get his leg over the side of the tub, then held her solidly next to him as he knelt down into the water.

"That's it, darlin'," Emanuelle murmured, flicking her tongue in and out of his right ear. "Now just sit down. We can have some fun whilst we cool off a mite."

Drugged with passion, Seth positioned himself on the bottom of the tub, then felt the water sucking between them as he once more began to work himself in and out of her.

Lowering his mouth, he circled one of her breasts with his tongue, dizzying even more as her teeth clamped down onto the flesh of his shoulder. As her teeth held, the heat inside him boiled into an inferno. First he felt the intense spasm of delight capture his full attention, then groaned out his pleasure as he felt his release inside her.

Still moving her body against him, Emanuelle worked

him up into another frenzy and smiled wickedly when he again spasmed in pleasure.

"God . . ." Seth groaned, resting his reeling head on her shoulder.

"Do you ever have dreams like that?" Emanuelle whispered into his ear.

"Good lord no," he said thickly. "No dream could be *that* real."

"You say your nightmare is," she taunted.

Pushing her away from him, Seth grabbed a piece of soap and began lathering his body. "You know how to ruin a man's enjoyment," he growled.

Emanuelle picked up a soft brush from the floor and began moving the lather across his stomach with it. "I just want you to get away from those mines, Seth," she argued. "We could make love all hours of the day and night. It could be such fun."

"Do you think life is supposed to be just fun?" he grumbled. He splashed the suds from his body and rose to his feet.

"I know how to make it so," Emanuelle said, eyeing him wickedly as she moved to her knees. Still in the water, she moved her lips seductively over the flesh of his legs, then looked up at him worshipfully as her lips moved to his renewed hardness. She licked and mewed like a kitten.

"We could do *this* all day," she whispered huskily. "Surely nothing could feel as good as *this*."

Placing his hands on her shoulders, Seth watched her manipulations of him. No woman had ever done this to him before. The pleasure she was giving him was so great, he couldn't question her as to how she knew such a trick as this. Instead he closed his eyes, hoping he was ready

135

for a third round in such a short span of time. His pounding heart threatened to engulf him. Her tongue teased and played . . . her lips nibbled and chewed. Then suddenly she stopped and stepped out of the tub, away from him.

Jolted, Seth opened his eyes. First he stared down at his throbbing hardness . . . then to her and the cold triumph in her eyes. "What are you doing, Emanuelle?" he growled. "Why did you stop?"

"To give you something to think about," she said, smoothly pulling a sheer robe over her shoulders. "I *will* find ways to convince you, Seth."

Covering himself with his hand, suddenly ashamed of how she could manipulate him, he stepped angrily from the tub. "You're a teasing bitch," he growled. "You'll pay for that."

He jerked his jeans on, then turned and glared accusingly at her. "And where did you learn such tricks?" he shouted. "In one of the cribs on the edge of town? Did I unknowingly rescue you from that way of life? Are you nothing but a cheap prostitute who fooled me with your fine clothes and pretty way of walking?"

Emanuelle blanched. She teetered a bit before settling into a chair. "Seth, my word," she gasped. "How *could* you . . . ?"

Seth placed his gun and holsters on, then his shirt. "I won't be paying for any more keep for you, Emanuelle," he growled. "As of today, you'd best look for another fool. I now know what you truly are, and I won't be suckered for another day."

Emanuelle rose from the chair and rushed to Seth and clung desperately to his arm. "Seth, how *could* you?" she cried. "And all because of me making you feel good in a different way? It doesn't make any sense."

"How quickly you forget," he shouted. "You teased me. Sure, what you were doing felt good, but you left me hanging like a cheap tramp would. Had you not resorted to *that* I might have believed anything you have to say. But now . . . no . . . I don't."

His angry eyes raked over her. "And, darlin'," he said mockingly, "only whores who get paid know such tricks as you just displayed."

Emanuelle's full color had returned as her anger grew. She stepped back away from Seth and swung her hand and slapped him across the face. "I am *not* a cheap whore," she hissed. "I'll have you know my husband taught me how to do . . ."

Seth saw red flash across his eyes as his hand went to where his flesh pounded from her blow. Clamping his teeth together angrily, he raised a hand and slapped her back, knocking her from her feet. Not caring that she lay sprawled clumsily across the floor, he threatened her further with doubled fists.

"No woman hits Seth Carpenter," he snarled. "Now just remember, Emanuelle, we're through. No matter what you say, we're through."

With tears rolling from her eyes, and rubbing her swollen cheek, Emanuelle rose slowly from the floor. "I only wanted . . ."

"I don't care what you want," Seth said, pulling his boots on. "Don't you think I know you've entertained men other than me here, at my expense? How many of them have you used your talents on?" He spat onto the carpet at her feet. "And to think I kissed you. The thought sickens me."

"Mister goodie goodie," Emanuelle screamed. "Well,

I'll show you. Somehow I'll *show* you."

"You frighten me, Emanuelle," Seth laughed, plopping his wide-brimmed Stetson hat on his head. He gave the room a quick once-over, then once more glared toward Emanuelle. "Yeah. Nice room I set you up in. Don't you think so?"

Emanuelle rushed to him and grabbed at his arm. "Seth, I was only joking," she cried. "Truly. I never had other men in my room. I lent the room out to a friend, and she had a man in here. Honest. Please believe me. I love only you, Seth. Only you!"

Seth jerked away from her. "Emanuelle, will you just shut up and leave me alone?" he said softly. Then, spinning around, he rushed angrily from the room, slamming the door loudly behind him. Suddenly regret flooded him. Had he been too hasty? She *had* been good for him. She *had* shown him ways . . .

"No . . ." he whispered, shaking his head back and forth. "I don't want to want her kind. I want someone sweet and tender. I want to find a wife. Then whatever we choose to share together will be only shared between *us*. Surely she was lying. Surely there were other men . . ."

Seth moved down the staircase from floor to floor, still thinking about his broken relationship with Emanuelle. He had felt safe with her. Until only recently she hadn't mentioned marriage. The word "marriage" had always frightened him, remembering how his father had deserted him.

"Kendra says I am like Father in many ways," he thought further to himself. "She says I'm gambling the same as Father but not with dice and cards . . . with my life."

He knew that she had also compared Aaron with their

138

father. He was a gambler too . . . also gambling with lives, as he continued to head the mining corporations in the area.

"If Aaron doesn't soon see to these mine inspections," he angrily whispered, "all the mines will experience in real life what I've only thus far seen in a dream."

He shuddered, thinking of the dangers, then decided that, in a sense, everyone was a gambler. And I am *not* my father's son, he thought. Surely if he found the right lady, he could settle down to love and keep her.

He finally reached the ground floor of the hotel. There was a rush of feet in and out of the dining room at Seth's left, and the aroma of food and coffee made a gnawing ache stir in his stomach. He removed his hat from his head and sauntered on into the dining room, frowning when he saw the long, narrow oak tables almost completely surrounded by hungry gents. Most of them ate their evening meal early so the rest of the evening could be spent in gambling.

The succulent aromas urged him farther into the room where he began his search for an empty chair. Moving from table to table, his eyes jumped when he finally saw an empty space.

"Excuse me . . . pardon me . . ." he said as he bumped into the elbows of the men eating on both sides of him, then breathed a heavy sigh of relief when he reached a hand to the empty chair. He glanced only hastily at the men on either side of him as he scooted the chair from beneath the table.

Placing his hat gently on his lap, Seth again glanced at the men at the table. All were quite engrossed in scraping their plates free of food as Seth, equally engrossed, began to fill his plate from the steaming dishes in the middle of the table. He heartily approved of this buffet style of serving food. It was in a way like being home in one's own dining room, choosing food from the center of the table. The main difference was, though, the smell and the language of the men who chose to eat here, without female companionship. The smell and the language of these men could have turned the devil from red to white.

Chuckling beneath his breath, wondering what Kendra would say if she knew he was eating amongst such a mixture of riff-raff and diamond-studded gentlemen, Seth continued to fill his plate full of food. With a watering mouth, he chose pork chops, collard greens, sweet potatoes, and hot biscuits and was already eyeing the apple pies lined on a shelf against the far wall.

"This coffee is strong enough to float a colt," a velvety voice of one of the men said suddenly from beside Seth.

Seth's fingers clutched with more earnestness onto his fork and a strange uneasiness washed over him. That voice had caused his peculiar surge of apprehension. There was something familiar about it . . . as though he had heard it somewhere . . . a memory festering in the deep recesses of his mind.

Slowly he turned his eyes to the gentleman who had spoken at his right side. A numbness now took over inside him. It had been ten full years, but the years hadn't erased the memory of his father from his mind. And now . . . here his father sat . . . right next to him.

Seth's eyes glistened with restrained tears as blue eyes met blue eyes and held. It cut him like a knife to realize that his father didn't recognize him, but he had to remember that he had only been a skinny eight-year-old when his father had last seen him.

"The coffee," Blackie said. "Hard. Terrible. Wouldn't

140

you say?"

Seth could hardly speak. His tongue seemed suddenly heavy as though it was a dead weight lying awkwardly inside his mouth. His gaze swept over his father, hating him, yet feeling the small flames of love that had been left to die with the departure of his father beginning to rekindle deep inside him. He couldn't help but notice that his father was still a handsome man, with few wrinkles disturbing his face. His eyes were as blue and his hair as golden as Seth remembered them, and his suit had been pressed to perfection. A diamond stickpin teased Seth's eyes from the folds of a cravat.

Yes, his father seemed to be doing quite well for himself. And it appeared that Aaron had been wrong. It seemed that Stanford Carpenter had settled in Virginia City . . . not in Reno, as Aaron had earlier reported having heard.

And what was it he now called himself, Seth further wondered.

"Blackie's my name, young man . . ." Blackie said, offering a handshake of friendship toward Seth.

Seth, still having not said a word, eyed this hand being offered him as though it were a snake, coiled, ready to inflict a wound as it struck. Then the name registered. "Blackie . . ."

Blackie for blackjack. His father was ashamed of his true name, or was it because he was hiding from creditors . . . ?

With wet eyes and embarrassed because he was a man shedding tears, Seth grabbed his hat, pushed the chair back and rushed, stumbling, from the room.

Once out in the open parlor, Seth stopped, panting, to lean his head on his arm against the wall. "Fool . . ." he whispered harshly. "Now didn't I make a damn fool out of myself . . . and over . . . over . . . *him* . . . of all people."

The velvet voice broke through his consciousness again and Seth knew that his father had followed him.

"Young man, is something the matter?" Blackie asked, placing a hand on Seth's heaving shoulder. "Are you ill? Or what?"

Once more Blackie was reminded of his children. Wouldn't Seth have been this young man's age? But surely Seth would have grown into a lean, long-legged man. He had been so damn skinny!

Tensing, afraid his father might put two and two together and realize just whom he was addressing, Seth turned slowly around. Once more he felt his insides pain, having the need to embrace this man, *not* hate him. Yet he very politely placed his hat on his head.

"I must apologize, sir, for my rudeness," Seth then said. "You see, I felt a sudden sick feeling to my stomach. I guess it's just the heat."

Blackie pulled a deck of cards from an inner jacket pocket and began shuffling them through his fingers. "You gave me a fright," he said, lifting his lips in a slow smile. "You *are* all right now, aren't you?"

"Yes, sir . . ." Seth mumbled.

"Blackie," Blackie corrected. "Just call me Blackie." He chuckled good-naturedly. "They call me Blackie for my skill at playing blackjack. Ever played the game, young man?"

Fresh feelings of dread were encompassing Seth. Gambling had always been his father's first love and apparently still was. "Yes, sir," he mumbled. "I've been known to play a decent game of blackjack."

142

Blackie leaned into Seth's face. "Will you quit calling me 'sir'?" he said. "It makes me feel old. Don't want to scare the ladies away by giving away my age."

Seth circled his fingers into tight fists at his side. He wanted to shout at his father! He wanted to tell him that his wife of so many years was dead! He wanted to accuse him of, oh, so many things! But he refrained from doing so. It was more important to him at this time not to reveal his true identity.

"And, young man," Blackie quickly added, stepping back away from him. "Suppose we compare our skills at blackjack? Do you have time for, let's say . . . just one hand or two?"

Beginning to feel trapped, Seth spied the door. Then something warmed his insides when he thought further about the challenge his father had just offered. *Yes.* He would accept the challenge! Wouldn't it be grand to beat the champion . . . and put him in his place?

What a sweet revenge *that* would be!

Smiling crookedly, Seth offered a hand to Blackie, cringing when flesh met flesh, feeling the smoothness of his father's hand. It was a fact that Stanford Carpenter had never seen hard labor in his lifetime. Living off the misfortunes of others all his life . . .

"Yes, Blackie, I would like to accept the challenge," Seth said dryly. "But at a later date. I've got to get back to the mines."

Blackie shook Seth's hand earnestly. "You just name the day," he said. "You'll find me most times next door at my new gambling emporium." He chuckled. "You can't miss it. Blackie's, with a capital B."

Seth eased his hand from his father's, tremulous inside, having warmed to the touch of this man whom he

143

had once so idolized. Yes, Aaron was wrong. Stanford Carpenter was not in Reno. He had moved on, as he had the habit of doing. Now it was Virginia City. Which city would be next . . . and . . . when . . . ?

"I'll remember that, Blackie," Seth said, then rushed on away without another word. A lump was in his throat, threatening to choke him. He swallowed and swallowed, stepping on outside into the heat of the late afternoon. His heart was thumping wildly. In one afternoon he had lost his female companion and had found his father. There were two alternatives awaiting him to help make him forget both. There was alcohol and there were the mines.

His jaw firmly set, he chose the latter and boarded the wagon that made trips constantly back and forth from the town to the Con-Virginia mine. Down in the blackness fear would erase all other thoughts from his mind. Yes, today he would *welcome* the fear. In it there was also the indescribable excitement that was always there wrapping its sleek cocoon around him. . . .

After the wagon had reached its destination and the men had unloaded from it, Seth couldn't get to the mine's entrance fast enough. As he approached its mouth he watched as the never-ending stream of prospectors roamed about with supplies loaded on burros. Daily, pack trains tottered over the Divide with wine, cards, incense, silks, and perfumes, enticing these wandering fools, who felt rich even when one minute silver nugget was dug from the mountainside. But most of them who had any sense realized that the remaining silver wealth lay in rich veins deep beneath the surface. All the rest had been overworked and exhausted—as if a youngster had aged into an old man in a span of only ten years.

Seth felt the ache in his leg muscles as he continued to climb toward the mine entrance, where men scurried to and from it, loading buckets of wealth into coal cars waiting on narrow tracks. From jagged fissures in the earth on one side of Seth, jets of yellow steam spurted with a forcible sound, like the hiss of a snake. The ground was red with cinnabar, yellow with sulphur, and black with tar. A stream of pitch-blackened fluid edged off into the desert, stinking worse than putrid eggs.

The tales of underground rivers of heat and sulphuric water had been true. In some locations, the men would be drenched for hours by heated fumes in the darkness a thousand feet beneath the surface. Rocks continued to fall both day and night. A man had to be very strong to lift the heavy timbers in the mines. Seth had learned to handle them like broomsticks and had developed the ability to bend a dime with his teeth and to crumple a silver dollar in his fist. He could even hoist a heavy man standing on a shovel as easily as he could wield a shovelful of ore.

Yet . . . he hadn't been able to control his emotions upon discovering his father!

Angry and disgusted at himself, Seth boarded the flimsy, hand-run elevator that carried him and his one companion beneath the ground. At first the mine had used a windlass and a bucket to lower the miners and to hoist them out again. But the deeper the mine had grown, the more the need for greater sophistication had grown.

"Goin' below so soon again, Seth?" the man, pale and gaunt, asked at Seth's side.

"Same as you, Lloyd, I guess," Seth grumbled. "You came out when I did."

"Nothin' keepin' me above," Lloyd said. "My lady's

waitin' in Missouri for me to return with my pockets full."

"She had a long wait?"

"Yep. And I'm 'bout to give up. And you?"

"I don't expect much anymore, either," Seth grumbled. "Not from anything or *any*one."

"You got family here and I hear tell they're wealthy, Seth. Why do you punish yourself by goin' underground?"

"I mean to make my own way in the world *some*how."

"The big cats with their fancy banks are eatin' up the takings, Seth. I'm just gettin' wise to that. We'll never see none of it for *us*."

"Yeah. Guess so," Seth said. "But I *do* have the need to busy my hands. This is better than movin' cattle from range to range."

"That's what your family does, eh?"

"Some . . ." Seth said dryly. He would not confess that Aaron was one of those "cats" the man had spoken so coolly of.

They heard a bump, and Seth felt the jar to his system and knew they had reached bottom. It was always twilight down in the mines, a soft gloaming, pricked by a thousand candles. There was no repose or peace in that mysterious region. There was always the blasting of dynamite, the ringing of picks, the clanking of shovels, and the dripping of water.

Seth and Lloyd lit the candles in their lanterns, then stepped out onto the rough terrain of the crude flooring with the rest of the miners already at work. With each shift of their candles, the walls and roofs and the gallery glistened like stars. Seth soon joined the other men whose heads were constantly in the clouds, clouds that had a silver lining. . . .

146

Chapter Nine

Though a full night had passed, the rain continued to fall. Kendra watched from the door for Lucas's return. He had awakened early and had told her that he had things to prepare and that he would come for her later.

Shivering from the impending chill of the morning, Kendra hugged herself with her arms. She ached for a warm, refreshing bath, and, for the first time in many weeks, longed for the looseness of a dress instead of the tight, confining jeans clinging damply to her legs.

She combed her fingers through her hair, sighing, wondering if she had been missed back at the Circle C. She silently prayed that nothing had happened to cause Aaron's early return. And, though she worried so much about Seth in the mines, she hoped that this one time he still was there. It would be very hard to explain away her overnight stay with Lucas. It would be even harder to tell her family about the band of Indians that were only a stone's throw from the Carpenter spread. She knew that Aaron hated the Indians almost as much as he hated the Confederate "Rebs". . . .

"He will never accept Lucas into the fold," she worried. "Never. He's a part of both ways of life that Aaron hates."

A blast of thunder caused the sandy floor beneath Kendra's feet to tremble, and the rain seemed to begin in even more earnest. Water dripped through cracks in the ceiling in various parts of the room and puddles were beginning to circle and build. An occasional sizzling of the flames in the fireplace was evidence that the pounding rain was sometimes even finding a path down the large stone chimney.

Kendra's insides did a sensual dance when she finally caught sight of Lucas racing toward the adobe house. Seeing the heels of his boots sinking into the sandy mire, she opened the door for him and stood aside, breathing easier when he dashed on inside.

"Spring can be like this in Nevada," he said, taking his sombrero from his head. He tapped it against his leather chaps, spraying water droplets in all directions. "And, Kendra, I'd not think about returning home today. Some Piutes have returned to the village with word of flash flooding in the lower valleys."

Fear laced Kendra's heart. "Aaron . . ." she whispered. Her blue eyes told her concern. "He's on the spring roundup. Do you think he's all right?"

Lucas bent a knee and reached for the coffee pot hanging low over the fire. He carried it to the table and poured two cups of steaming brew. "He's fine, I'm sure," he said, casting her a fast glance. "If he's skilled at what he does, he'll be fine," he qualified his statement.

Kendra went to the table, gladly accepting a cup of coffee from Lucas. "He's not all that knowledgeable about the cattle drives," she murmured. "For so long he

148

was just a banker in Boston."

"If he's hired on a smart head wrangler, that's all that's necessary," Lucas reassured.

Kendra sipped her coffee, studying Lucas with an arched eyebrow. "How do you know so much about it, Lucas?" she queried. "What *do* you do besides help these Indians?"

Lucas shook a heavy lock of wet, dark hair back from his eyes, evading her watchful stare. It still wasn't the time to tell her. She would find out soon enough.

"That isn't important," he said. He slammed his coffee cup down on the table. "What is important is the Indians and what I must now do, rain or no rain."

Kendra took one final sip of coffee, then placed her cup next to his. Though it was still confusing to her, she did admire Lucas's dedication to the Indians. Today, as always, his sun-bronzed face with its chiseled features showed great force and determination in the set of his jaw and the command in his steel-gray eyes. His virile handsomeness and his broad shoulders set on his tall and lithe figure made Kendra's heart race anew, and she hoped he didn't see the flush of her face as he handed her a deerskin cape.

"Drape this around you," he said. "And follow me."

He placed his sombrero over his dark hair, leaving only his thick sideburns exposed. He then pulled a deerskin cape around his own shoulders.

"Lucas, where are we going? Must you always be so mysterious about everything?" She pulled the hood of her cape up over her hair.

"You are about to witness a people in need," he said, opening the door for her, standing aside. "Then maybe you can go to your brother and tell him to use some of his

149

power to see that these Indians are helped by the government."

Kendra whirled around, her eyes wide. "Lucas, do you know my brother?" she murmured.

"Doesn't everyone know Aaron Carpenter?" he said dryly. He placed an arm about her waist. "Come on, Kendra. The Indians are waiting."

They stepped outside. Kendra ducked her head to the rain and leaned against Lucas as she felt her boots being suctioned into the wet ground. "Is it only the Piute who live here?" she asked.

"The biggest part are Piute," he answered. "But there are also a few Shoshonee and Washoe."

"They're all from this region?"

"Yes. These are the original dwellers of this area, before the trains and silver mines came."

"And how is Quick Deer today?"

"Heart Speak looks after him. He grows stronger each day."

"And can I see him?"

Amusement flecked Lucas's eyes into many shades of gray. He lifted his lips into a wry smile as he leaned his face down into hers. "Why, yes, Kendra," he said. "That was your reason for coming here, wasn't it?"

His amusement was contagious. Kendra laughed softly as she gave him a sideways glance. "Lucas, by now you know better than that."

Lucas jerked her closer to his side. "My dear, maybe you need to show me again this evening the true reason why you are here."

"By evening I shall be gone."

"I won't allow it. Not in this rain."

Stubbornly, Kendra lifted her face to the sky. "The

touch of the rain against my face is invigorating."

"The touch of my lips is not?" Lucas teased.

Again Kendra laughed and pulled the cape up over her head. She sobered when she caught sight of a long line of Indians standing in the rain outside another adobe house. She eyed Lucas questioningly, then followed him past the shivering, dripping Indians who were huddling beneath their own deerskin capes. She shook the cape from around her as she was guided by Lucas into the house the Indians stood in front of.

In awe at what she saw, Kendra looked slowly around her. She was reminded of the first day she had seen Lucas. He had overseen the loading of a wagon, and what Kendra was now seeing was most surely part of many such shipments by train since that time.

It was like a general store, yet it wasn't. Lined along the wall on shelves were dried fruits, coffee, leather, smoked hams, new cloth bolts, molasses, rope, and fresh-cut plug tobacco. Dill pickles floated in juice in open barrels and beef lay piled on a table.

Swinging around, Kendra looked toward Lucas. "What is this?" she murmured. "Is this some type of store?"

Lucas held the door open, motioning with a nod of his head for the Indians to begin filing in. "This is issue day," he said flatly.

"Issue day?" Kendra whispered as she watched now as Lucas began cutting up the beef and handing some large, then some small portions wrapped up in bundles to different Indians.

"This is called an issue house," Lucas said, adding other provisions to the Indians' arms as they spoke of their needs to him. "A week's allowance of beef has been butchered for the Indians and cut into portions according to the size of the families. The Indians have been taught to line up alphabetically, for their weekly supply of meat and other provisions."

"And you, Lucas, finance all of this?"

"Yes. But they work for what they get."

"How?"

"They each have their duties assigned them, to keep the community clean and free of trouble."

"Lucas, you are . . . you're unbelievable," Kendra said softly.

"If I didn't do this, no one would," Lucas said dryly. "But I would like to see Washington step in and take over. At least part way. Most Indians in other territories have at least been assigned some of their land back and are protected by the government."

"Reservations, you mean."

"That is better than being completely ignored."

"And . . . schools . . . ?"

Lucas glowered toward her. "Yes. Exactly. They need at least to know the simple basics of reading, writing and arithmetic. I've, personally, taught them enough of the alphabet for them to receive their weekly provisions."

"Lucas, I wish I could help."

"Talk with Aaron. Spread the word."

"He won't listen to me. He's a very stubborn man."

"Talk with him, Kendra," Lucas ordered flatly.

"All right. I'll try."

Kendra stood side by side with Lucas, suddenly caught up in the giving. As Lucas handed out meat, she handed out supplies from the shelves, enjoying being a part of this event. She could see a deep love and gratitude for Lucas in the depths of the Indians' dark eyes. Tears

152

sparkled in Kendra's own eyes as some Indians flung their arms about Lucas's neck and muttered in broken English of their thanks to him. Most eyed Kendra half-heartedly and with mistrust. But she understood.

When the last Indian had stepped past Kendra with his arms filled and smiling his thanks, Kendra went to Lucas and eased into his arms. "I love you . . ." she whispered. "I don't only love you, I respect you. You're such a fine, generous man."

Lucas laughed hoarsely, pushing her gently away. "Whoa. Now don't get carried away," he said. "I'm human, and all humans have their shortcomings. I'm sure the day will come when you'll discover what mine are."

Kendra thrust her hands into her rear pockets, eyeing him quizzically. "Do you have anything specific in mind?" she tested.

Avoiding her eyes, Lucas began gathering together more supplies in a basket, along with the last of the beef. "Now we must take Heart Speak and Quick Deer their weekly provisions," he said. "Quick Deer will be surprised to see Nurse Kendra."

Kendra sighed heavily. "Lucas, you have ways of avoiding questions," she said.

Lucas lifted the filled basket into his arms.

"Are you coming with me?"

Seeing Heart Speak was the last thing Kendra wanted, but she was anxious to see Quick Deer. She had never set a leg before and she did feel she should inspect it to see if any swelling or discoloration had occurred. She would just die if such a thing as gangrene set in!

"Yes. I'm coming, Lucas," she said, draping the hooded cape around her shoulders. She followed him out into the rain and sloshed through the grime of the grass-free paths and soon found herself inside another adobe house no better or worse than Lucas's. She had almost dispelled all worries of Heart Speak's being his wife. She didn't live with him. She didn't see to his everyday needs. And if Heart Speak wasn't his wife, then Quick Deer was not his son. Thinking this made being in the same room with Heart Speak at least a bit more bearable.

Heart Speak walked smoothly into the room, out of the bedroom, her dark eyes shooting sparks of dislike toward Kendra. And then, ignoring Kendra totally, Heart Speak went to Lucas and leaned a soft kiss upon his lips, accepting the basket from his arms.

"Lucas, did everyone show up for issue day?" Heart Speak murmured. "I thought possibly the rain might discourage the less needy."

"Every bit of beef was distributed," Lucas said, removing his sombrero. He shook water from it, then tossed it on a chair. He went to Kendra and directed a warm smile downward at her as he gently removed the rain-soaked cape from around her shoulders. "Ready to see Quick Deer?" he said in a near-whisper.

Kendra flashed Heart Speak a half glance. "Are you sure she won't care?" she asked, nodding her head toward Heart Speak. "I don't feel welcome at all, Lucas."

"You are welcome. Heart Speak is just a bit jealous, that's all."

Kendra's gaze traveled around the room, seeing Lucas's handiwork in the table and chairs and the shelves of supplies he had given *her*. Jealousy tore through Kendra, almost threatening to shred her insides. "I don't know why she's jealous," she said coolly. "She has you in everything she possesses."

154

Lucas chuckled a bit beneath his breath, seeing how so visibly Kendra wore jealousy. "Why, Kendra, you *do* care," he teased, whispering into her ear.

His hot breath caused a sweet ecstasy to thrill her insides. She gave Heart Speak a haughty look and locked her arm through Lucas's. "Darling, please do take me to Quick Deer," she murmured. "Then let's return to the privacy of your house. I believe we left something undone there."

It tickled Kendra to see the seething hate cause Heart Speak's hands to circle into tight fists at her sides. And as Kendra and Lucas moved toward the bedroom, Heart Speak began unloading the basket, slamming things on the table with loud bangs.

Thick padded mats made of layers of Indian blankets provided Quick Deer with a makeshift bed. Seeing this made Kendra give Lucas a glance of wonder.

"They haven't yet accepted beds into their culture," Lucas explained. "The ground has been their bed for so long that they mock the 'strange' use of a bed."

"Oh, I see," Kendra said, now feeling eyes on her as she drew closer to the small figure lying there so quietly. She let her gaze move to meet Quick Deer's, then smiled with relief when she saw that he recognized and welcomed her by the small circle of his lips lifting upward as he returned her smile. She couldn't help but remember the day she had helped him. There had been no smile. There had been no thanks. Only a cold, indifferent stare until he had drifted off into a fitful sleep.

"Well, hello there," Kendra said softly, falling to her knees beside him. She tentatively reached her hand to his copper brow and touched him there affectionately. "And how are you, my little friend?"

Her gaze took in a full impression of him now. He seemed healthier than the rest of the Indian children Kendra had seen and there was a marked intelligence in his bold, dark eyes. His coarse black hair was pigtailed and short, and straight bangs lay only inches from Kendra's fingers.

"Schoolteacher? You've come to teach in Piute village?" he finally said in broken English.

Kendra was taken aback. She laughed a bit awkwardly, glancing at Lucas, then back at Quick Deer. "Quick Deer, I'm not a schoolteacher," she murmured.

Lucas knelt at her side and placed an arm about her waist. He leaned closer to her. "He must've thought you were the schoolteacher that went with the schoolhouse. Just as I did," he whispered. "But this is the first I've even heard him mention it."

"You no schoolteacher?" Quick Deer said sadly. "Then why you come? Why you here?"

Settling more comfortably on her knees, Kendra placed her hands on her lap. Again she smiled, nodding toward his bandaged leg. "I've come to see you," she said. "To check on your leg. How does it feel, Quick Deer? Does it still hurt?"

Quick Deer shook his head. "It does not hurt," he said. "Mother doctors me. Every day. She put clean, white bandages strongly around it. It be all right."

"I'm so glad," Kendra murmured. Her eyes grew serious. "But can I take a peek, Quick Deer? I'd like to see."

"No. Mother good nurse."

"Oh. Well, all right," Kendra said, blushing a bit at his flat refusal.

"You good nurse when mother wasn't there," Quick

156

Deer added. "But mother here now. She smart." He lowered his lashes and set his face into a frown, then looked with determination once more toward Kendra. "Why not you teacher? You were at schoolhouse. You too old to be student."

"Well, thanks a *lot*," Kendra laughed, giving Lucas a quick, amused look, then looked back toward Quick Deer. "No one ever told me that I was old before."

"You be *my* teacher," Quick Deer said eagerly, his eyes suddenly shining. "You come. Teach *all* Piute, Shoshonee, and Washoe children how to read. Please?"

When Kendra gasped softly, she felt a soft nudge in her ribs and looked quickly at Lucas, imploring him with her eyes.

"It's not such a bad idea, Kendra," he whispered. "I had thought about asking you myself."

"But I'm *not* a teacher. . . ."

"Do you know how to read . . . ?"

"Why, yes . . ."

"Then you can teach children how to read," he said flatly. "A teaching certificate isn't necessary here in the Piute village. And, Kendra, you would feel the reward in your heart as I do each day I am with these people."

"Lucas, I don't see how . . ."

"Maybe one day a week you could come here. If you left at daybreak you would have time to teach a bit then be back home by nightfall."

"Lucas, am I really that close to my ranch? It seemed to take forever to get here."

"That is because I wanted it to appear that way in case you ended up not liking my Indian friends."

"It did seem as though we had traveled in one big circle. . . ."

157

"Exactly."

A nervous, soft laugh, then Kendra boldly accepted the challenge. "Yes, Quick Deer," she announced. "I will teach you how to read and spell."

"And maybe a bit of arithmetic?" Lucas asked, lifting a heavy, dark eyebrow toward her.

"I can't promise. . . ." she murmured. She giggled. "You see, I'm not all that skilled at numbers myself."

Suddenly her face took on a pained look. "I remember, as a child, my father first taught me my numbers by showing me his playing cards," she whispered.

Her face then warmed with color as she glanced at Lucas. "You see, he's a gambling man. He even taught me blackjack. Can you imagine, Lucas? A father teaching a ten-year-old how to play blackjack?"

"It could come in handy sometime," Lucas teased, chuckling.

When he saw the alarm in her eyes, he cleared his throat and rose to his feet. "Well, now that our plans are made for schoolin', perhaps we might leave Quick Deer to snatch a wink of sleep."

"Yes. You're right," Kendra said. Her eyes wavered as she felt the need to bend a kiss to this small boy's brow. But she already felt like an intruder in Heart Speak's house and wasn't sure if it was appropriate to provoke too much fondness in her son.

But, shrugging, no longer caring, Kendra kissed his brow and felt an intense warmth travel her spine when he reached a hand to her face and touched her softly and affectionately there.

"Me thank you," he murmured. "For everything, Ma'am Kendra."

"Ma'am Kendra?" she giggled.

"All Indian children address adult women as ma'am, always placing it before their proper name."

"Not only sweet but polite as well," Kendra said, kissing him again. "And, you're quite welcome, Quick Deer. Quite."

"When will schoolteaching begin?" Quick Deer asked, leaning up on an elbow as Kendra rose to her feet.

Kendra locked an arm through Lucas's, questioning him with her eyes.

"Kendra will return in a few days, won't you, Kendra?"

She smiled, then focused her attention back on Quick Deer. "Yes. I will," she said.

"Why not stay now?" Quick Deer worried.

"I must return home first. My people worry about me just as yours worry about *you*."

Quick Deer nodded his approval and understanding. "Me understand, Ma'am Kendra."

"Then I'll see you later, Quick Deer?"

"Yes, Ma'am Kendra. Later."

Feeling good and strangely fulfilled, Kendra floated from the room beside Lucas. But she quickly settled back down to earth when Lucas broke free from her and went over to Heart Speak, who stood solemnly alone before the fire in her fireplace.

Kendra's insides flashed cold as she watched Lucas draw Heart Speak around and into his arms and whisper something softly into her ear. The pleasure his words gave Heart Speak showed in the softness of her eyes and the way in which she quickly hugged him back.

Then as Lucas pushed her gently from him and gave her a tender kiss, Kendra rushed blindly from the house and began running. She didn't even notice that the rain

159

had stopped or that mud was splashing all over her jeans as she hurried her pace, frantically searching for where her horse might be.

Footsteps behind her made her stumble a bit but she cushioned the half fall by grabbing onto an open door and rushed on inside, breathing harshly. She could still see their embrace . . . their lips meeting . . . and at this moment she hated Lucas and all the Indians. Then she remembered her promise to Quick Deer.

Circling her fists to her side she whispered. "Oh, God, how *can* I? It will mean seeing *her* also, and maybe even Lucas with her. . . ."

Someone coughing behind her drew Kendra around with a start. Her eyes widened and her heart began to thunder against her ribs when she caught sight of a room of elderly Indian men, sitting crossed-legged on the floor in a large circle, all staring silently toward her.

Inching her way back toward the open door, Kendra smiled awkwardly back at them, then looked more closely at what they were doing. A fire in the fireplace and several lighted kerosene lamps glowed golden onto cards held in their shriveled hands. Small sticks were piled in the center of the circle, obviously the stakes they were playing for.

"Kendra . . . ?" Lucas said suddenly, from behind her.

Kendra stiffened and spun around, accusing him with her eyes. "Why don't you just go back to Heart Speak?" she hissed softly.

"Kendra, come on," Lucas said, offering her his hand. "You know you are being a bit foolish."

"I think I'll just stay here and play some poker with these gentlemen," Kendra said, nodding stubbornly toward the circle of wrinkled old men.

Lucas laughed amusedly and guided her out of the house. "So you want to play blackjack with the elders of the various tribes, do you?" he laughed. He drew her next to him as he directed her on toward his own house. "And will you also play the game of 'sticks' with them?"

"You mean the sticks they are using as money?" she asked, struggling as he continued to hold her tightly to him.

"No. There is a different game played by these elders who have done their part in life," he said. "The old men play 'sticks,' a sort of sleight-of-hand performance with a bit of wood in which the outside party guesses the hand that holds it."

"Why, that sounds so juvenile," Kendra gasped.

"Yes. But what else can these men do to pass the time away? Cards. Sticks. That is all they have. They had their land taken from them. They are the ones who had turned into scavengers until I brought them here."

"How sad," Kendra said, softening her defense. Then she set her jaw firmly. "But, Lucas, all of this talk of old men is just a ploy, to direct my attention from your having kissed Heart Speak in front of me."

She succeeded in pulling herself away from him and stepped before him, stopping his further approach to his house. Kendra doubled her fists to her side. "Lucas, you are two-faced. First you tell me you love me, then you kiss and hug and even whisper into Heart Speak's ear? Oh, how could you?"

Lucas's gray eyes hardened with feeling. "Kendra, I knew her way before I knew you," he said stiffly. "Do you expect me to ignore her now that I have found you? I can't do that, Kendra. She means too much to me."

Kendra stamped her foot, grimacing when more mud

161

splashed onto her pants leg. "How much *does* she mean to you? So much that you will choose her over me?" she said from between clenched teeth.

"Now, Kendra, you are being a bit ridiculous," Lucas said, moving on past her into his house.

Kendra stood still, stunned. Feeling a desperation rising inside her, she once more began looking around for signs of her horse, but all that she could see was a large herd of wild mustangs in the distance on the rise of a bluff, outside the Indian village.

Then her eyes traveled further to the back of the village and finally she saw many other horses, one of which was hers, grazing, unsaddled. Stubbornly, she took a step away from the house, to go to Domino, but was stopped when Lucas quickly put an arm about her waist and drew her into his house, closing the door after them.

"What do you think you're doing?" Kendra screamed angrily. She struggled against his hold. "Lucas, let me go. Let me *go*. I want to return to my ranch. Now! Do you hear me?"

"I can't let you do that," he said, bolt locking the door behind them.

Kendra grew quiet, eyeing the locked door. She rubbed her raw wrist when Lucas set her free. "Lucas, what do you want from me? It's obvious you have all you need here in this Indian village. I was foolish to think you cared for me. You used me. You . . ."

The sudden pressure from his warm, moist lips quickly stopped Kendra's flow of harsh, troubled words. She mellowed into his arms as he pressed his hardness against her, kissing her with force and determination. As his tongue made its entrance inside her parted lips, a soft moan emerged from the deepest depths of Kendra's

162

being, and once more she was lost to all but him.

"You little vixen . . ." Lucas said huskily, swooping her suddenly up into his arms, moving with her toward the bedroom. "I'll show you just how much I care. I use nobody! I *give*."

"Lucas . . ." Kendra sighed, placing her cheek on his chest, hating herself for her weakness. He was to be her *only* weakness, but a real one. Somehow it was easy to forget all her previous anger toward him. There was no Heart Speak . . . there was no doubt. . . .

"Kendra, darling, I love you, only you," Lucas said, lowering her to the bed. He stretched out next to her and drew her once more into his arms, kissing the hollow of her throat. "Let me prove my love. Undress. Let's make love as we never have before."

"But, Lucas . . ." Kendra said, her doubts slowly ebbing back. His lips were once more there, loosening her thoughts . . . warming her insides into a sort of pleasant mushiness. She traveled her hands over the corded muscles of his shoulders, lowering them to the broad expanse of his back. Then she let her hand move down into the back of his jeans and trembled when she discovered the tightness of his buttocks, stiffening even more as he so obviously enjoyed the tender caress.

Kendra closed her eyes to the rapture as his teeth began working at the top button of her shirt. And when he was working with the third, she couldn't help but reach her hands up to release the others, spreading her shirt open for his lips to have easy access to her breasts.

But she was disappointed when she didn't feel his tongue or lips. Instead she opened her eyes to find him disrobing himself, as the gray command of his eyes devoured her from tip to toe.

Smiling almost wickedly, Kendra slipped her blouse from around her shoulders, then leaned and removed one boot and then the other. She shivered as his fingers went to the waistband of her jeans and unbuttoned them and began working them over the thin taper of her waist and lower, to finally expose her nudity to him and his exploring fingers.

"You're next. . . ." she murmured.

He had already removed his bandana and shirt, leaving the rest for her eager fingers. Smiling up at him, she unfastened his gunbelt and let it fall heavily to the floor, then, breathing hard and anxiously, she unbuttoned his jeans and pulled them down over his hips, revealing his hardened, throbbing sex to her hungry eyes.

Blushing, she felt like a whore, but lay back and waited as he continued with removing his boots and pants and then stretched out on top of her, touching her exquisitely with the hardness of his manhood. It seemed to scorch her thigh where it lay. Her heart flamed . . . her insides were quickly set on fire with yearning for him.

Lifting her arms to him, she cried out her joy when he dropped his lips to her breast and began suckling it as though he was a hungry child and she the mother. A wetness formed between her thighs, causing her to open them to him. And her answer from him was his slow entrance inside her, where he then began to thrust easily, in and out. Lifting her legs around his waist, Kendra crept her fingers through his hair, tangling them inside, as the bliss of their union lit up her insides into a pleasurable, glowing sensation.

Slowly his lips traveled upward, stopping at her mouth. His lips were trembling as he kissed her softly . . . tenderly. His hands were gentle as he cupped her breast. His sweetness made Kendra grow lethargic, her head beginning to do a slow spinning. Then she opened more to him when she felt him increase his speed inside her and their spasms become as one as they clung desperately to each other while exchanging a heavenly moment of paradise.

Sighing, Kendra slowly came down from her height of happiness. She kept her eyes closed as his lips kissed her brow.

"I love you so," Lucas whispered huskily. "How could you *ever* doubt me, Kendra? Haven't I proven my love?"

"I'm like any other woman, Lucas," Kendra whispered. "I cannot bear to see my man with another woman. Surely you can understand this. Can't you?"

"As I, the man, could never bear to see you with another man," he said thickly, drawing away from her, drugging her more with the passion in his eyes.

"Kendra, yes, I do understand how I must have made you feel when I demonstrated my affections for Heart Speak in front of you," he said. "But she has been all I have had for so long. It is hard to turn my back on her so quickly. Please try to understand."

Kendra's anger filled her suddenly. She rose from the bed, grabbing her jeans, thrusting her legs into them. "Oh! Lucas! You are impossible," she cried. "When I leave, to return to the ranch, can I expect you to bring her in here, onto this bed, afraid you will hurt her feelings if you do not do this thing for her?"

Lucas jumped to his feet and grabbed her by the shoulders. "Listen to yourself," he spat. "You sound like a jealous witch."

"Shouldn't I?" she demanded. "Can you tell me you won't bring her back to your bed? You are so protective

165

of her, Lucas. If you truly love me, you will have to completely put her from your mind and especially your *bed*. I will not share you with her. I will *not*!"

A loud knocking on the door drew Lucas away from Kendra. He lunged for his jeans and stepped quickly into them, then just as quickly holstered his guns around his hips. Grabbing his shirt, he proceeded to button it as he moved to the door.

Kendra tensed and leaned an ear to the bedroom door as she began pulling her own boots on. She could hear some excited talk from an Indian . . . telling Lucas in Indian language something that must have happened that wasn't good. She cringed inside when she heard Lucas speak back to the Indian, also in Indian language. He still was as mysterious as before. She hadn't learned all that much more about him here in the Indian village. She had only strengthened her impression of how he truly felt about these people . . . especially the beautiful woman.

Now, knowing that she had to get away from this place, Kendra fastened her holstered pistols about her hips. She flipped her hair to hang long and lustrous down her back and was reaching for her hat when Lucas came back into the room.

"I've got to leave," he growled. "Kendra, don't you budge from this house until I return. I've got to get this damn thing settled with you once and for all."

He tied his bandana around his neck, secured his leather chaps about his legs, and plopped his sombrero onto his head. He then went to Kendra and clasped his fingers onto her shoulders.

"You did hear me, didn't you?" he said. "I will return as soon as I can."

"Where are you going in such a rush?" she said in a

166

near-whisper, seeing a burning anger in the depth of his gray eyes.

"It's a band of outlaws," he growled. "I have to teach them a lesson."

An iciness swam around Kendra's heart. "Outlaws? What's happened?"

"They've confiscated our supply wagon," he said. "It was coming from Reno. I've begun to let the Indians take more charge of things. I no longer travel to Reno to pick up supplies for the Indians. I feel they need the experience. I do have other business, besides, here in this village."

"You . . . do . . . ?" she whispered.

Lucas turned his eyes away from her, then looked forcefully toward her again. "You will stay, won't you?" he asked. "It could even be dangerous for you to try to travel back to the ranch alone now that those desperadoes are out there somewhere, causing Lord knows what kind of trouble besides takin' the supplies."

"Do you know who it is, Lucas?"

"I think I know from where they've traveled," he said. "There's a valley in the Pahranagat Range that has become a refuge for rustlers and outlaws. I'm pretty sure this is a part of their gang."

"Please be careful, Lucas," Kendra said, reaching her hand to his cheek, now more afraid for him than angry at him.

"You'll stay?"

"I would worry too much about you if I didn't," she murmured. "At least by staying I will see if you return safely."

He kissed her ardently, then swung away from her and toward the door. "I'll return as soon as I can," he said, tipping his hat before stepping from the door.

"I do love you, Lucas," Kendra whispered to the place where he had just stood.

With her head bowed, Kendra went to the fireplace and lifted a log onto the fire. The rain had left a chill in the air. But at least the rain had stopped. . . .

Kendra stiffened, feeling a sudden presence at her side. She turned and started when she found Heart Speak standing there, quiet and moody.

"Heart Speak," Kendra said dryly. "What do you mean coming here like this, unannounced? Do you make sneaking a habit?"

"You don't belong here," Heart Speak hissed. She raised a hand and pointed toward the door. "Go. Now."

Kendra straightened her back and laughed beneath her breath. "And do you think I'll do that just because you've asked me to?"

"Go . . ." Heart Speak said, much more firmly. "Now."

"Lucas has asked me to await his return."

"And my son has asked you to be his teacher," Heart Speak murmured. "I know. He told me. But you still must go. You will only bring sorrow into the Indians' hearts. All white men, but Lucas, have done this. You are no different, even though you're a woman."

"I have come here to be a friend," Kendra said, gritting her teeth, knowing she could never feel friendly toward the other woman in Lucas's life. But for Lucas and Quick Deer she had to push such bitter jealousies from her mind.

"Lucas is blinded by your fair skin and golden hair," Heart Speak said sourly. She reached a hand toward Kendra's hair, but was stopped by Kendra grabbing her angrily by the wrist.

"I wouldn't try that," Kendra warned. Then her eyes wavered and her heart plunged when she caught sight of the ring on Heart Speak's left hand. Kendra felt a dizziness seize her as she studied the ring. It was identical to Lucas's Indian ring. The turquoise flashed back at Kendra, mockingly.

"The ring . . .." she whispered. She raised her eyes slowly and caught the smug smile Heart Speak wore on her copper face, and suddenly Kendra felt the fool and had the need to flee all over again.

Having to force her tears to not surface, she rushed into the bedroom to get her hat. The sight of the bed saddened then angered her.

"And all the while *she* wears his ring . . . they wear matching rings . . . as a man . . . and wife . . . would!" she said aloud.

The knowing tortured her. Kendra tried to close her eyes to the truth, as she backed shakily from the room. When she heard soft laughter behind her, she plopped her hat angrily on her head and ran from the house.

Tears finally sprang forth. The milling Indians on all sides of her were only a blur as she ran, stumbling, in the direction where she had seen Domino. And when she finally reached him, Kendra leaned against his black and white spotted mane and let her breath return in small snatches.

"I'm such a fool, Domino," she cried. "Such a damn fool."

Domino pawed at the ground and whinnied. Kendra could feel the tightening muscles of her horse's stomach and knew that the desire for freedom itched away at him as though a million bugs were crawling on him.

"I know," she said, patting his nose. "I feel it also. Let's go, Domino. Let's get the wind against our faces again!"

Kendra rushed to the small stable and got her saddle blanket and saddle. She kept watch on all sides of her, now trusting no one. Lucas had fooled her so easily. Well, no one else would!

Once the saddle was secured on Domino's back, Kendra fit her foot into the stirrup and swung her leg over. She took one last, lingering look toward the village, then urged Domino onward, up and over the fence, then felt the breath of freedom wrap her once more in its safe cocoon.

"Never again, Lucas!" she shouted. "Never again!"

Chapter Ten

Aaron tightened his hold on the reins, keeping a close eye on the sky. The continuing downpour had slowed the drive north, and it appeared that a repeat performance was close at hand. The clouds were hanging low, gray, and ominous, with an occasional rumbling of thunder breaking through, like an animal growling.

Zeke drew rein next to Aaron. "Don't look good," he said, pushing his wide-brimmed sombrero back a bit from his brow with his thumb. "The damn storm spooked hell outta the herd last night. Think we'd best hurry them along? We don't need no stampede on our hands."

"Take it easy, Zeke," Aaron said, frowning.

"Aaron, I know this land up and down and know what the storms can do to a herd," Zeke growled. "You'd best listen. You hired me on as the head wrangler. You're not gettin' your money's worth if'n you don't listen to my advice."

Feeling a slow anger rising inside him, Aaron flashed Zeke a threatening look. "Head wranglers are a dime a dozen," he stated flatly. "Don't get too sure of

171

yourself, Zeke. And don't think I've not been watching you with Kendra. Hands off. Do you hear?"

Playing with his bushy, red sideburns, Zeke chuckled amusedly. "You scare the hell outta me, Aaron," he said. His dark eyes traveled over Aaron, causing a smirk to lift a corner of his lips. "You and your cowboy duds ain't foolin' no one. You don't know beans 'bout a cattle drive. So I'd not be shootin' my mouth off too much before gettin' the herd to proper grazin' land."

Aaron's face paled and his heart raced. He knew that Zeke was right. No matter how much Aaron tried, he still felt awkward out of Eastern clothes and dressed in jeans and boots. He had often wondered what his friends in Boston would say if they saw him so changed.

In Boston, Aaron had been the one leading the way, with his dark fashionable suits and silk top hats. Except during the war. Then he had proudly worn the blue captain's attire with its copper buttons always shining, and a sword at his side always gleaming.

But to be a cowboy? No. None of his friends would ever believe it.

"Well? What's it to be?" Zeke grumbled, leaning closer to Aaron. "Or do you want to turn chicken and return to the ranch?"

"Damn you, Zeke," Aaron growled. "One day you will push me too far."

"Yeah . . ." Zeke laughed, then circled his horse away from Aaron and rode back to the other cowhands and began shouting orders to move on, head 'em out. . . .

Aaron grimaced, hating Zeke. But he knew that Zeke *was* the best, and he had to put up with him. At least until a replacement could be found.

Clucking to his horse, Aaron followed alongside his

172

cattle, proud of the new calves that had grown enough to join the spring herd on the travel north. So many had scoffed at him . . . saying that if the heat of summer didn't kill them off, the cold of winter would. Well, so far, nature had been good to them. No two seasons had yet been too severe.

A streak of lightning suddenly zigzagged across the threatening heavens. Then another and another. Stiffening inside, Aaron lifted his raingear back up around his shoulders and tied the cape securely at his neck. He pulled his wide-brimmed hat more securely onto his head, then bent himself into the pounding wind that had just begun.

Circles of sagebrush rolled clumsily across the ground . . . funnels of dust spiraled into the air . . . and a blast of sand burned suddenly into Aaron's eyes. Wiping frantically, he tried focusing on the mountain pass up ahead. Beyond it was where he planned to leave the herd. They would be on higher ground, safe from flooding. There would be rich grasses there to fatten the cattle, and there would be steady, flowing water from the mountain streams for drinking, and the high walls of the mountain to protect them from the scorching heat and dry winds.

Yes, all that was needed was there and the land was his! Just a bit further, and then they could return to the ranch with one more job successfully out of the way.

Upon his return to the ranch his next plans were to see that the ready cattle had been taken to the railheads in Reno for shipping. Then he was going to search out this "Blackie," and see if he was his father.

But if he is, what will I do, he thought angrily to himself. When I tell him about Mother's death, will he even care?

There was a sudden flash of light a short distance away and a sickening sort of click, and Aaron watched in horror as one of his prized cows was jolted with powerful surges of electricity from the bolt of lightning. The ensuing crash of thunder and the cow falling dead on her side made a bitterness rise inside Aaron's throat. He knew that the other cows had been frightened and he also knew what to expect next. The thundering of frantic hoofbeats!

"God . . ." he said, as he watched his cows spread out in all directions, fleeing desperately for their lives. As though frozen to the spot, Aaron continued watching as the cows made a sudden turn and began racing toward him.

"Aaron, for God's sake, get outta the way!" Zeke shouted. "Aaron! You're going to get trampled!"

Aaron held onto his horse's reins, numb. When he saw Zeke streak up beside him and slap the rear of his horse, he suddenly came back to his senses and clung to his reins for dear life as he directed his racing horse around to head in the opposite direction, away from the thundering, wild-eyed cows.

Panting, he edged his horse out of the cows' path and sat, stunned, watching as Zeke and the rest of his men circled the cows and finally succeeded at getting the stampede stopped and the herd under control.

"I feel like a fool," he mumbled. "What must the men think?"

He was remembering another time on horseback when he had frozen. It had been after the battle of Gettysburg. He had come face to face with the captain of the Confederacy, away from where his other men could see him. Hating the Rebs as much as he did, he couldn't

174

understand why he hadn't been able to raise his gun to the man. But, somehow, he was now remembering the commanding look in the gray eyes of that Reb.

It had been nearing the end of the war, he thought now, sweat beads on his brow. That was why he hadn't shot the Reb. It would have been a useless death. It was probably why the Reb hadn't shot him.

He would never want to believe he had a trace of cowardice in him. In a sense, hadn't his father been a coward . . . ?

The sudden downpour of rain drew his thoughts back to the present. The rain was so heavy it was hard for Aaron to make out anything even two feet ahead of him, so he stayed his ground. He listened to the bellowing of the cows and to the shouts of his men. He huddled in the saddle, seeing the water getting deeper around his horse's hooves. And, to his chagrin, the rain continued to fall . . . and the wind to whine and whistle through the canyon passes.

"Aaron," Zeke shouted, drawing rein next to him. "The rain's spookin' the cows worse'n the lightnin' did. And I don't like bein' at the base of the mountain. Damn. Look at the rain rollin' off'n its sides."

"It's got to stop soon," Aaron shouted back. He wiped wetness from his face and lowered the brim of his hat over his eyes, to shield them. "Just sit this one out, Zeke. It'll pass."

"The water's gonna swallow us up," Zeke further worried. "Don' like it, Aaron. Not one bit."

"You ever experienced the likes of this before, Zeke, while herding for someone before me?"

"Once . . ." Zeke growled, spitting sideways.

"And . . . ?"

175

"Damn near lost my life!"

Goose pimples rose on Aaron's flesh. "You think it's that bad now?"

"Afraid so," Zeke mumbled, hearing the roaring of the water as it splashed through the canyon. "The streams are overflowin'. Looks *damn* bad."

"What should we do?" Aaron frantically asked. His insides were a mass of tremors as he felt the shimmying of his horse beneath him.

"I've already instructed the men to secure themselves to trees if'n it got worse," Zeke shouted. "And from the look and sounds of things, it's best *we* now do the same."

"Can't we get the herd to higher ground first?"

"We don't have time."

Aaron leaned a bit forward, trying to see the cattle through the steady sheets of rain. Only a blur here and there was evidence of cows fighting the mud at their feet and the force of the rain against their wide-eyed heads.

"And the herd?" Aaron asked wistfully.

"We'll take what's left after it's over, I guess," Zeke shrugged. His dark eyes wavered. "Sorry, Cap'n," he added.

His dislike of Zeke could turn into affection, Aaron thought. It made Aaron proud to be called captain, for so few remembered his fine command during the war. . . .

Aaron let his horse be guided by Zeke next to a piñon pine tree and nodded a thanks as Zeke tied a rope around Aaron's waist, then around his horse's middle, and then attached the rope to the tree.

"You won't be washed away now should the water come racin' faster through the pass," Zeke shouted. "Just hang on and pray, if you have a belief in the man upstairs."

Aaron hung on to the rope and thrust his knees more tightly into his horse's sides, watching Zeke secure himself to the other side of the tree, with another rope. And, suddenly, it was as though all hell had broken loose. A loud rumbling, shaking the ground ominously, was followed by a crashing of water through the canyon pass, lifting everything in its way up from the earth.

Groaning, Aaron watched cows float past him with their legs flailing. He would never forget their frightened, pitiful bellows. "I can't watch," Aaron whispered, closing his eyes, now feeling the suction of the water's force against his ankles, moving quickly upward in swirls, to stop at his thighs. Its coldness seeped through his clothes and lapped at the flesh of his legs. And suddenly Aaron's horse's hooves lifted from the ground and the horse was floating, yet still attached to the tree.

"Damn it . . ." Aaron cursed, slipping from the saddle. He clung to the horse . . . then the rope. He felt imprisoned now, wishing the rope wasn't there to confine him so awkwardly between the tree and the horse. He felt he was going to be crushed! He looked anxiously toward Zeke and saw that he was in the same predicament, cursing and shouting as he grabbed at his own horse.

Then the rains stopped and the heavens took on a quick tinge of blue as the clouds rolled quickly away, on upward, past the mountain peaks.

But the gurgling, rushing water continued. Aaron once more closed his eyes and said a silent prayer that his mother had taught him.

"Now I lay me down to sleep, I pray the Lord my soul to keep . . ."

"We'd best break loose now," Zeke shouted. "Come on, Aaron. Ain't time for restin' eyes. Get the ropes

177

undone. If you'll notice, the water's recedin'."

With a start, Aaron opened his eyes and was shocked to see that his horse was now standing firmly on the ground, and all that he had to do to get back in the saddle was climb on.

"This is the damnedest thing I've ever seen," he said, untangling the rope from around his waist. As he worked with the rope he looked slowly around him. The water had washed on down the slope and had left disaster behind. Everywhere Aaron looked he saw dead cattle. Some had drowned and others had been trampled in the rush for dry land.

Zeke walked his horse next to Aaron, his clothes clinging to him and his red beard dripping sparkles of water from it. Coughing and spitting, he wiped at his eyes.

Aaron tossed the untied rope aside angrily. He secured his feet on the ground and took a Colt from its holster and wiped it against his pants leg. "Useless," he grumbled. "Pants are too wet."

He shot Zeke a fast glance, slipping his revolver back into its holster. "How many we lose, Zeke?" he asked guardedly, afraid to hear the answer.

Zeke let his horse move slowly around him, silently counting the dead carcasses. "Twenty . . . maybe thirty head," he said.

Aaron shivered. "Damn," he muttered. He lifted a doubled fist to the sky. "Damn," he repeated.

"We'd best get busy and round up what's left," Zeke said, swinging himself up into his saddle. The wet leather groaned beneath his weight.

"I'll be along shortly," Aaron said. He looped his reins around his horse's neck and swung himself up into the saddle. "I'm going to travel on up to the crest of the hill. You know we were about there when the damn storm hit."

"Yeah. Tell me about it," Zeke said, then rode quickly away, already shouting out orders to the men as they gathered around the confused cows.

Aaron's horse blew out a snort as Aaron gave it a flick of reins and a nudge from his knees. Feeling the intense heat of the newborn sun fusing his wet clothes to his body, Aaron moved on toward the crest of the hill, from where he could see the rich grassland where he had planned to put hard weight on his cattle. Maybe if he could have managed to have gotten the herd there before the raging waters had come like the devil, plundering . . .

"What the . . . ?" Aaron said, spreading his hand above his eyes, shielding them from the blinding rays of the sun. His heart began a crazy pounding, disbelieving what his eyes were seeing.

"How . . . ? Who . . . ?" he whispered. His face grew red with anger and his temples pounded.

"Hahh!" he shouted to his horse. He raced to the crest of the hill and then jumped from the saddle, growing weak-kneed as his gaze traveled slowly around him. . . .

It was a grotesque, obscene scene! Many of his cattle had rushed up this hill, blind, yet sensing safety ahead. But they had been stopped by the ugly claws of barbed wire, which had captured them, entangling them in a fence that was stretched out across the fresh, green grass as far as Aaron's eyes could see.

A light-headedness seized Aaron. He leaned his full weight against his horse, clinging to the saddlehorn, his head lowered, suddenly feeling a need to retch. A fence! A goddamned barbed wire fence strung across this land that Aaron had thought was his! Had his claim stakes been placed wrong? How could this have happened?

Then a low growl surfaced from deep inside him as he stomped, heavy-footed, away from his horse and to the fence, trying not to see the bleeding, torn cows.

"Barbed wire!" he snarled. No matter whose land this was . . . no barbed wire had ever stood in the way of free grazing on this range. There had always been enough rich grass for all!

He grabbed a fence post and began yanking angrily at it. "A barbed wire fence means only one thing to me! Someone's bringing sheep in! I know it!" he yelled.

Hoofbeats approaching drew Aaron around, and he saw the dark pits of Zeke's eyes taking in this scene of inhumanity.

"Barbed wire, Zeke," Aaron growled.

Zeke quickly dismounted and walked dazedly toward Aaron. "How did this get here?" he said in his craggy voice. "Who's got the guts?"

"You know what it has to mean, Zeke."

"To me, many things," Zeke growled.

"So what are we going to do about it?"

"Tear the damn thing down," Zeke said, eyeing the dead cows. "And then find out who owes us."

"Do you get a whiff of sheep behind this, Zeke?"

"Seems that way."

"Have you heard gossip of any rancher planning to bring sheep in?"

"Not a word."

"Then I'm going to do some investigating on my own," Aaron said dryly, swinging himself back up into the saddle.

Zeke eyed Aaron. "What's your plan?"

"Can you handle this mess here? Get the fence down and get the herd settled in?"

"Yep . . ."

"Then, Zeke, I'll see you back at the ranch later."

"What's up, Aaron?"

"I plan to trace this fence and see if I can find me a responsible party."

"You could get shot."

Aaron slapped his holstered Colt. "In the war I defended myself well enough," he said proudly. "Out here it'll be no different, Zeke."

Anger spurred him on away from Zeke, determined to see that no other fences were planted, and for sure to argue hotly against sheep! No sheep could share grazing land with his cattle! No sheep would be allowed to ruin this rich, fertile land that Aaron had brought his prized herds to. Before long, there would be no grass left, because sheep were known to crop grass so short no cattle could follow along after them.

"No one is going to be allowed to build fences on this open range to limit pastureland," he growled to himself. "Till now we've all shared without problems. It will be no different now. I'll see to it!"

The sun beat unmercifully down on Aaron as he followed the thin line of fence over mile after mile of green, blowing grasses, with the cool shadows of the mountains now in the far distance. Up one hill and down another, and finally something else caught Aaron's eyes. He clutched more angrily to the horse's reins when he saw a small house nestled beneath a stray stand of billowing cottonwood trees.

The barbed wire fence ran along behind the house, adjacent to another line of fence that bent out to encircle

181

the house inside its own fence. This fence was made of wood, not wire.

The one-story house was unpainted. A wide porch stretched across its front. A small patch of garden lay peacefully at the back of the house, and a lone, tied cow and one horse grazed a little distance from it. A well was in the front yard, and by it stood the tiny figure of a woman drawing water from it.

Aaron slowed his horse's approach, lifting an eyebrow. "Is this homesteader the responsible party?" he wondered to himself. "Surely not. With no barn full of equipment they don't even have the means to spread fences across the land."

Cautiously, Aaron continued on his way toward the house, never taking his eyes from the woman. The closer he drew to her the easier it became for him to see her earthy loveliness. Hair braided and coiled atop her head didn't hide the bright reds of it, and now, as he drew rein next to the closed, locked gate, he could see the innocence of her widespread eyes and the childishness of the splotches of freckles sprinkling her nose and high cheekbones.

Something akin to passion stirred inside Aaron and for the first time in many years he felt stirred by a woman's presence. He had lost something with Holly, oh, so long ago, over her insistence about having a child.

"Hello there, ma'am," Aaron said, tipping his hat to the lady. His gaze traveled over her, seeing the high swell of her breasts filling out the tightness of her faded cotton dress and the tininess of her waist where her dress gathered and fell full to her feet.

Aaron smiled warmly as he saw the tapered fingers of one of her hands move self-consciously to her hair.

"Yes . . . ?" she said, resting the water bucket on the edge of the well.

In the bright of the sun, Aaron could see her eyes much more clearly and felt drawn even more to her, falling in love with the color . . . the color of amethyst.

"Is the man of the house in?" Aaron asked, dismounting. He frowned when he saw a quick, guarded expression flash across her face as she took a step backwards, causing her to lose a firm hand on the water bucket.

As it fell to the ground in a crash, spreading water in all directions like tentacles of an octopus, Aaron's gaze was alerted elsewhere. He saw a movement at the door of the house and swallowed hard when he caught the very identifiable shine of a shotgun barrel being pointed at him. His right hand moved quickly to his Colt, but a loud shout stopped him in midair.

"I wouldn't do that." A man's voice broke through the strained silence.

The roof of the porch and the shade of the cottonwoods shaded the man in the doorway, only a shadow to Aaron as he squinted, trying to focus, to see what the full danger was. But, still only seeing the shotgun's shine, he let his hand drop slowly to his side.

"I didn't come here to cause trouble," he shouted back. "I saw your house. Just ridin' by. Thought I'd stop and make your acquaintance."

"And where do you ride from?"

Aaron nodded with his head. "I own a spread of land close by here," he said. "Carpenter. Aaron Carpenter's my name."

There was a full minute of silence. Aaron's pulse raced, wondering what might happen next. He glanced toward the woman, seeing that she hadn't budged. She stood stark still, eyes wide, arms stiffly at her side, looking lovelier than ever as the breeze blew the skirt of her dress up and away from her tiny ankles.

Then Aaron's breath caught in his throat when he saw a small figure of a man roll himself out into view in a rickety wooden wheelchair. Suddenly he knew that this was not the man responsible for the barbed wire fence. This man had no legs.

"Aaron . . . ?" the man said shakily, in a weakened voice. "Is it really you? Captain Carpenter?"

Goose pimples rode up and down Aaron's spine. He narrowed his eyes, somehow remembering the voice. But the face . . . ?

"You know me from . . . the . . . war . . . ?" Aaron said, straining to get a better look.

"Hazel, honey, open the gate for Captain Carpenter," the man said, suddenly laughing gaily. He leaned his shotgun against the house and rolled himself to the far edge of the porch. "It's me. John Lassiter. I fought with you at Gettysburg."

"John? John Lassiter?" Aaron whispered. He lifted his hat from his head and suddenly tossed it into the air, shouting. "Johnny!" he yelled. "My right-hand man! The best shot I ever did see."

As Aaron's hat fell back between his fingers, his gaze settled on the vacancy below Johnny's knees. "But, Johnny, at the war's end you were . . ."

"Healthy in all respects?" Johnny said bitterly. "Yeah. I *was.* Even got out of that hellish war with my legs intact." He waved a hand. "Come on, Hazel. Get the lead out of your feet. Open the gate. Let my good friend in. We'll empty a bottle of wine and talk about

184

old times."

Aaron's eyes shifted lazily toward Hazel as she scampered to the gate to unlock and open it. "I'm sorry, sir," she said softly. "But with Johnny disabled I have to be so cautious about strangers. You just never know who might happen along with ugliness on their minds."

Aaron smelled a soft fragrance lifting from her skin as he moved past her, into the yard. He suddenly felt awkward and very self-conscious about his shining, bald head. Surely she must think him ninety! With trembling fingers he quickly flopped his hat back atop his head.

"You can place your horse in back with mine," Hazel offered, relocking the gate. "There's plenty of water and feed if your horse is in need of either."

"Thank you, ma'am," Aaron said, bowing slightly, feeling the heat in his loins building as their gazes met and locked. There was much hidden in the depths of the intense violet shades of her eyes. Was it a loneliness? Was it a need that an injured, helpless man could no longer fill?

A slow smile lifted Aaron's lips as he saw a blush rise to her cheeks. Yes, he knew her needs. They matched . . . his . . . own.

Guilt surging through him, Aaron focused back on Johnny, now seeing his war companion's full features. Though a young man of only twenty-five, his face was lined and haggard and his hair a solid, thick mass of gray. His shoulders were frail and hunched and his hands bony and white. A healthy lad of fifteen during the war . . . and now an aging man of twenty-five in a time of peace. An ache circled Aaron's heart.

"I'll be right with you, Johnny," he murmured. As he walked around the corner of the house he heard Johnny

185

excitedly telling Hazel to fetch a bottle of wine from the root cellar, that this was a special guest, this Captain Aaron Carpenter was!

Aaron's approach to the house had hidden a small shack behind the house. Inside its open door was a buckboard wagon, feed for the horse and cow and a few garden implements, but no tools with which to plant fence posts and no signs of leftover barbed wire fence.

But, of course, he had known he wouldn't find these things because Johnny was confined to his wheelchair and the genteel young Hazel probably had all she could do to keep the garden growing and the cow milked. A few chickens squawked from a smaller fenced-off area next to the leaning shack, and a hand plow lay rusting on the ground.

"Must be hard for the little woman," Aaron sighed, tying his horse's reins on the low limb of a cottonwood, next to the brown and white speckled mustang, whose ribs were hungrily showing through its matted coat. "Maybe I can do something about all of this."

With wide, heavy strides, Aaron hurried back around the house and up the rickety steps of the porch. He grabbed his hat from his head when he saw Hazel there, holding the screen door open for him.

"Why, thank you, ma'am," Aaron said, bending his back as he stepped across the threshhold and into a cheerfully bright room. It was nothing like he had expected. Feeling that his friend and wife most surely were dirt poor from all outward appearances, he was surprised to see pure silver candlestick holders shining from the fireplace mantel and sparkling crystal glassware reflecting in blues and purples from a glassed-in curio case. The table was spread with immaculate white linen,

186

and long-stemmed wine glasses and a newly opened bottle of wine sat waiting upon it.

Aaron tried not to show pity as he looked toward the shriveled form of Johnny sitting beside the table, waiting. "You have a nice place here," he said, smiling at Hazel as she took his hat and placed it gingerly on the table.

As Aaron settled down onto a chair he once more admired the room . . . the bright carpet and curtains, and the walls covered with a flowered paper. At one end, a kitchen had been established, and built-in cupboards with drawers and bins for flour and sugar underneath had been built along one wall. Next to that a potbellied stove sat with cooking utensils smoking atop it, but the largest portion of the room's outer wall was taken up by an immense stone fireplace that showed signs of last evening's fire in an occasional glow of orange showing through the gray ash on the hearth.

Then something else grabbed Aaron's attention. It was a small bed at the opposite end of the room. Aaron's gaze traveled to the door leading to the one other room of the house, and from this vantage point he could see another small bed. It was obvious that this man and wife shared everything but a bed.

Clearing his throat nervously, Aaron loosened the bandana at his neck, suddenly conscious of the bite of its wetness causing an itch where it had lain. Though the temperature had been scalding hot after the rain, the humidity had kept his clothes from drying properly.

"Now, Aaron, tell us. What brings you to our place?" Johnny asked, pouring wine into the three glasses. He nodded toward Hazel, a silent invitation for her to join them at the table.

Aaron watched as she eased onto a chair. As she

reached for a glass, he felt his gut twisting, seeing the roughness of her hands and the way her fingernails were broken and short, almost to the quick. Her fair skin showed a flakiness, probably the aftereffects of being under the heat of the sun while gardening and working with the animals.

"Why?" he finally said. "It's the barbed-wire fence, Johnny." He felt his skin draw tight as he tried to keep his anger from showing. "Where the hell did it come from? It's chokin' the land, Johnny, and I've already ordered my men to get rid of it. When that stuff was invented in seventy-three I didn't think much about it except that it would be a cheap substitute for wood fences. But that was when I was still in Boston and had no concern over how this cheap substitute could be used. Banking was all I had on my mind. Not land. Not cattle."

"Your men are cuttin' the wires, Aaron?"

"Sure as hell are," Aaron growled. "Now tell me, Johnny, who's responsible for this fence? It's mighty close to your own wooden one. Surely you saw who strung it."

"Have yourself a drink, Aaron," Johnny said, scooting a glass toward him.

"Johnny, you're evading the question."

"Not really," Johnny said, toying with the long stem of his glass. "It never meant a thing to me. I have my own little world here, and as long as nobody threatens me and mine I don't care what they plant in the ground, be it fence posts or corn."

"Corn?" Aaron said, lifting an eyebrow. He laughed scornfully. "Johnny, you'll see no cornfields out here. You should've settled in Iowa or Illinois." His eyes wavered a bit. "Johnny, how is it you *are* here? How did you . . . uh . . . lose your legs?"

Johnny tipped his glass to his lips and swallowed the wine in fast gulps. His washed-out blue eyes took on a distant stare. He slammed the glass down and rolled his wheelchair back from the table.

Patting his thin thighs, Johnny laughed bitterly. "Beats all," he said. "Go through the war . . . see our men shot to pieces . . . and thankin' the Lord as each day passes that leaves you whole. Then you come out West in search of wealth and lose your legs in a damn silver mine."

Aaron gulped hard. He looked away from Johnny, only to find Hazel's lustrous eyes watching him. It was as though she was seeing right through him . . . seeing the guilt he was feeling. How often had Kendra argued with him about the mine's hazards? Even Seth faced daily dangers! But Aaron had argued back, trying to make Kendra understand that he was only one man . . . and one man could do only so much among the many who ruled over the mines!

Lifting the glass to his lips, Aaron felt its bitter sweetness a blessing as it rippled down the back of his throat. He sat the glass back down and wiped the excess wetness from his lips with the back of a hand. "Sorry to hear it, Johnny," he mumbled. "Damn sorry to hear it."

"And you, Aaron? What brought you out West?" Johnny asked, refilling his and Aaron's glasses as he rolled back closer to the table.

"Mother died," Aaron said. "So I just up and moved the whole family out here, you know, for a change."

Johnny laughed hoarsely. "And quite a change, Aaron," he said. "From Massachusetts to Nevada. How's the rest of the family taking it? How's that sister of

189

yours? Kendra. Bet she's grown up into a beauty."

"Yes," Aaron said. "Beautiful and daring. God, Johnny, has she changed. She was the genteel lady of Boston, always dressed in ruffles and lace, and so dainty. Now she dresses in men's breeches and shirts, and sports pistols at her hips."

Johnny roared with laughter, then sobered. "Bet she keeps you on your toes, Aaron," he said. Then he gave Hazel a wistful glance. "My Hazel here, she's got it different out here, too. Since my accident, she has to do it all. She does both women's and men's chores each day. Don't you, hon?"

"I try my best, darlin'," she murmured, casting her eyes downward.

"She's from Tennessee, my little woman is," Johnny said. "Met her on my way out here. Her folks had died of cholera. I took her in under my wing and we've not been separated since."

"You've a nice place here, ma'am," Aaron said quietly, then laughed. "But I think I've already told you that."

"Aaron, I've noticed your clothes. They're mostly wet," Johnny said. "Were you caught in that downpour?"

"Yes, and I've never seen anything quite like it," Aaron grumbled. He twirled his glass around between his fingers. "Lost several head of cattle. Some drowned . . . some stomped to death . . . and some got hung up on that damned barbed wire." He set his jaws firmly. "Johnny, you never did say who it was you saw installing that fence."

"Can't say."

"Why the hell not?"

"I didn't talk with him," Johnny said sourly. "And I forbid Hazel from stepping outside while the stranger was there. No. Don't know who it was."

"Don't you even know who lays claim to that stretch of land?"

"Nope. I homesteaded my small strip here I've circled with my fence, and up to my accident that was all I needed 'cause I didn't have time to see to cattle or nothing else."

"So you just keep your nose clean, huh?" Aaron said, rising from his chair, stiffening when he heard rain pellets suddenly hitting the roof.

"Can't see that I have no other choice," Johnny grumbled. He looked toward the window, then to Hazel, who had risen quickly from the table and had thrown a shawl around her shoulders.

"Where are you going?" Aaron asked, seeing her rushing toward the door.

"I must get the horses and cow inside, to dry shelter," she said.

Aaron rushed to her side. "No, you don't," he said, taking her by a hand. There was an instant magnetism between them with the touch of flesh against flesh. Aaron's heart raced and his insides warmed. "I'll do it. I'm already wet. No sense in you getting out in the weather."

"Some sort of freak of nature, I suppose," Johnny said, guiding his wheelchair across the room. "I could've swore the sky was clear only a short while ago."

Aaron and Hazel's eyes wavered as they stood, immobile, exchanging vibrations between them. . . .

"The storm clouds must've made a full circle and returned," Aaron said thickly. "I hope Zeke has

191

everything under control."

"Zeke?" Johnny said, moving next to Aaron, staring upward, looking slowly from Aaron to Hazel, conscious of what was happening between his wife and his old friend. His insides quivered with sadness, yet with a strange kind of hope. Hazel had been without for so long. Maybe Aaron could help her. . . .

Aaron dropped Hazel's hand as though shot when feeling Johnny so close beside him. His face colored as he stammered out a reply. "Zeke's my head wrangler. I left him in charge while I've come in search of the person responsible for the fence."

"Sorry I can't help you with the fence, but I can offer something else to you," Johnny said guardedly.

"And what's that, Johnny?" Aaron said, watching as Hazel slipped the shawl from around her shoulders, revealing once more to his eyes the graciousness of her figure . . . the sensuous swell of her breasts. . . .

"Some dry clothes and a place to stay for the night," Johnny said. "Seems the rains may be here for a while now."

Aaron went to the door and opened it, seeing the total blackness of the sky. It did appear that day had passed into night while they had been talking and that the rain did seem to have set in for the night.

"You are most welcome to stay, Aaron," Hazel said softly, placing her shawl across the back of a chair.

Aaron turned and looked toward Hazel and something in her eyes made him say, "That's mighty nice of you both. I'll gladly accept the invitation. . . ."

Chapter Eleven

Hazel's hair looked like colors spun from a magnificent sunset as it hung, unbraided, clear to her waist. Aaron crept from the bedroom, buttoning his shirt. Could he really be seeing Hazel standing nude, dripping wet, in a wooden tub of water? Oh, how gracefully she was drying herself, like a delicate rose petal, blushed pink from a morning rain.

As she raised her arms over her head to toss the towel aside, Aaron feasted his eyes on the stiff peaks of her breasts. The nipples were dark and firm, and as she cupped one with a hand and moaned throatily, Aaron felt the heat growing in his loins and the tight confines of his jeans becoming almost unbearable.

Looking quickly around the outer room, Aaron saw no signs of Johnny. Where could he be so early in the morning? It had rained off and on until only a while ago.

But now Aaron remembered what had awakened him. It had been the squeaking of the buckboard wagon wheels and the neighing of a horse. Had it been Johnny leaving? And without assistance from Hazel?

Once more directing his full vision to Hazel, seeing her sensual demonstration sent worries of Johnny quickly from Aaron's mind. Instead he stepped back into the bedroom and became a voyeur as he watched a dazed look appear in Hazel's eyes as she closed them and enjoyed the touch of her own hands traveling delicately across her body. And when her fingers moved lower, Aaron's face flushed crimson and his heart threatened to swallow him whole into its thunderous poundings.

As though in a trance, still watching her, he unbuttoned his shirt and threw it aside, then shed himself of his jeans. With slow, yet determined steps, he went into the outer room and gently joined her in the tub, replacing her hand with his.

Cautiously, expecting to be ordered from the tub, he drew her silken body into his, trembling as her breasts made contact with his chest. When he found her agreeable, he fit his body more firmly against hers and rubbed his flesh excitedly against hers.

"Please," she whispered. "It's been . . . so . . . long . . ."

Her hands caressed the baldness of his head as his lips lowered smoothly over her mouth. His tongue became a spear, entering between her teeth, plunging deeply down her throat as she moaned and writhed against him.

His hands moved frantically over the smooth silk of her back, then lower, shaping them around the sensuous curves of her buttocks. With force he shoved himself up inside her and began working in and out.

"Take me to bed," she whispered. "I want to feel all of you against my body. I need to feel all of you. Please."

Guilt tore through him, as he remembered Johnny and his maimed body. Hadn't he been able to . . . ? Was that

194

why Hazel was so starved for this way of loving? But no matter, Aaron was too far gone to stop now. He only hoped Johnny wouldn't return and discover his wife's unfaithfulness.

"Where's Johnny?" he whispered into her ear as he removed his sex from inside her. He had to ask. He just didn't want to hurt Johnny! His tongue lapped at her neck . . . her throat . . . a breast. . . .

Hazel arched her neck backwards, sighing with intense ecstasy. "He . . . he does this," she murmured.

"Does what?"

"He gets moody. He will be gone for hours."

"Where does he go?"

"Out on the open range . . . to drive off his frustrations."

"What frustrations?"

Hazel's violet eyes were heavy with desire as she met his questioning gaze. "His sexual . . . frustration," she whispered. "You see, the accident took more than his legs."

"God . . ." Aaron groaned, almost choking. "Then that's why you were . . . why you are . . ."

She placed a forefinger to his lips, cutting off his words. "Yes," she whispered. "Sometimes the need gets almost unbearable for me."

Aaron drew her quickly into his arms and hugged her tightly to him. "Yes. I can understand," he said. "God. You're so young. You're so much a woman."

"I have to confess something to you, Aaron," she said softly.

"And what's that?"

"Johnny *doesn't* do this often, as I said that he did."

Aaron's eyes opened, stunned. He barely breathed as

he continued to hold her. "What do you mean?"

She whispered against his chest. "He doesn't truly go out on the range for hours."

"What . . . ?" Aaron said. He moved her gently from his arms and implored her with his eyes.

"He rarely leaves the house at all," she murmured, casting her eyes downward.

"Why on earth did you tell me that he did?"

"Because Johnny has planned it this way."

"Which way? What are you talking about?"

"Carry me to bed, Aaron? Let me tell you there?"

He couldn't resist the tone in her voice nor the look in her eyes. He lifted her up into his arms and welcomed her cheek against his chest as well as her arms locked about his neck. His heart beat furiously, feeling the soft sponginess of her breast against his left arm as he stepped out of the water. His wet footprints followed after him as he carried his delicate bundle into the bedroom. And as he started to release her from his arms, her lips stopped him with a long, hungry, passionate kiss.

Their bodies fused into one as Aaron leaned down onto the bed with her. Her teeth nipped at his lower lip as he tried to ease away from her. And as one of her hands traveled down across his abdomen, then lower, where his sex jutted solid and hard away from him, Aaron thought he would not be able to wait any longer as her fingers circled around him and began to move.

He groaned and stiffened, then shivered, as her lips also lowered and chewed on the stiff peak of one of his nipples. And as her one hand continued to move, making him feel as though he was encased in a bed of velvet, he stretched out and closed his eyes.

"As I was saying," Hazel whispered between trailing

kisses along his stomach. "Johnny planned this. He wanted you to make love to me."

Aaron's eyes shot wide open and he leaned up on an elbow. "What . . . ?" he gasped.

"You see, I haven't had a man since Johnny's accident," Hazel continued. "It's been two full years. And when you came along, someone he admired, trusted and even loved, he felt it only right that you give me the pleasure I have been deprived of for so long."

Aaron blanched. "This was all planned?" He grew suddenly angry and brushed her away from him. "No thanks . . ." he shouted. "You can get yourself another stud." He rose furiously from the bed.

"Aaron," Hazel cried, running after him. "Please. Don't leave."

"I've things to do," he said coolly. "Now that the rains have stopped, I must return to the ranch."

"Aaron, please," she whimpered, falling to her knees at his feet. "I only told you about Johnny so you wouldn't feel guilty about our being together. If I had known you'd get angry I wouldn't have told you."

"And that's supposed to be a comfort? Telling me is supposed to make it all right?"

"I was being honest," she said, wiping tears from her cheeks with the back of a hand. "I thought you admired honesty."

Aaron looked down at her, seeing her fully blossomed breasts just asking to be touched, and the ache was there again, torturing him. When she began trailing her fingers slowly up his legs, sensual tremors trailed up and down his spine.

"Am I forgiven, Aaron?"

Her fingers found his hardness and circled it. He

197

stiffened, closed his eyes and gritted his teeth. "I will take you," he said huskily. "Damn it, I *will*."

He forgot his gentleness and wildly drew her up into his arms and once more carried her to bed. Once he was positioned over her he entered her roughly and began working frantically as she lifted her hips to meet him, moaning and tossing her head fitfully from side to side. His hands cupped her breasts and his breath became short and laborious. He no longer cared why he was there . . . only that he *was* there!

"I can't wait. . . ." Hazel cried out. "I wanted it to last but I . . . can't . . . wait."

Aaron buried his face between her breasts as he felt her body twist and turn with her climax. Then he closed his eyes and let his passion build, then spill over inside her in a moment of intense release that left him winded.

He lay panting, his cheek against her breast, stiffening as he felt her lips press a kiss on the bald top of his head. He couldn't believe that he had actually gone along with this farce. But he had, and nothing could quell his sudden love for this woman, planned or not. He now knew that this wouldn't be the last time. She was now as surely a part of his existence as his ranch . . . his banks . . . his wealth.

"Come here, you wench," Aaron growled, drawing her roughly into his arms. She slinked her body into the shape of his and framed his face with her hands as she lowered her mouth to his. He could feel the trembling of her lips. He could feel the wetness of her tears upon her cheeks. Their exchanged kisses were soft and sweet. His hands explored her body, as though memorizing it, to carry with him in his thoughts when he rode away from her.

"It was beautiful, Aaron," Hazel whispered between a scattering of soft kisses across his face. Then she giggled, rubbing his stubble of whiskers with her nose. "But I do believe you need a shave, handsome man."

Aaron's blue eyes lightened. A slow smile creased his face. He eyed her amusedly and locked his arms about her, warming again inside as her luscious breasts pressed against his chest. "Handsome?" he chuckled. "Did my ears hear right? Did you call this man with a bald head and thick waistline handsome?"

Hazel's hands reached up and began a slow caress of his head. "I find it quite stimulating," she murmured. "A head without hair is quite sexy. Yes, my darling, you are handsome and I think I'm falling in love with you, and I *do* know the dangers of that."

"Johnny . . . ?"

Her eyes lowered. "Yes," she whispered. "I will always stay with him. Always."

"Hazel . . ." He fit a forefinger beneath her chin. "Hazel, I have an idea."

She raised her eyes slowly. They were sparkling with tears. "Yes . . . ?"

"You and Johnny could come and live with me and my family at my ranch," he said thickly. "There's plenty of room. I could even find something for Johnny to do with his time."

Hazel rose to her knees, her face flushed scarlet. Excitement danced in her violet eyes. "Oh, could we, Aaron?" she sighed. "I do get so lonely out here alone with Johnny."

"Yes," he laughed, reaching to cup a breast. "It could be done. And soon. You ask Johnny. Then I will come for his answer. Real soon."

Hazel plopped sullenly to the bed, her eyes now dull "He won't," she murmured. "I know that he won't." Then she leaned up on an elbow and placed a soft kiss on his lips. "And, anyway, if we were there with your family how could you and I . . . you know. Surely your family would find out if we met together in this way right beneath their noses."

Aaron chuckled greedily. "My land stretches far and wide," he said. "It could be arranged. It could be worked out for us to meet safely."

"But Johnny just won't," she further pouted. "He doesn't like to be around people. He doesn't like for them to see him. He's very proud."

"Then I will convince him. Somehow."

"He may suspect you are doing this for only me."

"And? Does that matter? He planned for us to be together in the first place."

"But only once. . . ."

"To hell with only once," Aaron growled. He leaned over her and began sending kisses along her flesh. "I'll even have you again right now if you'll have *me*."

"Aaron," Hazel whispered, trembling beneath his fresh assault of kisses pleasuring her anew. "What about your wife? Don't . . . you . . . love her?"

"Holly has become a nag," Aaron grumbled. "I hate nags. Please don't ever demand things of me. Just let's enjoy what we've found."

"You're truly no longer mad at me for going along with Johnny with this plan to seduce you?"

"God, no. Look what I would have missed. What *we* would have missed . . . had you not."

"So let's not waste precious time," she purred, urging him atop her. "Please, Aaron. Once more before you leave."

"My poor, love-starved kitten," he said, burrowing his nose in the thickness of her hair as he eased his sex inside her. "Purr for me, darling," he said huskily. "Make me hear your pleasure."

Hazel giggled, then moaned as she opened herself up more to him and let the ecstasy begin washing over her anew. It was as though she was on a cloud, soft and fluffy, getting dizzier and dizzier as she was being taken high up into the sky. . . .

Aaron held her tightly to him, melting into her, and shook violently as he once more filled her with his love. He leaned away from her and kissed her breasts, one at a time. "But I must leave now," he whispered. "Johnny would not be amused to find us this way. He would know that we've had much more than he planned for us to have together."

"Let me fix you breakfast. Surely you've a ways to go."

"And also I'd like a fast shave."

"For the moment we could pretend it's just you and me, Aaron," Hazel whispered, leaning up to cling to him.

"Yes, for the moment," he said huskily. He was suddenly wondering what she would think of him if she knew that he wasn't man enough to even father a child!

But he would never tell Hazel. Even Holly didn't know the truth. She just kept nagging and nagging and nagging. . . .

Chapter Twelve

All the terrain looked the same to Kendra, but she knew that she was already traveling on Carpenter land. She had checked the flanks of the grazing horses and had smiled when she found the Circle C brand. But at the same time she had been a bit dismayed to find that Carpenter land lay so close to the Indian village.

Yet, now remembering, she recalled Aaron's anger about this when he had first discovered it. Kendra just hadn't taken the time to check it out. She had been too involved in the activities of preparing the new schoolhouse. It puzzled her now, though, why she hadn't remembered the Indian village earlier when she had found Quick Deer injured outside the schoolhouse door. But so much had happened so quickly that day. First there had been Zeke's sudden appearance on the trail to slow her return to the ranch to get the buggy, and then there had been the sudden reappearance of Lucas into her life a short while later.

Not wanting her thoughts to linger on Lucas, she drew Domino to a halt. With the sun beating unmercifully downward, scorching her face and seeping through her clothes, heating her flesh, she drew her hat from her head and began fanning herself with it.

"Surely I don't have much further to go," she sighed. "I'm so hot."

Her thoughts once more moved lethargically to Lucas. Though she hated him at this moment, she knew that she loved him with all her heart, and she was now worried about his safety. Had he put himself in danger going in search of the desperadoes? And had she done the same herself, by leaving the Indian village so hastily, alone?

Kendra's hair rose at the nape of her neck as she thought further about being alone out there. She was just a small speck of humanity on this vast valley of green towered over by the Sierra range spreading out in purplish hues in the distance. Everything was strangely quiet. Kendra could hear each breath that Domino took. His breaths didn't match her own. Hers were coming in shaky rasps, suddenly afraid.

A sparkle in the distance drew her quick attention. Water. And beside this meandering stream was a thick stand of willow trees, and the shade they could offer her. Her throat was dry . . . her lips were parched. She would refresh herself and Domino and then head for home. She had to at least have the ranch in sight when night began to fall. No way could she spend a full night alone out in the open. This time she was without the assurance of Lucas's being on the trail ahead of her, as before. And even a campfire wouldn't offer her enough protection. A campfire could draw many things toward itself . . . !

Kendra patted Domino's neck. "Let's go, boy," she said. "Or do you already smell the water?" She had seen Domino's head lift and his nose wiggle a bit. She had even noticed his nervous pawing at the ground, cautioning Kendra to look quickly all around her. But then she felt foolish, seeing nothing.

Frowning, she placed her hat back on her head and turned Domino's head toward the water. "Come on, boy," she said, leading Domino into a brisk trot through the range grass, which was as thick and plush as a carpet.

Kendra tensed when Domino let out a loud, nervous snort and shook his head back and forth. "What is it, Domino? Do you see a snake . . . or what . . . ?" she whispered, fear truly lacing her heart now.

But Domino followed her lead and was finally drawing up closer to the stream. Kendra accepted with a sigh the relief the shade of the willows handed her. She bent her back and rode beneath their low branches and drew rein next to the winding, shallow blue water.

Eager to feel the coolness against her face, Kendra dismounted and led Domino to the water's edge. She smiled as he put his front feet into the stream and dipped his head downward, to take his deep drinks. Kendra had learned from experience that all mustangs always put their front feet into the water, but never their hind feet. From having been born wild and free, the mustangs had learned to keep their hind feet free at all times, so they could move in a hurry if threatened by man or beast.

Kendra would never forget watching Domino being tamed after he had been brought to the ranch. He had shown such strength and pride and had fought so hard to regain his freedom. Yes, he had made one hell of a noise screaming and stomping. He had turned on Zeke, over and over again, with snapping teeth and striking front hooves. It had been sad to see him lose his fight when

Zeke had finally succeeded at roping down the plunging mountain of bone and flesh. . . .

"Drink your fill, boy," Kendra whispered, hugging his powerful neck. "You deserve it."

Kendra then stepped back, eyeing the stream. Smiling, she tossed her hat aside and began unbuttoning her shirt. She would take a quick dip before going on her way. At this moment nothing else could feel as good. The sun had left its mark on her by burning her face and the exposed flesh at her throat. The shade of the willows over the water and the breeze whipping through their limbs would refresh her, and then she could make better time.

Unbuckling her gunbelt, she placed it gingerly on the ground and then quickly disrobed all the way and ran eagerly into the water. She shivered when she felt its iciness, knowing that it had tumbled lazily from the mountains where snow still crowned their tips. Hugging herself, Kendra stepped deeper into the water, laughing beneath her breath when the water nipped at her breasts.

Now used to the coldness touching her like a million icy fingers caressing her, Kendra began splashing the water on her face. Then she held her head back and let the water slowly seep into her long and flowing golden hair. She sighed pleasurably and closed her eyes. It was heaven! Oh, how glad she was she had decided to take the time to do this!

Domino's sudden whinny drew her eyes open. She looked toward him, wary. "What's wrong, boy?" she asked, shaking her hair from her eyes as it floated all around her, clinging.

But seeing no signs of intrusion or danger, Kendra shrugged and dove headfirst down into the water. Floating back to the surface, she took long, easy strokes and kicked her legs, enjoying herself almost to the point of feeling sinful. But a noise—this time definitely not Domino—caused her feet to once more make contact with the sandy bottom of the stream.

Tensing, she ran her fingers through her hair, hearing it again.

"Oh, no . . ." she thought wearily. She now recognized the sound of Spanish spurs from somewhere in the dark recesses of the low-hanging willows. And when Zeke emerged and stopped with his hands on hips to leer openly toward her, Kendra knew, somehow, that he had been there all along, watching her. Suddenly she felt dirty. Not even the water could make her feel clean as he strolled to the water's edge to stoop on one knee.

"Enjoyin' yourself, Kendra?" he chuckled. His sombrero didn't hide the evil lust in his dark eyes. The shade of the willows didn't even shadow his red whiskers and bushy sideburns. And it certainly didn't hide his burliness, a threat to Kendra even more now, since she had left her weapons on the ground, too far from her reach.

Trembling, she flashed him a forced brave look. "Zeke, what are you doing here?" she hissed. "I thought you were with Aaron."

"Aaron had business to tend to. He left me in charge of the herd."

"Well, then? Why aren't you with them? Or who did you leave in charge, so you could ride the range looking for meanness to get into, should probably be my question!"

"The herd is safely on their grazin' land," Zeke said, lifting his sombrero from his head. He began twirling it on a finger. "The boys are restin' a ways from here.

207

We're on our way back to the ranch. I was just checkin' to see if I could find me anymore barbed wire fences to report to Aaron.''

"Barbed wire . . . ?" Kendra gasped.

Zeke laughed throatily. "Thought that'd liven you up a bit," he said. He motioned with a hand. "Come on, Kendra. Come outta the water and I'll tell you about the barbed wire fence we found standing in the way of our drive north."

Kendra wanted to hear about the fence, but she feared he might be lying, just to lure her from the water. "Do you think I'm daft, Zeke?" she laughed bitterly. "You'd say anything to get me from the water." She lifted her chin haughtily. "If you want me, you'll have to come in and get me."

Rising to his feet, Zeke towered over her. "Don't tempt me, Kendra," he snarled. "The trail's been hot and void of women. Jumpin' in there after you could quench my thirst for everything."

"You wouldn't dare," Kendra hissed.

"Naw. I wouldn't," he said with a toss of his head. "Come on. I'll step back a ways into the trees whilst you get dressed."

"And watching all the while," she jeered. "Zeke, just be on your way, so I *can* get dressed and head for home. All you're doing is delaying me and causing me to maybe not reach the ranch before dark."

"You can travel with me, Kendra."

"I'd rather ride with the devil."

Zeke chuckled and then began walking toward the willows. "Get dressed, Kendra," he said from across his shoulder. "I'll see ya back at the ranch."

"I don't trust you, Zeke."

"That's *your* problem," he shrugged.

"If you so much as try to come back here, you'll be sorry, Zeke," she shouted after him.

His laughter faded as he disappeared from her sight, and when Kendra no longer heard the jangle of his spurs, she began inching her way from the water. But, still fearing Zeke, she kept her breasts covered with crossed arms as she broke free from the water. Scrambling, she gathered up her jeans, and, just as one leg was covered, the jangling of spurs was there again.

Kendra's heart began thumping wildly when she saw Zeke step back out into the open, smiling crookedly.

"You were foolish to think I'd let this opportunity to get a taste of you slip by me," Zeke chuckled, already unbuttoning his shirt.

Kendra looked wildly around her. Though there were clear passages reaching out to the more open range, she was not in a position to escape. Zeke had her at a definite disadvantage by catching her unclothed. Yes, she *had* been foolish to trust him. But she now realized that no matter when she had left the water, he would have been there . . . waiting.

Eyeing her pistols, Kendra began inching to where they lay. She had to forget her nudity and try her best to defend herself. She wouldn't be able to bear it if he succeeded at taking full advantage of her. She hated his coarse, rough hands. She hated his lips. She hated the smell of him!

"I see your game," Zeke snickered, catching sight of her pistols. "It won't work, Kendra. I'm much faster. And, darlin', you wouldn't shoot your ol' pal Zeke, would ya? Why, how would Aaron survive without me?"

As he stepped from his jeans, Kendra shuddered

violently and tried to cover her body with her arms and hands. "Aaron will kill you, if I don't first," she hissed.

"I think I've heard that threat somewhere before," he snickered. He took two wide steps and jerked her roughly next to him. Kendra cringed, feeling his swollen sex pressed against her thigh. And when his mouth bore down upon her lips, she began clawing and kicking at him. But all her struggles were in vain. He only held her more tightly, kissing her harder, probably bruising her.

"And now . . ." he said throatily. "What I've been waitin' for all these months." He grabbed her shoulders, digging his fingers into her flesh, and lowered her to the ground. "No more preliminaries, Kendra. I've waited long enough."

"Zeke, you mustn't!" she screamed, still fighting back. "Please . . ."

He sounded a throaty laugh as he lowered his mouth over a breast and moved his sex closer, but just as he was about to enter her, a loud shot rang out above his head.

Kendra jumped, then pushed Zeke from her as he was taken off guard, looking around to see who had fired the shotgun.

"Now get up, slow and easy from the lady," a gentle male voice ordered. "I think your fun is over for the moment."

Kendra inched away from Zeke, then raised her eyes to find a lone rider on a buckboard who was pointing the barrel of a shotgun dangerously toward Zeke.

Zeke rose slowly from the ground with his arms poised in the air. "Who the hell are *you*?" he queried angrily.

"Never you mind," Johnny said, motioning with the barrel of his gun. "Just you get your clothes on and be on your way."

"And if I don't?"

The shotgun was lowered a bit, directed toward Zeke's penis. "If you don't, I believe I could make you a very sorry man," Johnny laughed. "Now wouldn't that just take care of our problem good and proper?"

Kendra grabbed her clothes and began pulling them on, breathless, never taking her eyes off the stranger. She hadn't heard the buckboard's approach. But the thick stand of grass had surely muffled the sound of the wheels and the horse's hoofbeats.

Her gaze traveled over the man, tensing suddenly, seeing that he had no legs from his knees downward. Her gaze shot upward again, seeing his thick crop of gray hair, the lines of his face and the pain in his eyes. He looked old . . . but his voice was young. Had he lost his legs in the war? Pity washed through Kendra. And, oh, how very grateful she was to him for showing up at this time! A few moments longer and it would have been too late.

Kendra laughed to herself as she saw Zeke clumsily scrambling into his clothes.

"Kick your gunbelt toward Kendra," Johnny ordered.

Kendra's eyes widened. He knew her name. How?

"Out here on the open range a man's life ain't worth two cents without his revolvers," Zeke argued.

"Yours ain't either way," Johnny mocked. "With them you're dead, because I won't give you a chance to use them on me."

"Damn," Zeke grumbled.

"And no sense in thinkin' your rifle will be the answer," Johnny laughed. With his free hand he lifted a rifle into the air. "You see, I think of everything."

Zeke paled. He reached a hand out. "You've got my rifle," he shouted. "You got my rifle from my horse, you

211

bastard. I'll come huntin' for you. I'll get you for this."

"I'd suggest you hightail it clean out of the terri tory," Johnny growled. "When Aaron Carpenter hear about your takin' indecent liberties with his sister, you life won't even be worth spit."

Kendra's hands went to her throat. This man ever knew Aaron! Who *was* he?

Zeke fastened the last button of his shirt and begar walking carefully away from the stream. "No matte where I head today it won't be far enough for you," he snarled. He pointed a finger at Johnny. "You'd bes enjoy yourself while you can 'cause your days are nov numbered on this earth. I'll find ya. And when I do ya'll be sorry you ever laid eyes on me."

"I've been threatened by worse'n you." Johnn laughed. "And I've survived, ain't I?"

Zeke's gaze lowered and saw that where legs ha once been, now only jeans hung loosely away from Johnny's knees. He laughed sarcastically. "Looks a though someone's aim was good," he said. Then h glared, fists doubled. "But I'll see to it that more' that is missin' when I get through with you."

"Get the hell out of here," Johnny shouted.

Zeke tore into a fit of laughter as he disappeared from view.

Kendra fastened her gunbelt about her waist, lifted her hat to her head, then hurried to the wagon. "I'l never be able to repay you for your kindness, sir," she murmured. "How can I thank you?"

"Just you say howdy to Aaron for me."

"How is it that you know me and Aaron?"

"Aaron was my captain durin' the war. My name' John. Johnny Lassiter." He lowered his shotgun to hi lap and offered Kendra a bony white hand.

Kendra accepted the hand and something compelled her to squeeze it affectionately. "But how do you know *me*? My *name*?" she whispered. "How did you know we were even in this area?"

"Aaron came by my place yesterday durin' the storm," Johnny said. "We became reacquainted. He spoke of you quite fondly and said you'd grown up into a beautiful lady but that you were a bit too willful at times. And when I heard that man speak your name as he was about to . . . well . . . you know . . . I knew it had to be you. Aaron's sister Kendra. I figured you'd probably been out explorin' on the range when this man happened along and couldn't resist the temptation of a beautiful woman's flesh."

Kendra removed her hand from his and toyed with her hat. "That man is Zeke," she said bitterly. "He's Aaron's head wrangler. He's been pestering me since my first day in Nevada. I *do* owe you a debt of gratitude for what you did here for me today."

Johnny's face colored a bit as his eyes wavered. "Let's say all debts are taken care of," he murmured. "Aaron has a way of bein' kind that you'll never even know 'bout."

Kendra's eyebrows lifted quizzically. "You say you saw Aaron yesterday," she said. "What part of the range were you on when you saw him?"

"I was at my house. Like I said. He came by my place during the storm. I offered him shelter."

"Oh, I see," she murmured. "Then he left after the storm blew over?"

Johnny glanced away from her, but not before she saw added pain enter his eyes. "I'm sure he's on his way home

213

by now. . . ." he murmured.

"Johnny, did Aaron mention anything about a barbed wire fence?" she asked cautiously, remembering what Zeke had told her.

Johnny's head moved slowly around. "Why, yes," he said. "That's why he was travelin' by *my* place. Because the fence stretched out close to my piece of land. He thought I was responsible for the barbed wire."

Kendra kneaded her chin thoughtfully. "So Zeke was telling the truth," she worried. "Someone has brought barbed wire into the area."

"Yes. And lots of it, as far as I can tell," Johnny said. "That's why I'm so far from home. I was checkin' it out. But I haven't found any yet on this particular stretch of range. It's far back, closer to the higher valley ranges."

"Who could be responsible?" she said, knowing that barbed wire was a curse to all ranch owners.

"I'd say only a damn Reb would do somethin' as dumb as that," Johnny growled. "If you find a Reb in this area, bet your bottom dollar you've found the barbed wire fence lover."

Kendra grew cold inside. She knew a Reb, didn't she? Didn't Lucas admit to having fought for the Confederacy? But surely he wouldn't . . . ? Why *would* he . . . ?

"Why would you think a Reb would be responsible?" she murmured.

"Once a Reb, always a Reb," Johnny growled. "They like to stir up trouble. And plantin' barbed wire fences on open range is the worst kind of trouble, wouldn't you say? Those damn bastards just live for stirrin' up trouble."

Kendra's gaze went to his legs. "You must hate the Rebs even more than Aaron," she murmured.

Johnny patted his stubs. "Didn't get these durin' the war," he growled. "No. I rode side by side with Aaron, tall in the saddle, every inch of the way after Gettysburg, until Lee surrendered."

"Then . . . how . . . ?"

"The mines, Kendra," Johnny grumbled. "The damn silver mines."

Kendra's heart skipped a beat, remembering Seth. Large, handsome, jolly Seth! What if such a thing were to happen to him?

"I'm so sorry. . . ." she said in a quiet whisper.

Johnny peered upward, through the branches of the trees, seeing their fiery tips as the lowering sun cast shadows onto them. "You'd best be on your way, Kendra," he advised. "And I'd best also. We both have a pretty good piece yet to travel before dark."

Standing on tiptoe, reaching a hand, Kendra touched Johnny's pale cheek. "I hope we'll meet again," she said. "I do owe you for today. Maybe by the time I see you again I'll have thought of a way to repay you."

"Like I said," he said, patting her hand. "All debts are paid as of today. Your brother is all heart, you know."

"What do you mean? What's he done for you?"

Johnny's face colored again. "I must really go," he murmured, ignoring her question. He guided his horse and buckboard around, to head back the way he had come. "Get on home, Kendra," he yelled from across his shoulder.

"And you be careful of Zeke," she yelled in return. "He's been more than humiliated today. He's also lost his job."

Johnny held his shotgun up in the air. "I've all I need right here," he shouted. "It's even better than a pair o legs."

Kendra went to Domino and swung herself up into the saddle. Her mind was a jumble of questions. Could Lucas somehow be responsible for the barbed wire fence? Was he still that much . . . of . . . a . . . Rebel . . . ? Hadn't he been satisfied to leave the war behind him?

"For there surely will be a war over the fence," she whispered. She raised her eyes to the sky, praying silently that Lucas wasn't the one in question. . . .

Chapter Thirteen

Kendra watched as Aaron fastened his gunbelt around his waist. It had been a full month now since Zeke had disappeared and Kendra knew that Aaron had had trouble filling Zeke's shoes. But Aaron wasn't too disgruntled about this. In fact, he had said that if he so much as came across Zeke on his land, he would personally hang him for what he had tried with Kendra.

It had also been a month since Kendra had seen Lucas, and the longer their separation, the more she silently ached for him. But she had to forget him. She had no other choice.

"What are your plans for the day?" Aaron asked, fastening leather chaps over the legs of his jeans.

"I'm not quite sure yet, Aaron," Kendra lied, flipping her hair to hang in long golden streamers down her back. She pulled her bone-colored, satin robe more securely around her and slouched down onto a chair, watching the dancing flames in the living room fireplace.

"That's not like you," Aaron scoffed. "Are you sure you're not up to some more mischief? I still can't believe

217

you were so far out on the range that Zeke almost raped you. When Johnny told me where he had found the two of you, I almost died. Damn it, Kendra, don't you know not to wander so far from the ranch?"

"I can take care of myself," Kendra pouted. "Will you just stop worrying?" She sulked for a moment longer, then cast Aaron a quizzical glance. "This Johnny. Strange how you ran into him after all those years, wasn't it?" Kendra was quite aware of the flush of his cheeks as he avoided her eyes when he answered her.

"It's a small world, Kendra," he laughed awkwardly. "Or haven't you discovered that yet?"

"Are you going to ride out to their place today?"

"No. I'm planning to check to see if there have been any more barbed wire fences erected. Seems they pop up as fast as we pull them down. Damned barbed wire. It's going to destroy the open range."

"Have you found out who is doing it yet, Aaron?" Kendra asked cautiously, remembering Johnny's words about a Reb's probably being responsible. She had since scoffed at this. It was just the way of the men who fought for the North. They still had to blame the South for everything that went wrong. Well, she wouldn't believe that Lucas had anything to do with any of this. He was too involved in the Indian cause!

"Nope. Not a clue," Aaron grumbled, plopping his wide-brimmed Stetson hat onto his head. He went to Kendra and drew her gently up before him and held her at arm's length. "And now, Kendra, listen to what I say. I want you to stay close to home today. I'm tired of worrying about you."

"And Holly?" Kendra mocked. "Seems she's not obeying your orders. She's already gone for the day. Or hadn't you noticed?"

"Yes. She's gone into town to do a bit of shopping. But she's safe. She has Parker with her. Now do I have to hire someone to accompany you also, to keep an eye on your every move?"

Kendra angrily jerked away from him and swung around, placing her back to him, thinking of her real plans for the day and how quickly Aaron could put a stop to them.

She turned and glared toward him. "Aaron, don't you try that," she warned. "I won't stand for it. Maybe Holly won't fight you, but I will. I will have my freedom."

Aaron laughed gruffly as he drew Kendra back into his arms. "Hey. Don't get your dander up so much," he said. "You have to realize I worry about you. Where's my beautiful, gentle sister who turned all the gent's heads in Boston, when you dressed up in the latest fashions from Paris?"

"I'm still the same sister I was then, Aaron," she sighed, draping her arms about him, hugging him back. "I just dress differently. That's all."

Aaron pushed her gently from his arms and smiled down at her. "Well, baby sister, I'm going to take care of that," he chuckled.

"Oh, Aaron, what on earth do you mean now? Won't you ever give up?"

"We've been invited to a neighboring ranch. For a dance," he said. "Well? What do you have to say? Won't it be nice dressing up again? In fact, why don't *you* go into town today and buy you the sassiest dress you can find?"

A flutter of excitement lit up Kendra's insides. A dance! A social function! She *had* missed things like that. Then her enthusiasm was shadowed by doubts. "Oh," she said. "Do you mean a square dance, Aaron? That's the only type of dance given here at ranches, isn't it?"

"No. No square dance," he chuckled. "The invitation said dress formally. Black tie. The works. And I said, go buy you a new dress. A sassy one doesn't mean the type worn at a square dance."

"When is this dance, Aaron?" she said, feeling excited again, yet trying not to reveal her interest to him. She would not let him see that he had won her over in the least bit!

"One week from tonight," he said. "That should give you plenty of time to choose a dress and decide on how to wear your hair."

"And where is this dance to be held? Is it a new acquaintance? Which ranch?"

"No. No new acquaintance. I haven't even met the family yet. We received a formal announcement by mail yesterday. But this is a way to make new friends. I've been so busy with the herd and trying to run down this barbed wire fence character, I've been neglecting my other duties."

"But I thought you had met most of the neighboring ranch owners by now, Aaron. You *are* becoming a bit neglectful. You might be missing a chance to have them as clients at your banks."

She teased him further. "Tsk, tsk, Aaron. You had best get your mind on your business. If I didn't know better, I'd think you had found another woman besides Holly to scramble your thoughts."

Aaron's lips drew into a tight line and his eyes wavered. "That's damn crazy, Kendra," he said. He swung around and headed toward the door. "I'd best be going. I do have better things to do than to stand here jawing with you."

"Jawing?" Kendra said, laughing softly. "You're picking up some strange language, brother dear."

Aaron cast her an amused look across his shoulder, then rushed on outside.

Kendra followed him out. "Aaron, you never did say whose ranch we are going to be visiting for the dance. Whose?"

Aaron pulled himself up into the saddle of his horse. "Luke. A Luke Hall," he said, then tipped his hat to Kendra and rode away from her.

"Luke . . . Hall . . . ?" Kendra whispered. "Lucas . . . Luke . . . ? No. Impossible. And, anyway, Lucas is not the type to own a ranch or give dances."

Shrugging, she ran on into the house and up the staircase, already breathless over her day's plans now that Aaron was finally gone.

Seth had come home for a few days this past week. There had been some talk between him and Aaron. Quiet talk. In the library. But Kendra had heard. She had listened outside the library door. She hadn't felt she was spying. When her father's name had been mentioned, she had felt as though it was her right to know as much about his whereabouts as Aaron and Seth.

Well, she had heard all right! Seth had told Aaron that he had found their father. He was this man known as Blackie. But he was no longer in Reno. He was now in Virginia City and was the owner of quite an elaborate gambling emporium called Blackie's, located right next door to the fabulous International Hotel.

Seth had gone on to say that he hadn't revealed his true identity to their father and that he hadn't seen him since . . . that he steered clear of both the gambling emporium and the International Hotel . . . not wanting to converse with him again. Having met his father in such a cold, impersonal way had hurt Seth. He had said that knowing that his father hadn't recognized him when they were face to face had cut deeply inside him, as though razors were stripping him into raw bits of flesh.

"Well, Blackie, at first you won't know me either." Kendra laughed sarcastically. "Your own daughter . . . and you won't even know it. Father dear, I plan to play you a few games of blackjack. And I plan to *win.*"

With eager fingers, Kendra began coiling her hair tightly above her head, pinning it all in place, preparing herself fully for her little game. She had decided that this was the only way that would satisfy her. She would not wear a dress. Only breeches and a shirt and six-shooters at her hips. She would be a new cowboy in town, ready to lose all his earnings from his latest roundup!

"I will fool him," she hissed. "I will beat him at his own game. He only played a few games with me, but he taught me the game of blackjack very well!"

Dropping her gown from her shoulders, letting it flutter to the floor at her feet, Kendra gazed, frowning, at the swell of her breasts. Now that could be a problem! And what she had planned for them would be quite painful, but she had no choice but to do it.

Lifting a long stretch of cloth, she began wrapping it around her back, then on around her breasts, binding them as flat as possible to her chest. This was the only way! She had to look all man!

Kendra closed her eyes to the pain as she bound her breasts tighter and tighter. Then when she opened her eyes and studied herself, she knew that she could put up with a bit of pain to succeed at what she had planned.

Hadn't she had pain as her everyday companion ever since her father had left her, anyway?

Determination urged her onward. She slipped into her shirt, feeling it a bit awkward as it fit more loosely than before because of the absence of her breasts. Then she slipped into a man's pair of jeans, ones she had stolen from the bunkhouse from a cowhand who was fleshier than she. She had known better than to show up in town in her snug-fitting jeans, which revealed just too much of the shape of her legs. That alone would have given her away.

Standing sideways, sucking in her stomach, Kendra smiled coyly to herself. Yes, these breeches were much better. They hung from her hips loosely, and her knees had room to breathe!

"Thank God no one is home to see what I'm doing," she whispered. "They would think me daft for sure."

She reached for her gunbelt and slung it around her hips and fastened it. Laughing, she quickly drew both pistols from their holsters and pointed them toward herself in the mirror. She could even look legitimate if it was required of her. She most surely could outdraw any man in Virginia City. She had practiced enough this past week. Thank God Aaron had been gone. He would have become suspicious had he heard the rapid gunfire, day in and day out. . . .

"Now my hat," she whispered, thrusting her pistols back into their holsters. She placed her hat atop her thickly coiled hair. "And now my boots," she said, slipping into them. "And I'm ready to go."

With her head held high, Kendra strutted from her room, then ran outside and mounted Domino. She bent over and patted her horse fondly on the neck. "Come on, boy," she whispered. "We have quite a day ahead of us."

Kendra peered, squinting, toward the sky. She blessed the blue of the heavens, hating the threat of the continuing rains, yet she cursed the heat of the sun. She wished for a happy medium . . . but she knew that would be asking for too much in the heat-infested climate of Nevada.

She held her head high and her back straight, riding quickly out onto the open range and then onto a dirt road that was heavy with tracks from stagecoaches. In the far distance she could hear the shrill whistle of a train and was reminded of her first day in Reno. She would never forget the magnetic pull of Lucas's gray eyes. She would never forget the tingling it had caused at the base of her spine. Even now she could feel his lips heating her flesh . . . she could feel his hands sending her into a feverish glow. . . .

"I can't think of him," she whispered, setting her jaw. "I can't."

But her thoughts wouldn't rest. The trail was boring. The trail was long. . . .

"Luke Hall . . ." she whispered, frowning. "The neighboring ranch is owned by a Luke Hall."

She thought long and hard. "Lucas Hall," she whispered, trying the name on the tip of her tongue. "It *does* fit, somehow," she murmured.

She jerked her head angrily. "Why didn't I think to ask him his last name?" she worried. "How dumb can a body get! Make love to a man whose last name I didn't know?"

She laughed to herself. "Now wouldn't that make Aaron displeased with me?" she said. "He would disown me for sure, first for having let a man possess me without

224

wedding papers, then to find out that I didn't even ask the man's last name?''

She giggled some more, then fell into silence as she settled back and let Domino take over, leading her on, until she saw the first signs of Virginia City on the horizon.

The heavens were smutted with smoke. Kendra knew that this smoke was rising from the area of the mines. She tried to envision Seth there . . . sweating . . . laboring . . . remembering what he had told her about his long days underground. He had explained to her that the ore that he dug daily was assorted into two grades. The richest, the most promising, would run one thousand dollars to the ton or upward, and some was even sacked for shipment to England.

The second- and third-class stuff was piled aside for future milling. That which ran fifty dollars a ton or less was utilized in grading the streets of Virginia City. One could say that the roads leading up Mount Davidson were paved with silver.

The Comstock Lode had created the greatest mining turmoil in history, but now there was fear that the mines were being worked out. Kendra had to wonder why Seth still persisted at working them. So many men had ventured on south, to California, where talk was thick of gold still in the hills, there to be found by those who were patient. . . .

''But Seth is as stubborn as me,'' she thought to herself. ''Once he gets something set in his mind, nothing will change it.''

Kendra tensed as she moved into Virginia City, noticing how the city was built on tiers on the slope of the mountain. The better residences seemed to be above the

225

main street itself, which was called C Street, and then, further down the mountainside, were whitewashed cottages.

Kendra moved on into the center of town, quickly feeling like a part of the community. The dust-filled streets were busy with men on horseback, wagons being pulled by horses and mules, and an occasional stagecoach rumbling by.

The wooden sidewalks were a hubbub of activity. Women in colorful dresses and carrying parasols strolled along, mingling among the men, who appeared to be mostly stray cowboys. Probably the miners were all busy underground. For once, Kendra hoped that Seth was in the mines. She didn't need him discovering her and stopping her at her charade.

Suddenly worrying about the breast binder, wondering if it was doing the trick, Kendra slumped over on the saddle. Could she be singled out from all the rest of the cowboys on horseback because she had this one oddity about her?

Cautiously, she let her eyes dart from building to building on each side of the street, watching for the International Hotel. She would rein her horse there and walk casually on next door, where she hoped that she could enter the gambling emporium without drawing attention to herself. Her voice could be the ruin of her. She had to pretend to be too hoarse to talk. Surely that would do the trick! It had to! A low, throaty whisper, and she would be able to place her bets well enough while she played blackjack with her father.

"Father . . ." she whispered, clenching her teeth, grinding them together. "How can I even call him that? He hasn't been a father now for ten long years."

226

She tried to force her thoughts to other things, knowing she would have to confront this issue of "Father" much too soon. She only hoped that her hatred for him wouldn't show through. In the end, wouldn't it be fun to reveal her true self to him? She would slowly remove her hat . . . uncoil her hair . . . and then shake her long golden hair to hang down her back. She only hoped that she would have the courage to go through with it! She so wanted to get back at him . . . to hurt him as deeply as he had hurt her . . . !

Some of the buildings in Virginia City were much more modern than in Reno. Kendra knew that the wealth of the city had made this difference. Large brick buildings, four and six stories high, partly lined the main thoroughfare, some of them with wide balconies surrounded by black-painted iron balustrades. Underneath the balconies stretched a continuous, dark, irregular arcade, along which people walked. On the second stories there were galleries onto which French windows opened and upon which iron stands stood, filled with flaming red geraniums. Morning glories climbed over the eaves, and red flowering oleanders nodded ragged plumes against the walls. Chinese fruit vendors trotted about with fruit baskets, and organ grinders were grinding out music while costumed monkeys danced and begged at command.

The Territorial Enterprise Newspaper building was a handsome red brick iron-faced structure. It was said that Mark Twain had begun his career there as a reporter. Everyone in Virginia City had liked Mark Twain for his humorously exaggerated style of writing and had hated it when he had moved on to San Francisco, where it was known that he was now working for a newspaper called the *Morning Call*.

As Kendra rode on further, she was amazed by the number of saloons, general stores, hotels and gambling houses. She rode slowly past the Opera House. She had heard that many Italian light operas were given there yearly, as well as vaudeville acts, lectures, and Shakespeare's plays.

Another building caught Kendra's eye. It was a library. Seth had told her about the Miner's Union Library, and that she could feel free to go there at any time, to browse. This was her first time in Virginia City, and hopefully, not her last, for she definitely planned to visit this grand building filled with books.

There were blacksmith shops, more saloons, livery stables—and then her heart began a strange thumping when she saw the grand sign stating that she was fast approaching the International Hotel. Her gaze moved quickly past that, and she saw the bold red letters on a sign above the door of the next building. The sign said Blackie's, and she knew that soon . . . soon . . . she would be face to face with . . . her . . . father.

A lump grew in Kendra's throat and her eyes burned. She didn't want to be besieged by the memories of the old days, when she had sat on his lap and hugged and kissed him.

No! She wouldn't let these feelings take over! She would succeed with her plan. She wanted to see the expression on his face change to one of shock and dismay when she spoke her name. She closed her eyes, seeing it now. . . .

"Father, it is I, Kendra," she would say, lifting her hair tantalizingly into the air. "Haven't I grown into a lovely lady? And, Father, aren't you proud of the way I play your game of blackjack?"

Of course, this would be immediately after she had beat him. She would run away from him laughing . . . laughing . . . laughing. . . .

The sudden shaking of the ground, causing Domino to whinny and snort angrily, drew Kendra from her self-imposed trance.

"What is that . . . ?" Kendra whispered, feeling it again. She had read of earthquakes and how they felt. Could Virginia City be having an earthquake? She clung to the reins as she heard a low rumble and watched the street ripple ahead of her. But the strange thing was that no one else seemed to notice, or care. Everyone was just going on their way . . . mindless, it seemed, that the world seemed to be going crazy beneath their feet.

Kendra wiped cold sweat from her brow with the back of her hand when everything grew calm again. I don't know what it was, but I do hope that it doesn't happen again, she thought. At least until I am far gone from this place.

Dismounting, Kendra tied Domino's reins to a hitching post, then kept her head low, hoping the brim of her hat would hide most of her face.

She heard drunken laughter emerging from a nearby saloon, mingling with the tinkling from a player piano. Loud guffaws followed with the clinking of glass, causing Kendra's back to stiffen and her insides to tremble uneasily.

"But I mustn't become afraid," she said to herself, forcing a stiff upper lip.

Swallowing hard, she stepped up on the board sidewalk and walked on past the International Hotel, then paused momentarily outside Blackie's to glance quickly from side to side, then took one more fast step and entered the excitement of bright lights and spinning wheels.

Kendra was taken aback, never having seen anything quite like it before. It was a gambling house all right! All the wheels were going, all the dice were being shaken, and games of twenty-one were being flipped. Kendra watched as drunken miners, celebrating their few coins earned, swayed from table to table, where most were probably cheated in poker games by cardsharps who used marked decks of cards, or by the games that Kendra suspected of being rigged for the house to win. She watched as cards were slapped down on the tables, then the faces of agonized pain when the coins were pushed away from their owners. . . .

Slowly, still trying to hide her face in the shadow of the brim of her hat, Kendra strolled further into the room, wishing her heart would stop pounding so furiously. In every man's face, she looked for her father. But so far, she hadn't caught one glimpse of any man who resembled him.

With her hands resting lazily on her holstered pistols, she stepped up to a roulette game. Standing between the men who played their luck at this table were several bold-faced women decked out in gay dresses, brilliant feathers, and showy jewelry.

Kendra got the itch to play, but instead watched, wide-eyed, as the players put their money on spaces on the board corresponding to the numbers on which they wanted to bet. Then just as anxiously, as if she had bet and could win money for herself, Kendra watched as the man in charge, called a croupier, spun the wheel. As it turned, he released a ball in the opposite direction to the rotation of the wheel. The strain of silence at this table was thick as everyone waited, watching hopefully. When the wheel finally stopped and the ball landed in a pocket, a laughter of triumph rang out next to Kendra. She smiled, knowing she was standing next to a winner.

A loud shout from across the room drew Kendra quickly around. She felt an iciness circle her heart when she turned and saw a man enter the room with a lovely lady clinging to his arm. When his name . . . Blackie . . . once more rang out from an admirer . . . Kendra knew that she had finally found her father. But she had found much more than she had expected. She had also found . . . Holly.

Taking a step backward, feeling desperation rising inside her, Kendra let herself become hidden by some taller men. She took a peek around one of them and watched in wide-eyed frustration as her father moved further into the room. He was still as handsome! He even looked as young! In his face she saw herself, in the blue of the eyes, the shape of his chin, and the straight line of his nose. And when he smiled, she could see his familiar, beautifully white, straight teeth. Attired in a neat, black suit with a diamond stickpin at his throat, he indeed looked a man of fortune.

Then Kendra's gaze moved slowly back to Holly. Holly! Of all people! And with her own father-in-law? Did Holly even know? Had she not given her full name to *him*? And what on earth was Holly doing in such a place?

Feelings of rage engulfed Kendra, thinking of Aaron and how much faith he put in his wife. And all along, she did not deserve one ounce of this trust.

But above all else, Kendra knew that her plans had just gone awry. There was no way to play this charade out with Holly now being a part of the game. Holly would

231

quickly recognize her.

No. Kendra knew that she had not won at anything today. And Aaron seemed to not have, either. They had both lost . . . and because of the same woman!

Kendra began to slink away from the crowded room, glancing cautiously from side to side, afraid someone might grab her at any minute and reveal that she was a woman . . . not a man . . . and tell the world that she had once more been a fool!

"I'll pay Holly back for this," she whispered beneath her breath. "And I'll be back, Father, I'll be back. . . ."

Swinging around, she couldn't leave the room fast enough. Sweat beads sparkled on her brow. Her throat was dry and she felt a renewed burning in her eyes, so wanting to cry, now having tumultuous feelings about seeing her father. She hated him . . yet she . . . loved him. . . .

"Must it always be this way with men?" she thought. First Lucas . . . and then . . . her . . . father!

Chapter Fourteen

Knowing how the Confederacy must have felt after having lost a major battle, Kendra rode from town, head hung, feeling empty with defeat. She was hurting both for herself and Aaron, and Holly was getting the full blame. Had it not been for her, Kendra knew that at this very moment she could be playing blackjack with her father. But now when would she? Would the opportunity arise again when she would feel as daring, as bold as she had today?

Taking a different route from town than she had coming in, Kendra moved down the mountainside, weaving down the hillside studded with huge boulders and slipping and sliding down slopes of shale rock. In the far distance, she could see a band of wild mustangs moving at a short, choppy trot along a network of trails. They were a group of roans and sorrels, led by a black stallion looking powerful, watchful, and menacing.

In another direction, she could see the workings of a mine and wondered if it might be the Con-Virginia, where Seth worked. She could see a scrambling of activity around its entrance and she jumped as though shot, when a shrill whistle began sounding out long and eerie. Through the mountain passes cries rang out, echoing over and over again, reaching Kendra's ears.

"Fire?" she whispered, stiffening, straightening her back. "They're shouting something about a fire . . . !"

Her thoughts once more returned to Seth. If that mine *was* the Con-Virginia then he could be in danger!

"I must get to the mine, and fast," she whispered. "Seth might need me."

With a pounding heart, she cried out to Domino and thrust her knees deeply into his sides. "Come on, boy, let's really make time," she shouted.

She clung tightly to the reins and watched on all sides of her as Domino began slipping and sliding on down the slope. And when they finally reached a straight stretch of land, Kendra held on to her hat as Domino raced ahead, panting, snorting. Kendra kept her eyes on the scurrying of men around the face of the mine, more fearful now as billows of black smoke began filling the sky, blackening everything and everyone in their reach.

Coughing, Kendra reined Domino to a halt when she finally reached the area where men were being carried out of the mine and stretched lifeless in a row on the ground. Barely breathing, Kendra ran to the men and began inspecting their blackened faces one at a time. She frowned as the scurrying men nudged her in the ribs and back and kicked at her as they passed on by her with more men hanging limply from their arms and draped over their backs.

Feeling a twisting of her gut, Kendra continued to go down the long row of men, then stopped when she saw another man being carried out of the mine. She ran her eyes quickly over him and recognized the bulkiness of the shoulders and knew that that man covered in black could be her brother!

Stumbling over the legs of the outstretched men, Kendra ran up to the man, whose head hung limply and whose legs were being dragged as he was laid easily to the ground. Kendra gasped when she saw Seth's features beneath the black soot on his face. She dropped to her knees and lifted his head onto her lap and cradled it, crying.

"Seth," she whispered. "Oh, Seth . . ."

A low moaning surfacing from between his lips drew Kendra's breath from her. She reached a hand to his throat and felt a weakened pulse beat, then spoke his name with more strength, shaking him. "Seth," she cried. "Please, Seth, wake up. It's me. Kendra."

Seth coughed and rubbed at his eyes. His tongue looked strangely red against the black of his face as it began wiping his lips clean of soot. Then Kendra realized that redness was blood. Her heart ached when she saw even more blood start to trickle from his nose and from the corner of his mouth.

"Seth, how badly are you hurt?" she asked weakly, wiping the blood away with the sleeve of her shirt.

Seth slowly opened his eyes, then began blinking them wildly. "Who . . . ?" he said in a strained, drawn voice. "Who . . . are . . . you? What happened?"

Tears streaked through the black on Kendra's face. "Seth, it's me. Kendra," she sobbed. "Please tell me that you recognize me. Please tell me that you're going to be all right."

Seth lifted an eyebrow quizzically as his eyes moved slowly over her, seeing the flatness of her breasts, the larger jeans and her hair hidden beneath her hat. "Kendra! God, Kendra, what's ... happened ... to you ... ? What kind of game ... are ... you playing ... now ... ?"

Realizing that Seth was apparently going to be all right, Kendra hugged his head to her chest. "Seth, oh, Seth, thank God," she sighed, throwing her head back with relief.

Seth pushed away from her and rose shakily on an elbow, coughing and spitting more blood from inside his mouth. With the back of a hand he streaked the blood across his face and into his mustache. Then he once more looked toward Kendra and at her attire. "Kendra, what *are* you up to?" he asked.

Kendra's face turned a soft crimson color, remembering that in her haste to leave Virginia City and in her state of mind, she had forgotten about her bound breasts and her stolen jeans. She widened her eyes innocently. "Why, Seth, I don't know what you're talking about," she said.

Groaning, Seth rose to his feet, teetering. "I don't know what you're up to now, but this isn't the time to get into it," he grumbled. He ran his fingers through his hair as he slowly looked around him. "My God," he again groaned. "The mine's really gone and done it this time."

His gaze took in the long row of dead men. He was now remembering the heat of the flames ... the loud explosion that had preceded the fire. . . .

Then his legs buckled beneath him and he found that he could not hold his weight on them.

Kendra gasped loudly and grabbed at him. "Seth, what's the matter?"

Seth began running his fingers desperately over his

236

legs, growing more and more frightened by the minute. "My legs . . ." he whispered. "They're growing numb. I . . . can't . . . feel . . . anything . . ."

"Oh, no," Kendra cried, dropping to her knees beside him. "Why?"

Scratching his head, Seth began to shake it back and forth. "I don't know," he murmured. "I *did* get hit on the head. And I remember falling quite hard. Maybe when I fell I injured my spine. Who knows? Damn it, all I *do* know is that I can't stand. What am I to do, Kendra?"

"I've got to get you to a doctor," Kendra frantically said.

"No. No doctors," Seth growled. He hit at his legs, one at a time, cursing beneath his breath. "I can't stomach doctors. Especially the quacks who have settled here in this area."

"Seth, you *must* . . ."

Seth glowered toward her. "Do I go around telling you what to do?" he growled.

"You try . . ."

"Not often," he argued. "Not anymore, that is. And I don't expect you to try to run *my* life either. Take me home, Kendra. Take me goddamn home."

"But how? If your legs . . . are . . . dead . . . how can you ride?"

"Kendra, I can sit in a saddle," he shouted. He pointed toward the corralled horses. "You know my horse. Go and fetch it. Pronto. There's not much I can do around here with no legs." He glanced sourly around him, feeling helpless. He wanted to help the other men who were lying half alive. But now it was useless. It all seemed useless. . . .

Kendra rescued Seth's black mustang from the group

of horses and rushed it back to him. Seeing that everyone was too busy to help her, she had the job of getting Seth onto his horse without assistance. Struggling, groaning she lifted his heftiness from the ground and strained with his weight as he struggled to place a foot into the stirrup.

"Damn it . . ." he whispered. Then with his powerful arms he just pulled himself on up and one at a time positioned his legs on each side of the horse.

"Are you going to make it all right?" Kendra worried, eyeing him warily.

"Just get on Domino and let's get the hell out of here," Seth grumbled, snapping his horse's reins.

Kendra swung herself into her own saddle and began moving alongside Seth, keeping an eye on him, seeing a new sparkle of red trickling from his nose. "Seth, you *must* go into Virginia City," she begged. "You've just got to go and see a doctor."

"All I need is my bed and a few fast winks of shuteye," he said stubbornly. He glanced over at her and stared at her studiously. "Kendra, now that we're away from that commotion, tell me what you've been up to." His gaze traveled lower and once more studied her flattened breasts and then the looseness of her jeans.

Kendra guided Domino onto a straighter stretch of road, evading Seth's questioning stare. She just tilted her chin and rode on ahead, ignoring him. She grimaced when she felt his presence at her side again.

"You know you're going to have to give me an answer sooner or later," Seth grumbled. "It'd be best to just get it over with, wouldn't you say, Kendra?"

"Seth, it's no concern of yours. . . ."

"Everything that has to do with you is my concern," Seth said flatly. "You know that. Now tell me, Kendra.

238

What mischief have you been up to this time?"

She lowered her eyes and swallowed hard. "It's Father," she whispered.

"Speak louder, Kendra. I can't hear you."

She tightened her jaw and glowered toward him. "It's Father," she shouted. "Now. Did you hear that plain enough, Seth?"

Seth laughed. "Probably the whole county heard you that time," he said. Then his face drew shadows onto it. "What about Father?" he asked. "What did you do?"

"I didn't do anything, Seth." She sighed heavily.

"So you just rode into Virginia City dressed in that garb and did nothing, did you, Kendra?" he argued. "Now that doesn't make any sense at all. What'd you do, Kendra? I'll probably hear of it sooner or later, anyway. The men'll surely hear tell of this lady who was dressed as a man and some'll even find out that that fool lady was my sister."

"Fool is the right word to use, Seth," Kendra spat. "Always a fool."

"Kendra, what are you talking about? Who's a fool?"

Kendra lifted an eyebrow. "Me, Seth," she murmured. "Me."

"Get on with it, Kendra. What have you done that you feel foolish about, or need I ask? Don't tell me you faced Father dressed in that garb?"

"No . . ."

"What then . . . ?"

"I had planned to," she said softly. "But things went quickly awry."

"What things?"

Kendra closed her lips tightly, feeling a slow, sick feeling circling inside her. How could she tell anyone that

239

Aaron's wife was keeping company with Aaron's father?

"I don't want to talk about it," she said quickly, urging Domino on ahead. But again she tightened inside as Seth moved next to her.

"You're not making things any easier on me and these damn dead legs by playing this game with me," he growled. "Kendra, what don't you want to tell me?"

Kendra pleaded with her eyes. "Seth, please don't persist with this. I don't want to talk about it any longer."

"Did you see Father or not?" he growled.

"Yes . . ."

"Did he see you?"

"No . . ."

"Well, then, what's the problem?"

"If you insist, *Holly* is the problem," Kendra blurted, then covered her mouth with her hand, realizing what she had just let slip. Now what? She had thought maybe to not tell Aaron for fear of hurting him too much. But Seth would most surely tell him! Men had no way of keeping things to themselves. And as for Holly, she deserved being tattled on! But poor Aaron . . . poor, poor Aaron . . .

"Holly . . . ?" Seth said, completely in the dark.

Kendra could see Seth's face paling beneath the black soot. "Yes," she murmured. "But you mustn't tell any of this to Aaron. Let him find out for himself. Right now he's got so much else on his mind with the barbed wire fence problems and all."

"Don't tell Aaron what? What about Holly?"

"Seth, she was with Father," she said dryly. "She came into Blackie's gambling emporium with him. She was clinging possessively to his arm. For all to see. I don't see how this hasn't gotten back to Aaron. Yet . . . Aaron

240

hasn't taken Holly into town to show her off. I guess it would be impossible for the men to know her even if they did see her."

"Holly . . . with . . . Father . . . ?" Seth gasped. "Why, that bitch. And he's even old enough to be *her* father! What does the man think he's doing?"

He grew silent for a moment, then looked studiously back at Kendra. "Do you think he knows who she really is? Do you think he's doing this to cause more hurt to Aaron?"

"Seth," Kendra gasped. "Father may have deserted us for whatever reasons, but he was not a vindictive, evil man in *that* way. Why would he get pleasure hurting Aaron? Most surely Holly didn't reveal her real name to him."

Seth doubled a fist and raised it threateningly into the air. "How could she do this to Aaron? How?" he growled. "I knew that she was restless. But I didn't know *how* restless."

Then he paled even more. "And to think that I had planned to meet with him, to play him a game of blackjack," he murmured. "What if I *had*? What if he had walked into the room with Holly and I would've seen her with him? What if she would have seen *me*?"

"You had planned to play blackjack with Father?" Kendra murmured.

"Yes. I had agreed to, but then I changed my mind, not wanting to be near him again after that first clumsy experience of running into him like I did."

"Seth, how has Holly kept this so quiet? Surely the ranch hands from our Circle C have been in Father's gambling emporium."

"Think about it, Kendra," Seth growled. "How many

241

times has Holly gone anywhere near the ranch hands? She's never shown any sort of interest in what Aaron has done with the ranch. She stays pretty much to herself at home. Guess she doesn't want to dirty her hands by going out near the stables. Most of the men have just seen her from a distance, and even then she's mostly hidden beneath a hat or by an open parasol."

"Yes. I guess you're right," Kendra sighed. Then she gave Seth a quick glance. "Please don't tell Aaron, Seth. Not yet, anyway. Let's decide on a better way to deal with this. Please, Seth?"

"It'll be damn hard," he grumbled. "How can I be expected to sit down at the dinner table with her, knowing?"

"You're hardly home anymore to even do that," Kendra sighed. "So it shouldn't be so hard for you."

Seth hit at his numb legs. "You forget my legs so quickly?" he said darkly. "Looks as though I might be around for a while."

"Seth, I warned you and warned you about the mines," Kendra said. "You just wouldn't listen."

"Don't preach at me, Kendra," he said. "And I'll get these legs to workin'. You'll see. I'll force them to get feelings into them again. I'll be back in the mines again in a few days. You'll see."

Kendra blanched at the thought. She cast him an angry, confused look. "You'd go back? Even now?" she cried. "Didn't you see those men who died? You could be next, Seth. You're lucky to be alive today. I won't let you go back. I won't!"

Seth laughed. "You won't be able to stop me, Kendra," he said. "Like I said. I'll be back in the mines in a few days."

"Do you have a wish to die?" Kendra said hotly. "Is that it? Are you tired of living? Or what?"

"I live for excitement," he said. "And what more excitement than what can be found beneath the ground, tempting fate?"

Kendra groaned. She then turned her head with a start when she heard someone yelling behind them and a horse's hoofbeats approaching followed by the loud sound of buggy wheels bumping in and out of potholes in the dirt road.

"Who . . . ?" she whispered, casting Seth a quick look. She looked back toward the buggy, seeing a lovely lady plying a whip on and off the lone horse's back.

Seth turned his head and then set his lips firmly together, emitting a soft moan. Emanuelle! Why wouldn't she leave him alone? She had followed him around like a puppy since the day he had walked out on her. He was now even beginning to feel that maybe he had been wrong about her. Maybe she did love him for himself and not his money. And why the hell was she after him now? Had she heard about the accident? Had she come to check on him?

Kendra drew rein next to Seth as he pulled his horse to a halt. "Who *is* that, Seth?" she whispered, lifting her hat from her head, running her fingers across her sweat-soaked brow.

"Emanuelle," Seth sighed. "She thinks she's my girl."

A slow smile crinkled Kendra's nose. She *thinks* she's his girl? Surely he had given her reason for such an idea! Kendra was going to enjoy this. She watched as the buggy drew up next to Seth and closely observed the lady sitting behind the reins.

Beneath her stiff bonnet, a showing of blond hair

shimmered free, and hazel eyes set widely apart were the best feature of this lady's petite face. She showed strength in her jaw and the way in which she held herself, but her voice showed the weak side of her character as she began to drawl slowly in a deep southern accent.

This set Kendra's teeth on edge. It seemed that Seth had found himself a southern lady, and her kin had most surely fought for the Confederacy! Surely Seth couldn't be serious!

Then Kendra's face flushed. How could she be condemning Seth? Wasn't *she* in love with a man of the South . . . a man who had even fought up front . . . a captain?

"Seth, darlin', I heard the talk of a fire in the Con-Virginia," Emanuelle said, panting. "I just had to go and see if you were among the casualties."

"And when you found me not among them, you just *had* to come and pester me some more, huh?" he said sharply. "Emanuelle, how many times do I have to tell you . . . ?"

She cut his words short. "Seth, the men told me you were wounded," she said. "I asked where you were and some pointed this way and said you had refused to go to Virginia City for the services of a doctor. So I just had to come and see if you *were* able to return home 'stead of goin' to Doc Lawrence."

"Doc Lawrence's butt," Seth growled, lowering his eyes. He stared at his legs, silently cursing them. "I'll be all right, Emanuelle."

"You shouldn't be on that horse, darlin'," Emanuelle said, reaching a hand to one of his legs, touching it.

Seth shoved her hand quickly away. "Don't touch me," he shouted. "Go on back to Virginia City. Leave me alone. Do you hear, Emanuelle?"

"Let me take you on to your ranch in my buggy, Seth," Emanuelle pleaded, straightening the folds of her fully gathered dress. "It'd be a much easier ride for you."

"I'm doing just fine, Emanuelle," Seth argued, feeling a sudden throbbing at the base of his skull. The miles stretching out ahead of him *were* long, and the sun was mighty hot beating down on him. The fringe-trimmed, covered buggy might be of some help, yet he didn't want to appear weak by accepting the offer to ride in it.

Emanuelle secured her whip and climbed from the carriage in a huff. "Now you listen here, Seth Carpenter," she said stubbornly. "I insist that you let me help you into my buggy. This very minute."

"Emanuelle . . ." Seth growled.

Kendra dismounted and went to the other side of Seth's horse. "Maybe she's right," she said softly. "Let her take you home, then she can return to Virginia City. Seth, I'm so worried about you."

"You agree with *her*?" Seth said, eyes wide. "Someone you don't even know? I haven't even introduced you to her yet, and you take her side?"

"I don't care if you *never* introduce us," Kendra said, with hands on hips. "I do see that she knows what's best for you. Now, let us help you down from the horse and onto the buggy seat."

"Damn it . . ." Seth growled. He looked from Kendra to Emanuelle, then rolled his eyes upward in defeat.

"Kendra, best you come on over on this side and let us work at gettin' him off here. It's closer to the buggy," Emanuelle said, already steadying Seth's hand that he had placed on her shoulder.

Kendra took long steps and then positioned herself

next to Emanuelle. "You already know me?" she asked, tilting an eyebrow.

Emanuelle smiled. "Seth has spoken much of his sister to me," she said.

Kendra didn't return the smile. "Well, I can't say the same about you," she said dryly. "This is the first I've ever heard of you."

"That's because Seth and me've been havin' some trouble as of late," Emanuelle drawled. "But I 'spect to change that now. I plan to doctor him back to health if'n you'll let me stay on at the ranch for a few days."

Seth jerked his back up straight. "You what . . . ?" he shouted. "Emanuelle, so that's your game? You've finally found a way to get onto the Carpenter ranch? No. Get out of here. I won't have it. I knew there was something behind this. You just had to try it, didn't you?"

Emanuelle smiled coyly up at him. "It's only because I love you so much, Seth," she whispered. "Now place the other hand on my shoulder. Kendra is goin' to let you lean your body next to hers as you slip on out of the saddle."

"You both are impossible," Seth further growled. "It's a conspiracy. That's what it is. Emanuelle, didn't you hear anything that I just said?"

"Just be quiet, Seth," Emanuelle said. "We've got to get you to the buggy."

He grunted and groaned as he slipped between the two women and grudgingly draped an arm about each of their shoulders.

"That's it . . ." Emanuelle said softly. "We're almost there."

"Where do you usually make your home, Emanuelle?"

246

Kendra asked, puffing, helping to lift Seth onto the buggy seat.

"I originally was from Kentucky," Emanuelle said, also puffing. "But I followed my man out here to the mines. When he got killed, I stayed on. Then I met Seth. I've been hopin' . . ."

"She's been hopin' to latch on to the Carpenter money," Seth interrupted. "You can't deny that, Emanuelle."

"I love money just as much as the next person," Emanuelle sighed. "No denyin' that. But I love you more, Seth."

"For now, let's just see to getting Seth on home," Kendra said flatly.

"And I can stay a while?" Emanuelle asked, fluttering her thick lashes toward Kendra. "I wouldn't get in the way. Honest. I would just see to Seth's comforts."

"I bet you would," Kendra whispered, walking away from her. "We'll see," she said aloud, swinging up into her saddle. "We'll see."

Kendra dropped back away from the buggy as it began rolling on down the road. She didn't know about Emanuelle, whether or not she could be trusted. It was quite apparent that Seth didn't trust her. Well, it would have to be Seth who would make that final decision as to whether or not Emanuelle stayed on at the ranch. Maybe Emanuelle could even persuade Seth not to venture back into the mines! Maybe by her staying, coddling him, he might even learn to enjoy such treatment and think twice before wanting to live the crude, dangerous life of a miner again!

Feeling the sun beating through her clothes, Kendra became very conscious of the fact that she hadn't yet removed the binder from her breasts. Stopping Domino, she threw her shirt open and began untwisting the binder, roll after roll, until she felt her breasts spring free as they fell out into place and the blood began slowly flowing back inside them again.

Kendra closed her eyes and held her head back, sighing. Tossing the cloth into the air, she was reminded of the wasted day. But she would have another chance. Surely soon. She wouldn't give up that easily!

The sound of wheels and more hoofbeats behind her drew Kendra's hands into a frenzy of activity. She quickly buttoned her shirt, then slowly turned around as the big, stately black carriage of the Carpenters drew up next to her.

Feeling hatred burning her insides, Kendra watched as Holly threw open the carriage door. "Why, Kendra," Holly said, blushing. "Whatever are you doing so far from the ranch?"

Then Holly's eyes traveled up the road and saw the horse being led behind the buggy and recognized it as Seth's horse. "And Seth? Has something happened to Seth?" she murmured. "I did hear of some news of a fire at the mine he works."

"Oh, you did hear," Kendra mocked. "And whatever were you doing at the time when the news spread your way?"

Kendra watched as Holly's green eyes took on a desperate cast. She smiled wickedly to herself, oh, so wanting to lash out at Holly, but the time would come to do that. Later. But not much later!

"Why, I was shopping for a gown. To wear to the dance," Holly whispered. "Aaron did tell you about the dance we've been invited to, did he not?"

Kendra smoothed Domino's mane with a hand. "Yes," she said dryly. "He did. And, Holly, did you, my dear, find a dress to your liking? I would like to see it. Maybe I might go shopping at the same . . . uh . . . emporium as you have just come from."

Again she saw the look of . . . yes . . . it was a guilty look . . . in Holly's eyes! Kendra could hardly wait to accuse her face to face! But later. She would find the appropriate time. Maybe even in Aaron's presence, when Aaron's other troubles had lightened a bit.

Holly's fingers went to her throat. "Why, Kendra, I am sorry," she murmured. "I had no luck. I wouldn't advise you to even enter the emporium I shopped at today."

"I'm sure you wouldn't," Kendra said bitterly to herself.

Holly leaned forward, cocking her head a bit sideways. "What's that you said, Kendra?" she said, placing a cupped hand to her ear. "You'll have to speak up."

"I said let's hurry on," Kendra said. "The sun is melting me."

Holly looked on ahead, seeing the buggy moving quickly away from them. "Kendra, you didn't tell me. Was Seth hurt in the mine? That is his horse tied to the buggy ahead."

"Yes, if you must know. Seth was injured."

Holly gasped. "Badly? Was he hurt badly? He isn't . . . dead, is . . . he . . . ?"

"He's going to be all right," Kendra said. "But he does seem to have a problem."

"What sort of problem?"

"His legs . . ."

"Legs . . . ?"

"Seems they may have been paralyzed."

Holly blanched. "You mean . . . he may not be able to walk again?"

"I hope that his injury isn't that severe," Kendra sighed. "Seth seems quite determined about forcing his legs to work again. And, do you know? I think he'll do it. He has the will of an ox."

"And who is that in that buggy with him?" Holly asked. "She looks a bit familiar. It isn't. No . . . it can't be. . . ."

"A girl named Emanuelle?"

"Yes," Holly said softly. Her eyes widened. "If you know the name Emanuelle, surely it is she in the buggy with Seth. What is *she* doing with Seth, Kendra?"

"Seems she's another lady who is after the Carpenter name and wealth," Kendra said, shooting an accusing eye toward Holly.

Holly's lips set in a quick, straight line and her face reddened. "Kendra," she gasped. "My word! You aren't implying that . . . I . . ."

"I wouldn't have a few months ago, Holly," Kendra said dryly. "But today? Yes, I would be speaking of you. I now have reason to believe that you've never loved Aaron as you've professed to."

Holly slammed the carriage door in Kendra's face after shouting to Parker to take her on home.

Kendra laughed softly to herself as the dust flew after the carriage as it drove wildly on down the road. Then Kendra sobered. "Oh, Aaron, I wanted to be wrong about her," she whispered.

Lifting her hair from her shoulders, Kendra sighed and then sent Domino heading for home at a gallop, hoping for better things ahead, already thrilling over the prospect of the dance. Luke? Lucas? No. Surely not . . .

250

Chapter Fifteen

Kendra spun around in front of the mirror, laughing softly. She hadn't realized just how much the gentler side of her had missed the feel of silk against her flesh. Ruffled petticoats rustled enticingly around her legs as Kendra drew herself to a halt, to take one final look before meeting Aaron and Holly at the waiting carriage.

She had piled her golden hair high atop her head, leaving soft ringlets to frame her delicately chiseled features. Her eyes and lips were bright, and her bare white shoulders were gleaming.

Yes. This evening she was as delicate as a cameo, in her powder blue silk gown that enhanced the ocean-blue of her eyes. The gown's bodice clung sensuously to her figure, emphasizing the exquisite swell of her high, rounded breasts and the smallness of her waist. Delicate, pale blue velveteen ribbons were sewn crisscrossed across the bodice and around her waist, where the ends were tied to lie in a sensuous flutter down the front of the fully-gathered skirt of her dress. She had removed the squash blossom necklace, and in its place hung a sparkling diamond necklace that had been Kendra's mother's, and, to match the necklace, she had clipped tiny diamond earrings onto each of her earlobes.

"If Lucas saw me now he most surely wouldn't recognize me," she whispered, reaching for her white satin cape to sling around her shoulders. Tying it in place, she moved toward the door, stopping to pick up her matching purse.

"Oh, if Lucas *could* only be there," Kendra sighed, lifting the skirt of her dress and the hem of her cape up into her arms to glide down the staircase.

"I see you're all spruced up and rarin' to go," Seth said, leaning heavily against Emanuelle as he met Kendra's descent on the stairs. He chuckled, chewing aimlessly on the tip of his Cuban cigar. "Quite an improvement, Kendra," he said, letting his eyes rake over her. "I'd forgotten how beautiful my sister was. I imagine Aaron's proud as punch you've shed your blue jeans."

"I must hurry on, Seth," Kendra said, trying to avoid the envious stare from Emanuelle. Emanuelle had quite boldly spoken her desire to attend the dance. But no one had offered to escort her, and Seth had yet to regain all the strength in his legs, so was unable to offer his services.

"Aaron tapped quite impatiently on my door only moments ago," Kendra added. "He said that he and Holly were going on to the carriage."

"Holly . . ." Seth grumbled, tossing his head in disgust.

"Yes. Holly," Kendra said dryly. She gave Emanuelle a cautious look, hoping that Seth hadn't mentioned Holly's infidelities to her. It was a family problem. Oh, *what* a family problem it was! Strange how Holly had kept her liaison within the boundaries of the Carpenter family and didn't even realize that she had done so! What a laugh when she finally realized whom she had been bedding up with!

Seth leaned a kiss onto Kendra's cheek. "You quit worrying over Holly and Aaron," he whispered into her ear. "Just go and have fun, darling sister. You deserve it."

He straightened his back with a groan, then said, "And maybe you'll even meet an eligible bachelor to your liking at the dance."

"I'm sure Aaron has somehow arranged for Steven Teague to be there," Kendra sighed. "I will probably be pestered the entire evening by *him*."

"Maybe this Luke Hall is available," Seth said, wrinkling his mustache as he scratched absently at his chin. "It'd be kind of nice to join our two spreads into one. Think on it, Kendra. You might even make eyes at him."

"Oh, Seth," Kendra said, walking away from him. She gave him a quick glance from across her shoulder. "Anyway, if he's not married, he's probably old, fat, and boring. Bye, bye, now."

"Have fun," Seth shouted after her. He gave Emanuelle an affectionate squeeze around the waist. "We'll have our own private fun here at home, won't we, Emanuelle?"

Emanuelle gave him a silent, pouting glance and helped him back into the sitting room. He lowered himself into a chair, cursing his legs, yet thankful that at least he was able to stand and move about now. Neither the house nor Emanuelle would hold him prisoner much

253

longer. He was hungering for the shine of the ore . . . the dangers of the beehive underground. . . .

Kendra rushed on outside, seeing Parker waiting patiently beside the stately carriage. She thanked him as he helped her inside, then settled herself comfortably on the cushioned seat opposite Aaron and Holly.

"It's about time," Aaron growled, puffing on his cigar.

"I wanted everything to be just right," Kendra said, patting her cape onto her lap.

"I'm sure it took much effort," Aaron said. "You've not had much practice with silk and lace as of late."

"Don't start on me again, Aaron," Kendra said hotly. But one look at Holly and her red eyes and Kendra realized that Aaron's bad temper wasn't only because of herself. It appeared that Holly and Aaron had been arguing again. The strain between them was thick in the air. Kendra had begun to wonder if Aaron suspected Holly. Or did he have cause himself to feel guilty in the presence of his wife?

Something had caused a change in Aaron these past several weeks and Kendra didn't see this change as being associated with worry. There was a moodiness about him that she associated with someone who has found new love. . . . Kendra had seen this in her older brother only one other time and that had been when he had first fallen in love with Holly!

Smiling to herself, Kendra hoped that Aaron *had* found someone else. It would be a pleasure seeing Holly squirm when Aaron told her that he no longer loved her. But then, wouldn't Holly be relieved? Would she in turn tell Aaron of her new love and leave him to go to her Blackie?

Kendra shook her head and closed her eyes. Every-

254

thing about Aaron and Holly was becoming a bit much for her. Something splashed cold inside her, dreading the end results. . . .

"Are you all right, Kendra?" Aaron asked, leaning forward to take one of her hands in his. "You seem a bit concerned about something. Can I help?"

Kendra's eyes jolted open. She looked from Aaron to Holly, then back to Aaron. "No," she murmured. "Everything is fine. Just fine."

"Are you anxious about the dance, Kendra?" Aaron said, releasing her hand, to settle back against the cushion of his seat.

Kendra smiled. "Yes, I must admit, a bit."

In the late afternoon light, she admired the way her brother had chosen to dress for the evening. He looked his worth in his expensive navy blue velveteen evening coat over an immaculately white shirt, a matching blue silk cravat at his throat where a lustrous diamond stickpin sparkled from its folds. Though Aaron had thick shoulders and a large waist, he did look handsome with his silk top hat hiding the baldness of his head.

Beside Aaron, Holly sat stiffly, displaying her loveliness, her midnight-black hair hanging in glossy coiled curls from her crown. Beneath her cape she was attired in a shapely rose-colored satin gown that revealed most of her cleavage, where emeralds hung down long and enticing. Her green eyes wore her uneasiness in them, the only thing spoiling her usually quite alluring innocent face.

"Kendra, Steven Teague has been asking about you," Aaron said, holding his freshly lighted cigar between his fingers, staring at its burning tip.

"I'm sure he has," she sighed.

255

"You've been avoiding the schoolhouse, Kendra."

"I've had other things on my mind."

"Such as . . . ?"

Kendra felt her face warming and glanced quickly at Holly, seeing smugness stiffen Holly's lips. Had Holly somehow found out about Kendra's daring entrance into Blackie's gambling emporium? But surely not. Only Seth knew, and he wouldn't tell Holly!

"Such as shopping for this lovely gown and cape," Kendra finally managed to murmur. "You do approve, don't you, Aaron?"

Aaron's bushy brows lifted as he flicked ashes from his cigar out the carriage window. "Yes. Must say I do," he said. "And I'm sure Steven will, also."

"I doubt if Steven Teague even knows how to dance," Kendra said haughtily, lifting her chin. "I'm sure he has only mastered reading, writing, and arithmetic in his dull existence."

Aaron chuckled. "We'll soon see, won't we?" he said, once more chewing on his cigar.

Kendra fumbled with her purse. "Aaron, how much do you know about this Luke Hall?" she asked in a near-whisper. "Why do you think he's asked *us* to attend a social function at his ranch?"

"From what I've been told he's owned his stretch of land for some time now," Aaron replied. "But he has only recently constructed his ranch house."

"Don't you find that a bit strange, Aaron?"

"Not really. He's probably not had the need of a huge house until now. He's probably found himself a woman and wants to show her off."

"So you think a woman is behind his invitation?"

"More than likely. She's probably some delicate thing

from out of state, and lonesome as hell. He probably wants to get her introduced to you womenfolk. That's all."

"You sound awfully sure of your assumption, Aaron."

"Women are behind most of men's plans," Aaron grumbled, avoiding Holly's eyes as she quickly glanced toward him.

"It would be nice to make a new acquaintance," Kendra said. She gave Holly an icy stare. "Seems I lack for proper female friends myself here in this Nevada territory."

Aaron gave Kendra a puzzled look, then looked slowly toward Holly. When Holly glanced quickly away from him, avoiding the questioning in his eyes, something twisted at his gut. She looked damn guilty about something! He began tapping his fingers nervously on his knee, wondering. . . .

Feeling renewed tensions inside the small carriage, Kendra scooted closer to the window at her right side and stared from it. Out there, somewhere, was Lucas. Was he possibly thinking of her at this very moment? Sometimes he felt so close she could imagine feeling his breath on her cheek or his powerful arms about her waist. . . .

I mustn't let myself think about him, she thought sadly to herself. It was too painful.

Instead, she focused her eyes and thoughts on the beautiful landscape moving by her outside the window, looking at the mountains in the distance. The white tips that through the day mysteriously picked up the reflected blues of the sky were now giving way to browns and rusts, pinks and roses, glowing warmer and brighter as the sun sank. The backdrop of sky was slowly becoming a breathtaking spectrum of blues . . . turquoise, jade, indigo and violet . . . almost startling in their intensity.

The carriage moved deeper and deeper into Washoe Valley. Aaron leaned forward, touching Kendra on her hand. "We're almost there," he said. "From the directions on the invitation I believe we should be catching sight of the ranch house quite soon now."

Kendra watched almost breathlessly as the thick pines of the foothills blended into the openness of the valley, in a lustrous blend of greens, so undisturbed by man that it reminded her of the biblical descriptions of the home of the first disillusioned woman.

"The Garden of Eden . . ." she whispered.

"What's that you said, Kendra?" Aaron asked, tossing his cigar from the window.

Kendra blushed. She straightened her back. "Nothing . . ." she murmured. But she suddenly felt envious of whatever woman might be inheriting this with her marriage. Yes, the Carpenter spread was lovely, but *this* land had more peacefulness about it. So far no cattle disturbed the scenery. . . .

Then Kendra saw the house. Its two-storied magnificence drew a long sigh from between her lips. Its pillared front of long white columns reminded her of a southern mansion—it was nothing at all like what one usually found in the landscape of Nevada.

Aaron moved jerkily to the window. "What the hell . . . ?" he growled. "What sort of cowboy would build a house like that out here on the range?"

"Maybe someone who hasn't always been . . ." Kendra began.

". . . a cowboy. . . ." Aaron completed her sentence.

A slow heat began to rise on Kendra's cheeks.

Luke . . . ? Lucas . . . ? "It would seem to be a house built by someone who may have . . ."

". . . lived in the South . . ." Aaron helped her say. "What do we have here? A damn Rebel in our midst?"

Kendra felt the strangest excitement trembling her insides. "Do you think this Luke Hall may be a Southerner?" she whispered, clasping and unclasping her fingers together on her lap.

Aaron settled back against the cushion, crossing his legs. He thumped his fingers nervously on his knee. "I'm sure I'm wrong in my judgment," he said. "Just because we have us a southern mansion dirtying the view doesn't necessarily mean its owner is a Reb. Maybe he built the house for his woman. Maybe she's from the South."

His thoughts went to Hazel, causing his pulse to quicken. "It's been known to happen," he added. "A man with strictly devoted feelings for the Union falling in love with a lady from the South."

Kendra's eyes wavered and her hand went to her hair, pretending to check to see if it was still in place. "Oh," she murmured. "I didn't think about that. But most surely you're right."

She felt foolish to have for the briefest moment believed it might have been Lucas who was calling himself Luke on his personal invitations. No. It wouldn't have made sense. Lucas would be out of place in this house. He didn't appear to have the need for flashy houses, or for the clothes that would have to be worn in such a house.

The carriage moved alongside other parked carriages at the side of the house and stopped. Parker opened the door and assisted Kendra and Holly down. Aaron then offered them each an arm and they made a turn on the

259

drive and walked toward the front steps, then up them and to the large oak front door. Aaron lifted a heavy, silver knocker and let it fall once . . . then twice. . . .

While waiting, Kendra couldn't help but notice the silver doorknob and the silver hinges on the door. She had heard that most of these silver accessories used in Nevada were hammered out of bullion from Nevada's mills by San Francisco's silversmiths. . . .

The door jerked quickly open. A black butler dressed in a long-tailed white coat, dark breeches, and white gloves opened the door and bowed to them. Aaron and Kendra exchanged quick glances, then they all stepped on into the foyer where Aaron's hat and Kendra's and Holly's capes were taken and hung with all the other guests' personal belongings. Music from a four-pieced ensemble filled the air, along with the chatter of mingling men and women.

Behind the butler, Aaron escorted Kendra and Holly on through the foyer. They were directed into a huge room lighted brightly by hundreds of candles burning in several ceiling chandeliers.

Aaron bowed a silent hello to people whom he knew, and Kendra stood as though spellbound looking at the loveliness of the room and the beautifully gowned women waltzing around the center with their impeccably dressed escorts.

Kendra's gaze moved on around her, taking in the windows of Bohemian glass, richly etched, and an elaborate natatorium that had been built into a corner of the room. Hot water, probably from nearby thermal springs gushed out of the mouths of silver-headed mountain lions. Murals by the best California artists adorned the walls, and tropical plants in marble urns unfolded their fronds in other corners of the room. And to complete this atmosphere, a canary warbled in a brass-shuttered cage next to a staircase that led up to the second floor.

Aaron drew Holly to his side as the butler announced their entrance. Then he accepted a glass of sparkling Moselle from a lackey who was dressed in a formal broadcloth and gilt-trimmed suit.

"Thank you," Aaron murmured, nodding toward Kendra and Holly, who then also accepted the sparkling refreshment.

"Where *is* the chap who owns this ridiculous showcase?" Aaron growled, looking nervously about him.

"Aaron, really," Kendra scolded. "You're just jealous because this house is more unique than ours. I don't call this ridiculous at all. I call it lovely. It fits in with the 'Garden of Eden' feeling."

Aaron smoothed a hand over his shining bald head, raising an eyebrow quizzically in Kendra's direction. "Garden of what?" he mused.

Kendra's face flushed pink. "Nothing, Aaron," she murmured. "You must've misunderstood me."

Aaron's eyes lit up and he raised his long-stemmed glass into the air, motioning with it. "Ah, there's Steven," he said. He tried to catch Steven's eye.

Kendra grabbed at Aaron's arm. "Aaron, please . . ." she begged. "I'll be bored by him soon enough."

There was a stirring of the crowd at the foot of the staircase, and all eyes moved upward. Kendra's head took on a quick dizziness and her throat went suddenly dry when she saw the man responsible for all the attention at the head of the staircase.

"Lucas . . ." she whispered shakily, taking a step backwards. "Luke Hall . . . *is* . . . Lucas. . . ."

Aaron turned quickly to her. "Kendra? Are you all right? You look as though you've seen a ghost."

Kendra shook her head and blinked her eyes. "Yes. I'm fine," she murmured. To her it was the same as seeing a ghost! She shook her head and blinked her eyes. Her hand went to her brow and kneaded it, then slowly she turned her gaze back to Lucas, seeing how differently he was dressed than always before. His white frock coat, filled out so magnificently at his shoulders, caused his sun-bronzed face to appear even darker, and the pink ruffles at his throat and edging his shirt sleeves were such a contrast to his usual cowboy shirt and bandana!

His dark hair was combed to perfection and his sideburns were trimmed and neat. But again it was his eyes beneath the dark arch of his eyebrows that drew Kendra's attention. He had already singled her out from the crowd, and the command of his steel-gray eyes was once again there, causing Kendra's knees to weaken and her heart to thunder against her ribs. Her gaze traveled over his long, trim torso . . . his narrow hips . . . and his muscular thighs, where the dark breeches fit him so snugly. Had he ever been as handsome . . . as virile . . . as at this moment? Though he was dressed like an aristocrat, she could still see the free and untamable quality about him in the way he carried his tall and lithe body. His movements were easy, yet exact. And as he left the last step and was lost from Kendra's view for a moment, panic rose inside her. She had to expect now to see the woman of the house make her appearance at the head of the staircase. Would he really have the nerve to introduce Heart Speak as his wife? Was that also part of his plan to try and draw the Indians closer to the white community? Is that what this evening was all about? Had he built this house for her? For . . . Heart Speak . . . ?

Such were the thoughts that ate away at Kendra's heart. . . .

Aaron bent and spoke into Kendra's ear. "So that's Luke Hall," he chuckled. "Looks like a damn Reb all right, dressed in sissy pink with ruffles to boot."

Anger began to seethe inside Kendra. She couldn't help but defend Lucas. Though he could never be hers, she would always love him. "He is no sissy," she whispered back. "He's quite a man, Aaron, one you might take a few lessons from."

Aaron's eyes widened. "You speak as though you know this man. How could *you* have met him when even *I* haven't?"

Kendra tightened her fingers about the stem of her glass, cursing herself for having been caught out by her habit of speaking her mind. Now what was she to do . . . ?

"Welcome to my home," Lucas said, suddenly appearing from out of the crowd. He extended a hand of friendship toward Aaron, smiling, casting Kendra a quick sideways glance. He could hardly resist the urge to pull her into his arms and sweep her from the room, to demand an explanation as to why she had left the Indian village so abruptly and without a goodbye. He had worked only halfheartedly since he had seen her last. But going to her ranch to force her to see him was not the way he did things.

And, ah, didn't she shine in her loveliness above all the other women in the room this evening? Though her tight jeans had become her, the gown and its low-swept bodice were much more to his liking.

263

But, either way, she was one hell of a lady! And he loved her. . . .

Aaron shifted the wineglass to his left hand and accepted Lucas's greeting. "So you must be Luke Hall," he said dryly, raking his eyes over Lucas, assessing his worth. There was strength in this Luke Hall's handshake and his face was lined with force and intelligence, alerting Aaron to be cautious of any dealings with him. And wasn't there something strangely familiar about his eyes? Aaron had a sudden feeling that he had met Luke Hall some time in his past. But where?

"Lucas," Lucas said. "Call me Lucas." He released his hold and clasped his hands behind his back. "And you must be Aaron Carpenter."

Aaron frowned. Without a formal introduction, how had he known? Then he let his eyes follow Lucas's and saw the answer to his unspoken question. It was Kendra! Somehow Lucas Hall *had* made her acquaintance prior to this night! But how? Where? Was Kendra his sole purpose for asking him here?

But, no. More than likely not. The whole community had been invited. Had this man, somehow, gotten to Kendra first, hoping to use her for whatever his purpose was? Was this the man who . . . ? Was this the man who had brought the barbed wire into the community? Aaron stiffened at the thought and a slow hate began to rise inside him. . . .

"And your lovely sister Kendra . . . ?" Lucas said, taking Kendra's right hand. He kissed it gently and bowed, letting his eyes move slowly up to meet hers. "I'm pleased to make your acquaintance, ma'am."

He smiled devilishly up at her and had to hold back the strong urge to wink.

Kendra tensed and felt an ache around her heart when she saw the Indian ring on his left hand.

Fearing too much attention might be drawn toward them, Lucas stepped before Holly and performed the same courtesies he had given Kendra, though much more formally, and in haste, and without the mischievous glint in his eyes.

Aaron placed his empty glass on a table, then boldly faced Lucas. "All right," he said. "We've made our formal appearance as requested, but now I'd like to place all formalities aside and ask why you've gathered together most of the families this side of Reno. You don't fool me for one second. Not now that I've seen you and your damn, peculiar house."

Aaron leaned into Lucas's face. "You see," he whispered. "I smell a Reb. And I don't like seein' *no* Reb makin' eyes at my sister."

Aaron's gaze traveled to the staircase and back to Lucas. "I'll bet your bottom dollar there's no Mrs. Hall, is there?"

Kendra's eyes grew wider and wider. Aaron had never behaved so poorly after having just made a new acquaintance. She looked toward Lucas, seeing fire in his eyes and the cold, hard set of his jaw. Then she glanced back at Aaron, seeing the flush of his face. There had been an instant dislike between the two men who were the most important in her life.

"Aaron, please . . ." Kendra whispered, sidling up next to him. "We're guests in this house. Lucas was kind enough to include us in his invitations."

Lucas tried to ignore Aaron's arrogance. "Have a cigar?" he said softly. He hadn't any idea of what he had done wrong but he did understand the intelligence of this

265

man whom he saw suddenly as a rival . . . in . . . *many* things. . . .

Aaron grumbled beneath his breath, then accepted it.

"And maybe some more Moselle?" Lucas said suavely. "Or maybe you're hungry. Maybe you'd like some frogs' legs? Or maybe some caviar?"

Aaron lit the cigar and lifted an eyebrow as smoke circled upward into his eyes. "I'm only interested in getting to the point," he said. "I saw no cattle on your range. I saw no horses. What's your game, Lucas?"

"I only recently moved into this house," Lucas said, lighting his own cigar. "I've yet to move my herd."

"Where did you make your residence before?" Aaron prodded.

Kendra placed a hand to her throat, remembering the adobe house. Now she understood why he had had no change of clothes there. He had moved them into this new house already. Oh, so many questions were spiraling around inside her head! Lucas was such a complicated person. He seemed to have two personalities. She had yet to understand at which point these personalities merged to become one man . . . one Lucas.

She listened as Lucas skillfully evaded Aaron's continuing questions. It would be interesting to see who won this battle of words. . . .

"I asked you if there's a Mrs. Hall," Aaron persisted.

"Since you are my guest and I *am* a southern gentleman, I won't tell you that's none of your business," Lucas growled.

"And since you won't tell me that's none of my business, I will once again ask for an answer to my question," Aaron said smugly.

Kendra tensed, once more glancing at the ring on

Lucas's finger. Then a new voice broke into their conversation, throwing Kendra's heart into a thunderous pounding and her head into another frenzy. Why, oh why, did Steven have to show up at such an inopportune time?

"Kendra," Steven Teague said, pushing his way on toward her with an outstretched hand. With the other hand, he pushed his gold-framed spectacles back on his hawklike nose. "I'm so glad you've arrived." He grabbed one of Kendra's hands and held it possessively. "You've just got to dance with me, Kendra. Will you do me the honor now?" Steven gave Aaron an almost apologetic glance. "I'll bring her back soon, Aaron, and this will leave you free to dance with Holly."

Kendra moaned to herself as Steven pulled her out onto the dance floor among the whirling couples. She glanced across her shoulder, noticing that Aaron and Lucas had resumed their discussion, and she hated Steven with every fiber of her being for having intervened at such a time. Lucas had been ready to say whether or not he was married! She just knew it. He wouldn't have been able to have continued to evade Aaron's persistent questioning, because he *was* a gentleman and wouldn't want to draw attention to himself by arguing with a guest at his own party.

Grudgingly, Kendra lifted the skirt of her dress with one hand and rested the other on Steven's frail shoulder as he very expertly continued to spin her around the room. She couldn't help but feel Lucas's eyes on her, following her every move, burning a hole through her. . . .

"You look beautiful tonight, Kendra," Steven said, admiring her openly with a quick raking of his eyes.

"Thank you, Steven," Kendra said stiffly. She could have offered equally kind words to him, but he *wasn't* handsome in his usual plain broadcloth suit. His hollow cheeks and bony frame did not match the velvet of his voice. Yes, he had chosen the right profession. It was meant for him to stand before a classroom all day in a stuffy room where only the strength of the voice mattered.

"Why haven't you come by the school?" Steven queried softly. "You said that you would. You would see quite intelligent students who are a delight to teach."

"A delight . . ." Kendra mocked. She narrowed her eyes. "Steven, did you ever consider adding some Piute children to your classroom? Or Shoshonee or Washoe?"

Steven's glasses scooted farther down on his nose as he dropped his mouth open. "Kendra," he gasped. "Why would I even consider such a thing? Indians are not even allowed in the classroom."

"I know that," Kendra sighed. "I just wanted to see what you would say to the suggestion."

"Why would you want to do that, Kendra?"

Kendra held her head back and let her soft, flowing ringlets hang down her back. "You wouldn't understand," she sighed. "No one seems to . . . except for . . . one man."

As she whirled on around the room in time to the music she lifted her skirt and closed her eyes, and when she opened them again, she caught sight of Lucas moving toward her with wide, angry strides. When he placed his arm about her waist and swung her around and into his arms and away from Steven, she uttered, "My word, Lucas, whatever are you doing?" She glanced over her shoulder at a pale, gaping Steven.

"I've waited too long already to be near you," he murmured into her ear. "Did you think I was going to stand by and watch you enjoy yourself with another man?"

His hard thighs pressed against her and his hot breath on her cheek was causing a lethargy to take hold of her senses. But when she felt eyes on her and realized how closely Lucas was holding her, she began to squirm and to push at his chest.

"Lucas . . ." she whispered. "People are staring. Don't hold me like this while we're dancing. It isn't proper."

Lucas took a step backwards and placed one hand on her waist and clasped his other in one of her hands and guided her around the floor. "Now is this better?" he chuckled.

"Much," she said dryly, trying to avoid his eyes. Her insides quivered and her heart pounded. But she didn't want him to know how he still affected her. The ring on his finger was a constant reminder. Her gaze went to the staircase, watching it.

"And how is Heart Speak?" she murmured softly, hating to even speak the name.

"Heart Speak is well," Lucas said, eyeing her quizzically. "It's very generous of you to ask, Kendra."

"And when will she make an appearance?" Kendra asked shallowly. "Soon I would think. Is Quick Deer here? How is his leg?"

She moved her gaze slowly to his face, testing him now with a boldness in the flashing of her eyes and the set of her jaw. She would never forget how he had used her! Never! She squared her shoulders, awaiting his response.

A slow smile lifted Lucas's wide, seductive lips. "And

what makes you think they are here?" he said thickly.

Kendra was puzzled by the twinkling of his eyes. She found the subject of Heart Speak anything but amusing! The constant thought of Heart Speak and Lucas together had become a burden almost too heavy for Kendra to carry inside her heart.

"You built this house especially for a wife, did you not?" she finally murmured, almost choking on the words. She would wish it to be *her* Eden . . . not Heart Speak's. But instead, it was an elusive Eden . . . one never to be even within her reach. . . .

Lucas began dancing her toward an open double door at the far end of the room. "Yes," he said. "I must confess that I did."

Kendra's heart ached even more. "Then where *is* she?" she murmured. She lowered her lashes, as eyes followed their exit from the room onto the veranda. "And, Lucas, how is it that you've chosen to change your way of living? You seemed so content before."

"I had no reason for such a large house before," he said, guiding her down some steps, to a flagstone walkway lighted only by the moon.

"Before what . . . ?" Kendra asked as she followed beside him into shadows from a tall stand of pines.

"Before *you* . . ." Lucas said huskily. He stopped and drew her breathlessly into his arms and possessed her lips in a powerful kiss.

Feeling the ecstasy sweeping through her, Kendra returned his kiss, confused by what he had said. What had he meant? How could *she* have had anything to do with his building such a magnificent mansion? But his tongue entering her mouth and a hand cupping one of her breasts through her dress dimmed her worries and wonder.

Lacing her arms about his neck, Kendra let herself become lost in his presence. She ran her fingers through his hair as his lips lowered and kissed the hollow of her throat.

"I've missed you so, Kendra. . . ." he murmured. His lips lowered even more and kissed the upper, exposed flesh of her breasts, causing Kendra's breath to drunkenly escape her. "Don't ever leave me again, darling," he added huskily.

"But, Lucas . . ."

Lucas sealed her words with a gentle kiss to her lips. "I must first talk serious business with Aaron," he said, drawing away from her. "Then, hopefully, I will be free to explain everything to you."

Kendra leaned even further away from him, but, unable to lose all contact with him, she ran her fingers down each of his cheeks. "But what can you possibly have to discuss with Aaron?" she whispered.

"The Carpenter land lies adjacent to mine," he said. "It's important that we understand each other right away so we can live peacefully as neighbors."

Kendra laughed. "Having already seen you and Aaron together, I would tend to believe that impossible," she said. Then her smile faded. "And, Lucas, why didn't you tell me earlier that your land ran flush with ours? Why did you choose to keep that a secret from me? Why have you been so mysterious about everything since we've met? I doubt if I shall ever understand you."

He leaned another kiss to her lips. "Please be patient, darling," he murmured.

"And why should I?"

"Because I am asking you to," he whispered. "Because

I love you."

Kendra's insides rebelled, feeling once more drawn into his words that were most surely lies. Now, more than before, she felt his true motive was to use her. He apparently wanted something from Aaron, and to get it he would surely try to use her persuasion of her brother.

"Lucas, I believe I'd best return to the dance," she said stiffly. "I do believe I owe Steven the dance you so rudely robbed him of."

She began to walk away, but he stopped her with tight fingers on her shoulders, turning her to face him. Even in the moonlight she could feel the command of his gray eyes, and she felt her defenses against him crumbling.

"Who is this Steven Teague?" he grumbled.

"He is the new teacher for our schoolhouse," she said dryly.

"And what does he mean to you?"

"I'm not quite sure yet," she lied, flinching when his fingers tightened.

"Is he the reason you've chosen to avoid me these past weeks?"

"Maybe."

"What the hell does that mean, Kendra?"

"Lucas," she said, jerking free from his hold, "why don't you just go on and tend to your business with Aaron? The sooner the better. You see, I think I'm ready to return home."

"God. You're unpredictable," he growled.

"Maybe almost as much as you are," she said, breezing on away from him. Her heart pounded out each hurried step until she was back in the large room filled with music and laughter. But Kendra felt that she didn't belong. Lucas was playing word games with her. Why would he

272

try to make her believe he had built the house because of her? Why didn't he admit that Heart Speak was behind his every thought and move . . . ?

Seeing Steven Teague standing alone at the edge of the crowd, Kendra forced a smile and worked her way toward him. Out of the corner of her eye she saw Lucas step in from the veranda. For a moment he watched her intensely, then he swung around and made his way toward Aaron.

Kendra reached a hand to Steven. "I've returned," she said, forcing a giggle. "I believe we've a dance to complete, Steven."

Steven pushed his glasses back on his nose and smiled nervously. "Where did you disappear to, Kendra?" he asked, shifting nervously from one foot to the other.

"I needed a breath of fresh air," she sighed. "But now I'm refreshed and am anxious to dance again."

"Then I shall do the honors," Steven said, already guiding her out onto the floor.

Kendra lifted the skirt of her dress and swayed with the music. She searched and found Aaron and Lucas. They were nodding and talking, and then just as quickly Lucas had walked away from him and was once more headed toward Kendra.

Oh, no . . . she thought. Not again.

But this time he behaved like a proper gentleman. He waited until a particular song had ended, then bowed to her and then Steven. "I must request the next dance with Miss Carpenter," he said firmly. His lips quivered in an amused smile and his eyes shone in steel grays.

"Kendra . . . ?" Steven whispered, eyeing her questioningly.

"It's all right, Steven," she said softly. "I'll talk to

273

you later."

Steven bent his shoulders as he walked away from them. Kendra flashed Lucas an annoyed look. Her fingers worked nervously with her diamond necklace.

"Where's the squash blossom necklace?" Lucas growled.

"Don't you approve of my diamonds, Lucas?" she teased.

"I gave you the necklace for a true purpose."

"And since I didn't understand this true purpose I've chosen to leave it in a drawer until I do," she said stiffly. Her gaze moved around her. "And, Lucas, you've been neglecting the rest of your guests. You'd think the Carpenter family was the only family here."

"Oh, there's another guest here for sure," he growled. "Steven Teague."

Kendra giggled, loving his annoyance. "You invited him," she said. "Not I." Then her eyes narrowed. "Which leads me to ask . . . how was it you did ask Steven? Why, Lucas, you didn't even know him by name or face when you asked me who he was."

"I left the addressing of invitations up to Sam, my bookkeeper and manager. Since the purchase of my first ranch house on the other end of my spread, he's taken care of all my money responsibilities and personal affairs. He oversees my estate, hires and fires hands, and keeps books. This leaves me free to work for the Indian cause and to see to my own cattle and horses."

"So you make your residence somewhere full time besides the Indian village? You do have a ranch where your cattle and horses are kept?"

"Exactly," he said.

"You confuse me even more, Lucas."

"Until now, that is. Now I plan to make *this* my permanent residence. I must see to my other guests, Kendra," he said, leaning a kiss onto her cheek.

"But my brother. Did you settle things with him?"

"We are to meet at your ranch tomorrow evening," he said. "But before then I was hoping you would return here to my house and let me really show you around . . . alone."

"I cannot do that," she said, squaring her shoulders.

"And why not?"

"There are too many unanswered questions between us."

"And which is the one of the many that you'd like answered most?"

Kendra glanced toward the Indian ring, then let her gaze move slowly upward to search his face. "Lucas, why did you have to marry *her*? Why did you have to father a son by her?" she quickly blurted.

Lucas eyed her with intense disbelief, then guided her by the elbow through the crowd and back out onto the veranda. "Now, Kendra, what on earth have you been thinking?" he asked, framing her face between his hands.

"That you are Heart Speak's husband . . . that Quick Deer may even be your son."

"What?" Lucas said shallowly, then threw his head back into a fit of laughter.

"Lucas . . ." Kendra whispered.

Lucas's laughter died. He drew her roughly into his arms and kissed her ardently. Kendra responded with a quivering sigh as he molded his body into hers. Then her insides melted as he placed his lips to her ear and whispered, "My silly darling," he said. "I have never been married to *any*one. I want *you*. Only you. I want you

275

to be my wife."

Kendra clung to him, disbelieving. Tears rolled from her eyes as he then began kissing them away. "And all along I thought . . ."

"You thought wrong," he said. "Now I know I should've told you earlier. But I've worried about Aaron."

"And you were wrong about that also?" she said, sniffling. "You and Aaron . . . you will be able to settle things?"

"I'm not sure."

"Then when will you know?"

"Hopefully tomorrow."

Kendra sighed. Tomorrow! She always seemed to be endlessly waiting on tomorrows . . . !

Chapter Sixteen

"Seth, you shouldn't," Kendra argued. "You're not up to it." She gave Emanuelle a sour look, at least glad to know that *she* was leaving. Emanuelle's time with Seth had done nothing for anyone. Not even Emanuelle. Seth was even more determined to get back to the mines than before. He said that he had something to prove. . . .

Seth patted his legs. "Almost as good as new," he said. "I'll get by."

"You didn't feel like going to the dance last night," Kendra scoffed. "How did you so magically improve by this morning?"

"I'm sick to death of being stuck in this house," Seth growled.

"Even with Emanuelle seeing to your every want and need?"

Seth placed his wide-brimmed Stetson hat on his head, avoiding Kendra's reference to Emanuelle. He was anxious to be rid of Emanuelle. She still clung too possessively to him and her desire to acquire the Carpenter name. Once he had her back in Virginia City he would once more try to break ties with her. He didn't need . . . he didn't *want* her. Surely this time she would get the message.

"Let's be on our way, Emanuelle," he said flatly, cupping a hand beneath one of her elbows.

It pained Kendra to see Seth's slow, agonizing movements, and she couldn't help but silently admire Emanuelle's continuing devotion to him as she removed his hand from her elbow and instead placed an arm about his waist and helped him toward the door.

"Darlin', maybe we could stay here at the ranch for one more day," Emanuelle pleaded. Her hair lay in a circle of gold braids atop her head with a few ringlet curls at her brow, and her silk print dress showed her exquisite curves and petiteness. Next to Seth, she looked even smaller.

"Now that you've got a taste of fancy livin', you don't want to let go, do you?" Seth growled, crumpling his thick sandy mustache as he shaped his face into an accusing frown.

"Seth . . ." Emanuelle whined, giving Kendra a quick, innocent glance.

Kendra rested her hands casually on the pistols at her hips, then turned quickly on her heel as Aaron came down the stairs, buttoning his plaid cotton shirt. When he caught sight of Seth standing there, decked out in his regular jeans and work shirt, he was taken aback. He took quicker steps and stopped next to Seth. "Where do you think you're going?" he growled.

"I'm bored, Aaron. I've got to get out of here."

Aaron nervously caressed his bald head, lowering his gaze to inspect Seth's legs. "And this means all feelings have returned? You're strong enough?" he quietly said, trying to hold down his temper at the foolhardiness of this brother of his.

"Aaron, quit makin' over me like I was a baby," Seth grumbled.

"So you're going back to the mines?"

"Yes . . ."

"Seth, if you're going back to the mines just because you're bored, I can take care of that. I need help. There's more fences that need cuttin'."

"I don't like that barbed wire any more than you, Aaron, but you know I didn't come to Nevada with you to work on the ranch. That was *your* idea. Not mine. Now, big brother, I'll do my thing . . . you do yours."

Aaron threw his hands up into the air and stormed away. "I give up," he shouted.

"Come on, Emanuelle," Seth growled. "Let's get out of here."

Kendra rushed to him. "Seth," she said, reaching to place her arms about his neck. She hugged him tightly, feeling afraid for him this time more strongly than ever before. "I wish you weren't so stubborn."

"Listen to who's talking," he chuckled. "We were poured from the same mold, don't you know?"

Kendra kissed his cheek, then patted him there. "Yes. I know," she sighed. She held back the strong need for tears as she squeezed his hand and then watched as he winked at her, tipped his hat, and clung to Emanuelle as he walked from the house.

Wiping a tear from her cheek, Kendra went to the door and watched Emanuelle's buggy pull away. A shiver raced across Kendra's flesh . . . she did not know why. . . .

"So he's gone, I see," Aaron said, moving to Kendra's

side. He placed his hat atop his head and tightened his gunbelt a notch. "And where are *you* going so early in the morning, Kendra?"

Kendra's eyes wavered. "Where?" she murmured. "To see Steven," she quickly added, finding it easy to lie, with Lucas waiting for her. "I promised Steven last night that I'd ride out to see him and his students."

"That's commendable, Kendra. I'm proud. Tell Steven I said a big howdy."

Kendra laughed softly. "Howdy, Aaron? You're sounding more like a cowhand every day."

"If I ever get this barbed wire mess cleared up I could get away from the ranch for a while. I've things to do in Virginia City."

Kendra's smile faded. "Virginia City?" she whispered. "You're speaking of banking affairs, aren't you, Aaron?"

She doubted it. She knew that Aaron too had been counting the days until he could be free to meet face to face with their father. She knew that one day soon they *would* meet. Aaron would not do as she and Seth had done. Aaron would speak his mind. He would reveal to his father just who he was.

But something else kept nagging away at her. She knew that when Aaron went to Virginia City, he might possibly find not only his father, but his wife. The end result of this discovery could be disastrous. But Kendra could not put a stop to it.

"And a few other assorted items on my agenda," Aaron finally answered, thumping the brim of his hat nervously with his forefinger.

"Like seeing Father?"

"Like seeing Father," he stated flatly.

"What do you plan to do, Aaron?"

"Whatever my mind wills me to do at the time. Lord only knows I'd like to give him more than a piece of my mind."

"Yes, I know," Kendra whispered. And she *did* understand. She still had her own day of reckoning with her father to look forward to.

Aaron swung a powerful arm about Kendra's waist and hugged her. "I've got to run, Kendra," he mumbled. "You take care of yourself out there on the range. Those rattlesnakes have been hell lately."

Kendra leaned a soft kiss to his cheek. "See you tonight?" she murmured. "You'll meet with Lucas Hall?"

"Yeah. I'll meet with him," Aaron growled. "But I'm already suspectin' what's on his mind."

"And what's that, Aaron?" Kendra asked, pulling smoothly away from him.

"We've barbed wire fences springin' up at the same time this Luke Hall makes his first grand appearance to the community? Ha! I bet your bottom dollar he's the culprit I'm after. Lord have mercy if he is."

"You're wrong, Aaron," Kendra said softly. She couldn't tell Aaron that she knew that he had been in the Nevada territory way before the Carpenters and had owned his spread much longer than they had theirs. To tell Aaron this would be to reveal too much about her relationship with Lucas.

Yet she had had her own previous misgivings about Lucas, about many things! He was a Reb. And he *had* been shifty, in not revealing full truths to her from the beginning.

But none of these doubts would keep her from going to him this day. Her insides bubbled with delight. He was

281

truly free . . . he had *not* married Heart Speak. And he had even asked her for her hand in marriage!

Then her thoughts grew weary. "Aaron, if Lucas *is* the one, what will you do?" she cautiously asked.

"I will declare war," he growled. "I'll fight him every inch of the way."

Kendra's insides went cold. She leaned another fast kiss onto Aaron's cheek. "But you're wrong about Lucas Hall," she murmured, hoping he wouldn't hear the fearful tremor in her voice. "You'll see. You're wrong."

"You sound awful damn sure of that, Kendra," Aaron said, placing a hand heavily on her shoulder. "When are you going to tell me about your relationship with this man? How did it come about that you already know him?"

"I met him one day while I was riding Domino out on the range," she said, her eyes wide and innocent.

"There are *many* varieties of snakes crawling about out there, I see. Too bad you happened along on *that* one."

Kendra's face colored. "Aaron, I don't understand your attitude," she whispered. "Why *did* you have an instant dislike of Lucas Hall? It's not like you."

Aaron pushed his hat back and scratched idly at his brow. "It's not only him. It's something about his eyes. Damn it. I *know* I've seen their cold gray somewhere before. They penetrated my flesh last night like sometime before in my past." He pulled his hat hard in place, shaking his head. He turned and walked toward the door. "Sure wish I could remember. . . ." he murmured.

Kendra jumped when the door slammed with a bang. She didn't like this sort of moodiness in Aaron. She had witnessed it before, when he had been an officer for the

282

cavalry. This range war that seemed to be brewing. Would Aaron put his all into it . . . as he had done during the only other war he had ever fought in?

"Oh, what if it *is* Lucas?" she whispered. "I will have to choose between the man I love and my own brother!"

This saddened Kendra. During the war, brothers actually had fought each other. Loyalties had run strong on both sides.

"I'd have to be loyal to Aaron," she said aloud, hating the words. "It couldn't be any other way. Sister will not fight brother in this family, no matter how deep my love for Lucas."

She shrugged aimlessly, forcing a laugh. "Just listen to me," she said. "I've already declared war between Carpenter and Hall!"

Securing her hat on her head, Kendra rushed outside and mounted Domino. The day was bright and cheerful, which helped lighten her mood. She rode away from the house, glancing toward the bunkhouse. What a relief Zeke's departure from the ranch had been. Words between Zeke and Aaron hadn't been necessary. After Johnny Lassiter's threats, Zeke hadn't even returned to the ranch.

"And good riddance," Kendra whispered, tossing her hair, enjoying the wind against her face as Domino rode in a steady gallop through the waist-high valley grasses that stretched out in shades of deep green between the two ranches. She had left behind the sagebrush and the wind-sculptured sand dunes. Kendra could feel that she was entering the land of Eden again as the vast, undisturbed land stretched before her.

The mountains rose in purple hues in the far distance, and the deeper Kendra rode into the valley the thicker the pines grew on each side of her. Cooler breezes whispered around her, and a flight of chukar partridge roared up from the brush and winged away across the backdrop of the blue sky. A lone deer broke cover and bounded across Kendra's path. And as she reached another open meadow, the ground became a panorama of color with an assortment of wild, blooming flowers. Indian paintbrush, larkspur, shooting stars, and white and yellow violets intermingled at Domino's feet.

"It's so beautiful here," Kendra whispered. "What a wonderful place to raise children."

Realizing where her thoughts had taken her, Kendra's eyes widened. "Children?" she whispered. She laughed and urged Domino on even faster, until she caught first sight of Lucas's magnificent mansion. All that seemed to be missing was draping moss on towering oaks, which would have made the two-storied columned mansion a house right out of Georgia or South Carolina.

Kendra could so vividly remember Aaron's angry words. "Only a damn Reb would choke the land with barbed wire fence. You find the man responsible and you'll probably find yourself a Johnny Reb."

Lifting her eyes to the sky, Kendra uttered a soft prayer. "Please, God, don't let it be Lucas. . . ."

Loud thuds from hammers drew her eyes back open and her attention to activity at the back of the house as she made a turn on a freshly graveled drive. Corrals were quickly springing up, a barn was being erected, and far from the house a line of bunkhouses was being built. As far as Kendra could see, there was a hubbub of activity. Lucas's ranch was coming alive.

This made what had happened the previous evening even more real and Kendra that much more eager to see

284

Lucas. She would block all her and Aaron's worries about Lucas from her mind. At least for the present. This time with him would be theirs to share and, hopefully, it would not be the last.

Kendra edged Domino between several other horses lined up at the hitching rail in front of the house. When she heard footsteps on the veranda she felt her insides quiver, then let her gaze move slowly to meet Lucas's further approach. She felt a flush rise to her cheeks, and was suddenly a bit uncomfortable under his close scrutiny as he descended the stairs. He was surely expecting much from her today, as she was also desiring much from him. . . .

"I see Aaron didn't stop you from coming," he said, lifting his arms to offer her help from the saddle.

"Surely you know I didn't ask his permission, *or* tell him where I was going."

"I'm sure you didn't. He would have said that it isn't proper to come unescorted to my ranch," he said, lifting his lips into a wry smile.

"And what do you think of me for coming?" she whispered as his firm hands gripped her waist and lifted her down so close to him she could smell the rich aroma of a cigar on his plaid cotton shirt and see the aftershave still glistening on his freshly shaved, sun-bronzed face. "Do you think me a brazen hussy, Lucas?"

"You know better than that, Kendra. And have I made you uncomfortable asking you to come?"

"Nothing could have kept me away, darling," Kendra whispered, drawing in a deep breath as he locked her body against his.

"That's exactly what I wanted to hear you say," he said huskily, tipping her hat back. His lips came down upon hers in a soft sweetness as his fingers traveled over her back. Kendra twined her arms about his neck and locked her fingers together behind his head as his lips worked with hers, opening them, letting his tongue smoothly enter her mouth.

A voice spoke abruptly from behind Kendra. "Now isn't this a sight to behold," the man said.

Kendra's eyes flew open and she pushed at Lucas's chest. When Lucas released his hold on her, Kendra swung around, knowing that her face had to be crimson in color. It was as though she had been caught in a dark, ugly sin. . . .

"Sam, some timing you have, ol' man," Lucas chuckled, draping an arm back about Kendra's waist. He drew her possessively to his side.

"So this is Kendra," Sam said, lifting his gold-framed spectacles from his nose, squinting his eyes as he inspected Kendra more closely. His pale features brightened a bit as he showed his approval. "Yes," he said, smiling. "This must be Kendra."

"And, Kendra, this is Sam," Lucas said, gesturing with his free hand. "I told you about him last night. I'd be lost without his brains."

Kendra looked Sam over. He looked older than her father, pale and thin. He held himself stiffly in his dark business suit. He placed his glasses back on his nose and extended a thin, bony hand in her direction.

"Nice to make your acquaintance, Kendra," Sam said. The wind rifled through his thinning gray hair. "What do you think of what we're putting together here in the valley?"

Kendra let her fingers be circled by his. "It's lovely," she murmured.

"It shouldn't be long now and we'll be able to use the corral," Sam said, shaking, then releasing her hand. "It shouldn't take much longer now to get everything else ready to make the ranch complete."

"Sam, I'm going to show Kendra around inside the house," Lucas said, nodding toward it. "I think you've business overseein' things out here, don't you?"

"Sure thing," Sam said. He half bowed to Kendra. "I'm sure I'll be seeing you again. Soon." He walked stiffly away.

Kendra laughed to herself. It was as though Sam had starch in his underbreeches!

"Shall I escort you inside, ma'am?" Lucas asked, gesturing with his arm, as he showed her a half bow.

"My, my," she giggled. "I'm dressed in jeans but I'm being treated as such a lady."

"You *are* a lady," Lucas laughed. "Jeans don't make you less a lady."

Kendra tossed her head. "Aaron would tend to disagree with you," she said dryly.

"Well, it is a bit unusual for a woman," Lucas chuckled. He cupped her elbow and guided her up the front steps, onto the wide, shaded veranda. "But, honey, if you didn't do the unusual, I'd be disappointed."

"Sam is nice," she said, stepping across the threshold as Lucas opened the heavy oak door that led into the foyer of the house.

"He's quite capable of running my affairs," Lucas said blandly. "That's all that matters to me."

"He's not married?"

"No. I believe he was born with his nose already in books. He's the best bookkeeper in these parts, or, as far as that goes, probably anywhere."

Kendra grew silent as she walked into the parlor. Without the dancing couples crowding the room it showed its spaciousness and full grandeur. There were many gilt-trimmed chairs, and a matching velveteen sofa was graced on each end by an oak table. The Oriental carpet had been rolled up and away the previous evening but now was in place in the center of the floor. White satin drapes hung smoothly and gracefully at the many windows of the room.

"Not a typical ranch house, I know," Lucas said. "As I'm sure yours isn't, since you come from an elite Boston family."

Kendra ran a finger over the smoothness of a table. "I would guess this house is a replica of your family mansion that was destroyed during the war," she murmured.

"Exactly," he said. He gathered her close to him again. "Come. I'll show you a very interesting room . . . one that I think will raise your eyebrows just a mite."

"Hmm," Kendra said. "You've got my curiosity aroused. Lead the way."

They passed through the long hallway, and at the far end Lucas led Kendra into a room bright with morning sunlight. No curtains veiled the long and wide windows to block the full view of a magnificent pocket billiard table with a wrought-iron-trimmed light hanging low over it, from which globed candles stood tall and tapering. Green felt had been stretched tightly over the slate-topped table and billiard balls had been racked colorfully into the shape of a triangle at one end.

"Why, Lucas, you've a gameroom," Kendra said, looking all around her. There was a built-in mahogany bar at one end of the room, and behind it on the wall crystal glasses sparkled on shelves. Plush leather chairs edged the room, a cigar stand beside each, and along the one outside wall a stone fireplace had been built ten feet wide and tall.

"Have you ever played billiards, Kendra?" Lucas asked, already chalking the tip of a cue stick.

"Why, you know that I haven't," she laughed, blushing at the thought. "You only find such recreation where ladies are *not* allowed."

"Then let's take a few moments and hit a few balls around," Lucas said, lifting his lips into a soft smile as he saw her surprise at the suggestion.

He walked to a rack on the wall and tested the weight of one cue stick, then another, nodding as he finally found one that felt well-balanced for her. He went to her, lifted her hat from her head, tossed it on a chair, then fit the cue stick into her hand. "Come on. I'll show you how," he said. He then chose a cue stick for himself.

"Lucas . . . I . . ."

"Just a couple, Kendra."

"You'll have to show me exactly how to do it."

Lucas went to one end of the table and placed a cue ball on the green felt. "First I'll break to scatter the balls, then I'll show you from there what to do," he said. As he shot, balls rolled and spread in all directions. Lucas smiled smugly as a ball rolled into a side pocket.

"Come on, darling," he said, gesturing with his cue stick. "We'll play a game of solids and stripes. I'll be shooting for the stripes, since the ball that rolled into the pocket is striped."

As Kendra moved to his side he bent and aimed again. "Now I'll continue shooting until I miss, then it will be your turn," he said. He took three more successful shots and then he missed.

"And, now, Kendra, it's time for you to try to get some solids into the pockets," he said. He placed his cue stick on a chair and went to her side.

"Lucas, the stick feels so clumsy," she argued. "How on earth do you expect me to do anything with it?"

"Kendra, I haven't seen you *not* be able to do *any*thing," he laughed. He fit her hands on the cue stick. "Now your first concern is the proper grip on the cue stick. Grip it in the right hand. Now place your left on the table like this." He showed her. "You must determine the balance point of the cue stick by laying the cue stick across your fingers and sliding it along your fingers until the weight of the butt end balances the weight of the shaft."

Kendra sighed and did as he guided her.

"Now, Kendra, grip the cue stick lightly with your thumb and first three fingers . . . make sure your head is over the cue stick in the line of aim . . . face the direction of your shot . . . stand back from the table one foot and bend forward at the hips. Grip the cue stick lightly but firmly with your right hand, with your wrist joint loose, and shoot at the cue ball."

"Which am I to aim for?" she asked, lifting an eyebrow quizzically.

"The solid red, number three," he said, leaning, resting his weight against the mahogany edge of the table.

"All right," she murmured. "If you insist." She eyed the ball and shot, and to her surprise the cue ball made contact with the ball she was aiming at and rolled slowly into an end pocket.

Lucas kneaded his chin. "Well, I'll be damned," he grumbled.

"Is that right, Lucas?" Kendra asked, her eyes innocently wide. "What is the object of the game?"

"To make all of your balls before I do and to get the eight ball in a pocket," he said. He once more leaned against the table. "Go on, Kendra, it's still your turn."

Kendra bent forward at the hips again, aimed and watched another ball roll casually into another pocket. She smiled wryly and shot again, then frowned when she missed.

Sighing with relief, afraid she was going to make a fool of him with her very first game, Lucas strolled to the table with his cue stick and began shooting, succeeding ball after ball. A confident smile spread across his face when only the eight ball remained for him to make to be the victor.

He pointed with his cue stick. "Left side pocket," he murmured. "If I get the eight ball in, I've won."

Kendra placed her cue stick on a chair, shoulders heavy. "Well, there's no doubt about the results of *this* game," she said. "No way you're going to miss."

Lucas bent, aimed, and shot. Then his face grew ashen in color as he saw the cue ball bounce off the eight ball and roll into the pocket instead of the eight ball. "Damn," he growled. "Damn! I scratched!"

Kendra went to his side. "Why, Lucas," she said. "The wrong ball went in."

Lucas turned and glared down at her. "No. Really?" he grumbled.

A slow, teasing smile lifted Kendra's lips. "Lucas, does that mean that you lose? Did I win?"

Lucas silently took his cue stick and placed it on the rack on the wall, then likewise Kendra's.

Kendra followed him and stood behind him. "Lucas,

darling," she further teased, climbing his back with her fingers. "Are you a poor loser? You haven't even admitted to losing."

"Would you like to see the rest of the house, Kendra?" he asked, straightening his shoulders as he half looked at her.

Kendra giggled amusedly and placed an arm through his. "What other gamerooms do you have, Lucas?" she whispered. "I liked this one."

"Kendra, will you just quit rubbing it in," he growled as they moved back out into the hallway.

Forming her lips downward into a pretended pout, Kendra sidled more up against him. "I'm sorry, Lucas," she whispered. "And, yes, please do show me the rest of your house."

She was shown the kitchen, an office, a library, and then Lucas began guiding her up the long walnut staircase leading to the second floor. When they reached the second floor landing, Kendra stopped, amazed at what she saw. It looked as though they had stepped into a sunroom—but, in fact, she was only looking at a well-executed painting where lilacs bloomed in the dooryard and aspens quivered at a gate.

"It's beautiful, Lucas," she marveled. "The mural on the wall looks so real."

"I went to an enormous expense to capture sunshine and imprison it in paint on this dark stair-landing," he sighed. "A painter from Europe who now makes his residence in San Francisco was hired to paint this for me." He hugged her tightly to his side. "I'm glad you approve, darling."

Leaning into his embrace, Kendra once more felt herself being caught up in the magic of him. She followed him into a bedroom where a grand four-poster oak bed was the prominent focus of the room. A draped navy blue velveteen canopy shrouded this bed . . . the largest bed that Kendra had ever seen.

Smiling slightly, she turned to meet Lucas's commanding stare, and all else was lost to her as he drew her into his arms and embraced her fiercely, hungrily demanding. His lips devoured hers, his hands searched feverishly over her. Then he whispered into her ear.

"Take off those damn guns," he said. He flicked his tongue across her lips. "Then everything else, Kendra." He kicked the door shut behind them.

"The guns are to protect me," Kendra teased.

"You don't need them while you're with me," Lucas said flatly, already unbuttoning his shirt. "Take them off."

"Yes, sir," Kendra purred. "Whatever you say, sir."

She unbuckled her gunbelt and placed it on a chair, then, with heat rising inside her, matched his movements. They first removed their shirts, then continued on down until they stood nude, admiring each other.

Then Lucas's gaze stopped at her throat. "Where's the squash blossom necklace, Kendra?" he asked thickly.

"I told you," she whispered. "I refuse to wear it until you tell me its meaning."

"That doesn't make any sense," he growled, reaching to lift her hair, then letting it ripple slowly back to her shoulders.

"But that's the way it's to be, Lucas."

"I would tell you now, but from the very beginning I had decided on the proper time to tell you its meaning, and I remain firm on that decision."

"Then I've for sure met my match," she laughed softly.

"Meaning . . . ?"

"You're also as stubborn as a mule."

Lucas laughed and quickly scooped her up into his arms. "Why are we wasting time talking?" he murmured. He began walking toward the bed. Lowering his head, he fit his mouth firmly over one of her nipples and let his teeth work on it until it was firm and erect. His hand circled around and enfolded the other breast, squeezing it gently.

Kendra placed her head against his chest, enjoying the soft cushion of hair against her cheek. She closed her eyes rapturously, already feeling as though she was floating above herself—and their loveplay hadn't really even begun.

The soft warbling from down below in the parlor made her remember the canary she had seen the previous evening. She smiled to herself and turned her lips to kiss Lucas's neck. This man she was in love with had many sides to his character. The one that outshone all else in her eyes was his gentleness. The canary was evidence of it . . . his love for the Indians was evidence of it. . . .

Lucas lowered her to the bed, then knelt down over her. Kendra lifted a hand to his face and traced its outline, becoming consumed with need for him.

"Lucas, you are so handsome," Kendra whispered. Her fingers traveled on down, across his chest, circling one of his nipples, then lower, to where the heat of his sex lay swollen against her thigh. She traced its outline and smiled seductively up at him as she felt his body tremble beneath her feather-light ministerings.

In turn, he kissed her eyelids closed, then the hollow

of her throat, and then worshipped a breast with flicks from his tongue. His hands molded her thighs, then let his fingers splay open and begin a slow descent until a hand lay on either side of the golden-colored, soft crown of hair at the base of her abdomen.

Sighing lethargically, Kendra relaxed her hands at her side. She grew intensely quiet when she felt his tongue leave a warm, sensuous trail across her abdomen and lower. And as his fingers opened her, his tongue softly flicked in and out, torturing her, then he positioned himself fully over her and lowered his sex into her.

Moaning, Kendra opened her legs more widely to his entrance, almost wild from the ecstasy wrapping her in its delicious embrace. She clung . . . she twisted . . . she responded to his eager thrusts.

His breath seared her flesh as his lips moved in a frenzy on her face. She placed her arms about his neck and pulled his chest to hers, crushing her breasts against him. Then her head began to reel as he once more kissed her passionately . . . hotly . . . until the familiar tremor began inside her, threatening to drown her as all feelings exploded inside her into a momentary cessation of time, where only the pleasure took over in place of the rest of reality.

"I love you . . . love you . . ." Lucas groaned as he worked harder inside her. And when he gripped her to him and held her as though in a vise, she waited for his spasms to end, knowing that once more they had shared the ultimate of raptures. . . .

As he lay there panting, she cradled his head against her breasts. She stroked his hair, she kissed his brow. She could never love him more than at this moment. Then when he lifted a hand drunkenly to her face, to gently stroke it, she was jerked back to reality, once more seeing the Indian ring. Had it not matched Heart Speak's there would be no cause for jealousy. But it *did*, and Kendra was at this moment going to find out why he chose to wear such a ring!

Inching from beneath him, Kendra leaned up on an elbow. She watched as he turned to lie on his back, looking contentedly toward her.

"I do love you," he said huskily. "God. I didn't think I could ever love a woman as I do you."

"Then why do you wear a ring that matches Heart Speak's?" Kendra asked, quietly accusing.

Lucas pushed himself up on an elbow, facing her. Then he placed the ring before her eyes. "You're speaking of this ring?" he asked, eyeing the ring fondly.

"I don't see any other ring on your fingers, Lucas," she said dryly. "You know I am making reference to your Indian ring. Heart Speak wears one that matches. Why? I had thought it was because she was your wife. But now I at least know that's not true."

Lucas chuckled amusedly. His gray eyes gleamed.

Kendra rose to a sitting position. She angrily crossed her arms across her chest. "You find the most peculiar times to be amused," she said sourly. "And you choose the most peculiar subjects to be amused about. Why is that, Lucas? I'm deadly serious."

Lucas placed a forefinger to her lips, sealing them. "Shhh," he said. "Just listen. Then you may feel a bit foolish for being so angry about something I would have explained to you that first day we were together, had you asked."

Kendra eased her arm from her chest and waited anxiously for his explanation. She trembled inside as he lowered his finger to trace a circle around a nipple.

"My darling, this ring signifies loyalty to the Piute," he murmured. "Heart Speak's father gave it to me on his deathbed. Strong Bear, Heart Speak's father, was the elderly Indian who saved my life. He's the one who just happened along immediately after I was bitten by that rattler. If not for the speed of his knife, I would be dead now. You see, he cut and sucked the poison from my body. Then he took me to their makeshift house dug into the ground, where Heart Speak and he nursed me back to health."

Guilt for having ever doubted Lucas swept through Kendra. She snuggled down into his arms, and listened further.

"Strong Bear placed his ring on my finger on his deathbed," Lucas continued. "He looked to me as his son. I looked to him as a father."

"But you felt more than sisterly love for Heart Speak," Kendra whispered, tensing.

"Heart Speak came to my bed one night and offered herself to me. She gave me what I didn't search out on the streets of Reno or Virginia City. Her love was clean. Her love was sweet."

Lucas's words were now cutting away at Kendra's heart as though he had taken a knife to it.

"And you?" he continued. "Your love is a mixture of all those things and even more. You're the one I want as my wife. I've never asked another."

The ache in Kendra's heart faded as he kissed her long and sweetly, twining his fingers through her hair. "Will you?" he whispered, drawing gently away from her.

"Lucas, what about . . . what about Quick Deer?" she dared to ask. "Whose . . . ?"

"Who is his father?" he asked, smiling softly toward her.

"Yes."

"Quick Deer's father died when he was a baby," he said, lowering a soft kiss to her lips. "And now that you have so many answers to your questions, darling, how about giving me the answer I am seeking."

"Lucas, please ask the question again," she said, feeling the thunderous beats of her heart.

"Will you be my wife?" he asked huskily, watching her, studying her. . . .

Forgetting Heart Speak . . . Quick Deer . . . Aaron . . . and all other doubts . . . swept away in her desirous love for Lucas, Kendra whispered breathlessly, "Yes . . . yes, Lucas. Oh, yes!"

Enfolding her in his arms, he kissed her again. He traced the silken flesh of her back with trembling fingers and pushed her body gently, fully, into the shape of his, entering her from below. Her hips strained upward, her arms circled his neck. She returned his kiss, surrendering herself wholly to him. With passion, he held her tightly to him, placing his lips to her throat.

The intensity of the moment grew like wildfire, spreading inside Kendra. She clung to him. His each thrust sent her mind into a rapturous whirling.

"Lucas . . ." she whispered. "Can this be real? Am I in a dreamworld?"

"No dream can be so beautiful," he murmured.

He bent his mouth to her breast and kissed it gently, then moved back to her lips and kissed her long and hard as their bodies exploded together into shattering climaxes.

Kendra twined her fingers through his hair as he

continued to lie on top of her, limp and spent. "When, Lucas?" she whispered.

He lifted his gaze to meet hers. "When . . . ?" he whispered, lifting his eyebrows quizzically. "What . . . ?"

"You silly," she giggled, kissing him. "Do you forget so quickly that you've proposed to me? When *are* we to be married?"

Lucas moved gently away from her and rose from the bed. He went to the window and pulled back a heavy navy blue drapery. "Kendra, let's set the date tomorrow," he said thickly, not turning to face her.

Hearing caution in his voice, Kendra crept from the bed and went to stand beside him. She draped an arm about his waist and leaned against him. She placed her face gently against his flesh. "Darling, why can't we set a date now? Right this minute?" she murmured.

Lucas slid an arm about her waist and touched her breast familiarly. "Do you forget that Aaron and I are meeting this evening?" he asked.

"Why should that have anything to do with this?" she whispered, fearing she already knew the answer. She could feel the tension in his body. She could see the uneasiness in his gray eyes as he directed them down at her.

"We'll just wait until tomorrow, darling," he said, lowering a soft kiss to her nose.

Kendra swung away from him and began dressing in angry jerks. Her jaw was set, her eyes flaming. "Always tomorrow," she said. "Why is it always tomorrow with you, Lucas?"

"I hadn't realized that it was," he said, eyeing her questioningly.

"Tomorrow . . ." she grumbled. "Always tomorrow."

With everything else on, she then swung her gunbelt around her waist and fastened it. "One of these days there won't even *be* a tomorrow, Lucas."

A loud crash from outside the window drew Kendra's attention. She leaned closer to the window, looked from it, and down, and grew cold inside when she discovered from where the noise had come. With fury in her eyes she swung around and faced Lucas, her hands pressed tightly to her hips.

"Lucas, how *could* you?" she accused him. "All along it *was* you! Now I understand why you feel it's necessary to wait until after tonight and your meeting with Aaron to make plans for our wedding. You know that Aaron will never agree to my marrying you, if you're even being truthful about wanting to marry me. Has all of this romance been a ploy, to get closer to Aaron?"

She rushed for the door but faced Lucas one more time. "I doubt now a wedding between us can ever be possible!"

With her head hanging and her spirits dragging, Kendra ran from the room, down the stairs, and into the billiard room, where she grabbed her hat. She slammed it down onto her head, tears blurring her vision as she glanced toward the pocket billiard table. While they had been enjoying an innocent game of pocket billiards, Lucas's men had been out on the range challenging Aaron in a much riskier game!

Almost blinded with tears now, Kendra rushed from the house, stopping to look at the many rolls of barbed wire that had been unloaded and dropped from the back of a buckboard wagon.

"Lucas . . ." she whispered. "Oh, why . . . ?"

His voice crying out her name as he ran, half-dressed

from the house only hastened Kendra's escape. She quickly mounted Domino, wheeled him around and urged him quickly away.

"What am I to do now . . . ?" she whispered. Her feelings were battling inside her. She didn't want the barbed wire to make any difference, but she knew that it did. She knew what it meant to Aaron, and she knew that she *had* to be loyal to *him*.

"That damned barbed wire," she cried. "It's not only choking the land, but my love for Lucas . . . !"

Chapter Seventeen

With the setting of the sun, Kendra paced the floor in the parlor, hands clasped tightly behind her. The swoosh of her skirt caught Aaron's attention as he sat drumming his fingers on an armchair while he reviewed the latest figures in his bookkeeping journal. He raised his eyes and watched Kendra. She was like a tigress in a cage, trapped. He knew the reason why. Lucas Hall. If Lucas Hall was a man of his word he would be arriving at the Circle C Ranch at any moment now. He was not a visitor Aaron would welcome with open arms. He didn't trust Lucas Hall. He seemed to be hiding too much behind the gray veil of his eyes.

Aaron ran his hand nervously over his bald head. "Damn those eyes," he pondered to himself. "I *know* I've seen them somewhere. . . ."

Kendra glanced toward the clock on the fireplace mantel, then toward the door. She unclasped her hands and let her fingers work with the severe, coiled bun atop her head. This hairdo matched the severity of her high-throated cotton dress, which matched the severity of the tumultuous feelings clamoring around inside her. She hadn't told Aaron about her discovery of the barbed wire at Lucas's ranch. It had become impossible to say the words. She had just decided to let him find out and settle it in his own way. She would be a silent bystander, observing her world slowly falling apart.

Flipping her skirt angrily, Kendra resumed her pacing. She kept her ears peeled to the outdoors, listening for the approach of a horse. How could she face him again so soon after . . . ?

She shook her head slowly back and forth. "No. I just can't," she worried further to herself. "I just can't."

"Kendra, will you stop that damn pacing," Aaron finally said. He slammed the pages of his journal closed and laid it aside, then rose from the chair.

Kendra turned with a start, flushing. "Oh? Have I disturbed your bookwork, Aaron?"

"Indeed you have."

"Then I'm sorry. . . ."

"He's in your system, isn't he, Kendra?"

Whirling around, Kendra placed her back to him to avoid his eyes. "Who are you talking about, Aaron?" she murmured. She went to the fireplace and picked up a poker and began toying with the logs on the hearth, knowing that wasn't a good enough diversion, since there wasn't even a fire lighted. She replaced the poker and strolled as casually as was possible to the window, to look out of it.

Aaron laughed cynically. "Lucas Hall is due to arrive at any moment now . . . you're pacing like hell . . . and you innocently ask what man I am referring to? Kendra, give me some credit for being smarter than that."

Turning slowly to face him, Kendra cleverly changed

the subject. "I wonder how Seth is doing?" she said softly. "Aaron, he has no business in the mines. His color was poor before the accident. Now he looks like a walking ghost. Why couldn't you have stopped him? He *is* your responsibility. If anything should happen to him . . ."

Aaron removed a cigar from a gilt-trimmed case. He quickly lighted it, flipping the match into the fireplace. He straightened the lines of the jacket of his dark, heavy suit, then answered Kendra.

"Kendra, he's no longer my responsibility when he bullheadedly does as he wishes," he growled. "I lost control of him the minute he set foot on Nevada soil, and you know that."

"But, still . . ." Kendra interjected.

Aaron glowered toward her. "No buts," he said flatly. He fit his hands inside his front breeches pockets, standing as stiff as the cold expression on his face. "If he's old enough to be beddin' up with a lady under our own roof, then he's old enough to do anything else."

"I wouldn't call Emanuelle a lady," Kendra said bitterly. "I'm sure you know what I *would* call her."

"Whatever," Aaron said, shrugging. "That's beside the point." He drew from his cigar, then took it from between his lips, letting smoke billow out in gray, circling clouds. "The point is, I am no longer my brother's keeper." He frowned toward her. "As I am no longer *your* keeper, it seems, Kendra."

Kendra smiled coyly toward him. "I didn't think I would ever hear you admit it," she said softly. "I do appreciate that, Aaron."

Aaron drew her into his arms. "I love you, Kendra," he murmured. "God knows how much I love you and Seth. But I can only do so much. The rest is up to you two."

He then held her gently away from him. "And, hon, you look pretty in that dress. You should always wear a dress. It's only proper."

Kendra threw her head back in a soft laugh. "Aaron, you will never give up on that, will you?" she said.

He chuckled and drew away from her. Then they both grew tense and quiet when a horse's hoofbeats approached and stopped outside the house. Kendra and Aaron exchanged quick glances. Kendra's heart began to thunder inside her. She felt panic rising. She could not face him. She would surely weaken when she saw him.

"Will you excuse me, Aaron?" she murmured. She lifted the skirt of her dress up into her arms and began edging from the room.

"Why, Kendra?" Aaron said with arched eyebrows. "What is this? Don't you wish to see Lucas Hall? Has something happened between the two of you?"

She shook her head slowly from side to side. "No," she said. "Nothing has happened. I just don't wish to see him. It's your business matter. Not mine."

Swallowing hard, she fled from the room and up the stairs, stopping at the second-floor landing. She hid herself in the darkness of the hallway and listened.

Aaron mashed his cigar out and went to the door and opened it, meeting Lucas's approach up the front steps. Aaron extended a stiff hand of welcome. "I see you came," he said dryly. "Come on in. We'll talk in the library."

Lucas nodded his head, clasped Aaron's hand, and released it just as quickly. "Lead the way," he said. He removed his hat and placed it on a coat tree just inside the door, then let his gaze move slowly around him as Aaron led the way down the hallway.

Lucas took a quick look into the parlor, scanning the room with his eyes, feeling the plummeting of his heart when Kendra was nowhere in sight. He was surprised that Aaron had met him at the door in any sort of cordial manner. He had thought Kendra would most surely have rushed back to the ranch and told him all about the barbed wire. But now he doubted that. Aaron was still ready to talk. If he had known that it was he . . . Lucas Hall . . . who had been spreading the barbed wire all across the range . . . then Lucas could have expected to be met by a shotgun aimed at his face.

Aaron stepped aside and bowed stiffly, gesturing with his hand. "My library . . ." he said. "Let's get on with this. I have better things to do with my time than idle it away talking."

"I'm sure you do," Lucas said, making his way into the paneled room. He stood with his back to the unlighted fireplace, watching Aaron pour two glasses of wine into long-stemmed glasses. He then looked toward the hallway, thinking he had heard light footsteps just outside the door. He ached at least to get a glimpse of Kendra. But he now doubted they would ever see each other again on any sort of friendly terms. Especially now . . . after he told Aaron the truth of the matter.

"Thank you," he murmured, accepting the glass of wine. He tipped it to his lips, half watching Aaron as he removed two cigars from a cigar box.

"And a fine cigar," Aaron said, offering one to Lucas.

Lucas placed his wineglass on a table. "Appreciate it," he mumbled. He swirled the end of his cigar around on his lips, wetting it. Then he leaned into a match as Aaron offered this also to him. He stepped back and inhaled deeply, looking toward a chair as Aaron gestured toward it.

Nodding a silent thanks this time, Lucas sat down, crossed his legs, and lifted the wineglass again. Tilting it back and forth between his fingers, he waited for Aaron to settle down into a chair also, and, when he did, leaned forward and said: "I'm sure you're wondering why I've come."

"I'm afraid to take a guess at that," Aaron said, taking a long, slow sip of wine. Then he rested the glass on his knee. "So why not just get to the point?"

"Aaron, I want to bring sheep in," Lucas stated quickly, flatly. "That's what this meeting is all about."

Aaron rose quickly from the chair, feeling as though someone had splashed cold water onto his face. He began a slow trembling inside, so close to the truth now, he almost felt ill to his stomach. He tried to look calm as he placed his glass on the table and his cigar into an ashtray, then swung slowly around and coldly faced Lucas. When he saw Lucas staring unwaveringly back at him with those gray eyes, a slow recognition began to dawn inside Aaron. He had seen those eyes . . . damn it . . . no, not . . . him. . . .

He cleared his throat nervously. "Sheep, did you say?" he said. "So that's what this is all about. Luke . . ."

Lucas interrupted him. "Lucas," he said. "Please call me Lucas."

"Lucas . . ." Aaron said blandly. "Why do you come to me with this declaration? I'm only one man in this community."

"I felt the need to have your approval above all others," Lucas said, uncrossing his legs. He placed his glass on the table and rose to his feet. He inhaled from his cigar, then smashed it out into an ashtray.

"Why *me*?" Aaron grumbled, lifting a heavy eyebrow.

"Your land . . . and mine . . . well, they do run together," Lucas murmured. "I think it important that we work together. I wanted you to approve, though I don't necessarily *need* that approval to do what I want with my own land."

"As long as you do it only on your land," Aaron growled.

"Though much of the land is marked off to be yours and mine, still there is the open range to consider," Lucas said flatly. "I have felt the need to fence some of it off."

Aaron stomped angrily across the room to Lucas and glowered into his face. "So it *was* you," he spat. "What do you mean by using barbed wire? My cattle are used to roaming free. They are used to going to whatever watering hole is the closest. Now they will have to wander much too far to get their fill of water. And sheep destroy the grazing land. They clip the grasses too short. What do you think you're doing by bringing such animals and barbed wire into Nevada?"

"It's something I want to do and I plan to do it whether or not you approve," Lucas said. "There's good profit made selling meat. I'm all for making profit."

"To hell with profit," Aaron shouted. "You will *not* add anymore fence to the horizon. I will see to it they are all torn down. And whatever sheep happen onto my land will be shot. Mark my word. I have warned you."

"Then war is what you want, is it?" Lucas asked. "I had hoped we could settle this peacefully."

Aaron leaned more into Lucas's face and grew even colder inside. "War?" he said quietly. "The war! Damn it! Now I *know* where I've seen you before. Gettysburg!"

Lucas took a step backwards, blanching. "Gettysburg?" he said shallowly. "What . . . about . . . Gettysburg?"

Aaron laughed awkwardly. "Damn it. I'm right," he said. "You're the Reb . . . the officer . . . that I came face to face with after the battle of Gettysburg. We both stared at each other for a brief moment, then we both turned on our horses and fled."

"Was . . . that . . . you . . . ?" Lucas murmured, raking his fingers through his hair.

"Damned right," Aaron said, turning on a heel, away from Lucas. He began pacing, shoulders slouched. "Now I remember it all. So many had already been killed. We ran across each other as we were on the edge of the battlefield, inspecting each of our losses. I guess you refused to shoot me for the same reason I chose to not shoot you. We had already seen enough deaths."

"Yeah," Lucas mumbled. "Exactly."

Aaron swung around. "It was your gray eyes," he said. "They have haunted me since. But when I came face to face with you the other night, everything seemed to go numb inside me and I couldn't remember *where* I had seen those damn, colorless eyes."

"Watch it," Lucas threatened, raising a fist to Aaron.

Aaron smirked. "We showed you, didn't we?" he bragged.

"If you're talking about Gettysburg, we showed *you*," Lucas growled. "Gettysburg was a great Confederate victory."

"Like hell it was."

"Lee was too smart for the Yankees."

"Hell!" Aaron shouted. "Gettysburg broke the back of the Confederacy. Hundreds of thousands of your soldiers were left lying in hospitals sick . . . wounded . . . dying. It was the North's victory!"

"There were as many in number of Yankees wounded," Lucas growled, doubling his fists at his side.

Aaron ignored Lucas's last statement of fact. "There was quite a Yankee victory at Vicksburg also," he laughed. "Grant knocked hell's bells out of Pemberton's wheelhorses!"

Lucas stiffened. He straightened his hair back in place. "We could go on all night comparing notes on the war," he said dryly. "This is now. I ask you. Is it another war you want? Will it be the South against the North one more time? If so, I will show you who is the strongest. I will win. I *do* plan to bring in my sheep. I've already fenced off a portion of the land for them. I plan to fence off even more. You will not stop me."

Aaron's face twisted with rage. "If not for that damned fence many head of my cattle would be alive today," he said. "The cattle could have escaped on to higher ground. No. I cannot approve of such a hellish thing as that fence. It also tears hell out of the hides of horses and cows if they run against it. They're used to open range. They don't know how to watch out for the likes of barbed wire."

"Aaron, if you would just stop and think, you'd know that we could work together on this thing. Sheep do not ruin a range. Instead they are even more delicate grazers than either cattle or horses. I plan to have sheep and cattle at the same time. And if you would not be so bullheaded about the sheep being brought in, I wouldn't have to erect so many fences. That is what it all boils down to. I knew what your reaction would be. This is why I had the need to begin raising the fences. You see, tomorrow I bring in the first load of my sheep."

"Tomorrow? Tomorrow, you say?" Aaron repeated.

"They are already on the train, traveling this way."

Aaron pointed to the door. "Get out of my house," he hissed. "Now. Do you hear?"

"Sorry we couldn't come to some sort of understanding," Lucas said. He rushed out of the room and rescued his hat from the coat tree. Having been certain he had heard light footsteps outside the library door while he and Aaron had been talking, and knowing for certain that it had to have been Kendra, Lucas turned and took a sweeping glance of the hallway as he placed his hat on his head. But there were no signs of Kendra. Maybe he had been wrong.

Aaron stepped from the library. "Lucas, what is the delay?" he asked, taking wide steps in Lucas's direction.

Lucas set his jaw firmly and rushed outside. He stopped to take in a deep breath, gazing unhappily into the sky, feeling as though he had truly fought the Civil War all over again. And he *had* in his mind, while Aaron had been rehashing those unhappy, fruitless days and nights of his life.

"He loved rubbing in the loss of the South," he growled to himself. "Well, this is one battle I cannot let him win."

With determination in his steps, Lucas went on down the steps, glad that Aaron hadn't followed him outside to create anymore disturbances. If Kendra had chosen to stay in her room, so be it. Lucas didn't want to cause her any uncomfortable moments just in case she might be at a window, watching his departure. He didn't wish for her to see him and Aaron get into it. She surely had heard enough as it was!

Lucas untied his horse's reins from the hitching rail,

then tensed when he caught a movement out of the corner of his eye. In the moonlight, had he seen the flash of a skirt at the stable door? The neighing of a horse being disturbed caused him to turn around and eye intently the open door of the stable. With slow, cautious steps, he guided his horse in that direction. Then he jumped as a horse dashed on past him, carrying Kendra away from him.

"Kendra?" he said in a whisper. "What the . . . ?"

The skirt of her dress was riding high above her knees and her hair was half fallen from a bun on top of her head, its loosened strands lifting loosely in the wind.

Kendra held her head high, trying to stifle the sobs rising in her throat. She had so hoped for some type of understanding between Lucas and Aaron. But none had been reached. Now she had to do the inevitable. She had to forget Lucas. It pained her deeply. She felt as though her heart was going to tear from inside her.

She had the need to get away. Far, far away. To think this through. But she already knew what she had to do. She had to be loyal to Aaron. She *had* to. All Carpenters stuck together. This had been an unspoken pact since their father had deserted them. No Carpenter would desert another Carpenter as long as any of them had breath remaining inside him.

With the moonlight as her guide, Kendra rode fast and furiously, knowing that Lucas had seen her. He would surely come after her. Oh, why had she chosen that particular moment to leave the stables? Only a few moments longer and he would have been gone.

A throbbing at her temples . . . the dryness of her throat . . . and the tears burning at her eyes made her dig her knees into Domino's side, wanting to ride faster . . .

313

faster . . . faster. . . .

Lucas quickly mounted his horse and gave chase. He pushed at his hat, causing it to cling more snugly to his head, watching her shadow beneath the golden rays of the moon. What the hell did she think she was doing? Didn't she know the dangers of running away like that in the dark of night? He had to get to her and stop her. Urge her to return to the ranch.

"And maybe I can even get her to listen to me this one more time," he whispered. "Oh, God, how can I go on without her? Why was Aaron so damn stubborn? Why didn't he at least try to understand? As he loves his cows, so shall I love my sheep. . . ."

Lucas felt his heart thumping wildly as he drew closer and closer behind Kendra. He saw her glancing over her shoulder, then he hurried even faster until he drew beside her. "Kendra!" he shouted. "Stop! Where are you going? Stop!"

"Leave me alone," she shouted back. She refused to look his way. She wouldn't be put under his spell again. Beneath the romantic glow of the moonlight she wouldn't be able to look at him without giving him whatever he wished of her. No matter how much she wanted to forget him . . . even hate him . . . she knew that it was impossible. He was inside her . . . He *was* her heart. . . .

Kendra gasped when Lucas grabbed the reins from her hands and drew Domino to a shuddering halt beside his own panting horse. "I said stop, damn it," Lucas growled. He reached and grabbed Kendra from her saddle and onto his lap. He held her tightly against him as she began slapping at him, all the while kicking and flailing her legs.

"Lucas Hall, what do you think you're doing?" she screamed. "Let me go."

"Kendra, settle down," Lucas grumbled. "Why are you doing this? I'm not the devil. I happen to be the man who loves you."

"Lucas, it's impossible," she cried, losing the strength behind her blows. "I heard. I heard it all. I was out in the hallway. It's no use. Let me go. I don't want to ever see you again."

Lucas forced her face around and covered her lips with his, holding her head in place as she continued to try to fight him away from her. Then he felt her slow surrendering and breathed easier when he felt her arms slacken and twine about his neck.

He pulled slowly from her. "That's more like it," he said huskily. "Kendra, you know how much I love you. What are we going to do? I understand your loyalty to your brother."

Kendra hung her head and shook it sadly back and forth. "No. No you don't," she whispered. "And, Lucas, please let me go."

"Is that what you really want?"

"I have no other choice."

"Will you return home?"

"I'm not sure."

"Then I can't let you go until you promise," he said softly. "There's too much meanness going on. I never did find the thieves who stole my horses. They may be wandering about right this minute. Wouldn't they have fun if they found *you*? They would forget horse thieving quite fast."

"Lucas, I needed time to myself," she murmured. "When I'm on Domino, I feel the freest. I can think more

315

clearly. And, please remember, I can take care of myself."

"You seem to have forgotten your pistols," he said, raking his eyes over her and taking in the way she was dressed. "And, darling, you look so beautiful tonight."

Kendra began to squirm again. She was beginning to feel the same sensual attraction for him that always seemed to steal her senses away from her. The warmth was rippling away at her insides. Soon she would be lost, and she couldn't allow it.

"Lucas, let me go," she whispered. "Just let me go."

An approaching horse drew Kendra's head quickly around. She squinted and strained her eyes, then recognized the figure of Aaron silhouetted against the horizon. "Aaron . . ." she gasped. "God, Lucas, it's Aaron."

Lucas lifted Kendra back into her saddle, then leaned a kiss onto her lips. "Always remember, I love you," he confessed, then rode away.

Tears streamed down Kendra's face as she urged Domino around and into a trot toward Aaron. And when he had drawn rein at her side, she gave him a set-featured look and rode on past him with her head held high.

Somehow, she couldn't help but blame Aaron for her misfortune. But she was a Carpenter. She had to keep telling herself that. She was a Carpenter. . . .

Chapter Eighteen

Ripples in his flesh followed along after Emanuelle's sharp fingernails ran down Seth's chest. His heart beat wildly against his ribs and he breathed erratically as her fingers lowered. The bed shook beneath his heavy weight and the aroma of Emanuelle's perfume clung sensuously to her sheer silk chemise.

"Seth, darlin', I have somethin' to tell you," she murmured. She watched him guardedly as she added, "Darlin', did you hear what I said? I have a surprise. Don't you want to hear about it?"

Seth's shoulder muscles corded as he reached for her and stretched her atop him. "I've got to get to work soon," he said thickly. "I don't intend to waste time talking, Emanuelle. You keep using your tricks to keep my interest in seeing you again. I'm afraid to hear about any surprises. Hon, I think you've sprung all of them on me already."

He cupped both her breasts and eased his sex inside her. "Now just shut up. I don't want to hear anything you have to say now except sweet nothings in my ear," he growled.

Emanuelle's hair fell from around her shoulders and tickled Seth's nose. He grabbed a handful and inhaled its sweet fragrance. "Yeah, hon," he whispered. "I no longer even care where you learned your tricks, just as long as I'm the only one you use 'em on now."

Slinking up a bit so that her lips could graze the flesh of Seth's neck, Emanuelle whispered: "Seth, you're the only one," she murmured. "For a little while longer, that is."

Seth framed her face between his hands and studied her hazel eyes. "And what's that supposed to mean?" he grumbled.

"It means that in about six months there will be *three* of us," she giggled. "You'll be sharin' me with a baby, Seth."

Seth let out a loud growl and shoved her roughly from him and rose from the bed in a huff. His blue eyes blazed with hate, changing quickly to contempt. With doubled fists at his side he glared down at her. "I hope I heard wrong," he fumed.

Emanuelle saw his anger and began inching away from him, across the bed. "Seth, don't look at me like that," she cried. "You look as though you could kill me."

"If you're telling me you're carrying my baby I just *might* kill you," he stormed. "Now let me hear you tell me again whose child you're carrying."

"It's . . . *our* . . . child, Seth," Emanuelle murmured. "No lie."

"You can't be sure. . . ."

"Seth, you may have thought I've been unfaithful to you, but I haven't," she whined. "I've told you that. Over and over again."

318

"You're lying!"

"No. I'm not! The child is *yours*."

Seth stepped into his jeans and jerked his shirt on. "So you've finally found a way to claim the Carpenter name and wealth, after all," he shouted. "Well, it won't work. I won't marry you. Do you hear me? I won't."

Emanuelle drew herself up into a ball as she sat up and hugged her legs closely to her chest. Tears sparkled in her eyes. "You have to marry me," she sobbed. "It's your child. You wouldn't do this to your own child."

"Wouldn't I?" Seth laughed. "You'll see." He jerked his boots on.

Emanuelle rose from the bed and went to him and began pounding on his chest. "You bastard," she screamed.

Seth grabbed her wrists and held them tightly. "Correction," he said. "It is *you* who will have to worry about a bastard."

Emanuelle blanched. "You're serious, aren't you, Seth?" she whispered. "You won't claim this child as yours."

"Never!" he growled into her face.

She tilted her chin haughtily. "Then I have no choice but to go to your brother Aaron and tell him about the child," she threatened. "As devoted as he is to family, he will not turn his back on his flesh and blood. He'll make you marry me."

Seth threw his head back into a fit of laughter. "Aaron?" he said. "Make me?" He sobered and leaned his face down into hers. "Aaron can't make me do anything. Seems you've picked the wrong man to give you an easy life, Emanuelle. I will never, no, never marry you."

He shoved her away from him, causing her to trip and fall in a heap on the floor. She began beating her fists against the floorboards, crying hysterically. "I hope you die," she cried. "I hope you die, Seth Carpenter."

"That's another wish you won't get," he laughed. He shoved his hat down onto his head and stormed from the room, slamming the door noisily behind him and rushed on down the stairs.

He cringed as he discovered that her crying could be heard in the hotel lobby and was causing a frenzied stir. But he just ducked his head and hurried outside, feeling a strange emptiness. It seemed to be gnawing at his insides. He couldn't help but envision a child . . . a son . . . *his* son . . . and remember the hatred he had felt for his own father for having deserted *him*.

Was this the same thing?

He stepped out into the thick of activity on the streets of Virginia City. He moved around a pile of horse dung and buzzing flies. He kicked at an empty whiskey bottle. When a voice broke through the sounds of horses' hooves and rattling buggy wheels, he let his gaze follow the voice and tensed when he saw his father waving for him to come to him.

"Young man . . ." Blackie shouted. "May I have a word with you? You seem to avoid me purposely. Might you tell me why? I've been waitin' for that game of blackjack with you."

Seth groaned inwardly, not needing this now. One mishap a day was all he could handle. He still had spells of weakness in his legs and sudden throbbings at his temples.

And seeing his father was a fresh reminder of what Emanuelle had just confessed to him. The word

320

"desertion" kept pounding away inside his brain, making him grab his head and grit his teeth. He was *not* like his father! How could he be deserting a child that wasn't even born yet?

Blindly, Seth began to run, still holding his head, torn between what was right and wrong. And instead of fooling with his own horse, he climbed aboard the buckboard wagon that carried him along with a dozen other men to the Con-Virginia mine. He ignored the exchanged jokes and offers of hand-rolled cigarettes. He stayed at the far end of the buckboard, his legs dangling over the side. And when they reached the mine, he went down into the shaft with pick in hand, just as alone. And, still deeply disturbed, he followed the soft glow of candles from the tin sconces that lined the wall, hanging back from all the rest. He was one thousand feet beneath the earth's surface, where six hundred miles of underground workings of crisscrossed tunnels, inclines, shafts, slopes, drifts, and winzes intertwisted and intertwined in the underground world.

Where he now walked with back bent, the timbers were wrapped in muffling mold. The walls dribbled with a monotonous splash. Above his head, the roof was smothered in monstrous dew-distilling growths. Fungi of uncanny forms clung with moist fingers to distorted posts and depended with sticky, slimy tails from beam and lintel. Up from the oozy, miry flooring, mineral fungi sprung, efflorescent with earthy crystals.

Seth's eyes narrowed and his head lowered, barely breathing, seeing something beneath his feet that no one else had seen as they passed over it.

"God . . ." he whispered. He fell to his knees and began running his fingers desperately over a network of silver strands widening into solid wedges.

The candle's light danced and shone in the silver, hypnotic in its gleam, and Seth rose back to his feet and followed this gleam. It took him around a bend, beneath lower beams, and to where most of the men had been warned to not enter.

Seth tensed when he felt some loose earth crumble slowly onto his head. A low rumbling followed, but Seth moved onward. Seeing a wall of earth yet to be invaded only a few yards ahead of him, Seth stopped and began slowly picking at the silver at his feet. But, not being able to see well enough, he went and got a wall sconce and set it on the floor beside his feet.

Perspiration laced his brow. On this end of the tunnel, air seemed to be more scarce, and there was a faint gaseous aroma. A fine dampness bathed the moist walls in an unearthly, corpselike pallor next to him. Yet he continued to pick and inspect.

"This isn't getting me anywhere," he grumbled. He wiped his brow free of dust and perspiration with his shirt-sleeve, then inched his way on to the end of the tunnel. He moved his gaze slowly around him, tapping his pick here and there, thinking there surely was more silver behind the dreaded wall of fallen rock and debris. Then he placed his pick on the ground and began tossing rocks aside, one by one.

Breathing hard, he stopped for a moment, and once more wiped at his brow, mopping it free of perspiration.

"Maybe I'd better get back with the rest of the men," he whispered. "I'm not making any progress here and this is a bit stupid being alone. Anything can happen."

He bent to pick up his pick. "But in my frame of mind no one would expect me to do anything rational," he said further.

A movement beneath his feet caused Seth's heart to skip a beat. "Rock. Shifting rock," he murmured. "That shouldn't be doing that."

He started to inch away when the earth shuddered and shook violently, causing him to lose his balance. With a loud thud, he fell to the earthen floor. Shaking his head, stunned, he rose slowly back to his feet. Then suddenly the ground beneath him gave way. Grabbing, but not succeeding at reaching anything, Seth let out a loud yell as he found himself falling, caught in a caving mass of splintering wood and rocks. When he finally stopped he found himself buried in the debris. His hands and arms were pinned to his body. Only his head and neck projected above the rock.

He gasped for breath . . . he blinked his eyes free of the dust . . . and he suddenly realized that all was pitch black around him. The candles had been blown out on all sides of him. He was alone. He was trapped. The earth sucked at his feet. The rock weighed heavy against his chest, testing the strength of his lungs as he battled now for each and every breath.

"Help!" he yelled, hearing his own voice echo back at him. "Someone! Anyone! You gotta hear me."

Panic was rising higher inside him. Then he remembered something, filling him with even more dread. "The nightmare . . ." he whispered. "This is what happened in my nightmare."

He tried to wiggle his toes. Nothing. He tried to move his fingers. Nothing. He tried to turn his head. Nothing. The only thing that was moving on him were the steady streams of tears rolling down his cheeks.

"Surely I can't die like this," he cried. "Maybe it's

even the nightmare again. Maybe I'll wake up as I always have before."

"Emanuelle!" he screamed. "Wake me up, Emanuelle! I'll marry you! I promise. Just wake me up. God, Emanuelle, wake me up. I don't want to die!"

His eyes widened and he gasped as he felt the rock shifting around him, sinking him a bit further. A part of his chin was now hidden. It was even hard for him to yell again, but yell he did, over and over again. He took long breaths and tried again. And when he heard voices and saw a light flickering toward him, tears flooded his face.

"I see your light!" he cried joyfully. "I'm glad you're coming for me."

He laughed insanely, then grew quiet when the walls around him began cracking, settling, and sliding. Flakes of earth kept falling on his head. And when the men saw the danger that they too could be buried alive, no one would venture within twenty feet of him.

"Come on . . ." Seth pleaded, eyes wide. "What the hell you waitin' on? Start digging me out!"

One man crept closer. He was only a silhouette in the dark to Seth. Seth didn't even recognize the voice when the man began to speak.

"Is that you, Seth?"

"Yes. It's me. Thanks for coming," Seth cried. "Come on." He laughed. "I'm waiting on you. You see, I'm not going anywhere."

"We can't, Seth," the man said. "We'd all go with you. None of us would make it."

"You can't leave me here to die," Seth cried.

"We'll try to think of something."

Seth tried desperately to move when he saw the man retreat, to stand with the rest. He licked his lips, he blinked his eyes, thankful at least that he still had the freedom to do that. Then once more he found himself sinking, and he knew that if the men didn't work fast, he was a goner.

"Good Lord," he yelled. "What are you waiting for? If I was there and you were here, I'd not let you die."

"Seth, it's impossible," one man yelled back at him. "What the hell were you doing this far from the rest of us anyhow?"

Seth laughed awkwardly. "Questions?" he shouted. "At a time like this? Get your shovels over here. Start digging."

This time no one answered. A cold touch of death seemed to dance across Seth's face. He sobbed. He choked.

"Dennis?" he cried.

"Clint?" he cried. "Surely you'll help me."

"Dave?"

"Lloyd?"

"Tom?"

He closed his eyes and swallowed hard. They were all ignoring him. None wanted to risk his own life to save his. He had to wonder what he might have done to cause their indifference toward him. He had always exchanged jokes and cut up with them. Only today had he ignored them. But he had had too much on his mind.

"My child?" he whimpered. "Lord. I was ready to turn my back on my own child. Now I know that I was wrong."

"Daddy?" he cried. "Oh, Daddy, where are you? I'll talk to you now. I'm sorry I ran away when you called out to me a little while ago."

Seth's mind swirled. He was now remembering all

things pleasant in his life, making him smile drunkenly.

"Kendra," he whispered. "Sweet Kendra. Will you miss me?"

"Oh, Aaron," he howled aloud. "Why? Why?"

"Seth?" a voice yelled, bringing him back to the present.

His good humor was still intact. "Still here," he laughed nervously. "And you?"

"We're going to saturate a ball of oakum with coal oil and roll it toward you to give us light to work by."

Hope swelled inside Seth. Tears of joy rushed from his eyes. "Anything," he said. "Anything you want to do is fine with me."

His eyes blinked wildly when the bright flare of fire rolled toward him. He choked and gagged from the strong stench of the coal oil.

"Dave's gone for a rope," Clint shouted.

Seth's mouth dropped open. "A . . . rope . . . ?" he gasped. "What good is a rope? If you try placing it around my head it'll be the same as hanging me from it. One jerk and I'm gone. That's dumb as hell, Dave."

"Clint," Clint shouted. "It's me. Clint. Not Dave, Seth."

"Well, Clint, I'll tell *you*," Seth shouted back. "A rope is dumb as hell. A shovel. Bring a shovel!"

"It's the only way, Seth."

"Okay. Okay," Seth shouted desperately. "I've been known for being bullheaded. Maybe my head will be hard enough to pull me through this one."

"Seen a mighty purty singin' lady enter town this morning on the stagecoach," Lloyd shouted. "She's gonna be singin' at the Silver Spur Saloon. Seth, she had the larges' knockers I ever did see. When we get you outta there we'll go and take a grab."

"Shame on you, Lloyd," Seth said. "What about the sweet thing waitin' back home for you?"

"It's been too long, Seth," Lloyd said, then laughed awkwardly. "Anyways, we'll both go and at least see her. What do you say, Seth?"

"Yeah . . ." Seth chuckled. Then he said, "No. Can't do that, Lloyd."

"Why not?"

"Because there's a weddin' in my future."

Several voices rang out in unison. "Wedding? You, Seth?"

Then Tom laughed. "So you're gettin' hitched to Emanuelle, are you?"

Seth was finding it harder to breathe. His chest ached from the pressure closing in on him. But he knew that the only thing keeping him sane now was the talking.

"She's a beauty, ain't she, Tom?" Seth said, raspy.

"Tiny little thing. A southern lady, I'd say," Tom said solemnly back.

Seth knew that Tom was just humoring him. He knew what most of them thought of Emanuelle. Though she was pretty, her reputation had been tarnished way before he had come along. But he would marry her, for the baby's sake. He had decided he'd make one damn good father. And he'd never enter another mine once he was set free from this one. He could visualize a house out on the range surrounded by a white picket fence. Emanuelle would grow flowers. Their son Mikey would have a swing . . . a dog . . .

"Seth, you still there?" Lloyd shouted.

"Now ain't that a damn question?" Seth growled.

"You joked about it last time you were asked," Lloyd

said. "Just thought I'd give you another reason to joke."

"My joke's are runnin' out," Seth said quietly. "As is my life, I'm afraid."

"A man like you don't give up, Seth!"

"A man like me dies just the same as any other man," he grumbled. He licked his parched lips. "Where's the damn rope? I'd like to get outta here before Christmas."

"How's Kendra, Seth?"

"Kendra . . . ?" Seth said softly.

"Hear tell she sports six-shooters on her hips."

Seth knew the questions were to keep him alert. That wasn't helping much, though. He was finding it harder and harder to do. Things were growing fuzzy in his head. Even the fire meant to lead the men to his rescue was a haze. But he blinked his eyes and kept his courage.

"Kendra's one damn sister," he finally replied. "You'll never find another one like her anywhere."

"Hey, Seth!" Lloyd shouted. "Hear a shipment of sheep rolled into Reno before daybreak. Know who's bringin' them in?"

"Aaron and me don't talk much about ranch business," he said, panting. Perspiration trickled down from his brow and glistened like diamonds on the tips of his mustache. "But now I plan to do nothin' *but* ranchin' once you fellas get me out of this mess."

"Play blackjack, Seth?" Lloyd shouted.

Seth closed his eyes and he felt an ache circle his heart. He knew that when there was a mention of blackjack in Virginia City, Blackie's name always came up. He didn't want to talk about his father. He didn't want to let his thoughts wander again. . . .

"Seth? I asked if you've ever played blackjack," Lloyd persisted.

"Yeah."

"Pretty good at it?"

"No."

"Well, I've got to brag a bit," Lloyd laughed. "I beat this big shot callin' himself Blackie the other night. I beat him at his own game of blackjack. How's that for a laugh?"

"Funny as hell," Seth groaned.

"When you get outta there, I'll challenge you to a game," Lloyd persisted. "Better yet, we'll go and both beat the hell outta Blackie at the same time. How's *that* sound?"

"I'm thirsty . . ." Seth groaned. "Someone. I'm thirsty. . . ."

No one replied. Everything went stone silent.

"Can't someone bring me a drink of water?" Seth cried.

His head began spinning. He was suddenly beginning to feel drunk. He laughed crazily. Then he began crying. Then he laughed again. His whole body was numb. It even seemed that his heart was beginning to slow a bit. . . .

"No!" he cried. "I don't want to die."

"You're not going to die," Lloyd yelled. "Stay awake, Seth. Somehow we'll get you out."

"How can you if you just stand there doin' nothing?" Seth screamed.

The sound of scurrying feet made Seth's heart beat faster. "Clint?" he shouted. "Is that you? You got that rope?"

"It's here," Clint shouted back. "Now I'm going to get as close as I can and throw it around your head. Then we'll all pull."

"It isn't going to work," Seth argued. "A shovel. Get a goddamn shovel."

"All right, Seth," Clint said. "I will."

Seth's eyes widened. He had finally found a man brave enough to risk his life for him. Tears rolled from his eyes again. "Thank God," he whispered.

Rock crumbled beneath Clint's body as he crawled on his stomach toward Seth. "I shouldn't have waited," he grumbled. "I should've done this from the first. Knew all along no rope would do it."

"Then why did you waste time going for it, Clint?" Seth growled.

"Time, Seth," Clint said dryly. "I thought maybe we'd come up with somethin' more substantial. Guess I was wrong."

"Thanks for offering to dig me out, Clint."

"No offer. I'm doin' it."

Seth watched with a racing pulse as Clint rose slowly to his feet and began shoveling one shovelful at a time away from Seth.

"It'll take all night doin' it that way," Seth cried. He looked beyond Clint. "What are you guys? A bunch of chicken Rebs? I bet most of you fought for the South, didn't you? Or you'd be brave enough to get in here and help Clint try and save my life."

"That ain't fair, Seth," Lloyd argued.

Clint continued shoveling. The walls groaned. Rock fell. Then pebbles and rocks began to fall more steadily. Seth began choking and coughing. The level of debris was building, now to his lower lip.

"Be quick, Clint," Seth muttered in a muffled voice. "I'm smothering."

"Lloyd! Dennis! Help me!" Clint yelled, desperation

330

sharp in his voice.

Feet rushing forward gave Seth reason to hope again. His lips were now covered. He couldn't speak a thanks. But it appeared all was useless. As the men scraped rock, more fell.

"It's all gonna come in on us," Tom shouted. "I'm gettin' the hell out."

Seth slowly closed his eyes. He could feel his life ebbing away. He sobbed to himself, hating this helplessness, knowing these were the last moments of his life. He focused his thoughts on his mother. Then, strangely enough, she seemed to be there. She was standing in a bright ray of light. Her gown of pale blue satin was billowing around her . . . her hair of golden silk was long and flowing. He wanted to speak her name but couldn't. But he could feel a part of him reaching out to her, and she responded with outstretched arms to him, beckoning him to enter the light, to follow along after her. . . .

"I'm coming, Mother," he thought hazily to himself. "I knew you'd be there waiting for me."

A loud roar and rumbling filled his brain as a great mass of clay, rock, and timbers gave way above him. . . .

Chapter Nineteen

As another fence fell clumsily to the ground, Kendra flinched. She sat slouched in the saddle watching Aaron's cowhands rope more posts and snip more wire. She had even planned to assist, to openly prove her loyalty to Aaron. But she hadn't been able to lift that first finger against Lucas.

"Oh, why does Lucas have to be so stubborn?" she whispered. She doubled a fist at her side. "Why does he insist on bringing sheep to Nevada?"

Then she had to remember Aaron's stubbornness. Had he agreed to first give Lucas's sheep a try, then no fences would have become necessary.

"But Lucas knew from the beginning what Aaron's answer would be," she further thought. "That's why he went ahead and began placing the fences on the land before his meeting with Aaron."

She flung her hair back across her shoulders and straightened her back. "Those darn sheep," she grumbled aloud. "Darn Lucas."

Wheeling her horse around, Kendra sent Domino into

a gallop away from the ugly scene of man battling barbed wire. Beyond that, the world was the epitome of peace and calmness. The only movement was the stirring of the range grasses in the breeze of the early morning, and, high above, silhouetted against the turquoise sky, Kendra could see an eagle, soaring silently, its white tail feathers spread out like a fan.

Kendra rode on past some stunted piñon pines and clumps of junipers, then realized where she was unconsciously leading Domino. To the Piute Indian village. She knew that she shouldn't, but her needs drove her further on, and when the sun was directly overhead she rode quietly into the village of silent adobe houses.

Barely breathing now, Kendra leaned over to pat Domino's neck, letting her eyes explore slowly around her. In the doorways of some houses she could see Indians sitting with arms crossed and heads bowed. They all seemed to be asleep, and Kendra's eyes brightened with her slow smile, realizing they most surely were taking a noon siesta.

Horses neighed and pranced in the corrals at the far end of the village and mules brayed and tossed their tails lazily.

"Why did I come here?" Kendra whispered. With a pounding heart, she searched for signs of Lucas, knowing the answer lay with him. But neither he nor his horse was anywhere to be seen. Then she remembered. He was receiving his first shipment of sheep today. That was where he was. Seeing to his own personal needs. Not the Indians'.

"Ma'am Kendra?"

Kendra drew her reins tightly, having heard the small

voice behind her. She wheeled Domino around. "Why, Quick Deer," she said. "How are you?" She eyed the makeshift crutch beneath his left arm.

"My leg is almost well," he said. He looked up at Kendra with curious, dark eyes set into his small, square, copper face. He wore only deerskin breeches, trimmed with fringe. "Why you come, Ma'am Kendra?"

Kendra's heart warmed. He trusted her now. It was good, feeling this trust. "Why, Quick Deer, I've come to see *you*," she said, knowing there wasn't any need to tell anyone the true reason why she had come. In a way, she was glad that Lucas wasn't there. What would she have said to him, had he been? Nothing had changed. And the war had just begun between Aaron and Lucas.

"Ma'am Kendra, to teach?" Quick Deer said, hobbling toward her. "You did promise to come and teach."

Pushing her hat back, Kendra frowned. How could she tell Quick Deer that that plan had been altered by circumstances? He would once again mistrust her. And she couldn't risk that. But she didn't have any books. How could she teach him anything today? Then she remembered the sandy floors of the houses! She could use a stick and make impressions in the sand!

"Yes. I've come to teach," she said, dismounting.

"You have come here uninvited by my people," Heart Speak said suddenly from behind Kendra.

Kendra whirled around and dropped her horse's reins. She faced Heart Speak with a pounding heart. "Heart Speak," she said, laughing awkwardly. "You startled me."

Heart Speak's dark eyes were cold, filled with mistrust and hate. She pointed toward the far end of the village. "Go. You are not wanted here," she said.

Quick Deer moved between Heart Speak and Kendra He raised his face to his mother. "Me want her here," he said stubbornly. "She teach me read and write. She must stay."

Heart Speak's expression remained cold and untouched. "She will go," she argued. "Heart Speak says who stays and goes. She goes."

"Lucas wants her stay," Quick Deer argued back.

Heart Speak's eyes wavered, then she clasped her hands onto Quick Deer's shoulders. "You are disobedient, my son," she murmured. "You go to house. You stay there the rest of the day. For being disobedient to your mother, you cannot play with your friends."

Feeling responsible, Kendra reached a hand toward Quick Deer, then reconsidered when Heart Speak lifted her gaze and challenged Kendra's intentions.

"Yes, ma'am," Quick Deer whispered. He hung his head and began walking away, stopping only momentarily to give Kendra a quick, backwards, hurtful glance.

Kendra placed her hands on her hips, anger flashing in her eyes. "You're not being fair to Quick Deer," she said dryly.

"You know you not come here for Quick Deer," Heart Speak said bitterly. "You come for Lucas Hall." She tossed her head and tilted her chin. "He is not here. You have traveled this far for nothing. Now go. You have your place. We Piute have ours."

"You're unreasonable," Kendra said, whipping herself angrily up into the saddle. "You will lose respect from Quick Deer. You'll see."

Kendra wheeled Domino around and was glad when the village was only a dot on the horizon, quickly left behind her. She was being drawn in a different direction now, one that was not familiar to her. She suddenly wanted to see these sheep that were the cause of friction wherever they happened to show up. She would see firsthand the animals that Aaron had taken such a disliking to.

"Surely Lucas won't mind if I take a peek," she whispered. "I'll stay out of sight. No one will even know I'm there."

Traveling over foothills, through deep canyon gorges, and then back out on the open range again, Kendra ran across two prospectors, walking their loaded burros along a dust-infested trail. They both were sun-blackened. One had a bristle of gray beard and wisp of a hand-rolled cigarette stuck in the corner of his mouth. The other had a tobacco-chewing stained mouth and face so scarred by the sun and wind that his wrinkles were like tiny black ravines on his face. Both tipped scraggly hats to Kendra as she rode on past them.

Then she came to a barbed wire fence, one Aaron had not yet come across. She stopped Domino, now seeing for sure a reason to hate such a thing. It was an obstacle to her further ventures. She looked from side to side. The fence was strung out on either side as far as the eye could see. There were no visible openings anywhere.

"I can now see Aaron's point to the argument," she whispered. "Well, the fence will not stop *me*."

She jerked her hat more securely onto her head, then began inching her way along the fence, checking the sharp points sticking threateningly out in all directions. If she didn't completely scale the fence, Domino's beautiful hide would be scarred for life.

"As *I* might even be," she worried.

Patting Domino's neck, Kendra rode away from the fence, then turned Domino to face it. She noticed his nervous pawing of the ground, as though he knew the challenge ahead. He jerked his head and snorted, then at Kendra's command, rushed toward the fence. Kendra fit her feet snugly into the stirrups and her knees into Domino's side, bent over, and held onto the reins with all her might, then felt herself being lifted into the air, still snugly in the saddle. She enjoyed the jerk to her body as Domino's hooves made contact with the ground on the other side of the fence.

Sighing with relief, Kendra hugged Domino's neck. "See? I knew you could do it," she said proudly. "I can always depend on you."

Smiling smugly, Kendra went on her way. The grass was thicker and greener, and a trickling stream broke the monotony with its sparkle and splash. Kendra led Domino to the water's edge and let him inch his front feet into it. As he bent to drink his fill, she dismounted and removed her hat to fan herself.

Squinting her eyes against the bright rays of the sun, Kendra let them slowly scan the land around her. A stirring in the distance, on the horizon, drew a quick breath from her. She took a step forward and cupped a hand over her eyes and looked more intently. It was a lone man, walking with a wooden staff in one hand, and every once in a while Kendra caught sight of a dog . . . a collie . . . leaping over the tall grass beside the man. Then she gasped more loudly when she saw her first sheep moving over a rise.

"Why, there must be at least a thousand," she whispered. "And who is that man? It most certainly isn't Lucas."

338

She quickly bent to her knees beside the water and splashed some onto her face. She licked her lips, shook her hair back, and replaced her hat. "There's only one way to find out who that is," she said. "I'll ride and meet the man."

Swinging herself up into the saddle, Kendra forged onward. The closer she drew to the slowly moving sheep, the more distinct their bleating became. The barking of the dog reverberated through the air continuously and Kendra could now see it and how it kept moving on all sides of the herd, as though it was the one in charge.

Kendra drew her reins tightly and felt her heart skip a beat when a lone horseman suddenly appeared over the rise from where the sheep had just come. The way he sat in the saddle . . . so tall and proud . . . made Kendra quite aware of who it was.

"Lucas . . ." she whispered. She was torn. A part of her told her to retreat and a part of her told her to go to him.

Her heart urged her forward. There was no denying this need that always led her to him. And she was slowly coming to the realization that her need for Lucas would win over her loyalties to Aaron. Not Aaron or any other Carpenter could give her what Lucas could. Her insides melted into sensual tremors just thinking about what his lips and hands could do to her. There was no denying that where Lucas was concerned she had already relinquished the freedom that she had so determinedly fought for. When she was with him, in thought or in actuality, freedom was the last thing on her mind. She now knew that she wanted to be his . . . wholly his. . . .

As Lucas grew closer, Kendra's heart pumped more wildly. Though his sombrero shadowed his face, she could see the chiseled features, the set of his jaw, and the command of his eyes as he caught sight of her.

His revolvers glistened on his hips beneath the glare of the sun . . . the leather chaps on his legs flapped in the breeze . . . and he bounced smoothly in the saddle . . . until he drew rein next to Kendra. His horse remained skittish beneath him as he eyed her.

"What are you doing way out here all alone?" he growled. "Kendra, don't you ever listen to anybody?"

"Don't grumble at me about anything," she said dryly. "I see you've got your sheep." She tossed her hand into the air. "You've even more barbed wire strung than Aaron will *ever* be able to find and destroy."

"That's the idea. . . ." Lucas said flatly. He wiped his brow free of dust and perspiration with the back of his hand.

Kendra tilted her chin haughtily. "Well, Lucas Hall," she bragged. "You see that your fence didn't hold *me* back."

"And I'm supposed to be annoyed at that?" he chuckled.

"Well? Are you?" Kendra challenged. "I *am* trespassing."

"How can that be?" he said huskily. "You're on land that's already been offered to you by me. Once we're wed, it will also be yours."

Kendra's gaze moved on past him. "And also the sheep?" she said with a cautious air.

Lucas's face drew worry wrinkles into it. "Yes," he said softly. "Also the sheep."

"And by that you mean I will even have the power to say what should be done with them?"

Lucas wheeled his horse around and faced the sheep.

"Damn it, Kendra, quit playing word games," he growled. "You know damn well I will have full charge of all herds, be they sheep, cattle, or horses. I would expect that once we were married you would choose to truly behave like a lady and leave the man's work to me."

Kendra glared at him. "You have a tendency to contradict yourself, Lucas," she hissed. "First I'm a lady and then I'm not. Which *is* it, Lucas? You've never objected to how I've chosen to behave before. Why would you now, or when or *if* we get married?"

"I wouldn't want you to marry me just because you think it will give you the power to help Aaron in some way," he argued, now facing her.

Kendra threw her head back in an exasperated sigh. "Good Lord. Would you think me capable of doing something like that?"

"Kendra, you must admit that you thought I was using you to get to Aaron, didn't you?"

A slow flush rose to Kendra's cheeks. "Well, yes," she murmured.

"Then I would say we're even on *that* particular score, wouldn't you?" he said. "Let's call a truce, hon. Now that you're here, let me show you the beauty of sheep."

"If Aaron knew I was here . . ."

"He won't, Kendra."

"I feel so guilty. . . ."

"Don't."

Lucas nodded toward the grazing sheep. "The sheep," he said. "Come. Let me introduce you to Alfredo."

"The sheepherder?" she murmured. "Lucas, you don't waste time. You were supposed to have brought the sheep in only this morning."

"Yes, and now the sheep are acquainting themselves

341

with my land."

"And the sheepherder?"

"Alfredo is a Basque," Lucas said, flicking his reins, urging his horse into a soft trot. Kendra joined him at his side. "I sent for him some time ago. He's from Spain. All Basques are reliable. They're very proud of their heritage as sheepherders. I know that this man will stay with my sheep no matter what might happen."

Kendra gave Lucas an angry look. "Lucas, you've known for a long time you were going to do this," she murmured. "Why did you wait so long before bringing the issue of sheep up to Aaron?"

"Do you really have to ask such a question?" he asked. "Didn't you see Aaron's immediate reaction?"

"Then why did you confront him at all about it if you already knew what his answer would be?"

"Because of you," he said thickly. "I had hoped . . ."

Kendra lowered her eyes. "I had also . . ."

"But he didn't," Lucas said tightly. "And we must now make the best of the situation."

"I won't be able to do this again, Lucas," Kendra murmured. "Come to see you. It isn't fair to Aaron."

"What's fair?" Lucas commented dryly, tossing his head. "Don't you realize that you're not being fair to yourself by refusing to accept the truth that you and I were meant for each other, no matter what that damn brother of yours wants to do with his life? Do you want to throw away the happiness we have found? Kendra, it doesn't make any sense whatsoever for you to refuse to see me."

"Lucas, I should even be ripping down those darn fences," she said, gesturing toward the line of fence that ran along the one side of them. "I can*not* agree to such an ugly thing. This is why my loyalty to Aaron must stay firm. How can you think that fencing in the land is right? How?"

"I would remove the fences myself if Aaron would not be so stubborn and would accept the sheep on the range," he said. "Once he realizes that my sheep are not destroying anything, then maybe we can come to some sort of compromise."

"Until then, I shouldn't see you," she said softly. "You must understand, Lucas. I hardly have any other choice in the matter. You and Aaron have in a sense really declared war on each other."

"A war I will in the end win," he said stubbornly. "The fences stay until Aaron backs down and says he is wrong."

Kendra set her jaw firmly. "Why must you be so stubborn?" she hissed.

Lucas chuckled. "Because, my darling, that's just the way I am, and you know that you love me for it."

Kendra nudged her knees into Domino's side and moved on ahead of Lucas, wishing the pounding of her heart would slow a bit. It was at times like this that she loved *and* hated him! He had such a way of confusing the issues! And, yes, she did admire his stubborn streak. He wouldn't be the man she knew him to be if he handled this situation in any other way. He believed in what he was doing. And he was standing behind this belief all the way!

Now so close to the sheep she could see their lazy, dark eyes, Kendra drew Domino to a halt and studied the bundles of fur. As they continued to graze so peacefully, several slowly lifted their heads and looked at her, studying her back. And it was then that Kendra felt a slow liking for these peaceful-looking animals. Their chewing was lazy, their eyes friendly and their fur beautiful!

"So? What do you think?" Lucas asked softly, drawing rein alongside her.

"What am I supposed to think?" she said dryly. "They're sheep. Nothing else. Most people hate sheep, you know."

The sheepherder made his way to Lucas and stopped next to Lucas's horse. He was attired in a crude garb and cap and clasping onto his walking stick. He was of medium height, with a prominent nose and a narrow, craggy face. His complexion was dark and his eyes were warm and friendly.

Lucas leaned down and patted Alfredo on the back. "Alfredo, I'd like for you to meet the future Mrs. Hall," he said, smiling toward Kendra. "And, Kendra, this is Alfredo."

Kendra cast Lucas a doubtful glance, not allowing herself to think of marriage at this time and wondering how he could. Then her attention focused back on Alfredo. She leaned forward and offered him a hand.

"I'm very pleased to meet you, sir," she murmured.

His hand was rough and dry and his grip hard as steel. Kendra laughed inside when he shook her hand vigorously, then dropped his back to his side.

"I likes American peoples," Alfredo said with a heavy foreign accent. "I think I will likes the solitudes of the American West." He nodded toward Kendra, but looked at Lucas. "You have yourself a beautiful womans here," he said. "You lucky man."

Kendra and Lucas exchanged smiles, then Lucas patted Alfredo once more on the back and said, "I'll have to agree with you there. And I'm sure you'll be happy with Nevada."

The collie came loping toward Alfredo and looked admiringly up at him. "Good dog," Alfredo said. He once more looked up at Lucas. "You chooses fine dog. We are already friends. We'll take care of things for you. Don't you worry about a thing."

Lucas tipped his hat to Alfredo. "I wouldn't have hired you had I had any misgivings," he said. "I must be on my way for now. I'll be checking back again. Don't *you* worry about a thing."

"Alfredo doesn't worry," Alfredo laughed good-naturedly. "I've got me some sheep and a beautiful dog. I'm happy."

"Good," Lucas laughed. He wheeled his horse around and rode alongside Kendra. "I'm going to ride with you for a while. At least until you get near your own spread."

"That's not necessary, Lucas."

"Are you saying that you don't want to be with me?"

"I didn't say that, did I?" she challenged him with flashing eyes.

"Well, then, just come along," he said. "Maybe we can even find a place to rest and water our horses before having to say goodbye."

"Yes, I'd like that," Kendra said. She pushed her hat more firmly onto her head and held her back straight as she began traveling beside Lucas. It gave her a secure feeling. She wished her future could be filled with many times like this. She felt more alive when she was with him. She indeed felt more content. It was easy to push all worries from her mind when he was at her side. She would enjoy it now. She would savor each and every minute of it!

They soon left the grazing land behind and entered a canyon. And though it was afternoon, bright with sunshine, the trail they were now following through a break in a cliff lay in deep darkness. Kendra welcomed the swirling, cooler air around her that was touching her face and moving down the front of her half-buttoned shirt. She closed her eyes and inhaled the fragrance of fresh dampness and knew that a stream wasn't far ahead somewhere past the boulders and wild rock.

Then, much too soon, Kendra found herself once more being engulfed by blazing heat as they began moving out into open spaces. The heat seemed even to be intensified by the fiery red rocks and cliffs on each side of them.

A sparkling on the horizon ahead and a thick stand of willows and pines caused the hair to rise at the nape of Kendra's neck. She had been there before! Zeke had also been there. Had it not been for Johnny Lassiter . . .

Lucas cupped a hand over his eyes. "Ah hah!" he exclaimed. "I see water ahead. And a place to rest our weary bones. Those trees are a blessing from the Lord."

Kendra smiled awkwardly. For some reason, she felt that it might not be safe at that particular watering hole. What if Zeke . . . !

But, no. He most surely had traveled hundreds of miles in a different direction. Had he not, though, he would remember his humiliation of that day and possibly return to try again.

"I'm being foolish," she thought to herself. "This range is so large. And he wouldn't dare return."

Lucas lifted his sombrero from his head and scratched aimlessly at his brow. "Kendra, is something wrong?" he questioned. "Suddenly you seem troubled."

Forcing a laugh, she cast him a quick glance. "It's

nothing," she murmured. "Truly. It's nothing."

Silence accompanied them until they reached the stream. The clear blue water blended with the blue sky overhead, making it almost impossible to see where one stopped and the other started. Then a fluffy white cloud blew across the horizon and set the two apart.

"It's a beautiful place, isn't it?" Lucas asked, dismounting. His gray eyes looked intensely toward her. "The water looks good enough to jump right into, wouldn't you say?"

Kendra couldn't knock her feeling of dread and apprehension. "Lucas, why not just hurry up and water our horses and be on our way?" she murmured, looking from side to side, cautiously.

"Kendra, you're more skittish than a horse near a rattler," Lucas grumbled. He stepped around his horse and stood beside Domino, looking up at her. "Are you going to tell me about it?"

Kendra's face flushed crimson. She avoided his eyes as she led Domino into the water. Only Domino's front feet were hidden by the water, leaving room for Lucas to move next to Kendra, where he lifted his arms and slid her quite determinedly from her saddle.

"Lucas, what *are* you doing?" she asked, squirming against his hold. "I really don't want to stay here."

Fitting her into the curve of his arms, he leaned his face down into hers. "I'm not going to let you down until you tell me what's the matter," he said. His breath against her cheek burned desire inside her. She felt her defenses weakening.

"I don't want to tell you," she said stubbornly.

His mouth came down on hers suddenly, in an onslaught of passion. His fingers dug into the flesh of her

347

arms as he held her even more tightly against him.

Unable to control the delicious warmth taking over her insides, Kendra slowly laced her arms about his neck and kissed him back hungrily. She was burning even more with consuming need of him. She twined her fingers into his hair and then reached to knock his sombrero from his head, succeeding as it flew to the ground.

She laughed inside when he used his head to knock her hat also away from her. Then she settled in leisurely against the steel frame of him, and when his lips strayed and began moving across her face, she leaned her head back and closed her eyes.

"Tell me, Kendra," he whispered. "Tell me why you don't want to stay here."

"Only if you promise we will leave soon after," she murmured.

"Before even taking a dip in the water?"

Kendra's eyes opened with a start. "What . . . ?" she gasped, as Lucas was working with her gunbelt, then dropping it to the ground. "Lucas, what . . . ?" she said again, as he scooped her up into his arms and began walking toward the water. With one swing he had her thrown into the water, clothes and all.

Kendra rose to the surface, stunned. She wiped wet strands of hair from her eyes and blew water away from her mouth. "Lucas?" she screamed. "I never know what to expect of you next! Why would you do such a thing?"

Lucas just laughed as he began removing his clothes.

"Lucas!" Kendra screamed. "What are you doing?"

"I'm going to join you," he chuckled.

"But what if someone . . . ?"

"There wasn't anybody for miles. We would have seen."

Kendra knew that wasn't necessarily so. She hadn't seen Zeke that time, and *he* had been there.

"My clothes," she sighed. "Darn it, Lucas. What am I to do about my clothes?"

"Take them off," he said, stepping into the water.

"Oh!" she said. "You know what I mean. How will I be able to explain away my wet clothes?"

Lucas swam to her and worked with the buttons of her shirt. "In this heat, everything but your boots will be dry before you reach the ranch," he said. "And no one will notice the wet boots but you."

"That's one person too many," she argued. She tingled when one of his hands brushed against her breast as he removed her shirt. She watched it fly across the water and onto the ground.

"You'll have to remove your boots," he said, splashing her playfully with water.

"I doubt if I can," she said, already struggling. "They're so wet."

Lucas dove beneath the water and swam down to where her boots were resting firmly on the sandy bottom. He lifted her feet, one at a time. One jerk, then two, and he had them removed. He popped to the surface with a boot in each hand.

Kendra giggled, her mood finally lightening. "This is a day I'll never forget," she said..

Lucas swung the boots to the shore. "Something to tell our grandchildren, huh?" he laughed.

"Grandchildren . . . ?"

Lucas drew her into his arms. "There will be children, who will give us grandchildren," he said thickly. His lips moved gently to hers. Trembling from building desire, his hands moved over her breasts beneath the water, then lower. She wriggled her hips as he lowered her jeans. And when they were also tossed on the ground, Lucas drew her nude, silken body into his.

"Lucas, darling Lucas," Kendra whispered. She welcomed his roaming hands . . . his scorching lips at the hollow of her throat. When she felt the hardness of his sex against her abdomen, she lifted her legs up around his waist and welcomed his hardness inside her.

With her face buried against his chest and her arms locked about his neck, she worked with him, enjoying the caress of the water against their moving bodies.

Lucas molded her breast with his hand and flicked her nipple with his thumb. Kendra moaned, growing feverish with building rapture. His lips traveled over the creamy white silk of her shoulder. Then he eased her face away from his body and quickly consumed her lips with a fiery, lingering kiss as the magical glow began inside her.

Kendra dug her fingers into Lucas's neck as the pleasure mounted and exploded inside her. She clung . . . she trembled . . . she cried out as he released her lips. And when he stiffened and held her even more tightly, she knew that he was being smothered in his own flames of rapturous release.

"Lucas, it was beautiful," she whispered into his ear, then flicked her tongue inside it."

"Sorry now that I threw you in?"

"Well, now, I didn't say that," she laughed. She pulled free of his hold and began swimming away from him, teasing him with her eyes as she gave him a quick glance from across her shoulder.

When she saw him dive beneath the surface of the water, she took wider strokes away from him. She laughed and felt tremors of joy work across her flesh when she felt his hand reach and touch her leg beneath the water. She felt her heart start beating faster as his fingers moved smoothly upward and stopped at the soft cushion between her legs.

A painful ache tore through her, wanting him again. She reached for him and pulled his head up above the water and kissed him long and hard. The familiar melting inside her and the reeling of her senses invaded her again as she felt his hardness probe and find her.

Hands sought hands . . . tongue sought tongue . . . and a lethargic dizziness took over inside Kendra's head as once more they shared the ultimate of pleasure between man and woman.

"Kendra . . ." Lucas said, panting, as he drew away from her. He reached a hand to move stray hair from her cheeks, then framed her face between his hands. He gazed at her with intense love.

"We will be wed, darling," he murmured. "Sooner or later we will be man and wife. No love like ours can be stifled, no matter what obstacles are standing in the way."

Kendra glanced upward at the angle of the sun. It was already leaning too much toward the mountains. The shadows of evening would soon be upon them. "And, speaking of obstacles," she murmured, "Aaron may be home, worrying about me. I have to go, Lucas."

Lucas swept her up into his arms. She twined her arms about his neck and lay her cheek against his chest. She had never felt so at peace as at this moment. She felt so perfectly content, it was sinful! Oh, if it could only last. . . .

The sound of approaching hoofbeats in the distance very quickly dispelled all of Kendra's happiness. "A horse . . ." she whispered, tensing.

Lucas hurriedly carried her from the water, dripping wet. "Yes. I hear it," he growled. "Hurry, Kendra. Get into your clothes." He quickly pulled his jeans on.

"Lucas, I cannot be seen with you," she said, breathless as she worked desperately into her wet clothes. "Please hurry. Leave. What if it's Aaron?" Then her thoughts returned to Zeke! What if . . . ?

"I can't leave you here alone."

Kendra buckled her gunbelt on and patted her pistols. "I'm not alone," she said. "I have my friends here."

Lucas pushed his hat on his head, completely dressed now. He took his horse's reins. "I'll hide over there in the thickness of the trees," he said. "I refuse to leave you before I know who it is approaching."

"All right. If you must," Kendra sighed heavily. "But, please hurry. We already have enough problems with Aaron."

Lucas nodded. "I'll be right here," he said. "I won't let anything happen to you."

Kendra watched him duck into the cover of the trees, then swung around when the rider came into view. She squinted her eyes, trying to focus on the face. She already knew that it wasn't Zeke or Aaron.

"Mike . . ." she suddenly said, now recognizing Aaron's newly hired head wrangler.

"Miss Kendra . . ." Mike shouted, drawing rein next to her. His dark eyes roved over her, seeing her wet disarray. "Finally. I've been searchin' and searchin' for you. Everyone's out lookin' for you. Aaron has men combin' every inch of the land. I've not been around long, but do you make it a habit to travel so far from the ranch . . . to . . . take a swim fully clothed?"

Kendra placed her hands on her hips and glared at the bewhiskered man. "That's none of your concern," she said, blushing. "What does Aaron want? Is this a new way to keep rein on me?"

Mike tipped his hat back a bit. His fingers kneaded his whiskered chin. "No. Nothin' like that," he mumbled.

Kendra flipped her hair around, down her back. "Then what? Why have you come so far, looking for me? Why does Aaron have so many other men looking for me?"

Mike removed his sombrero and rolled it around and between his fingers, avoiding her questioning gaze. "It's bad news, Miss Kendra. . . ." he murmured.

An icy coldness swept through Kendra. She doubled her fists at her sides. "Mike, it's not Aaron. . . ." she whispered. "He's not been . . . hurt . . . ?"

"No, ma'am . . . it's not . . . Aaron. . . ."

Kendra's mouth went dry . . . her eyes burned. "Then, who . . . ?" she whispered again.

"Seth. Ma'am, it's Seth."

Kendra's heart plummeted, and her voice became strained as she asked, "What about Seth . . . ?"

"Ma'am, the mines . . ."

A bitterness rose inside Kendra's throat. She swallowed and swallowed, yet couldn't rid herself of the taste.

"He's dead, ma'am."

"No . . ." she whispered. "Oh, no. God, no. Not sweet Seth."

A rush of memories flashed before her eyes. Seth . . . catching fireflies with her as a child. Seth . . . teasing her when she had worn her first low-swept dress. Seth . . . his comforting arms when she had had childish hurts. . . .

Tears rushed from her eyes. She bowed her head into

her hands and shook her head slowly from side to side, the ache so strong inside her, and this time no Seth there to ease the hurt away. . . .

"Ma'am, are you all right?" Mike asked.

"Please go . . ." she sobbed, not looking his way.

"What'll I tell Aaron?"

"I'll be there. Shortly."

"Yes, ma'am . . ."

She listened to his horse's hoofbeats fade away, then swung around when Lucas moved from his hiding place. He was only a blur as he moved toward her. Anger rose inside her. She wiped the tears from her face and eyes and glared toward him.

"All the while we were making love, Seth lay dead," she cried. "I should have been with him. Had you not sidetracked me I *would* have been."

"Kendra, I'm sorry about Seth, but what you're saying makes no sense," he said sadly. "You can't blame me. . . ."

Kendra ran to Domino and swung herself up into the saddle. "This place is a jinx to me," she screamed. "The only other time I was here I was almost raped by that beast Zeke, and now to be told here that my brother is dead . . . *was* dead while you and I . . ."

Lucas blanched. "Almost raped? Zeke?" he said, shock registering in his eyes. "Who is Zeke?"

Kendra wheeled Domino around and began riding quickly away from Lucas. She closed her ears to her name being yelled after her. . . .

Chapter Twenty

Organ music played over the soft voices of the crowded room of people who had come to the memorial for Seth. The smell of roses softened the air with their sweetness and a few candles flickered low.

Dressed in full black with her hair swept severely up into a bun atop her head, Kendra moved to Aaron's side and slipped an arm about his waist. He had never looked as old as he did at this moment. His eyes were dull and his face was lined with new, tiny wrinkles. His lips were set into a narrow, straight line, and his dark suit appeared too tight and burdensome.

"I'm so glad I was able to get the organ for tonight," Kendra whispered to Aaron. "It only seemed right that we should have an organ."

"Nothing is right," Aaron said.

"Aaron, please . . ." Kendra sighed. "We've done all that's possible. We can do no more."

"But there's not even a body to bury," Aaron said with a crack in his voice.

"I know . . ." Kendra whispered. She wiped a tear

from the corner of her eye.

"Buried one thousand feet down," Aaron said. "There's *got* to be a way to get him."

"The men tried. Over and over again," Kendra said. "Aaron, more lives could be lost. Please forget it. You really have no other choice."

"But to have no body to place in a grave?" Aaron whispered, running his hand over his bald head. "It's sinful, Kendra. We can't even have a proper funeral."

"This memorial will suffice, Aaron," she tried to comfort him. "Just look at the people who have come to pay their last respects. Please be comforted by that. They're still continuing to arrive. You've *so* many friends in the community now, Aaron. Please take comfort from their presence."

A shuffling of feet on the far side of the room drew Kendra's attention in that direction. She watched as more people stepped aside and made room for the wooden wheelchair that rattled into the parlor.

"Johnny," Aaron whispered. His face then flushed pink as he saw Hazel enter behind Johnny. Their gazes met and momentarily held, then Aaron broke the semitrance by crossing the room to meet them.

He took Hazel's hand. Tears burned his eyes as she looked sympathetically up into them. "You didn't have to come," he whispered. He bowed and kissed her hand, then grudgingly released it to step in front of Johnny.

Bending his back, Aaron placed his hands on Johnny's frail shoulders. "This is mighty fine of you, Johnny," he said thickly. "I know how hard it must be for you. I know how you have avoided people since your accident."

Johnny lifted his hand and placed it on top of one of Aaron's. "I hadn't thought much about it before, Aaron,

356

but I guess I'm damn lucky to be alive," he said. "I guess it's taken Seth's death to make me realize that."

Aaron swallowed back a lump in his throat. "Well, Johnny, I'm glad to hear it," he said thickly. "At least Seth's death has worked for the good of somebody."

"Something should be done about those mines," Johnny growled, patting the two stumps of his legs. "Tougher regulations. And they should be strictly enforced."

Aaron's eyes wavered as he paled. He lifted his hands from Johnny's shoulders and ran a finger nervously around the inside of his stiffly starched white collar. "I'm sure you're right, Johnny," he mumbled.

Guilt caused an emptiness in the pit of Aaron's stomach. First Johnny . . . now Seth. Would he ever be able to forget that he was partly responsible for both their tragedies? But he had to keep reminding himself that he was only one man and shouldn't elect himself judge and jury, condemning only himself over and over again. Many were at fault. But mainly *greed* was the culprit here!

With swooshing skirts, Kendra moved to Aaron's side. She bent her back and kissed Johnny softly on the cheek. "It was so nice of you to come, Johnny," she whispered. "And this gives me the opportunity to once more thank you for coming to my rescue that day. I shall always remain grateful and in your debt."

"Should've shot him," Johnny growled. "Lord knows what meanness he's up to now."

"Zeke is gone. At least we can be thankful for that," Kendra sighed.

Straightening her back, Kendra smiled toward Hazel, then felt a strange stirring inside her when she caught

Hazel and Aaron exchanging looks that were more tha those of friends. The passion passed from one to th other, evident only in their eyes. Kendra knew only on reason for such silent admiration. They most surel shared more than Hazel's husband's devotion. Ha Aaron fallen out of love with Holly and in love with Haz Lassiter?

Kendra glanced quickly down at Johnny and saw hir looking from Aaron to Hazel. He also saw it, she was sure But he didn't show any shock or annoyance.

Feeling the need to quickly clear the air, Kendr reached her hand toward Hazel. "And you must b Hazel," she said. "I haven't yet had the pleasure c meeting you." She silently appraised the petite womar whose hands reflected anything but a life of gentleness i their coarse roughness. Dressed in black, her red hai pulled back and held in place with combs, she looked th role of an innocent, faithful wife. It was apparent that sh did the outside chores, because her fair skin showed dried flakiness that only the harsh winds and sun coul cause. But, oh, the violet shade of her eyes hadn't bee affected by misfortune or weather. They were beautifull intense in color and strength as Hazel challenged Kendr with a set stare, having apparently read Kendra accusing thoughts.

"Yes. I'm Johnny's wife," Hazel murmured. "And yo must be Kendra. I've heard so much about you it's a though I already know you."

"Oh?" Kendra whispered.

Hazel flushed a bit. "Johnny has told me about you, she quickly interjected. "He says that you were Aaron main topic of conversation during the war."

"Oh, I see," Kendra said softly.

358

"And then there was that day," Hazel added. "Johnny told me about how he stopped that awful man."

"Yes. Zeke," Kendra said. "As I told Johnny, I'll forever be grateful."

"Where's your wife, Holly, Aaron?" Johnny asked, scanning the room with a careful eye.

"She's been feeling poorly of late," Aaron said, glancing toward the staircase. "But she promised she'd join me soon."

"What seems to be the problem with her, Aaron?" Johnny asked, squirming, trying to rearrange himself more comfortably in the wheelchair.

Aaron ran a hand over his head. He leaned down into Johnny's face. "Damned if I know," he said.

"Maybe it's Seth's death."

"No. It began a day or two before that."

"Hope it's nothing serious, Aaron. The doctors in these parts aren't the best, you know."

A flutter of skirts and the rustling of a petticoat drew Aaron's attention to Holly, who suddenly appeared on the stairs, moving slowly downward. Her midnight-black hair, hanging long and free around her shoulders, framed a face pale and gaunt. The black, fully gathered dress even deepened this paleness, and her usually sparkling eyes were disturbed by black, sunken-in rings beneath them.

Johnny followed Aaron's gaze. A slow smile lifted his lips. He reached for Aaron and drew him down to whisper into his ear. "I think I can tell you what might be ailin' your wife," he said.

Aaron's eyebrows lifted. "And what might it be?" he asked.

"She looks like my sister Paula looked when she was

first found to be with child."

"What . . . ?" Aaron gasped.

"She's as pale and drawn in the face," Johnny whispered back. "Caused by upchuckin'. Most women do when they're first pregnant. I had six sisters. I ought to know."

Aaron grew cold inside. He was remembering when he was nine . . . when his mother was first pregnant with Kendra. His mother had behaved identically to Holly!

But . . . how . . . could Holly be? He knew his condition too well, and he knew she couldn't be carrying *his* child.

With hate grabbing at his insides, Aaron watched Holly as she began making her way toward the crowd, toward him. He watched her hand move to her stomach and place it there as the chalky pallor increased on her face. When she came in a gliding sort of fashion to his side, Aaron, hating it, placed his arm devotedly about her waist, knowing that introductions were in order.

"My wife, Holly," he said stiffly, still intently studying her. He caught her downcast glance and read guilt in her eyes. "And, Holly, this is Johnny Lassiter and his wife, Hazel."

"So this is the pretty wife from Boston," Johnny said. He took her hand and lifted it to his lips and kissed it. Then he smiled up at her as he let her hand go. "Hear you've been ailin'. Sorry to hear it."

"I'm perfectly fine," Holly said softly. Her eyelashes fluttered toward Hazel. "And I'm glad to make your acquaintance, Mrs. Lassiter."

Hazel had heard the men's whisperings. She glanced down at Holly's stomach, then icily accepted Holly's indignant stare. "And I, yours," she murmured. Then hating the thought of anyone but her carrying Aaron's child, she had to ask, "And, your illness? Is it because you are with child?"

Johnny cast Hazel a quick, uneasy glance. "Hazel," he scolded. "That is not a proper thing to ask. Whatever gave you the notion to be so openly inquisitive?"

Hazel clasped her hands tightly together before her. "I thought maybe knowing there was to be a new baby in the family just might ease Aaron's pain over the loss of his brother," she lied. "So often it happens, Johnny. A birth of a child . . . to replace the loss of a family member."

"I feel faint," Holly gasped, placing fingers limply to her brow. "Aaron, help me to a chair."

"Excuse us, please," Aaron grumbled. His jaw was set hard and his thoughts whirling with rage. All those times Holly had gone into town . . . had it been to meet a man? Was she with child? He had to know. And *now!*

With urgency, he directed her to a dark corner and eased her down onto a gilt-trimmed green velvet chair. Then he knelt down before her with one knee supporting him against the floor. With his need to know burning his insides, he took one of her hands in his and pretended a caring sort of interest, though he didn't quite know what he would do, if she did confess a pregnancy to him. He might even kill her! To dirty the name of a Carpenter was to him the same as blaspheming God!

"Holly, are Hazel's suspicions correct?" he whispered. His heart pounded. His pulse raced. Beads of nervous perspiration sparkled on his brow.

"Aaron, this isn't the time or place."

"Holly, your illness. Is it because you are with child?" he insisted.

She lowered her lashes and dabbed at her nose with her

handkerchief. "And what if I were?" she murmured. "You've always refused to discuss children."

A sick feeling impaled Aaron's insides. "Holly, I want to know. Are you with child?"

"Aaron, let's discuss it later," she begged. She was suddenly afraid of him. She knew his moods well. She also could read his eyes. She could see a seething anger in them this time and had to believe he knew more than he was letting on. Had someone seen her with Blackie and conveyed the information to Aaron? Or had Seth's death caused Aaron such grief that she was confusing torture with anger in his eyes?

"I must know now," he said flatly.

"Will you hate me if I tell you we are to have a child?" she murmured. No matter what, she would, to the end, say the child was his, though she knew the child was in truth Blackie's. She knew when the child had been conceived . . . a child that would give her purpose . . . keep her from being so lonely.

Yes, she would say the child was Aaron's. There was no room for her or any other woman in Blackie's life. Gambling was his mistress. Holly was only a passing fancy with him. Her usefulness would run out as soon as he saw her begin to swell with child. And how would Aaron ever know that the child wasn't his . . . ?

The organ music . . . the flowers . . . the milling, whispering people reminded Aaron where he was. No matter what the next few moments revealed to him, he had to remain calm and deal with this problem later. He had his reputation to uphold. He couldn't let the whole community realize his wife had been unfaithful to him. He couldn't let people know that she was carrying a child that was not his.

He swallowed back his anger and pride and nodded. "No. I won't hate you," he said in a strained voice. He looked up into her green eyes, suddenly thinking of Hazel. He needed Hazel now. Somehow he knew that soon he would need comforting for more than the loss of a brother. His manhood was going to be severed as surely as if someone had taken a knife to his testicles. . . .

Trembling, Holly reached a hand to Aaron's cheek. Her chin quivered as a nervous smile broke loose. "Then, Aaron, my love, I would like to make the proud announcement that, yes, I *am* going to have a baby," she whispered.

Her eyes searched his face, desperate for signs of approval. But she saw him flinch, and then the pallor that quickly followed her announcement, and she knew that to him the news was *not* good.

She dropped her hand to her lap and watched as he rose and moved slowly away from her without a word of approval or disapproval.

Kendra had stood watching the tense scene between Aaron and Holly and now watched as Aaron moved away from Holly with his fists doubled at his sides. They never ceased to amaze her. Their feuding continued no matter the time or place. They both needed manners taught them. Sometimes even older brothers needed scolding!

Working her way across the room, Kendra finally stopped beside Aaron, who stood looking blankly out of a window. "Aaron, please, don't you and Holly have a scene now," she whispered harshly.

Aaron's head hung and his shoulders slumped. He didn't answer. Though he had also been unfaithful, at least he didn't have embarrassing proof that would show outwardly, as Holly did. What was he to do? The truth, when it was known to the community, would kill him. He would never hold his head up proud again. It would be common knowledge that Aaron Carpenter hadn't been man enough to keep his wife from straying.

"Aaron?" Kendra murmured, shaking his arm. "What on earth is wrong? What did Holly say to you?"

Aaron looked jerkily toward Kendra. His heart hammered against his chest. He now knew the full brunt of his fears. Why, he couldn't even tell Kendra! No one but he . . . knew he couldn't father a child! Maybe that was the only way out. To *lie*!

He hung his head again, shaking it back and forth. No. He couldn't lie. And he couldn't tell the truth. He was caught in the middle of Holly's deceit. "It's nothing, Kendra," he finally replied.

Kendra placed a hand on his chin and forced his eyes to meet hers. "Aaron, I know you," she whispered. "More than Seth's death is suddenly eating away at you. And I know it's to do with Holly. What did she say to make you so distraught?"

Footsteps behind Kendra drew her quickly around. Her heart raced crazily when she looked up into Lucas's gray eyes. "Lucas . . ." she gasped.

Aaron turned quickly on his heel, rage reflected in the squint of his eyes. "What the hell are you doing here?" he growled. "You shouldn't set foot on my land, much less inside my house."

"This is a memorial for Seth, is it not?" Lucas asked, lifting his sombrero from his head, to hold it down before him, clutching tightly to its brim.

"What the hell does that have to do with you?" Aaron asked hotly, taking a step toward Lucas. He placed his face into Lucas's, sneering. "Johnny Rebs aren't welcome here. Get out. Do you hear?"

Kendra looked desperately from one to the other. She placed a hand on one of Aaron's arms, and her other on one of Lucas's. "Please," she softly begged.

The lines on Lucas's face softened, as did the expression in his eyes. "Kendra, I'll be here for only a moment," he murmured. "I heard about Seth's death. I wanted to pay my condolences. And I was worried about you. You talked so fondly of your brother. I know how close you were."

Aaron gave Kendra a puzzled look. "Kendra, how does he know so much about you?" he whispered. "You haven't . . ."

Kendra placed a forefinger to Aaron's lips. "Aaron, one day I'll explain it all to you," she murmured. "But for the moment, please, let's treat this evening as it is meant to be treated. It's for Seth. Remember. Above all else, it's for Seth."

"Kendra, can you walk me to my horse?" Lucas asked, ignoring Aaron's continuing angry stare.

"Yes," she replied, avoiding Aaron's low gasp. She could feel his eyes on her as she placed an arm through Lucas's and they slowly made their way through the crowd. Out of the corner of her eye, she could see Lucas's handsomeness. He was dressed in a neat, dark suit. He was the perfect man, with his wide shoulders, tapered hips, and muscled legs. Some of his hair spilled down over his forehead in a slight wave, and his sideburns appeared to have just been freshly trimmed.

But it was the classic, chiseled features of his sun-bronzed face that attracted many a woman's eye this evening, and Kendra felt proud that he was at her side. She knew that she had much to explain to Aaron. But for now, nothing mattered except that Lucas had cared enough for her to worry about her in her grief . . . enough to risk even his life to come to her to be at her side, to comfort her during her time of sadness.

Stepping out onto the front porch, Kendra welcomed the moonlight. "Lucas, you didn't have to come tonight," she whispered. "You really did take a chance. You know how Aaron feels about you."

"I had to, darling," he murmured. "For you."

Going on down the wide steps, Kendra clung to Lucas until they came to his horse. "Lucas," she said, stepping before him.

Lucas looked from side to side and when he saw no one threateningly close he drew Kendra into his arms. "Yes, darling?" he said, bending a kiss to the tip of her nose.

"Now that Aaron has so much grieving to put behind him, I will have to stay closer to home, to help him," she murmured. She twined her arms about his neck and placed her cheek on his massive chest. "I'm sure you understand."

"I know," he said thickly. "I *do* understand." He lifted her chin with a forefinger. "And, darling, will you be all right? You do seem to be taking this so well. Is it because the full truth hasn't sunk in? Will it come harder, later? Please watch that. It can be devastating. It happened when I discovered the deaths of my family. At first I was in a state of shock. Then, later, it almost became the end of me. Only traveling out West . . . coming to Nevada . . . helped me to leave my grief behind me. But it took many months. Please, Kendra, watch your feelings at this time."

"Lucas, if I find the grieving more than I can bear, can I come to you? Would you mind terribly if I came to you?"

Lucas's insides warmed. "Kendra, I would be honored if you would do that," he said huskily. "I am always here. You know that. And more than that. Please be thinking of our marriage. Aaron will learn to accept that also."

Kendra swallowed hard. "Marriage?" she whispered. "No. Not at this time." She looked up into his eyes. "And, Lucas, you do remember how I felt the last time we were together."

"Yes. You blamed yourself and even me for your not having been with Seth when . . ."

She sealed his lips with her finger. "Yes," she murmured. "I did. I felt that I should've been there for Seth. But I've had much time to think about that, and I know that I was wrong. I'm sorry I yelled at you and left you in such a way."

"I understood," he said. He wanted to ask what she had meant about the rape she had mentioned, but he knew this was not the time.

"You always seem to understand everything," she sighed. "You are a complex man, Lucas Hall. First stubborn . . . then mellow, like a soft, falling snow."

Lucas chuckled. He traced her face with his finger. "That's the first time I've ever been compared to snow," he said. "Maybe a mule, but never snow."

"You know what I mean," she laughed.

Lucas drew her closer to him and hugged her tightly. "There. A laugh from my darling," he said. "That sounded so good, Kendra."

"Lucas, I really must get back inside," she murmured, trembling at the thought of the reason for the crowd of people. It still seemed unbelievable that Seth was gone. Her dear, sweet brother. Tears began flowing from her eyes. "Oh, Lucas," she cried. "Please hold me. Darling, hold me. I miss him so. Seth, my sweet brother. Why did it have to happen to him? He never did harm to anyone. Never. He was so gentle . . . so kind. . . ."

Her body shook with the tears. "Let it all out, Kendra," Lucas whispered. "Cry, darling. Then you will feel much better. Then all your days will be filled with laughter. You'll see. Seth wouldn't want you to mourn forever over him. Cry now. Get it all out. Then try and start putting it all behind you."

Kendra clung. She cried. She sobbed. Then, suddenly, it was as though a heavy weight had been lifted from her shoulders. She sniffled and drew gently away from Lucas. Wiping her nose with the back of her hand, she looked up into his eyes, remembering the first time she had seen them. They were soft now, caring. Yet the command was still there. There was such strength in his eyes. And she would take some of that strength from him at this moment and try and help Aaron get through the rest of this evening without any more mishaps.

"Thank you, Lucas," Kendra said, gently framing his face between her hands.

"For what . . . ?"

"For being you. For being here. I could never love you as much as I do at this moment," she said, yet she knew that she felt the same way each and every time she was with him!

"The Piute Indians were lucky to have found a man like you to help them with their cause," she added, smiling sweetly up at him.

"Things are looking better for them, Kendra," Lucas said. "The legislature is discussing placing the Piute on reservations."

"Exactly what will that do for the Piute?"

"There will be special areas set aside for them," he said flatly. "The government will own the land and hold it in trust for the Indians. It will be tax-free land. Some tracts of land will be held by a tribe or be divided into individual plots. They will be free to farm the land or raise livestock."

"Are you pleased?"

"I would think the Indians should be able to *own* their tracts of land, just like the white man," Lucas growled. "But this will be better than nothing. And they are talking of organizing a sort of Bureau of Indian Affairs. They will have jurisdiction over the reservations and also will have charge of helping the Indians relocate, to settle and get jobs."

"Lucas, it sounds as though you may have won," Kendra said anxiously.

"In a sense," he said. "And, also, it is said that the Indians may be able to borrow money from the government for improvements."

"I'm so happy for you and the Indians," Kendra said, hugging him to her. "I'm sure you're relieved. You will now be able to devote more time to your ranch."

"And to my sheep," he said matter-of-factly.

Kendra stiffened. She drew slowly away from him. "Yes. And your sheep," she said quietly. She swirled the skirt of her dress around and began walking away from him. "I really must go," she said from across her shoulder. "Aaron. He needs me, Lucas."

Lucas took two wide strides and took her shoulders and swung her around to face him. "Does the mention of sheep cause a wall to go up between us so quickly, Kendra?" he said angrily.

"I had almost forgotten about the sheep, Lucas," she murmured. "Now that I have been reminded, I remember my reasons to be loyal to Aaron. It isn't only for Seth, but for all Carpenters. Please. Just go."

"Can you forget so quickly how you were feeling just moments ago?" he demanded. "You even talked of coming to me if you needed comforting. Now you turn from me because of my mention of sheep? Kendra, *you* are the complex individual here. I'll never understand you."

Lucas released his hold on her and stormed away. Kendra felt as though she were dying inside as she watched him swing angrily into his saddle and ride away from her in a huff. She watched until the darkness of night swallowed him in its total blackness, then hung her head sadly and began inching her way back to the house. But the sound of approaching carriage wheels drew her back around. She squinted her eyes, peering into the darkness, then tensed when she recognized the passenger inside the carriage and her thoughts were once more returned to Seth.

Emanuelle stepped from the carriage dressed in all black, with even a sheer black veil half hiding her face. She moved sullenly toward Kendra, then stopped before her. Lifting her veil, she looked teary-eyed into Kendra's stiff face. "Kendra, I had to come," she whispered. "Please don't be ugly to me."

"Emanuelle, you are not needed here," Kendra hissed. "Seth is dead. You may as well forget about the Carpenter name. It cannot be yours now that Seth is dead."

Emanuelle lifted a lace-trimmed handkerchief to her nose. She sniffled into it. "I loved him, Kendra," she said. "Please let me pay my last respects. Surely you can grant me at least that."

"You have no business here," Kendra argued. "Please, Emanuelle, go on back to Virginia City. Your presence will probably upset Aaron even more than he already is."

"Seth would want me here," Emanuelle said stubbornly, sniffling even more loudly. "I refuse to leave. I will go on inside and be one of the mourners and friends. You won't stop me."

Kendra swung around and watched in mortified silence as Emanuelle proceeded on her way. "Emanuelle!" she whispered loudly after her.

Emanuelle gave her a quick, stubborn glance from across her shoulder and went on up the stairs and inside the house.

Desperation seized Kendra's insides. "Aaron . . ." she whispered. "If he sees her . . ."

Lifting her skirt, she rushed up the stairs and inside, looking desperately around her, but saw that Emanuelle blended in well enough with the rest of the crowd, and that Aaron hadn't yet become aware of her presence in the parlor. He was still at the window, peering gloomily from it. Kendra went to a corner and leaned against the wall, sighing. Whatever else could happen this evening? Who *else* could show up? Would the evening ever end?

She glanced toward the door as a man entered the parlor. Kendra took a quick, second glance and then felt a slow reeling inside her head. She steadied herself against the back of a chair as he began moving toward Aaron. . . .

"Father . . ." Kendra whispered. "No . . ."

With a weakness in her knees, she moved hurriedly

371

toward Aaron and took his arm, swallowing hard when her father stopped before Aaron and removed his black silk hat from his head to hold it behind him.

Kendra devoured him with her eyes, puzzled by his sudden appearance. He showed a deep remorse in his blue eyes, and the lines on his face had deepened to make him look more his age—fifty—than the last time she had seen him. His black suit fitted him well, and his hair showed vague signs of graying in its thick blond waves.

"Aaron . . ." Blackie said hoarsely. "Son . . ."

Aaron took a step backwards, becoming even more pale than he already was. His mouth dropped open into a loud gasp and his eyes widened in muted horror. "Father . . . ?" he whispered.

"Yes, Aaron," Blackie said, humbly lowering his eyes. "I heard. I had to come. I had no idea that you were in the area. No idea at all. Or I would've come sooner."

"How did you find out . . . ?" Kendra said flatly.

Blackie's eyes traveled slowly over Kendra, up and down, then back up again. "Kendra?" he murmured. "It *is* you, isn't it?"

"I haven't changed in looks all that much, Father," she said icily. "I've filled out in the proper places, but my face has remained the same."

"So it is you," Blackie sighed. "My little Kendra."

"I'm not your anything," Kendra hissed. "And I'll ask you again. How did you find out about Seth . . . about us . . . ?"

"The talk is thick in town of Seth Carpenter's death," Blackie mumbled. "No one knew Seth was my son. As I . . . also didn't—the few times I spoke with the young man."

Aaron laughed cynically. "You . . . didn't even . . . know your own . . . son," he said. "And you come now? Wouldn't you say you are ten years late, Father? Seth is no longer with us to be the recipient of your deep devotion, Father."

The bitterness in Aaron's words cut away at Kendra's heart. At this moment she felt as sorry for her father as she did for Aaron. She knew what this had to be doing to him. What it would do to *any* father, no matter what kind of father he was.

Yet she knew that he deserved all the bitterness and hatred handed him. He had deserted them. Many years ago! To them, he had been the same as dead. . . .

But she knew better than that. She knew that—though she hadn't wanted to admit it aloud to anyone—finding her father had been a goal for both her and Aaron. Each of them had had a separate and secret plan to find him and hopefully to humiliate him in some way. So far, all of Kendra's plans had gone awry. And now she knew she would never be able to play the game of blackjack with him, as she had planned.

"Please let me explain," Blackie pleaded, placing a hand on Aaron's shoulder, which Aaron quickly brushed aside.

"Why bother now?" Aaron growled.

"I know. I should have. Long ago. But your mother. She always stood in the way," Blackie said. "She forced my hand, Aaron."

Blackie's eyes slowly scanned the room. "And where *is* your mother?" he asked. "I imagine she's taking this quite badly. Seth, being the youngest, was her favorite. Or maybe you didn't know that. Perhaps I have spoken

373

out of turn."

"Everything you have to say is out of turn," Aaron grumbled. "And as for Mother, well, you don't have to worry about her any longer."

"And why is that?" Blackie asked, nervously shifting his weight from one foot to the other.

"Because she is dead," Aaron said flatly. "That is why we came to Nevada. When Mother died, we had nothing holding us in Boston."

"Dead . . . ?" Blackie harshly whispered.

Aaron laughed cynically. "Don't act so shocked," he said. "You know you never cared or you wouldn't have left her. You wouldn't have *deserted* her."

"Aaron, you're wrong," Blackie said, then silenced his own words. This wasn't the time to reveal the truth to Aaron and Kendra. Their minds were too filled with grief to even understand what he had to tell them, much less believe him. Instead, he said, "Did you hear of my being here? Is that why you came to Reno, Aaron?"

Aaron threw his head back into a fit of laughter. "You give yourself much too much credit, Father," he said, sobering, glaring toward Blackie. "No. We didn't know you were here. You had nothing to do with our move. This was something we all wanted to do. We did it for ourselves. We just happened to hear recently about this man who called himself Blackie who played a winning game of blackjack. I knew it must be my gambling father."

"And Seth knew about me?"

"Yes. He *was* your son, wasn't he?" Aaron said flatly.

Blackie wiped at his brow with the back of a hand. "All along he knew and he didn't let on," he mumbled.

374

"Damn. Damn . . ."

"Seth told me about running into you," Kendra said icily. "And, yes, he knew it was you. It almost broke his heart that you didn't recognize *him*."

Aaron quickly placed his back to Blackie. "Get out of here," he murmured. "We've gotten along just fine without you this long. We sure as hell don't need you now."

"Aaron, you must let me explain something to you," Blackie pleaded, reconsidering. He couldn't bear the hate his son was feeling for him. Surely if Aaron and Kendra knew the truth . . .

"No," Aaron growled. "Just leave. Leave me to my mourning. I don't need you to cloud my mind with words that couldn't mean hell to me."

Blackie turned to Kendra. "Kendra . . . ?" he whispered.

Kendra lowered her eyes. "Father, it *is* best if you leave," she whispered. A movement next to her brought her head abruptly up. She looked toward Holly as Holly inched toward Blackie. . . .

Panic seized Kendra. All hell could break loose if either Blackie or Holly spoke the other's name. There was *no* way they could know one another. Aaron would have to ask a question that at this time he was not prepared to hear the answer to. As Blackie's head slowly turned and he showed recognition of Holly in his eyes, Kendra stepped between them.

"Holly, may I introduce my and Aaron's father to you?" she said in a quick slur. "And, Father, this is Aaron's wife, Holly."

Blackie's face dropped . . . Holly's hand went to her

head . . . and suddenly Kendra was kneeling over Holly, who had fainted to the floor, lifting her head to her lap. "Holly," she whispered.

Aaron dropped to a knee. "God," he gasped. "Holly, what happened?"

Kendra looked at Aaron, so relieved that his back had been turned and he had not seen the look of dismay on his father's and wife's faces when they discovered who each of them was. "She's fainted, Aaron," she said softly. "I guess she's . . . uh . . . much sicker than we thought. Please. Lift her and take her to her room."

Aaron scooped Holly up into his arms and moved quickly from the room. Kendra turned to her father. "I hope you're satisfied," she said accusingly.

"I don't know what you mean," Blackie lied.

"I believe you do," Kendra said flatly.

"You seem to know all the answers, Kendra," Blackie said dryly. "You tell *me*."

"I've seen you with Holly," she whispered. "I've known for a while now. How *could* you? Your own son's wife."

Blackie lowered his eyes. "I didn't know," he said. Then his gaze moved quickly up. He pleaded with his eyes. "You've got to believe me, Kendra. God. Do you think I would do such a thing as that?"

"Surely you knew her name."

"She didn't give me the name Carpenter," he said, shaking his head, disbelieving all of this. "I had no idea. No idea whatsoever."

"And she's young enough to be your daughter," Kendra further accused. "What kind of man *are* you?"

"Kendra, please let me explain," he said solemnly. He

reached for her hand, which she refused him. "I've come tonight not to cause trouble but to plead my case as your father. I've so much to say to you. Things I should have said long ago, but your mother forced my hand. . . ."

Kendra doubled her fists to her sides and gritted her teeth. Then she said, "This is not the time for confessions, Father. Seth is dead. Mother is dead. You *are* a bit late. I think it best that you go. Now. It would be easier for everyone concerned."

"Holly . . . ?"

"Yes," she laughed cynically. "What about Holly? How are you going to explain this one to Aaron should he find out? You seem to be getting in deeper and deeper, Father. Aaron would never forgive you if by chance Holly does decide to tell him the truth."

"She won't," Blackie said. "It wouldn't prove a thing."

"Only that you are not only a gambling man, but also a cheap womanizer," Kendra said angrily into his face. She lifted her hand and pointed toward the door. "Please leave, Father. I don't think I can bear another minute of this conversation. It's making me sick."

Blackie placed his hat on his head. "Kendra, you will listen to reason. Sooner or later," he said bluntly. "Now that I've found you and Aaron, I will get you to listen to me."

"Ah, and also Holly?" Kendra laughed bitterly.

"Holly and I were drawing apart anyway," he said. "There seemed to be something standing in the way as of late. So I'm sure she won't mind that we no longer are together . . . in that . . . uh . . . way."

"Oh!" Kendra said, stomping a foot. "Get out. Just

377

get out."

With blurring eyes, she watched him saunter from the room. And when she heard the horse's hoofbeats fading into the night, once more she felt as though a part of her heart was being torn away. She had found her father, only to lose him again. She now regretted having been so coldhearted to him. Maybe she should have listened to what he had to say. Yet she had to make herself remember that there was now more than just his desertion standing in their way. There was also Holly!

"Kendra?"

Hearing Emanuelle's voice drew another deep sigh from inside Kendra. She turned slowly and found Emanuelle standing next to her. "Emanuelle, are you still here?" she whispered.

"As you have seen, I have caused you no embarrassment," Emanuelle whispered back, looking cautiously from side to side.

"Not yet you haven't," Kendra said. "But I'm afraid that at any moment you may. Emanuelle, what do you have to say? Be quick with it. I must go see to Holly."

"I know why Holly reacted in such a way when she heard that Blackie was Aaron's father," Emanuelle whispered into Kendra's ear.

A slow red began creeping up Kendra's neck, onto her cheeks. "And what do you think you know?" she said tersely.

"Not think," Emanuelle corrected. "I *know*. I've seen Holly with Blackie. Several times. They have frequented his room together many times. You see, he has a room in the same hotel where I have made my residence."

"Emanuelle," Kendra said, paling. "You wouldn't tell . . ."

378

"No. Not if you do as I ask," Emanuelle said with a break in her voice as she once more looked cautiously around her.

Kendra's eyes went upward. Her heart pounded against her ribs. Blackmail! She knew Emanuelle was capable of many things. But blackmail? Oh, how had Seth gotten tangled up with her? How?

Kendra crossed her arms and gave Emanuelle a cold stare. "You wouldn't . . ." she said flatly.

"Oh, wouldn't I?" Emanuelle laughed.

"You would," Kendra sighed. "So what is it you want?"

"To move in with you Carpenters. Here. At the ranch," Emanuelle whispered. "And soon, Kendra. Soon."

"Good Lord . . ." Kendra gasped. "You don't think I . . . ?"

Then Kendra took Emanuelle by the arm and began guiding her toward the door. "No. I *won't*," she said flatly. "You're going to leave, Emanuelle," she added. "And if you cause any trouble here at Seth's memorial, I will personally flog you. Do you hear?"

"I'll be back," Emanuelle whispered harshly. "Kendra, you'll see. And I will be living here with you. I haven't told you all that has to be told. . . ."

Kendra gave Emanuelle a gentle shove out onto the porch. "You hush. Right now, Emanuelle," she said. "I warn you. If you cause this family any more problems, especially now, with Seth just having died, I will see to it that you will be sorry."

Emanuelle tipped her chin haughtily. "I'll be back," she hissed. "And soon. You'll see. And when I do, you will have no choice but to let me stay here. When I tell you that I . . ."

379

Kendra flung her skirt around and rushed back into the house, breathless. She leaned heavily against the door as she closed it behind her. "She *will* be back," she thought angrily to herself. "And what else does she have to tell the family?"

She hung her head and began going up the stairs, heavy at heart.

Chapter Twenty-One

Aaron watched from his upstairs bedroom window. The carriage was pulling away from the stables, carrying Holly. "She sure did get well fast enough," he grumbled, clenching and unclenching his fists. "I'm sure she isn't going into town to pick up the gown that she said that she ordered from New York. I bet she's going to meet with him, and even in her black mourning clothes. Well, I'll catch her."

He strapped his gunbelt around his waist and patted his revolver. "I think I just might be needing this," he mumbled. "No man makes a fool of me twice."

Fitting his wide-brimmed Stetson hat onto his head, he rushed down the stairs and to the stables. "I've got to keep back a bit," he whispered. "She can't see me following her. I've got to catch them in the act. Surprise the hell out of them."

He placed his saddle on his horse, secured it, then swung himself into it. He still hadn't figured out how he would handle this "child" Holly was carrying. He had thought about this and had at least decided that he could not draw attention to himself and his inadequacies.

"And getting involved in a shooting may be the wrong approach," he grumbled, clucking to his horse. "Well, I'll do whatever has to be done when the time comes. First, I have to find out who's been making the fool out of me."

He slouched his shoulders. "Besides my own wife, that is," he gloomily added.

Kendra drew her curtain aside and watched as Aaron rode from the ranch. She placed a finger to her lip, wondering where he might be going so early in the morning. He hadn't mentioned any appointment in town. And she knew that he was in no mood for anything else. He was still too torn up about Seth and this problem with Holly, whatever it was this time.

Then Kendra tensed. She was now remembering hearing Holly's carriage leave only moments before Aaron's departure from the house. "Oh, no," she gasped. "Surely he's not following her. If he is, he will find out about her and Father. This isn't the right time."

She lifted her eyes to the ceiling. "Please, God, don't let Holly be foolish enough to go to Blackie this morning. Aaron mustn't find out in this way. He mustn't."

But she knew that she had to also follow. If this was the case, then someone had to intervene who could talk to them with a level head. "And an open heart," she whispered. "I must remember that Blackie is my father. My *father*. My true flesh-and-blood father. Maybe Aaron won't remember that in his rage. Aaron might even . . ."

Shaking her head, she tore into her clothes. She pulled her boots on, fitted her gunbelt around her waist, and pulled on her Stetson hat. Smoothing the legs of her jeans, she kept remembering the expressions on both Holly's and her father's faces at the memorial.

"Yes. I guess Holly would have to go to him. I'm sure she has plenty to say," Kendra sighed. "Wouldn't anyone, caught up in such a situation?"

Kendra glanced sadly toward the black mourning dress draped over a chair. She hadn't planned to place her mourning for Seth so quickly behind her, but for now, the living needed to be dealt with.

With a determined stride, she went out to Domino, saddled him, and rode in the direction of Virginia City.

The carriage felt like an oven today. Holly fanned herself with her handkerchief, feeling sinful for many things. She seemed to be mocking her mourning attire by going to the man she had fallen in love with. But her feelings of rage were stronger than her guilt over her deceit. The man with whom she had shared many sinful days and nights was in truth her father-in-law.

"Oh, the shame of it," she whimpered, blinking tears from her eyes. "Poor Aaron. Should he ever find out, it will be devastating to him."

Placing her hand on her abdomen, a sob tore from deep inside her. "This child I am carrying is Aaron's father's child," she cried. "How can I live with the knowledge of that? How can I?"

She covered her mouth with her hands. "I feel sick," she whispered. "Disgustingly sick. It seems I've brought nothing but more heartache into my life. How can I pretend this child is Aaron's now that I know who Blackie is?"

The heat caused her temples to throb and her throat to become dry. She proceeded to fan herself again, glancing from the carriage window. It was a hot, golden day. The air was so bright her eyes had to draw into a squint. She could see whirling yellow dust clouds building on the range and sage dotting the land under the glare of the morning sun. It was a drowsy sort of heat and it added to Holly's burden, oppressive in its muggy weight, making her wish for Boston and its beautiful, wintry snows.

"Maybe that's what I should do," she whispered to herself. "Return to Boston. Have my child there. Alone. Then no one would ever have to know whose it really is."

A sluggish smile lifted her lips. "That has to be my answer," she sighed. "I'll go back to Boston. My child and I will have a life of our own. Everyone in Boston will believe it's Aaron's. They will just believe we've naturally separated. It was common knowledge there that Aaron and I quarreled quite frequently."

Resting her head back against the plush-cushioned seat, she closed her eyes and whispered: "Yes. That's what I'll do. I'll . . . go . . . home."

Her head bobbed as she half-dozed. Then when she heard the noise of the city she became quickly alert and watched the International Hotel come into view. Parker knew where to take her. He had now done this many times. He still had his own pleasures in the gambling houses and saloons.

Feeling the carriage coming to a halt, Holly tensed. It saddened her thinking of the other times she had come to this hotel. How different she had felt then! She had always looked forward to seeing him with such exuberance. Guilt had never entered into what she was

384

doing. But now? Dread flooded her senses. She didn't even know what to expect. Would he be as outraged . . . as . . . she . . . ?

With her head held high, she stepped from the carriage and entered the lobby of the hotel. Without stopping to inquire about whether or not Blackie was in his room, she began climbing the stairs, stopping and trembling before his door once she had reached it.

"Can I really do this?" she whispered, clasping and unclasping her hands. She straightened her back and swallowed hard. "Yes. I must," she murmured. "I must."

Lifting her hand, she tapped lightly on the door. She stood numbly, waiting. When couples floated by behind her, she placed her hand at the side of her face, hoping not to be recognized. Before, it hadn't really mattered. She had, at one time, even begun having hopes of a lasting relationship with this man. But when it had become a reality, with her being with child, she knew that it could never be. With his lifestyle, a child would only be in his way.

I hadn't planned to become with child or to fall in love, she thought gloomily to herself. And she most certainly hadn't planned to fall in love with her own father-in-law.

Not having received any response from her knocking on the door, Holly cleared her throat nervously and knocked again. She sniffed. She could smell cigar smoke circling from beneath the closed door. She knew he was there. Why didn't he come to the door?

Glancing from side to side, making sure she wasn't being observed, Holly placed a hand on the doorknob. Barely breathing, she began turning it.

"It's not locked," she whispered, continuing to slowly

turn the knob. "Thank God, the door isn't locked."

When the knob had made its full turn and the door had begun to creep slowly open, Holly peeked her head around its corner. She stifled a sob with the back of her hand when she saw him stretched across the bed, unshaven and hollow-eyed.

A bottle of whiskey lay empty at the foot of the bed and a cigar hung limply from between his lips. He lay fully clothed, even to his boots. It was apparent that when he had left the Carpenters' Circle C Ranch, he had returned to the hotel and had decided to drown his sorrow and unbelievable discoveries in alcohol.

The deep love Holly felt for Blackie washed through her in a tormented agony, knowing that what they had had was never to be again. She wasn't even sure if she could live with that fact. But she *did* have their child. A part of Blackie would always be with her. . . .

Creeping into the room, Holly went to the bed and kneeled over Blackie, placing a hand to his cheek. "Blackie," she whispered. "It's me. Holly. Darling, I'm so sorry."

Blackie rolled from the bed on the opposite side. He teetered toward a table where another bottle of whiskey sat, half-emptied. He smashed his cigar out and poured some whiskey into a glass. Tipping it to his lips, he emptied it in one fast swallow. A shudder visibly rolled through him as he slammed the glass back down onto the table. And, with accusing eyes, he swung around and faced Holly.

"Why did you lie, Holly?" he said thickly. "Why didn't you tell me your real name? God. You're my . . . son's . . . wife."

Holly's dark hair swung around her shoulders as she

turned and put her back to him. She placed a knuckle to her teeth and bore down onto it, wincing with the pain she was purposely inflicting.

Blackie pulled his frock coat off and let it drop to the floor, then he tore the ascot from his throat and slung it across the room. "Damn it, Holly," he grumbled. "Why were you being unfaithful to my son? Didn't he give you everything you needed? The Carpenters have money. Money can buy most anything."

He unbuttoned his shirt and jerked it from his body and went to a wooden wash basin. "Except respect, that is," he growled. "You seem to lack that now, my daughter-in-law."

He stooped over the basin and began splashing water onto his face, then combed some of it through his hair with his fingers. Grabbing a towel, he walked slowly toward Holly. "Why have you come?" he asked. "You should know that I don't want to ever see you again."

Tears ran in rivers down Holly's face. She wiped at them, sobbing. "I said that I was sorry, Blackie," she said.

"Stanford Carpenter is my real name," he said bluntly.

Holly swung around. Her green eyes suddenly held a cold anger in them. "See," she accused. "I wasn't the only one not being truthful. If you had told me your true, full name, I would have known you were Aaron's father. As it was, I only knew you as Blackie. How can you accuse me so unjustly? You are guilty of the same sin as I. Blackie, please. You mustn't hate me. You mustn't."

"But, Holly, *why*? Isn't my son man enough to hold his own wife at home?"

"Aaron has much on his mind," Holly said, lowering her eyes. "He just doesn't have enough . . . time . . . for me. That's the problem, Blackie." She would not speak of the child ever to Blackie. He would never know that the child was . . . his.

It would be useless . . . telling him.

"So you just went looking for companionship and just happened to choose me," he said dryly.

"If I remember right, you had a bit to do with our first time together."

Blackie ran his fingers through his hair, arranging it in gold waves. "Yes," he said quietly. "I guess I did."

"What are you going to do now that you know about Aaron?"

"What *can* I do?" Blackie demanded. "Now that you are involved, what the hell *can* I do? He can never know about us."

"Kendra already knows."

"I'm aware of that," he said. He went to his wardrobe and chose a fresh shirt and slipped into it.

"You are?" Holly whispered, her green eyes wide. "Did Kendra talk to you about . . . uh . . . me and you? Is that how you know she knows?"

"Exactly."

Holly paled. "And? What did she say? What must she . . . think . . . ?"

Blackie's blue eyes narrowed. "What would you think if you had found out that your father was bedding his son's wife?" he growled.

Holly hung her head and slouched down onto a chair. "Oh, Blackie, I am so sorry," she whispered.

"Quit saying that," he shouted. "You're sorry. What good is that? I've surely lost all my daughter's respect all over again. And if Aaron should find out, God. What

388

would *he* do?"

Aaron drew his horse up next to Holly's carriage and dismounted. As he tied his horse's reins to a hitching rail, he caught a fast glimpse of Parker as he stepped from Blackie's Gambling Emporium, headed toward the saloon next to it.

"So he's a part of the deceit," Aaron said angrily to himself. "All along Parker has known and has continued to aid Holly in her deceit. And in Virginia City, of all places. I had thought all along she was doing her shopping in Reno."

Taking wide strides, he moved to Parker's side and grabbed him by the wrist. Urging Parker around to face him, Aaron glowered into his face. "Where the hell is Holly?" he hissed.

Parker's eyes wavered. He looked nervously toward the International Hotel. "Damned if I know," he murmured. "I just bring her to town. Nothin' else."

"You're lying," Aaron growled from between clenched teeth. "Now you tell me or you're going to feel my six-shooter in your ribs."

"Aaron, my God," Parker gasped.

Aaron forced Parker between the buildings. "How long have you been in on this thing, Parker?"

"I don't know what you're talking about."

"Yes, you do. You know that Holly isn't shopping. She's with a man. What man, Parker? Where?"

Aaron's hands went to Parker's throat. He circled his fingers around it. "I don't intend to put up with lies much longer. Now tell me . . . or else . . ."

Parker's face was growing red. He struggled and began pushing against Aaron's chest. "I can't tell, Aaron," he gasped. "Holly. I promised Holly."

"Who's payin' your wages, Parker?" Aaron said, removing his fingers from around his neck. He placed his hands on his revolver and pulled it threateningly from his holster.

Parker looked down at the revolver pointing directly at his stomach. "Why, *you* pay my wages, Aaron," he said thickly. "You do. And, Aaron, don't do anything foolish. I'll tell. I'll tell you all you want to know. Just place that revolver back in the holster."

Aaron stuck the cold barrel of his revolver into Parker's stomach, nudging him with it. "Not until I get all the information I'm after," he growled. "Now. Start talking."

Parker inched back against the brick wall. "All right," he said, panting. "Just give me time. It's not every day that I've had a revolver stickin' in my guts."

Aaron eased away from him and lowered the barrel of his revolver. "Is that better?" he grumbled.

"I'd say," Parker laughed nervously. He wiped nervous perspiration from his brow with the back of his hand.

"I'm waiting. . . ." Aaron growled, tipping his hat back with the barrel of his revolver.

"She's with a gambler," Parker said anxiously. "He goes by the name of Blackie."

Aaron took a step backwards, clumsily tripping over an empty whiskey bottle. His heart began pounding wildly and his stomach lurched. He began to shake his head slowly back and forth. "No," he murmured. "You must be wrong. You're surely mistaken."

"No. There's no mistake. There's only one man in town who goes by the name of Blackie and who plays the game of blackjack so well," Parker said solemnly.

"No," Aaron once more said. "It can't be."

"Why, Aaron? Do you know him?"

"Huh?" Aaron said, raising his eyebrows.

"You act as though you know this Blackie," Parker said.

A slow ache was beginning to circle Aaron's heart. His own father. His own father . . . and . . . Holly . . . !

Then he felt a raw sort of sickness invading his senses. Holly . . . was pregnant . . . and with . . . !

"Parker, I saw you come from a gambling emporium," he said hoarsely. "Is this Blackie in there now?"

"No. He and . . . uh . . . well . . . uh . . . Holly, well they are probably in his room," Parker said. He hung his head. "Damn it, Aaron. I hate to tell you all of this. Why did you make me?"

"Where does he make his residence?" Aaron asked dryly.

Parker's gaze moved slowly upward. "In the International Hotel," he said.

"That's all I need to know," Aaron said. "I owe you a thanks, Parker, for telling me. But, instead, Parker, pick up your last paycheck from the Circle C when you arrive back at the ranch today."

"Aaron, you can't fire me over this," Parker begged.

Aaron repositioned his hat in place and dropped his gun inside his holster. "It's already done, Parker. You *are* fired," he said. "You betrayed my trust in you when you chose to join in with Holly in her deceit of me. As I said, your last paycheck will be written out for you when you get back to the ranch later in the day after you do

391

your one last deed for me, the owner. You will take Holly home this one more time. Then clear out your things and don't let me ever see or hear from you again."

"I ought to leave that damn Holly stranded," Parker said, straightening his dark frock coat.

"Then you wouldn't draw your wages coming to you," Aaron said flatly. "So I would suggest you go sit in that carriage and do only what you're getting paid for, Parker. Holly will be ready to leave shortly. I can assure you of that."

Turning on his heel, Aaron moved from between the buildings. He straightened the gunbelt at his hips, cleared his throat nervously, then headed toward the International Hotel. He strolled slowly to the front desk, dreading having to ask for Blackie's room number.

"My own father" kept rolling through his mind, over and over again. "Holly . . . and my . . . own father."

Asking for Blackie's room number was simple enough. It seemed to Aaron that everyone knew Blackie's name right away when it was mentioned. Yes, his father had brought his reputation clear from Boston. He was a man full of charm, wit, and skill. And somehow he had duped Holly with all three of these qualities.

With weak knees and a dry throat, Aaron crept up the stairs until he came to the first landing. He stopped to inhale deeply, looking down the full length of the long, narrow hallway. In one of these rooms, his father and his wife were . . . what . . . ? What were they doing? After last night, surely they knew better than to . . .

Had Holly used a fictitious name? Had Blackie not given her his last name? How could such a thing have happened? Aaron was torn. He wasn't sure what he was going to do now that the "other man" had proven to be his own father.

A door opening only a footstep away drew Aaron quickly into a dark corner, breathless. He wasn't ready to be discovered. But would he ever be? Holding himself steellike against the wall, he watched as a clinging couple strode on past him, quite unaware of his presence. And as they moved on down the staircase, Aaron stepped back into the soft, mellow glow of the candles in the wall sconces.

"I must get this thing over with," he whispered. "Or I shall surely have a stroke from the worry."

Stepping gingerly along the highly polished, hardwood floor, Aaron checked the numbers on the doors. And when he found the number that corresponded with the name of Blackie, a dizziness of sorts suddenly enflamed his head, causing him to reel and grasp onto the doorknob, to balance himself against it. But as he grabbed, his fingers turned the knob, and he suddenly found himself falling into the room that housed his wife . . . and . . . his father.

Holly rose quickly from the chair and hurried behind it as she watched Aaron pick himself up from the floor. She hid herself behind the back of the chair and slowly peered from around it. Her temples were throbbing . . . her mouth had gone dry . . .

"Aaron," Blackie gasped, taking a step backwards. "My God, Aaron." He cast a quick glance toward Holly, seeing her cowering behind the tall-backed chair, and shame coursed through him.

"I would never have believed it," Aaron said, straightening his back as he found his full weight back on his feet. He looked slowly from the beautiful, round face of Holly as she looked up so innocently at him, and then

393

at the guilt-lined face of his father.

"Father, first you desert me, let ten years pass before I ever hear from you again, and then when you *do* make yourself known in my life again it happens to be with my wife," Aaron said, laughing absently, kneading his chin. "Father, you're one for the books, you are."

Holly rose slowly from the floor and began inching toward Aaron. "Aaron, please. Let me explain," she murmured. She flinched when she saw his hand go to his revolver. Then she sighed when she saw that his only intention so far was to rest his hand heavily on it.

"And, you, Father," Aaron growled. "What sort of explanations do you offer?"

"I had no idea that Holly was your wife," Blackie said. He went back to his whiskey bottle and poured himself another drink. Tipping his glass to his lips, he emptied it in one fast swallow.

"Getting drunk isn't the answer here," Aaron growled. He walked quickly across the room, picked up the bottle, and threw it angrily against the wall. "Yet, I don't guess there are any answers, are there?" he added, turning his attention to Holly.

"And what you confessed to me last night," Aaron growled. "What do you have to say about that?"

Holly covered her mouth with her hands and began shaking her head desperately back and forth, glancing, horrified, toward Blackie.

Aaron's insides turned cold. Holly hadn't told Blackie yet. He didn't even know that she was carrying his child! Well, Aaron thought to himself, I won't be the one to tell him. Let the fool find out for himself, from someone else. No sense in letting *any*one know. Not yet, anyway.

"What's that?" Blackie said, eyeing Aaron, then Holly.

"It was something to do with the ranch," Aaron growled. "Nothing at all to do with you."

Why should Blackie know? He would just desert this child as he had his others. No. Blackie wouldn't know about this child. It was quite evident that Holly had chosen to not tell him. This gave Aaron a small ray of hope. Though he hated Holly with all his being at this moment, he still had to hope she would think of the Carpenter name and the shame she had already brought to it, without telling all around about an illegitimate child!

"Aaron, son," Blackie began, taking a step toward him.

Aaron interrupted him. "Don't call me that," he snarled. "You don't have the right to call me son. You haven't been a father for way too long now."

"I see that you call me Father," Blackie argued. "So you haven't forgotten that I *am*."

"What else am I supposed to call you?" Aaron said. "Fool? Cheat? Deserter? Which of those names suits you best?"

Blackie reached a hand out to Aaron. "Please, Aaron," he sighed. "I know you have much bitterness inside you for everything. But, believe me, I had reasons why I left Boston." He lowered his eyes and raked his fingers through his hair. "But I had no reason other than an attraction to a beautiful lady for having been with your wife." His eyes lifted. "But you know damn well I didn't know she was your wife. I didn't even know you were in Nevada." He glowered toward Holly. "Had *she* been honest . . ."

Holly went to Blackie and spoke into his face. "Had *you* been honest, don't you mean," she accused. "I didn't know who you were. Why on earth did you lie to *me*?"

"I've left a trail of gambling debts behind me, Holly,"

he said flatly. "I've chosen a different name in each different city I've been in."

"You haven't changed, have you, Father," Aaron growled. "In Boston, Mother was always having to bail you out with her money. What surprises me is why you gave that up. Wasn't that easier for you, having someone to pay your gambling debts?"

"Aaron, that's why I wanted to talk to you last night," Blackie pleaded, gesturing with both his hands.

Seeing Holly and Blackie standing so close together, and seeing so much in Holly's eyes when she looked up into Blackie's face, made Aaron suddenly see red. It was as though something had snapped inside his brain. He drew his revolver from its holster and directed it toward his wife and father. He shook his head angrily. "I don't want to hear any more," he said. He nodded his head. "Look at the two of you. Lovebirds. My wife and father. Maybe you'd even like to die together. How would you like that?"

Holly paled. "Aaron, you wouldn't," she said, inching next to Blackie, suddenly clinging to him around the waist.

Kendra dismounted quickly next to Aaron's horse. She looked desperately from side to side, wondering which way Aaron might have gone. Then she spied Parker standing stiffly next to the family carriage. With a furious heartbeat, she rushed to him.

"Parker," she said, tipping her hat back as she looked up into his face. "Where is Aaron? Have you seen him?"

She heard a groan come from Parker as his eyes rolled back into his head. Then he slouched his shoulders and leaned closer to her.

"Why are you looking for him?" he asked sullenly.

"Parker," she said flatly. "That's none of your business. Now, if you know where he is, tell me. This instant. This could be a matter of life or death."

Parker glanced toward the International Hotel, then back to Kendra. He nodded toward the hotel. "In there," he grumbled. "Aaron went in there."

Kendra's insides grew tremorous as she glanced toward the hotel. Then she directed her eyes back to Parker. "Did he say why he was going in there?" she asked dryly.

"Kendra, not you too," Parker groaned.

"What on earth do you mean, not me too?"

"Kendra, it's best you just climb back on Domino and head back home. Let Aaron do what needs to be done. You have no place gettin' mixed up in his private affairs."

"You're a hired hand, Parker," she said angrily. "I don't take orders from you. Now, Parker, will you tell me, or will I have to fire you?"

Parker threw his head back, laughing boisterously. "Fire me?" he said. Then he eyed her. "Kendra, Aaron has already done that little thing today."

Kendra's mouth dropped open. "What?" she gasped. "Why?"

"Let Aaron tell you," Parker growled. "I'm just doin' what was told me now. I'm standin' here waitin' on Holly. I don't plan to do nothin' else."

"Then you *do* know why Aaron went in there?"

"Yep . . ."

"Parker, please tell me."

"Nope . . ."

"Then I'll have to figure it out for myself, I guess," she said flatly. She swung around and began walking toward the hotel, knowing that the answers to her questions had to lie there. More than likely her father and Holly were also in that hotel. The thought of what might be happening in one of the hotel rooms right now made shivers ride her spine.

"Kendra," Parker said, rushing to her, taking her by the arm. "You'd best not go in there."

"And why not?" she asked, jerking free of him.

"If you must know, Aaron is checkin' on Holly and this guy Blackie she's been seein'."

Kendra closed her eyes and shook her head sadly. "That's what I thought," she murmured. She nodded toward the carriage. "Go on back to the carriage," she whispered. "I know what I'm doing. Don't worry about me."

"Aaron was damn mad," Parker said, glancing upward at the windows that lined the front of the building. "He was wearing his revolver. He even pulled it on me and threatened me with it. If I hadn't given him the answers he wanted, no tellin' what he'd have done."

"Good Lord," Kendra gasped. She whirled around and ran into the hotel. When she learned Blackie's room number from the desk clerk, she took the steps, two at a time, until she found herself standing outside Blackie's room. Without even knocking, she turned the knob, pushed the door open, then stood, wide-eyed and wordless at what she had stepped into.

"Aaron!" she whispered, inching toward him. "Put the revolver away."

The hair rose at the nape of her neck when she saw that he wasn't going to listen to her. Instead, he continued to stand there, glaring at Holly and Blackie, hate etched across his face.

"Aaron," Kendra pleaded. "You mustn't. Your reputation. Remember the Carpenter reputation. This will spread like wildfire. I will never be able to hold my head up again in this town or any other town. You will be hung and I . . . well . . . I . . . will forever be shamed. You mustn't kill Father . . . or Holly. Put the revolver away. Let's go home. There's no need to carry this thing any further. We should be home, mourning Seth. Nothing more. Please . . . ?"

She held her hands out to Aaron, watching his eyes beginning to waver as tears began seeping from their corners. Then Kendra closed her eyes momentarily, and she took a deep breath of relief as the revolver slowly lowered.

She then rushed to Aaron and slung her arms about his neck and hugged him tightly to her, feeling the cold, hard steel of the revolver against her arms, thanking God that she had been in time.

"Aaron, oh, Aaron," she whispered. "I know how you must feel. It seems as though your world is crumbling around you. First Seth . . . then Holly."

"How did you . . . ?"

"I've known for a while now, Aaron."

"And you didn't tell me?"

"I didn't want to hurt you."

Aaron pulled free from her embrace and slipped his gun into its holster. "I've got to get out of here," he said thickly.

Blackie took two wide strides and suddenly clasped his

hands onto Aaron's shoulders. "By damn, Aaron, you're going to listen to me before you go anywhere," he said.

Blackie watched Aaron's eyes lift to his, flinching when he saw the empty coldness there. But he had to tell Aaron now. He knew that he wouldn't be given another chance. Not after this morning and its revelations.

"I told you before. I don't want to hear anything you have to say," Aaron said, void of feeling or expression.

"But you *will* listen to what I have to say."

Kendra stood quiet, looking from her father to Aaron. Strange. They did resemble each other, and it did seem that they both had the same stubbornness.

"Aaron," Blackie said, then glanced toward Kendra. "Kendra?" He then focused back on Aaron. "You were never told the full truth of why I left Boston. From your attitude toward me I know that your mother failed to tell you that she ordered me from the house. I had no choice *but* to go. You do know that it was *her* house . . . *her* money . . . *her* land. I was only there, a *thing* for her pleasure, whenever she chose to seek me out for that pleasure."

Kendra blushed and lowered her eyes, stunned at what he was confessing to them. She moved to Aaron's side and placed an arm about his waist. They needed each other's comfort at this time. They had clung together through all the years and now it was even more important that they do so. It would be a shield of sorts against what else might be told to them.

Blackie drew away from Aaron and began pacing. He held his hands clasped behind him and kept his head bowed. "You see, I couldn't resist the cards even then," he said shallowly. "But you know that. And, yes, I *did* go to your mother, many times, for her to bail me out when I

400

lost at blackjack."

He cleared his throat nervously and stopped to stare blankly from a window. "I squandered her wealth. I was obsessed to the point that I went days without eating. I didn't show up at the bank to see to my duties. I didn't even sleep. I just played blackjack. It was the same as being an alcoholic. It was something I could *not* do without."

He turned and eyed Kendra, and then Aaron. "As it is even now with me," he said. "But this time, I have *made* money. Not *lost* it. So I invested in the only thing I knew how to do. I purchased the gambling emporium. And, damn it, I've done quite well."

Aaron jerked away from Kendra, glowering. "What the hell does that have to do with us?" he snarled. "Come on, Kendra. Let's get out of here. I need some fresh air."

Once more Blackie stopped Aaron with the firm grip of a hand. "No. You haven't heard it all," he said. "Aaron, what I've been trying to tell you is that your mother gave me no choice *but* to leave. Please listen. It's time that you cast your stubborn streak aside and listen instead of telling. I am not one of your cowhands, ready to be brushed aside casually, as though I don't exist, except for you and your damn orders."

"So what you are saying is . . . is that you let Mother chase you off?" Aaron growled. "That you didn't have the backbone to stand up to your own wife and fight back? You didn't care enough about your family to quit playing blackjack? You are some man, Father. One I hope never to be."

Blackie strode to a table and lifted a half-smoked cigar from an ashtray. He lighted it and slouched down onto a chair. "I can understand your thinking such a thing," he murmured. "But you haven't heard it all. Maybe you will understand that I had no choice but to leave. And without a goodbye to you children."

"Let's hear it all," Aaron sighed, settling down onto a chair opposite Blackie. "Now that you're opening up wounds, we might as well get it all over with."

"Kendra, please come and sit beside me?" Blackie asked, motioning with a hand.

"I prefer standing," Kendra said stiffly. Holly moved next to her, eyes wide.

"All right," Blackie said, swallowing hard. He took a deep puff from his cigar, then held it, smoking, between two fingers. "To continue. Your mother quit letting me have any money. So I started . . . started . . ." He raked his fingers through his hair, finding the words hard. He shook his fingers away, then continued. "I started stealing from the bank," he said in a slur.

Aaron's face went blank, then a slow laugh began to rise from inside him. "I had thought as much," he said. "I figured you had done that, Father."

"Your mother caught me at it," Blackie continued, ignoring Aaron's sarcasm. "She threatened me. She told me to leave. She said that I couldn't tell you children goodbye. She said that if I involved you at all in what she had chosen to do about me, she would turn me in to the sheriff. She would see to it that I was sent to jail. So I had to promise to forget you children. As much as it tore at my heart, I had to promise her that, to keep my freedom."

Aaron rose from the chair just as angry as before. "This is what you had to tell us?" he said, laughing sarcastically. "And you think telling us that would make us feel sorry for you? Never, Father."

"No. Not sorry. I wanted you to just understand," Blackie pleaded. "Your mother was *not* the gentle soul she presented herself as. Only I knew the true woman. She ruled me with an iron glove. She was cold inside. Ice cold. I was glad to be away from her. I don't know how I stood her as long as I did. But I guess I *do* really know why."

Kendra moved to Aaron's side. "Let's go, Aaron," she whispered. "I think I've heard enough." It felt good to be able to reject her father. In a sense, she and Aaron had become the victors in this emotional conflict, after all. Leaving their father pleading seemed cruel . . . yet right. . . .

Blackie choked on tears. "So you can't understand or forgive?" he said, looking from Kendra to Aaron.

"Forgive?" Aaron said, placing his hand on his revolver. "I still feel a bullet is what you deserve."

Kendra gently moved Aaron's hand from his revolver. "Come on, Aaron," she whispered. "There's been enough sadness in our family already. There's no point in going on with this with Father."

Aaron shook his head, looking as though he were drunk. "You're right," he said. "Let's go home."

"Aaron? Kendra?" Blackie pleaded, following them to the door.

Kendra turned and glowered at Blackie. "Father, don't you think it's time for you to move on? I've heard about this place called Las Vegas. Why not try your luck there? Seems you've lost here."

She gave him a smug look, then placed her back to him and walked quickly from the room alongside Aaron.

Chapter Twenty-Two

Packed valises were piled by the front door. Kendra and Aaron exchanged slow glances. Then Kendra watched as Aaron settled down into a chair, placing his fingertips together before him. Kendra sat down next to him, leaning a hand to his knee. "Aaron, it's best this way," she tried to reassure him. "Holly has never been happy here."

Aaron raked his eyes quickly over Kendra, amazed that nothing seemed ever to change her. She was still strong, yet sweet in a gentle sort of way. A warmth spiraled through him, no longer caring that she wore those damn jeans and shirts. She was lovely . . . no matter what she wore. In his life, she had been the best thing yet for him.

"Aaron?" Kendra said, slowly smiling. She felt a flush rise on her cheeks, seeing his appraisal of her in the faded blue of his eyes. "Why are you looking at me like that?"

"Oh, it's just that you always seem to be here, my pillar of strength, though you are ten years younger," he laughed hoarsely. "Nothing takes away from your strength. I admire you for that, Kendra. Damn admire you."

"I hurt, Aaron," she whispered. "But I wear my hurt well, so to speak. But I *do* hurt."

Her thoughts went to her father . . . to Lucas . . . to Seth. Yes, she had felt many hurts these past several weeks. But she had seen that she was needed by Aaron and had managed to keep all *her* hurts inside her. Now she was glad that she had. She could see the pride in Aaron's eyes and could hear it in his voice. It gave her a peaceful feeling inside.

"I'm sure you do," Aaron said, shaking his head. "I'm sure you do." He lowered his eyes. "And do you plan to see . . . ah . . . Lucas Hall again?"

"You know I do, Aaron," she said dryly. "I love him. I can't help but love him."

"Kendra, you know that I shall never be able to give you my blessing," he said, furrowing his brow. "Not as long as . . ."

Kendra shook her head. "Yes. I know," she murmured. "Not as long as you and Lucas continue to have your differences."

"You do see the impossibilities of this situation, don't you, Kendra?"

"I tend to lean both ways now," she said, avoiding the shock in Aaron's eyes. Then she met his gaze with a determined force. "You see, Aaron," she continued, "I have seen the sheep. . . ."

Aaron leaned forward, dropping his hands. "You . . . what . . . ?"

"Lucas showed me the sheep," she continued. "I even met Alfredo, the Basque sheepherder. Aaron, I think you're wrong about the sheep. It was such a beautiful scene out there on the range. The sheep are beautiful. They are so peaceful. I don't see why . . ."

Aaron rose quickly from the chair. "Because they ruin the grazing land," he shouted, flailing his arms into the air. "I've told you that. Over and over again. Why do you continue to close your ears to the truth?"

"Aaron, please," Kendra said, flinching. "Don't get so angry. It's not good for you. You've already been through so much. You must watch your temper."

Aaron slunk back down onto the chair, holding his head in his hands. "How did we get on the subject of sheep?" he said quietly. "That's the *last* thing I want to discuss this morning."

Kendra bowed her head. "I know," she whispered. "I'm sorry."

Recently Kendra seemed always to be finding the need to say that she was sorry. She wished this time in their life could be blotted out . . . that it was all behind them.

"Holly is surely taking her time," Aaron grumbled. "The carriage has been waitin' now for at least a half an hour. If Holly just hadn't . . ."

"But she did," Kendra said flatly.

"Maybe if *I* . . ."

Kendra flung her hands into the air. "Stop it, Aaron," she cried. "Just stop it. Nothing you say will change what has happened. And you know you would do nothing different if you had the chance to live your life over again. You have your responsibilities to the ranch *and* to your banks. Holly just couldn't accept it. That's all."

The sound of carriage wheels approaching drew Kendra to the door. She opened it and grew cold inside when she saw Emanuelle being helped to the ground by a coachman. In her fully gathered silk dress and with her lace-trimmed bonnet tied snugly beneath her chin, she looked the picture of respectability.

"Who is it?" Aaron asked, rising. He went to the door and looked out, then stiffened. "Oh, no. Not her. Why doesn't she give up on us? Seth is dead. Why can't she let him rest in peace?"

"It isn't Seth she wants to disturb, Aaron," Kendra said dryly. "I believe she wants to bother us. The living."

Aaron swung the door open and stepped out onto the porch. He placed his legs wide apart and crossed his arms over his chest. "Why have you come here again?" he snapped. He watched in disbelief as Emanuelle tilted her chin haughtily and began climbing the stairs toward him.

"I must speak with you. In private, Aaron," she said flatly.

"I don't have time to speak with the likes of you," he growled. "You've wasted your time. Just get back aboard the carriage and head back in the direction of Virginia City."

"No. I won't do that," Emanuelle said, her eyes flashing. "I wish to speak to you. And today. I won't leave until you listen to what I have to say."

Kendra moved to Aaron's side. "You're a bit too late," she laughed. "You can't blackmail us to get your way. Aaron already knows about Father and Holly. So you see, Emanuelle, you *have* wasted your time by driving out here today."

Aaron questioned Kendra with his eyes, but said nothing. It seemed she knew *much* more than he ever had. He shook his head sadly, then directed his attention back to Emanuelle. "So you planned to blackmail us Carpenters, eh?" he spat. He pointed toward the carriage. "I don't know what that was all about, but seems your little plan backfired. Go on, Emanuelle. Leave now. We've got things to do."

Emanuelle moved on past Aaron and Kendra and into the house. She whirled around, and, with a set stare, met Aaron and Kendra's advance toward her. "If you won't speak to me in private, Aaron, then I must tell you also, Kendra," she said icily.

"Whatever you have to say to me, Kendra is quite free to hear," Aaron said. "So spit it out, Emanuelle. Seems you're determined to cause us trouble until we're in *our* graves."

Emanuelle looked sheepishly from Aaron to Kendra. "I want to stay here. Live with you," she murmured.

Kendra sighed heavily. "Emanuelle, we've been through all of this before," she said. "Now if that's all you've come for, you have indeed wasted your time."

"You wouldn't want Seth's child to be born without a proper home, would you?" Emanuelle quickly blurted, tensing when she saw the looks of horror register in both Aaron's and Kendra's eyes.

"Child?" Kendra and Aaron said in unison, sounding as though an echo of one another's voices.

"What are you talking about, Emanuelle?" Kendra asked, taking a step toward her. "Is this another scheme? If it is, it won't work."

"I'm pregnant. With Seth's child," Emanuelle said flatly. "He knew. But only the day he was : . . the day he . . . died." She lowered her eyes. "I had just told him. Then he went off and had . . . to . . . die."

"Jesus Christ," Aaron mumbled, crumbling down onto a chair. He lowered his head into his hands, shaking it back and forth. "What else?" he mumbled. "What else can happen?"

"So you see?" Emanuelle said. "I *do* have a good reason to live here. Since you and your wife haven't had a

409

child, then it will be Seth's child who will be the Carpenter heir. You have to let Seth's child have that chance in life. He belongs *here*. With your family. With Seth's family."

A slow rage began to rise inside Kendra. "You probably planned it," she hissed. "You probably planned to trick Seth into marrying you by getting pregnant with his child." She placed her hands on her hips and tilted her chin. "And how do we know it's not somebody else's child? You have a reputation, you know."

"I was with no other man after Seth and I began living together," Emanuelle said icily. "Seth believed the child was his. It *is* his. And it deserves to have all the comforts in life that the Carpenter money can give it. And since the child will be the heir to the Carpenter fortune, you *must* be fair to both me and the child."

The word "heir" kept running through Aaron's mind. Now that it had been brought to mind, yes, with his condition, there would be no heir born from his union with a woman. And now to find out that Seth's whore was carrying the only Carpenter heir? It sickened him. It dumbfounded him. How could he keep it from happening?

Then a slow smile curved his lips upward. No one knew the truth about Holly's child except Holly. This child she was carrying was going to be mistaken as his, anyway, wasn't it? Yes! That was the answer! He did have an heir after all!

He rose slowly to his feet and faced Emanuelle, who stood wide-eyed, waiting for an answer. "Let me think for a minute here," he said, kneading his chin.

"Aaron, there's nothing to think about," Kendra argued. "She can't stay here."

Aaron went to Kendra and clasped her shoulders. "Kendra, we have to believe that the child Emanuelle is carrying is Seth's," he whispered. "And you know as well as I that we can't turn our backs on the child. Now can we?"

"If it *is* Seth's," she softly argued.

"I think I have a way to make sure," Aaron said, leaning a soft kiss onto Kendra's cheek. "Just you let me take care of this."

"Well, all right, Aaron," Kendra murmured.

Aaron went to Emanuelle and took her by the elbow. "Emanuelle, please be seated," he said. "I think we have much to discuss here."

Emanuelle nodded and let herself by guided into a chair.

Aaron settled down next to her and leaned a bit out from the chair, his elbows resting on each of his knees. He clasped his hands together tightly and directed a set look toward Emanuelle. "So you say this child is Seth's," he said softly.

"Yes," she said in an almost-whisper.

"Then, my dear, you can stay here with us," Aaron said, giving Kendra a frown when he heard her gasp loudly at his side.

Emanuelle reached out and wrapped her fingers about Aaron's hands. "Oh, thank you," she sighed. "Thank you. Thank you. Seth would've wanted it this way."

"Emanuelle," Aaron said flatly, brushing her hands away from his. "You didn't let me finish." He rose from the chair and began slowly pacing. "I said that you could stay here. But I didn't say for how long." He swung around and faced her.

"What do you mean?" Emanuelle whispered, rising

411

from the chair, going to him.

"Emanuelle, you can stay here until the child is born. Then you must leave it here and go on your way," Aaron said, smiling to himself when he saw her falter and her face pale in color.

"You can't mean . . ."

"Yes. Exactly," Aaron corrected. "I mean to say that you can be a part of our lives until the child is born. Then all we will be interested in *is* the child. Seth's child. You will then go on your way and forget you had the child. Do I make myself clear?"

"No!" Emanuelle screamed. "No!" She stomped a foot and grew red in the face.

"You have forgotten the child's welfare so quickly?" Aaron said, arching his eyebrows.

"You are cruel," Emanuelle hissed. "You are despicable!"

"This is the only way you can stay with us for any amount of time," Aaron said coolly. "Let me repeat. You can stay here until the child is born, then you will leave, and without the child."

"Why would you do this to me?" she cried. "What have I ever done to you?"

"You come to me in the shape you are in and can ask that?" Aaron growled.

"Seth had a part in my getting pregnant," Emanuelle sobbed. "It wasn't a plot on my part."

"No matter," Aaron said smoothly, strolling to a table to lift a cigar from a cigar case. He lighted the cigar and puffed leisurely on it. Suddenly everything seemed to be falling into place for him. Yes. Things would work out for him. But he did have Holly yet to convince. But knowing Holly and what she wanted out of life, that would be

412

simple enough.

"Where would I go?" Emanuelle sobbed further.

"We would pay you well," Aaron said. "You could go to Europe. You can live a life of luxury."

Emanuelle went to Aaron and eyed him closely. "You would do this for me?" she whispered.

"I would do this for Seth's child," he said flatly.

Emanuelle whirled around and went to Kendra. "And you? Do you agree?"

Kendra smiled toward Aaron, nodding. Yes. Her brother was a smart one all right. She would never have thought of such a scheme. She then directed her slight smile toward Emanuelle. "Yes," she said. "I would agree. I think it's quite a nice plan."

"But my child," Emanuelle said, turning once again to face Aaron. "I don't want to give up . . . my . . . child."

"From this moment on you wouldn't think of the child as yours," Aaron said. "You would just think of it as an inconvenience until you have the child. Then when we place the money in your hands you won't be sad about having to leave. You will gladly say goodbye to this 'inconvenience' . . . this small interruption in your life."

"God . . ." Emanuelle gasped, shaking her head slowly back and forth. "You are nothing like Seth. Nothing at all. He was the sweetest . . . kindest . . ."

"He was also taken in by you, which made him a bit of a fool," Aaron said. "Emanuelle, what is it to be? What is your answer? Do you agree with what I have offered you? For, you see, if you don't, I will have to tell you that I never want you or the child to set one foot on my property again, or I will have you arrested."

"Only because this child is Seth's will I agree to this,"

Emanuelle hissed. "Only because I feel I can't ever give my child a decent life. My child will have all he needs with you. Only because of this and because of Seth's memory will I agree to such a terrible thing."

"Then we understand one another?" Aaron said, smiling smugly.

"Yes," Emanuelle murmured.

"You will sign an agreement?"

Emanuelle placed a hand to her mouth. "You will even ask that of me? You trust me so little?"

"Exactly," Aaron said dryly.

Emanuelle lowered her eyes. "Then, yes. I guess I have no choice but to do everything that you ask."

"When can we expect you to bring your things and get settled in?" Aaron asked matter-of-factly. He crushed his cigar out in an ashtray, eyeing her closely.

"I'll return some time tomorrow," she murmured.

"I will have the papers ready by then," Aaron said. "You won't bring one article of your clothing into this house until you have signed your name to all I have asked of you."

"Oh!" Emanuelle said, whirling the skirt of her dress around to leave, then rushing from the room.

Aaron chuckled beneath his breath. Then his eyes wavered when Kendra sent him a questioning glance.

"What you've asked of her," Kendra murmured. "And to know that she has actually agreed? None of it is believable."

"But she *did* agree," Aaron said, glancing toward the staircase, knowing that Holly had to be talked to before she came down ready to say her goodbyes to Kendra. "And that is that. We shall say no more about it. We will raise Seth's child. We will see to it that Seth's child *does* get the

414

best. Seth will live on in his child."

Kendra swallowed hard. Yes, Aaron was right. She hadn't thought of it in that way. She looked toward Aaron as he took quick steps toward the staircase. "Where are you going, Aaron?" she said. "I thought you and Holly, well, had said all that was to be said between you."

Aaron gave her a quick glance from across his shoulder. "No. Not quite," he said, smiling. "I believe Holly is going to change her mind. She's *also* going to stay. I'm going to see to it. She won't refuse. I won't give her that chance."

Kendra lifted an eyebrow. "But, Aaron, *why*? What made you change your mind? What makes you think *she* will?"

"Life itself and its little surprises," Aaron said. Then he stopped and turned to face Kendra. "Trust me, Kendra. Everything I do, I do for family."

"Yes. You always have," Kendra murmured. She watched him as he disappeared at the top of the stairs, then went to the window and watched as the carriage carried Emanuelle away. She shook her head sadly and murmured, "Without Seth, it's going to be so hard living here with her around. . . ."

Aaron opened the bedroom door and looked across the room at Holly, who was closing the last of her valises. With a confident stride, he went to her and reopened the valise and began emptying garments from inside it.

"What are you doing, Aaron?" Holly gasped. "Aaron, it's taken me all morning to pack. Now you're . . . unpacking . . . ? What on earth are you doing that for?"

Aaron looked at her out of the corner of his eye, knowing that he should hate her, but in her he saw the only means of his survival. With a quick raking of his eyes, he saw her loveliness. She looked so damn innocent in her low-swept, lace-trimmed silken dress with its tiny waist and fully gathered skirt. Her hair hung in lovely, black coils across her shoulders and was pulled back behind her ears, from which tiny diamond earrings sparkled. Her face was a healthy pink and her eyes were bright. He had to believe that her pregnancy was the cause of this. He had heard that most women were more beautiful during that delicate time in their lives. He vividly remembered how lovely his own mother had been when she was pregnant with Kendra.

"You're not going to Boston," he stated flatly. He went and opened drawers and began replacing her dainty underthings inside them. "You're going to stay with me. Where you belong. I'll have it no other way."

"But, Aaron . . ." she murmured. "Why would you even want me? After what happened . . . ? After . . . your . . . father? You *know* I am carrying his child. I thought you hated me, Aaron."

Aaron swung around and took one of her dainty hands in his. "I've been wrong about so many things in my life, Holly," he said, hoping he was sounding convincing enough. He would say anything now, to get her to stay, to bear him *his* heir!

"Wrong . . . ?" Her green eyes became awash with sudden tears. "I've been the one who has been wrong, Aaron."

"I neglected you, Holly," he murmured. "I'm sorry about that."

"But . . . the . . . child . . . ?"

"We will pretend the child is *ours*," he mumbled.

"Why would you do this?" she whispered.

He couldn't tell her that he needed the child to make him look more a man than he felt that he was. He wanted the community to *see* that he was virile . . . to know that he could sire a son. Even if it was a daughter, the child would be proof of his manhood! Not to him . . . but to all who mattered! Even Kendra wouldn't know.

"Aaron, you didn't answer me. Why?" Holly persisted.

"We've shared much in our marriage," Aaron mumbled. "I am sorry I wasn't the one who gave you your first child. But no one needs to know this. We will just go on as if nothing ever happened. We will remain as man and wife. We *have* to keep the family intact. We've already lost one member. Please. We don't need to lose another. Please stay, Holly? Will you?"

Holly lowered her eyes and sniffled. "But, Aaron, don't you see? Things wouldn't be any different," she whispered. "You would still be busy with business. I would be neglected."

"I would try to change," he said. "And there is the child. You wanted a child to fill your lonely days. You will *have* a child. If you stay, Holly, I will make everything up to you."

Holly lifted her gaze to meet his. "Aaron, do you really want me to?" she whispered. "Do . . . can . . . you love me again, as before?"

Aaron drew her quickly into his arms and buried his face in her shoulder. "God, Holly," he said hoarsely. "I've already missed you too much. I don't want to have to live without you."

"Aaron," Holly cried. "Oh, Aaron." She twined her

arms about his neck and sobbed softly against his shoulder. "I'm sorry I betrayed you with another man."

"Let's never speak of it again," Aaron whispered.

"But your father . . ."

"We will forget about Father being . . . the . . . well, you know . . ." he mumbled. "He's gone. That's what's important."

"Darling, if you love me, *that* is all that matters," Holly whispered. "I will be good to you. You'll see. I *do* want to stay with you. I *do*."

"Not only because it is the most convenient thing to do?"

"No. Because I *want* to," she whispered. She reached a hand to his cheek. "And I want to thank you for giving me this second chance. You won't be sorry."

Aaron took Holly by the elbow. "Let's go share the good news with Kendra," he said, smiling broadly.

Holly took a step backwards. She paled. "Kendra isn't going to think this is good news," she said. "Kendra hates me."

"Right now everyone is filled with *many* sorts of feelings, Holly," Aaron said. "Just you give Kendra a chance to get used to our new way of life. Things will work out. You'll see."

Holly turned and faced him. "Then we are to say this child I am carrying is yours? Is that the way you really want it?" she whispered.

"Yes. That's the way I want it."

"When shall we tell Kendra?"

Remembering Emanuelle and her announcement Aaron smiled coyly. "We shall also break that piece of news to her at the very same time we tell her you are staying," he said.

Holly tensed. "Do you think that is wise? Might not she suspect it isn't our child?"

"I will tell her it is my child and she will believe me," Aaron said stubbornly. "How does she know we haven't been sleeping together much these past weeks and months? Who knows? Maybe the child is truly mine after all."

Aaron didn't look her way, for fear that she might read the lies by the sadness in his eyes. Instead, he guided her from the room, down the stairs to where Kendra still stood at the window.

"Kendra?" Aaron said quietly. He smiled toward her as she turned slowly around.

Kendra set her lips into a straight line and her eyes flashed when she saw Holly clinging so possessively to Aaron's arm. "Yes?" she said dryly.

"Holly has changed her mind," Aaron said, reaching to pat Holly's hand. "There are many reasons why she should stay."

"And what might those reasons be?" Kendra sighed.

"First, she is still a Carpenter. She is still my wife," Aaron said. "Second, there has been enough sadness in our lives without adding another. It's only right that Holly stay at my side during the continuing weeks of mourning for Seth. And, third, she is going to have my child, Kendra. Her place most definitely is at my side. Wouldn't you say?"

Kendra's fingers went to her throat. She felt the usual weakness in her knees that she felt whenever she was caught off guard. "A child . . . ?" she murmured. She gave Holly a disapproving look. "Aaron, why didn't you tell me earlier?"

"Because Holly was determined to go back to Boston,"

he said. "And now that she has changed her mind and has decided to remain here, as my wife, I thought you should know."

Kendra lifted a brow, hearing something in Aaron's voice. Somehow, she knew that he wasn't being truthful with her. If he had known about the child, *his* child, there would have been no way he would have let Holly go back to Boston.

No. None of it made any sense. But what did, anymore? First Emanuelle's announcing that she was with child . . . possibly the heir to the Carpenter fortune . . . then Holly's springing this same surprise on everyone.

A slow coldness began to grab at Kendra's insides. An heir! Emanuelle . . . then Holly . . .

She gave Aaron a twisted smile, then walked away from them. This heir, Aaron's child . . . maybe, just maybe, it was the child of another Carpenter. Possibly Blackie . . . Stanford . . . Carpenter . . . ?

Which one was being deceitful? Aaron . . . or . . . Holly?

Suddenly Kendra just didn't care. She flew from the house and mounted Domino. She had a terrible need to see Lucas. "And see him I will," she said stubbornly. "If everyone else around here gets their way about everything, so shall I . . . !"

Chapter Twenty-Three

On her search for Lucas, Kendra found herself riding past the schoolhouse. Not wanting to get into any sort of conversation with Steven Teague, she began to ride on past, but she stopped Domino abruptly when she saw a movement beneath one of the school's windows. Through a thick stand of prairie grass and sagebrush, Kendra caught sight of even more movement. Then she watched as the tiny head of Quick Deer rose slowly from the grasses and moved closer to the glass of the window and began peering inside.

"Quick Deer," Kendra whispered to herself. Compassion for the tiny Indian tore at her heart. She suddenly realized that she hadn't kept her promise to Quick Deer. She hadn't returned to the Piute village to teach him and his friends the skills of reading, writing, and arithmetic. And the legislature hadn't yet passed any rulings that would enable the Indian children to attend the white man's schools.

Kendra let her gaze take in the number of horses hitched to the hitching rail. There were many children attending school this day. She smiled coyly. "Maybe they need just one more student," she murmured.

Clucking to Domino, she led him to the hitching rail and secured her reins with the others. Tiptoing, she crept to the corner of the building and peeked around it, then stepped into full view when she saw Quick Deer hurriedly limping away in a half-hopping fashion toward a stand of piñon pine trees where he had left his pony.

"He must have heard my horse," Kendra whispered. "I scared him off."

Holding on to her hat, she began to run after him. She couldn't yell at him. She didn't want to draw attention to herself or Quick Deer. At least not until *she* was ready to!

Seeing Quick Deer stumble and fall made Kendra rush on even faster. When she reached him she dropped to her knees and lifted his face from the ground where he had purposely burrowed it out of fear of whomever was in pursuit of him.

"Quick Deer. It's me. Kendra," she reassured him. "I'm sorry I frightened you."

Quick Deer's eyes opened with a start. When he saw Kendra smiling down at him he wrapped his arms about her waist and sighed. "Ma'am Kendra. I'm so glad it's you," he murmured. "If anyone else would've caught me at the window I could've been in lots of trouble."

Kendra leaned her face down onto the stiff bristles of his dark hair. She patted his back affectionately. "Yes. It's only me," she whispered. "I'm here. And no one is going to scold you just for looking in a school window."

"Me thought maybe to see you, Ma'am Kendra. That's why Quick Deer came. To see you."

"Quick Deer, I've told you that I'm not a schoolteacher. I'm not supposed to be there."

"You were, that one other time," he softly argued.

"I also explained why, Quick Deer," she said. "I was only there to see if all the school supplies were in place. That's all."

"Why haven't you returned to the village, Ma'am Kendra?" Quick Deer asked. He pulled away from her and eyed her with wide, trusting eyes. "You said you'd come. You were going to teach us to read."

Kendra touched his cheek gently. "Much sadness has entered my life, Quick Deer," she murmured. "This is why I had to place Quick Deer from my mind. But you've never been out of my heart."

"Quick Deer sorry you've been sad," he said, lowering his eyes.

"And, Quick Deer, how is your leg?"

Quick Deer stretched his copper-colored bare leg out before him. He ran his tiny fingers over it. "Quick Deer well enough to ride pony, so Quick Deer well enough to do *any*thing."

Kendra laughed. She rose from her knees. "Good," she said. "I'm glad. And that means you are well enough to go with me to visit the teacher and students in the schoolhouse, aren't you?"

"Quick Deer . . . inside . . . schoolhouse?" he whispered, rising slowly to his feet.

"Yes," Kendra said. "Quick Deer inside schoolhouse." She reached a hand to him. "Come on. I'll take you."

Quick Deer frowned. He began shaking his head slowly back and forth. "No. Me no go," he murmured. "Indians not allowed in white man's school."

Kendra went to Quick Deer and forced one of his hands inside hers. "We will see about that," she said

423

stubbornly. She tugged at him, but he refused to budge.

"Come on, Quick Deer . . ." she sighed.

"Me get in trouble . . ."

"No. You won't. I'll be with you."

She could feel him pulling against her as she coaxed him forward. But she kept urging him onward until they were at the open door with many eyes turned and staring unbelievingly toward them.

With her head tilted stubbornly, Kendra met Steven Teague's questioning glance, then half pulled Quick Deer further into the room. Ignoring the whisperings being exchanged between boys and girls on each side of her, Kendra moved with Quick Deer to the front of the room.

Steven Teague removed his spectacles and took a quick step toward Kendra. "What *are* you doing, Kendra?" he whispered harshly. He gave Quick Deer a lifted-eyebrow look, then once more questioned Kendra with his eyes.

Kendra placed her hands firmly on Quick Deer's shoulders and faced him toward the class. "Children, this is Quick Deer," she said firmly. "He is of the Piute Indians. Please make him feel welcome. He's been wanting to visit you all for some time now."

Steven inched his tall, thin figure next to Kendra. He leaned over and whispered into her ear. "Kendra, why are you doing this foolish thing? You're disturbing my class. Please take the Indian boy and go."

Kendra cupped a hand and whispered back. "I thought you were different, Steven," she said. "I thought you were kind. Not thoughtless."

Steven shifted nervously from one foot to the other. His face flushed. He looked awkwardly from Kendra to Quick Deer. "This just isn't proper, Kendra," he said. "You know that Indians are *not* allowed to participate in our school's activities."

"And, Steven, what could it hurt?"

"Life is governed by set rules," Steven argued back. "I *never* break the rules. Now get the Indian out of here."

"You're despicable," Kendra fumed. "You're a *bore*."

"Just get him out of here, Kendra."

A looming shadow appeared suddenly at the door at the back of the room. Kendra's heart fluttered when she saw the silhouette was undeniably Lucas's. She watched as he stepped into the room and took wide strides toward them and jerked Quick Deer to his side.

"What do you think you're doing, Kendra?" he asked.

"Quick Deer was peeking into the window," she murmured. "I thought he deserved better than that. I decided to bring him inside to introduce him to the students."

Lucas placed his back to the class. "Didn't you realize the harm you could inflict by doing that?" he asked in a lower murmur.

"Lucas, I didn't mean . . ."

"Until the question is settled about schooling for the Indians, all that is directed toward them is ridicule," he argued. He looked across his shoulder at the smug looks on the children's faces. He nodded toward them. "Take one look, Kendra. What do you see?"

Kendra moved her eyes slowly from face to face. She didn't see acceptance or friendship ready to be offered Quick Deer. "I'm sorry, Lucas," she whispered. She looked with a sad longing at Quick Deer.

"We must go. Now," Lucas growled.

Kendra gave Steven Teague an angry, displeased frown, then followed Lucas from the building. She sighed deeply with relief when they were once again out in the fresh air. She pulled her hat more securely in place, then untied Domino's reins and swung herself up into the saddle. She followed along behind Lucas as he led Quick Deer to his pony, alongside of which he had secured his own horse.

"Lucas, I thought I was helping Quick Deer," Kendra murmured.

Lucas lifted Quick Deer onto his pony's back. He gave Kendra a sideways glance. "I'm sorry for doubting your intentions," he said hoarsely. "But I just had to get Quick Deer out of there. He had no business being there. If I hadn't happened along, no telling what could have happened."

"It's all so unfair," Kendra sighed. "Why does the color of the skin make such a difference?"

"The color of skin will always make a difference," Lucas said.

"As it did during the war, Lucas?" Kendra tested, cautiously. She watched a bit of color flame his cheeks.

Lucas swung into his saddle. "I'd like to return Quick Deer to the village," he said, ignoring her reference to the war. "It's still early in the day. You'd have time to travel with us, Kendra, if you'd like."

Quick Deer hastily spoke. "Please, Ma'am Kendra? You *did* promise."

"I'd love to," she murmured. "The past several days have been hard."

"And Aaron?" Lucas questioned. "I imagine he's already out on the range, searching out my fences."

"Aaron has more problems than just those you've caused him," Kendra said. She clucked to Domino and rode next to Lucas, who rode between her and Quick Deer.

426

"Aaron's stubbornness is Aaron's main problem," Lucas grumbled.

Kendra tossed her head angrily. "Listen to you," she said. "You're the one who chose to go against everyone's wishes. You're the one who brought the sheep in."

"After seeing the sheep, I had thought you felt differently about them."

Kendra's eyes wavered. "Lucas, please," she murmured. "I don't care to get into this again. I need to think about less challenging things today. I've so much on my mind."

She cast her eyes downward. "It's going to take a long time for me to get over Seth's death," she whispered.

"But time does heal all hurts," Lucas tried to reassure her.

"I hope you're right, Lucas," Kendra sighed.

As they rode from a canyon pass, Kendra looked quickly into the distant sky where smoke was blackening the horizon. "Lucas . . . ?" she said softly. "Do you see the . . . ?"

"Smoke," he said, before she had a chance to.

"What could be . . . ?" Kendra murmured, leaning a bit forward in her saddle. She cupped a hand over her eyes and squinted against the sun's fiery rays.

"I know of nothing in that direction," Lucas scowled. He lifted his hat from his head and scratched his furrowed brow.

"There are a few stray homesteaders living in that region," Kendra said.

"Yeah," Lucas said, placing his hat firmly on his head. "You're right. I forgot about them. I did run across a few while I was setting up fence posts."

"You think you own the whole range, don't you?"

Kendra said dryly. Then her voice weakened as her eyes lowered. "Sorry, Lucas," she murmured. "I only say these things because of Aaron. But you know that."

Lucas drew his horse to a halt, tensing when he saw more black smoke billowing into the sky. "I don't like it," he said. "I'd best check this out."

"I want to go with you," Kendra said, tightening her hold on her reins as Domino began acting skittish.

"No. You'd best not," Lucas said. He directed his gaze to Quick Deer. "Quick Deer, you go on ahead to the village. Don't stop for anything or anyone. Do you hear?"

Quick Deer nodded his head. "Yes, sir," he said. He looked questioningly toward Kendra. "Ma'am Kendra, are you going to village with me?"

Kendra wheeled her horse around as Domino snorted and pawed at the ground. "Quick Deer, I'm going with Lucas," she said. "Someone may be in trouble. Maybe I can help. You remember how I helped you. I may be able to help someone else."

"Kendra, I don't want you to go with me," Lucas argued. "Who knows what I'm going to come across. It has to be a raging fire to put out such intense smoke."

"I *am* going," Kendra said stubbornly. She nudged Domino with her knees and clucked to him, racing away from Lucas. When she heard him close behind her she bent lower in the saddle and yelled even more loudly to Domino.

She kept riding at the fast, steady pace, until she began to smell the strong stench of charred wood. The smoke suddenly made a dark screen, one Kendra had to force her way through. Her eyes burned and her nostrils flared. She coughed and wiped at her eyes. Then there was a break in the smoke and she was able to see from where the smoke had been surfacing. She placed a hand to her mouth, feeling a bitterness rising inside her throat. She closed her eyes and turned her head quickly away, feeling a completely sick feeling overcome her.

"God," Lucas gasped as he drew rein to her side. "Who could have done this?"

Tears were rolling from Kendra's eyes. She shook her head back and forth. "It's so terrible, Lucas," she whispered. "They've been massacred."

Lucas helped Kendra from her horse. "Darling, you stand back while I check this out," he murmured. "I've got to see if . . ."

"They're dead . . . ?" she whispered.

"Well, there's hardly any doubt of that," he mumbled. "But I *do* have to check."

Kendra glanced toward the charred ruins of the house and outbuilding, the slaughtered cow, horse, and goat. Then she forced herself to once more look toward the bodies lying on the ground, almost choking from the gory scene laid out before her.

"Do you know who this might be, Kendra?" Lucas asked hoarsely, as he also surveyed the scene.

"I haven't any idea," she murmured, wiping tears from her eyes. Then she grew cold inside. The discovery had been too shocking for her to look more closely at the bodies. But now that she was, she could see the stubs that had at one time been legs, and, next to it, the charred remains of what had most surely been Johnny Lassiter's wheelchair.

Kendra's insides twisted; she teetered a bit. She grabbed for Domino and leaned against him. Then, after finally composing herself, she frantically reached for

Lucas's arm. "Lucas, I *do* know these people," she whispered, her eyes burning as the tears were once more there, flowing freely.

"You *do?*"

She gulped back a growing knot in her throat. "The man served with Aaron during the war," she murmured. "I didn't recognize him . . . right . . . away. Without a scalp . . . and with . . . all that blood . . ."

Lucas drew her into his arms. He hugged her tightly to him. "I know this is a nightmare for you, darling."

"Lucas, it can't be the Piute Indians who did this terrible thing, can it?"

"Nor the Shoshonee or the Washoe," he stated flatly.

"But the arrows," she whispered. "The scalp? That's the way of the Indians. Not the white man."

"Darling, didn't you notice that the woman's scalp had not been taken?"

"Hazel," she sobbed. "That's Johnny's wife."

Kendra's heart sank. She was suddenly reminded of Aaron. This would devastate him! Oh, why did so much sadness have to happen? She had heard that all misfortunes came in three's. Well, it seemed true enough for Aaron. First Seth . . . then Holly's infidelity discovered . . . and now the loss of his friends, Johnny and Hazel. . . .

"No Indian would massacre a family, scalp the man, and leave the woman's hair intact," Lucas grumbled. He eyed the outstretched female's body. Her hair was spread out around her head in its bright reds, with blood seeping onto it from an inflicted head wound. By the way her dress was hiked up about her waist and her legs outspread, it was obvious that she had been raped. Lucas had to wonder if this vile deed had been done before or after she had been slain.

"Then *who*, Lucas?" Kendra whispered. "Who could have done such a thing?"

"It appears to be an act of vengeance," Lucas mumbled. "Someone who had possibly had a run-in with the dead man. Someone who most surely hated him."

"Who could hate someone *this* much?"

"A man's mind can cause him to do crazy things, Kendra," Lucas said, drawing away from her. He lifted a hand to her cheek. "Now will you be all right while I check things out?"

"The Indians are going to be blamed, Lucas."

"Not if I have a say in the matter," he said flatly. "And I *will*. You'd best believe that. You see, whoever *is* responsible has purposely done this in this way, to make it look as though the Indians *were* responsible. That's all the Indians need. More trouble. Just as the legislature is finally hearing their pleas for justice."

"But . . . who . . . ?" Kendra murmured.

"I will find the one responsible and personally see to it that justice is done, all right," Lucas said. "I'll personally swing the rope over a tree limb." He strode off.

Kendra shuddered violently as she watched Lucas kneel over Johnny's body. Tears once more swelled in her eyes, remembering his kindness. Had it not been for Johnny, Zeke would have . . .

Kendra's eyes widened and her throat became suddenly dry. "Zeke . . ." she whispered. "Zeke threatened Johnny." Once more a strange coldness rippled through her. She began slowly shaking her head. "No," she whispered. "Surely not. Not just because Johnny stopped him from raping . . ."

Kendra's icy gaze went toward Hazel's outstretched

body, watching as Lucas gently lowered the skirt of her dress over her nudity. "Raped . . ." she whispered. "Hazel was raped."

She closed her eyes and gritted her teeth. Could Zeke have . . . ? Was he truly such an evil person? Had she too been in danger these past weeks since Zeke's departure?

"He could have done the same to me," she thought further to herself.

Then she forced her eyes open and laughed awkwardly. Here she was condemning a man who must surely be innocent, and who most surely was in California by now, or maybe even in New York State, stirring up his trouble there.

The smoke cleared some more. The sun began to shine through in a hazy sort of mist. Kendra coughed to clear her throat and wiped at her eyes, breathing easier now. When she again slowly looked around her, something twinkling back at her from a thick stand of grass drew her attention. Bending, she reached for the object and gasped loudly when she discovered what it was.

"A spur," she whispered. "Someone has lost a spur from his boot."

She placed it in her outstretched hand and studied it, growing numb inside. It wasn't just a spur . . . just anybody's spur! It was Zeke's Spanish spur. It had to be! She had never seen anyone in this area wear anything similar. She had hated its loud jangle, yet it *had* always warned her that he was near, hadn't it?

Feeling a deep hatred, she wrapped her fingers about the spur and glanced toward Lucas. "Lucas . . ." she said tremulously. "I've found somethng."

Lucas rose from his knees and walked toward her. He

432

pushed his hat back from his brow. "What is it?" he asked, then took the spur from her hand. "Oh. It's only a spur."

Kendra doubled her fists to her side. "Lucas," she said from between clenched teeth. "That's not only *a* spur. It's Zeke's. The head wrangler Aaron recently fired."

Lucas studied the spur, then Kendra. "Hon, there are many spurs worn in this Nevada region," he sighed. "Most cowhands wear spurs. Why on earth would you single this man named Zeke out from all the rest?"

"Lucas, study that spur in your hand, then look at yours," Kendra said flatly. "You will see quite a difference."

"I don't have to do that, Kendra," Lucas said dryly. "This is a Spanish spur. Are you saying that this Zeke fellow always wore Spanish spurs?"

"Always."

"But, Kendra, *many* cowhands wear Spanish spurs," Lucas said, shaking his head. "We can't blame this on any one man until we have more proof. And there *has* to be a motive. Why on earth would this Zeke want to harm this family?"

Kendra lowered her eyes. "Because Johnny . . . this man who lies terribly murdered . . . stopped Zeke from . . . from raping me," she managed to say, hating to say the words. She hadn't wanted to speak the word *rape* to anyone . . . much less to the man she loved.

Lucas's face colored a splotchy red. "What?" he gasped. "Kendra, are you saying . . . ?" Was this what she had meant the day she had angrily spoken of rape?

"Yes," she murmured. "Not long ago. I was swimming, you know, where you and I . . ."

"And this man Zeke . . . ?"

"He invaded my privacy. He was in the process of trying to rape me with Johnny appeared and stopped him."

Rage lined Lucas's face with angry, dark shadows. "Damn," he growled. "Damn, damn . . ."

Kendra went to him and twined her arms about his neck and placed her cheek on his chest. "Darling, oh, darling, if it hadn't been for Johnny . . ." she said, then lifted her eyes to Lucas's. "I know this was done by Zeke. He threatened Johnny. He's mean enough, Lucas. I just know he's mean enough. And when Aaron fired him that made him get even meaner. I know it was him."

"Well, it will be the last time he'll have the opportunity to do anything like this," Lucas growled.

"What are you going to do?"

"Go after him."

"We must return to the ranch and tell Aaron," Kendra said, pulling free from Lucas.

"I don't need Aaron," Lucas said flatly.

"He will want to help find Zeke," Kendra said softly. "You see, as I said before, Johnny and Hazel were important to Aaron. He will have the need to seek his own type of revenge. You must include him. You must."

"He won't want me to join in," Lucas grumbled. "You know how he feels about me."

"At times like this such feelings are surely forgotten."

"Well, they have to be, Kendra," Lucas said flatly. "I have *two* reasons to hunt this man down. To clear the name of the Indians and to get the man who tried to violate you."

"The third reason should be for Johnny and Hazel, Lucas," Kendra murmured.

"Above all else, for them," Lucas said, touching her

434

softly on her cheek. "But for now, Kendra, I must do something quite unpleasant. I'm sure you won't want to watch."

"What . . . must . . . you do . . . ?"

"I believe we must take the bodies with us. To see to it that they get a decent burial in Reno," Lucas said, eyeing the dead bodies, feeling an even stronger hate as each minute passed. "I will place them on the back of my horse. You may want to ride on ahead and tell Aaron that I'm coming."

Then he quickly shook his head. "No. You can't do that. Zeke may be out there waiting for you. You'll have to stay with me."

"I would be all right, Lucas," Kendra said stubbornly. "You do forget that I carry six-shooters."

Lucas nodded toward the house, then at the bodies. "And I'm sure your brother's friends had more than one gun in the house for protection," he growled. "It didn't help them any, did it?"

"No," she murmured. "It didn't."

"Then you do as I say," Lucas said flatly. "This one time you *will* do as I say, Kendra. Your stubborn streak won't do you one damn bit of good this time."

"All right, Lucas," she humbly said. "But I surely must help you."

"No, darling," he said. "You just go stand by Domino. I'll take care of it."

"All right."

She stood silently by as he took the saddle blankets from both their horses and carefully wrapped the bodies inside them. And when they were slung across the back of Lucas's horse and tied securely in place, only then did Kendra mount Domino and ride away from the scene of death. She wouldn't look Lucas's way for fear of seeing the wrapped bodies. It was hard to envision the delicate Hazel and the gentle Johnny Lassiter inside the blankets. They had only a short time ago been living, breathing, laughing, loving. . . .

A deep sob tore from inside Kendra, suddenly realizing that life was too short to waste another moment of it. She let her gaze slowly move to Lucas. When he looked her way, she could see a sadness etched in the gray depths of his eyes and knew that he must be feeling the same.

"I love you," she murmured. "Oh, Lucas, I love you so."

"And I you," he said.

Kendra straightened her back and focused her eyes ahead of her, dreading having to tell Aaron what had happened. She could remember the looks exchanged between Aaron and Hazel. She had realized very quickly that there had been more between them than what they would ever admit to. Just how would he take this?

"How much more can he stand?" she thought sadly to herself. "He's only one man, and one man can take only so much pressure."

The rest of the trip was made in silence. And when the Circle C Ranch came into view, Kendra's eyes wavered and her heart pounded nervously against her ribs. She could see Aaron in the corrals where his men were working with some wild mustangs.

Aaron's bald head shone beneath the bright rays of the sun and his thick shoulders were cording as he rode his horse with a rope in his right hand, ready to throw it over the wild mustang's head. He seemed to be taking his anger and frustration out on the horse. And when he roped the mustang and everyone cheered and let out loud

436

whoops of laughter, Kendra saw the look of pride cross Aaron's face. For a moment, he was happy again. For a moment, he had forgotten. . . .

"Kendra, maybe it's best for you to go ahead now, tell Aaron first, before I ride in with the bodies," Lucas said, drawing rein beside her.

Kendra removed her hat and smoothed some damp perspiration-streaked strands of hair from her brow. "Yes," she murmured. "I'm sure you're right."

She held her hat on her lap with one hand and the reins with the other as she rode on away from Lucas. She wished she didn't have this chore to do . . . but better she than Lucas. One look at Lucas and Aaron could have gone into a fit of anger before Lucas even had the chance to talk.

But yet . . . there were the bodies. They would probably be cause for silence . . . a strained silence.

"No matter," Kendra sighed. "It is best this way. Maybe Aaron will take it better if I tell him."

"Kendra!" Aaron shouted, riding his horse to the corral fence. He lifted a corner of his neckerchief up to wipe sweat from his face. "I got him! The wildest mustang we've ever brought back to the Circle C. Did you see?"

Kendra looked back over her shoulder, seeing that Lucas had stepped his horse back behind the barn. Then she directed a nervous smile toward Aaron as she drew rein opposite the fence from him. "Aaron . . ." she murmured. "That's nice."

Aaron's broad smile lessened as he saw the pain in her eyes. "Kendra? What's the matter?" he asked, leaning closer, over the fence. "You look as though you've seen a ghost. Did a snake spook Domino?"

"No," she stammered, lowering her eyes. "Nothing like that."

"Then what?"

"Aaron," she said, raising her eyes to meet his studious stare. "I've something . . . something terrible to tell you."

"What? What's happened?" he asked dryly.

"While I was out on the range I happened onto a terrible, terrible thing," she murmured, clearing her throat nervously. How could she tell him? It was the same as living Seth's death over again, having to tell Aaron of other loved ones having died. It gnawed at her insides, inflicting a raw pain, one that she thought might never end.

"Kendra, what on earth are you talking about?" Aaron said, stiffening in his saddle.

Kendra's shoulders slouched. She shook her head slowly. "Oh, Aaron, how can I find the words . . . ?" she whispered.

"Who . . . ?" Aaron said, his eyes moving slowly from Kendra to the approaching figure in the saddle.

Soft, slow hoofbeats behind Kendra made her aware that Lucas had seen her dilemma and had decided to come out in the open . . . to let Aaron see. . . .

Kendra inched Domino on away from the fence, letting Lucas's horse take Domino's place.

"Aaron, we found Johnny Lassiter and his wife Hazel," Lucas said thickly. "They didn't have a chance. They were dead when we . . . when Kendra and I . . . found them."

Aaron swayed in his saddle and began seeing double as things began swimming in his head. He grasped onto the saddlehorn of his saddle and swallowed back a heavy, growing lump in his throat. Then he composed himself and rode straight-backed from the corral and around to where Lucas sat with the bodies.

Kendra dismounted and went to Aaron and took his arm as he slowly moved from his saddle. "Aaron, I'm so sorry," she murmured.

"I've got to see," Aaron whispered, walking toward the wrapped bodies.

Kendra tugged at his arm. "No, Aaron . . ."

But Aaron was already lifting the blanket from one body. He flinched and jerked quickly away, covering his mouth with a hand. "God," he gasped. "Who would . . . do . . . such a . . . thing . . . ?"

"It was Zeke," Kendra whispered. "I found his Spanish spur close to the bodies. I know it was his. He's the one, Aaron."

"Zeke . . ." Aaron growled. He set his jaw firmly and looked squint-eyed toward Lucas. "And you say Kendra was with you . . . ?"

"You'd better be glad she *was*," Lucas growled right back. "She's probably the next on this madman's list of vengeance. It's not safe for Kendra to be *any*where alone."

Aaron took a step back toward the horse and slowly threw the blanket back over the exposed face of Hazel. His eyes burned and his throat tightened. Their times together had been sweet . . . but so short. Why did life continue to be so unfair to him?

He then lifted a corner of the blanket away from Johnny's face. He blanched and turned his eyes in another direction. Then he stepped quickly away from everyone and leaned his head down and retched until he felt as though he didn't have another thing left in his stomach. Then he swung around, fists clenched, and faced Lucas.

"It had to be Indians," he shouted. "This man's been scalped!"

"It's meant to look as though an Indian did it," Lucas said dryly. "It's to turn suspicion away from the guilty party."

"You only say this because you protect the Indians," Aaron accused.

"You had to notice that Hazel Lassiter's hair was very much intact," Lucas said. "No Indian would leave a beautiful head of hair like that if they were truly out for scalps."

"Maybe the Indians were frightened away."

"Indians do not frighten so easily," Lucas insisted. "And if an Indian chooses, for whatever reason, to take only one scalp, the Indian would have chosen the woman's hair over the man's. No, Aaron. This is *not* the work of Indians. It is the work of a crazed man . . . this Zeke you once employed on your ranch. He had a run-in with Johnny. Kendra said that he had threatened Johnny."

Aaron smoothed a hand over the baldness of his head and lowered his eyes. "Zeke," he grumbled. "God, Zeke. I had thought him a decent sort. Yes, he seemed a decent sort until that incident with Kendra."

"Aaron, Hazel was . . . raped," Lucas mumbled. "She wasn't just murdered. She was raped by that animal."

A low growl rose from deep inside Aaron. He walked stiffly toward his horse. "Bring the bodies into the barn," he said. "We will see that they are taken to Reno for a proper burial. But later. For now we have a job to do, don't we, Lucas?"

"We . . . ?" Lucas asked, tipping his hat back from his brow.

"I'm afraid it's going to take more than the men in my employ to round up the murdering sonofabitch," Aaron shouted. "You go to your ranch, get your men, and start searchin' on your end. My men and I will start combing the territory on *this* end."

"So you want to work together on this?" Lucas said, leaning up in his saddle.

"At times like this everyone should stick together. I'm sure you agree."

"Wholeheartedly."

Aaron turned to Kendra. "Now, Kendra, you stay put. You get in the house and don't go *any*where," he ordered. "I'm giving you an order this time. I'm not askin'. I'm *tellin'*. You go in and wait. We'll be back as soon as we can. Then we're goin' to have us a hanging."

Kendra pulled her hat more firmly onto her head. "I'm *not* staying here, Aaron," she argued. "I have as much right as any man to go searching for Zeke."

"Kendra, it isn't safe," Aaron growled. "The only safe place for you is here. I won't take no for an answer. You will *stay*."

"Aaron . . . ?" Kendra pleaded.

Lucas dismounted and went to her side. "Kendra, what Aaron is saying is right," he said. He clasped her shoulders. "Remember what I said about that stubborn streak. You'd best forget that side of your character until we have this thing cleared up. Seems Zeke has turned into some sort of maniac."

Kendra blinked her heavy lashes upward at Lucas. "Lucas, I can ride as well as the men," she said softly. "I can shoot. You know I am capable of taking care of

441

myself. I could even ride with you. We could ride side by side. I don't want to stay here."

"It's best," Lucas said flatly. He leaned a kiss to the tip of her nose. "And did you see?" he whispered. "Aaron wanted me along. Maybe this is a beginning for us. Maybe he will reconsider about the sheep once this thing is behind us."

"It's too bad that it took two deaths to soften Aaron up," she murmured. She swung her arms about Lucas's neck and kissed him swiftly, then moved away from him. "All right," she said. "I'll stay. But, please hurry. I'll be waiting."

After getting Zeke's full description and helping Aaron into the barn with the bodies, Lucas swung himself up into his saddle, tipped his hat to Kendra, and rode away.

Kendra moved slowly to the house and stood in the doorway as she watched Aaron and his men ride away in the opposite direction. Suddenly she felt too alone. . . .

Chapter Twenty-Four

Kendra leaned her back against the side of her wooden tub and closed her eyes. The bubbles from her bath were clinging to her breasts, sparkling in shining blues and purples as the light from the window settled onto them. She lifted her hair from her shoulders and let it fall back again. It seemed a bath was necessary. Only it could remove the stench of death from her skin. But nothing could erase it from her thoughts. The death scene was etched onto her brain as surely as a leaf fossilized onto a stone.

She shivered involuntarily at the thought of Johnny and Hazel wrapped in blankets, waiting for their proper burial.

"They were both so young," she whispered. "It shouldn't have happened."

Tears burned at the corners of her eyes. She had begun to feel responsible for this tragedy. If she hadn't been at the watering hole alone . . . if she hadn't so stubbornly continued to travel alone out on the range, then Zeke wouldn't have had the opportunity to take advantage of

443

her aloneness. And if Zeke hadn't been there, ready to rape her that day, then Johnny wouldn't have had to become involved.

Shaking her head, she whispered, "I am at fault. I know I am."

A creaking of the floorboards outside her bedroom door was cause for Kendra's eyes to fly wide open. She had checked on Holly and Emanuelle and they had both been napping. And it wouldn't be Aaron. He wouldn't have found Zeke this quickly. And if it had been Aaron, Kendra would have heard Aaron's men return with him.

Another creaking drew Kendra quickly from the tub. Dripping water across the floor, she went to her wardrobe and pulled a robe quickly on. She eyed her pistols. The gunbelt was hanging over a chair, out of reach. She took a quick step toward them, then stopped in midstep when her bedroom door burst suddenly open.

Kendra's heart went wild with fright when she saw Zeke standing there sneering at her, pointing a revolver in her direction.

"Zeke . . ." she whispered, paling.

"Watched Aaron ride out," Zeke said, stepping into the room. He kicked the door shut with his boot.

Kendra noticed that his Spanish spurs were missing. Her suspicions were confirmed. "You were here all along," she hissed. "You were just waiting for me to be alone."

"I've had plenty of chances 'fore now," he laughed. "I've kept an eye on you. But I knew if I waited long enough I'd have you just where I'd want you."

"And here . . . now . . . in my bedroom . . . is what you've waited for?" she dared with flashing eyes. She glared at him as he moved closer to her. His red whiskers and sideburns were thicker and more unkempt than in the past. It appeared that he had been living in the rough, because his tight-fitted jeans and red flannel shirt were covered with a layer of dust and his sombrero and the red bandana at his throat were sweat-stained.

Zeke chuckled amusedly, using the barrel of his revolver to push his sombrero up from his brow. "Cain't think of a better place than in a bed," he said. "Now, kin you?"

"I won't let you, Zeke," Kendra hissed, taking a quick glance at her pistols. She began to inch toward them sideways.

In two wide strides, Zeke had Kendra by the wrist. "Don't try it," he growled. He flung her roughly on the bed. "Take off the robe. I've waited long enough."

"I'll claw your eyes out if you try it, Zeke," Kendra said from between clenched teeth.

"Then maybe I'll have to tie you to the bed," he snarled. "Is that gonna be necessary, Kendra? Or are you gonna decide to cooperate?"

"Never," she hissed, creeping back on the bed. "I'll fight you to the end, you murdering, no-good . . ."

Zeke lunged onto the bed, kneeling down over her. He placed the revolver to her abdomen. "Just shut up," he growled. "And I told you to take that damn robe off."

In one quick movement of his left hand he had her robe pulled open. He chuckled and placed a hand to her breast. "Hot and soft," he said. "Just the way I like 'em."

Kendra cringed, feeling the rough coarseness of his fingers. She eyed the gun, then the dark pits of his eyes, remembering Hazel and Johnny. If he had shot them . . . then what would keep him from shooting her? She had to try to get away from him. She couldn't let him rape her.

She would rather die first!

As he was caught up in a building passion, fondling and kneading her breast, Kendra quickly raised her hand and knocked his gun away. And with his being off guard as he was, she was able to make a fist and hit him in the jaw and lift a knee hard into his groin.

When he rose away from her, yowling, Kendra stumbled off the bed and rushed to where her pistols hung and grabbed one from a holster. With trembling fingers she pointed the gun toward Zeke, who was too quickly composing himself, and aimed.

Placing a finger to the trigger of her pistol, Kendra felt consumed by heartbeats, then turned her head as she began to squeeze. . . .

Gunfire quickly erupted in the room. Kendra jerked her head quickly around and watched Zeke grab at his chest and crumple to the floor. Puzzled, Kendra looked toward the barrel of her pistol. There was no sign of smoke, and her finger had yet to pull the trigger.

"How . . . ?" she whispered.

A movement behind her made her turn with a start. She dropped her pistol to her side and watched wide-eyed as Lucas came through the bedroom door toward her, repositioning his spent revolver into his holster.

"Lucas!" she gasped. "Did you . . . ?"

"Yeah. I shot the bastard," he growled. He clasped her shoulders and eyed the gaping gown, seeing the velvet pink of her skin. "Was he about to . . . ?"

Kendra placed her pistol on the bed and fell into his arms, now breathless from the ordeal. "Yes," she murmured. "He was. But I did my best to stop him." She placed her cheek on his chest and drank in his closeness.

He caressed her back with his powerful hands,

chuckling. "Seems your best was mighty damn good," he said. "But, Kendra, seems I beat you to the draw. I'm the one who can brag of plugging him."

Kendra looked up into his gray eyes. "You can tease at a time like this?" she snapped. "Lucas, I was almost raped. A man lies dead in my bedroom. How can you make fun of it?"

Lucas traced her features with his forefinger. "Darling, I'm not making fun," he murmured. "I'm just so damn glad I got back here in time."

"Lucas, how did you know to?"

"It just didn't seem right leaving you here alone. It seemed a bit too risky leaving you unguarded in this big house," he said. "It just made sense that Zeke would try something like this. So the more I thought about it, the more I was convinced that I'd best check the house and grounds thoroughly before headin' on out."

"So you circled back . . . ?"

"That I did."

The sound of hoofbeats drew Kendra to the bedroom window. She pulled aside a curtain and looked down. "Why, it's Aaron," she said. "I wonder why he . . . ?"

Lucas laughed softly. "He probably returned for the same reason I did," he said. "Seems you got two men lookin' out for you, darling."

Kendra turned slowly around, shuddering when her gaze fell on Zeke. A pool of blood stretched out beneath him and his dark eyes were staring lifelessly ahead. "He *was* the one who killed Johnny and Hazel," she said. "His Spanish spurs are missing. And his coming here, threatening to rape and kill me, are even more proof."

Lucas stepped over Zeke and pulled Kendra's robe closed. "He won't be bothering anyone else, darling," he said hoarsely. He placed an arm about her waist. "Come on. Let's go meet Aaron."

"Maybe this will be the end of all our nightmares," Kendra whispered.

She leaned into Lucas's embrace as they moved toward the door. As they began to step across the threshold, Aaron appeared at the door with fists doubled at his side. He glared from Kendra to Lucas.

"So this is what I find on my return home," he growled. "I had thought to maybe find Zeke here, sneaking around, but, instead, I find you two taking advantage of my absence."

Aaron's gaze raked over Kendra, taking in her attire. He shook his head slowly back and forth. "Kendra, you disappoint me," he murmured. "Have you no respect . . . ?"

Lucas stepped between Aaron and Kendra. His face was red with building rage. "You're going to eat those words," he growled. "Don't you know Kendra better than that?"

"I suppose not," Aaron argued. "What *are* you doing here, Lucas, if not for what it appears?"

"I circled back for the same reason you did. And it's a good thing I did." He gestured with an arm. "Take a look inside Kendra's room, then see if you still condemn her or me."

Aaron's eyebrows lifted quizzically. "What are you . . . ?"

He took one step into the room and immediately saw. He removed his hat and ran his fingers over his bald head. "Well, I'll be damned . . ." he murmured, paling. Then he swung around and faced Lucas with wavering eyes. "You . . . ?"

"Yes," Lucas nodded. "I shot him."

Aaron's gaze moved slowly to Kendra, apology etched across his face. In two wide strides he had her in his arms. He burrowed his face into her shoulder. "God, Kendra," he said thickly. "Hon, I'm so sorry. I didn't mean all that I said. I didn't know." He hugged her tightly.

She hugged him back. "I know," she whispered. "You've been through so much, Aaron. It's only natural that you'd not be thinking so clearly."

Aaron drew away from her, holding her hands. He raked his eyes over her, feeling cold inside. If she was in a robe, then she had to have been when Zeke . . . "Did he . . . ?" he murmured.

"He tried," she whispered.

"But, he didn't . . . ?"

"No, Aaron. He didn't get the chance," she again whispered.

Aaron's gaze moved to Lucas. He now realized that he owed him. He had saved Kendra from . . . he closed his eyes and shook his head, not wanting to think of what might have happened if Lucas Hall hadn't been there.

Slowly he raised his hand to Lucas and looked directly into those gray eyes of his past. "I must apologize and thank you at the same time," Aaron said. He saw Lucas eye the hand being offered, then slowly raise his own hand and clasp it tightly to Aaron's.

"Accepted," Lucas said, smiling. Then he chuckled as he gave Kendra a proud, lingering look. "But I think Kendra was taking care of the problem quite well on her own before my arrival on the scene."

Aaron's eyebrows lifted. "Oh?" he said. "And how is that?" He gave Lucas's hand one more shake, then eased his own hand away.

"She had Zeke at a disadvantage," Lucas said, drawing Kendra next to him. He circled his arm about her waist. "If I hadn't shot him, she would have. She had her pistol drawn and ready to shoot when I entered the room."

"Well, I'll be damned . . ." Aaron said, kneading his chin.

Kendra sighed heavily, looking from Aaron to Lucas. "I've told you both, over and over again, that I could take care of myself," she said. "You just wouldn't listen."

A slow smile lifted Aaron's lips, and then he broke into a fit of laughter, joined by Lucas. Kendra stepped away from them both with her hands on her hips. "What do you find so funny?" she snapped.

Aaron wiped at his eyes. "Kendra, the change in you," he said. "In Boston, you were such a genteel lady, flitting around in lace and silk. And now? You truly *do* know how to defend yourself, don't you? You *can* handle a pistol as well as a man."

Kendra blushed and laughed softly. "I imagine Mother would be quite horrified if she could somehow know how I've learned to behave," she said.

"Yes, I believe so," Aaron said, muffling another laugh behind his hand. Then he sobered and faced Lucas directly. "But it was you, Lucas, who came to Kendra's rescue," he said. "And, for that, I owe you."

"I love Kendra," Lucas said dryly. "I would even die for her. You have to know that, Aaron."

Aaron lifted his hat to his head. He stepped between Lucas and Kendra and placed an arm about each of their waists, urging them toward the staircase. "Yes. I know that now," he said. "Come. After we see to Hazel and Johnny's funeral, just maybe we can sit down and talk about the future. Let's see what we can compromise on.

If you're to be my brother-in-law, we don't want barbed wire coming between us, do we?"

Kendra's heart raced as she glanced first at Aaron, then at Lucas. "The sheep, Aaron?" she murmured. "What about the sheep?"

"I hate sheep," he growled. "But I guess . . . I guess I can learn to live with them. There's lots of grazing land out there to be shared."

Kendra smiled, first to Aaron, then to Lucas, hope glowing brightly inside her. Maybe in time she could forget the tragedies that had brought her brother and the man she loved together, uniting in their love for her. . . .

Chapter Twenty-Five

Lucas was dressed handsomely in a white frock coat
and dark trousers, looking, indeed, the perfect groom.
"The guests are finally gone," he said, closing the door
behind him. He turned and gazed passionately toward
Kendra. "Mrs. Lucas Hall," he whispered. "My darling
wife." He took her outstretched hands and let his eyes
move slowly over her. "You've never looked lovelier."

Kendra smiled and glanced down at her gown. Yards
and yards of white silk fell in heavy gathers from her tiny
waist and were held out away from her by even more
yards of petticoats.

Ruffled lace lined the low-swept bodice, matching the
lace that circled the skirt of her dress. She had piled her
hair high on her head and had placed tiny pink rosebuds
into its folds. Diamonds sparkled at her throat and at her
earlobes, but these in no way matched the sparkle in her
sky-blue eyes.

She slowly lifted her eyes to Lucas and smiled warmly.
"I could have been married in my jeans," she teased.
"Surely you wouldn't have minded, darling."

Lucas laughed amusedly. "Hell, no. I wouldn't have minded," he said. He swooped her up into his arms and held her tightly to him. "I would have married you even if you had worn only a fig leaf."

Kendra's eyes widened. "A . . . fig . . . leaf . . . ?" she said. Then she giggled and twined her arms about his neck as he headed toward the staircase of his mansion. "It was such a lovely wedding, Lucas. And, thank you, darling, for understanding about the mourning period. It wouldn't have been proper to have wed any sooner."

"Two months wasn't too bad," he said. "But I couldn't have waited longer."

"Aaron *is* acting civil toward you now, isn't he?"

"I don't believe we'll ever really care that much for one another," he murmured. "Nothing can change his feelings toward sheep, and I absolutely refuse to remove them from the range."

"Well, at least he's agreed," Kendra sighed.

Lucas chuckled. "Darling, he knew that he had no choice," he said. "From the very first he knew this. The incident with Zeke . . . with me rescuing you . . . well, hon, that gave him a way to back down, to act as though he did so because he owed me. In truth, he did it because he damn well had no other choice."

Kendra felt a slow anger rising inside her. Though she loved Lucas and was now his wife, her loyalty to Aaron . . . to all Carpenters . . . still ran deep. But then she had to remember! She was no longer a Carpenter. She was a Hall! And her loyalties had to lie with her newly given name.

She forced her thoughts elsewhere. As Lucas set his foot on the first step of the staircase, Kendra glanced down the hall and remembered the billiard room. A slow smile lifted her lips. "Lucas, care to take a moment to let me beat you again at pocket billiards?" she teased. "You do know that I have a bit of my father in me. Isn't pocket billiards a form of gambling?"

"Kendra, I have better things on my mind," Lucas murmured. He leaned a kiss to her cheek. "As it should be with you, darling." He eased a hand over one of her breasts and cupped it. "I believe it's time to shed that beautiful gown, don't you?"

Kendra gave him a sideways glance, smiling coyly. "Oh? So I can slip back into my jeans?" she further teased.

Lucas laughed softly and carried her on up the stairs and into his bedroom. The large oak bed had been made up in orchid-colored satin sheets with matching pillowcases, and long-stemmed, tapered candles flickered romantically from various spots in the room.

The strong aroma of roses filled the room from a bouquet placed on a nightstand next to the bed, and on the other nightstand a crystal decanter filled with wine sat next to two tall-stemmed crystal glasses.

"Now, darling, do you honestly believe jeans would be the appropriate attire to wear tonight?" Lucas asked, kissing her softly on the tip of her nose.

Breathless, Kendra let her eyes once more appreciate the way Lucas had chosen to prepare the bedroom for their wedding night. It was so romantic it seemed unreal . . . as though she might have been fantasizing . . . instead of living it.

"It's so lovely," she whispered. "Lucas, it's absolutely breathtaking."

Lucas looked toward the closed, dark draperies and the drab color of the canopy overhanging the bed. "Thank you," he murmured. "But, darling, I do hope that very soon you will put a woman's touch to this room. Make it more *you*. I don't feel the darker colors are for a woman."

"I'd love wallpaper with tiny rosebuds on a white background," she said. She hugged his neck. "Oh, yes, Lucas, I'll have fun doing it."

"Then you'll enjoy playing the role of a wife instead of a gunslinger?"

Kendra giggled. "Yes, yes," she whispered.

"Then let's not waste another moment," Lucas said huskily. "I know the fastest and best way to initiate you into that role."

Kendra looked lovingly at his face, once more enamored by his handsomeness. "And that is . . . ?" she whispered.

"And that is by making love to you, darling. How long has it been now? So much has stood in the way."

"But everything is fine now," she reassured. "The future is ours. All ours."

Lucas eased her from his arms and to the floor. His fingers went to her hair and began slipping pins and rosebuds from it. And as her hair fell loosely to her shoulders, she shook it away, to hang long and lustrously down her back, shining like satin beneath the soft glow of the candles.

"We will spend the full night making love," Lucas whispered huskily. "For tomorrow we must begin our long journey to Washington."

"Do you think the legislature will even listen to you?"

"Yes," he said flatly. "And who else could argue the Indian cause better than I? Yes. They will listen."

Lucas plucked the earrings from her earlobes and dropped them to the floor, then unfastened the necklace and tossed it aside.

"In my things I've brought from my house I have something I want to show you, Lucas," Kendra murmured.

"Not now," Lucas whispered. "Darling, I have to have you. Please undress while I remove my own things." His hands were already busy, first removing his impeccably pressed white frock coat, then the slate-gray cravat at his throat.

"But, Lucas," Kendra softly argued. "I want to show you . . ."

Lucas reached over and placed his forefinger to her lips, sealing her words. "Shh," he said. "Later. We've already spent too much time talking."

"All right, darling," Kendra murmured. Flames of passion were rising inside her, almost scorching her with their intensity. She trembled as she began working her way out of her gown, being caught familiarly under the spell of the command of his gray eyes.

Her heart beat out the moments until they shared their nudity, and, after a few moments of mutual admiration, Lucas reached for her and pulled her body against his.

Kendra stood on tiptoe and twined her arms about his neck, trembling as her breasts made contact with the steel frame of his body. She fit her slender form even more snugly against his, gasping when she felt the hard readiness of his manhood pressed into her abdomen.

Gently his lips lowered to hers and explored her mouth with soft, sensual kisses, while his fingers worked through her hair and forced her mouth even harder against his. His tongue flicked out and teased the soft flesh of her lips. As she parted them and welcomed his tongue inside her mouth, she groaned.

She gave completely in to him as he once more lifted her into his arms. And when he stretched her out on the bed, she reached her arms out to him and welcomed him as he snuggled next to her, pulling her to face him, breast to breast, hip to hip.

His hands began their magic, easing their bodies only inches apart. He took the breath from Kendra as he cupped both breasts. And when he repositioned himself and let his lips devour her breast while his hand lowered to where she ached painfully, yet sweetly, between her thighs, desire for him tore away at her insides.

"Lucas, please," she pleaded. "You're torturing me so. I must have you. Now."

Lucas lowered his lips to her abdomen and kissed her there. "The pleasure is heightened by the waiting," he teased. His fingers continued to work their magic on her breasts, and his lips lowered to touch her where she opened so fully to him. Lucas felt the pounding in his temples and the heat rising higher in his loins.

"But what the hell," he grumbled. "I can wait no longer either, darling."

Slowly, he rose to be above her, eyeing her intently, then lowered himself inside her. Closing his eyes, he moaned. The softness of her . . . the warmth enfolding his sex made waves of rapture wash through him.

Kendra tangled her fingers through his hair, her lips enjoying the tender kisses he was raining upon her mouth, eyelids, and cheeks. Her heart was beginning to race out of control. She arched her hips upward, meeting the sudden demand of his thrusts.

As her senses swam deliciously, the warmth began spreading through Kendra until she felt her spasm of delight match the trembling and arching of Lucas's body, as he also was being sent into a magical world of release.

"Lucas, oh, how I love you," Kendra whispered, kissing the corded muscles of his shoulder. She could feel his skin shudder as her fingers moved across his chest, tangling into the dark fronds of his chest hair.

"And I you, darling," he murmured. He kissed her breasts, worshippingly, one at a time, then rose from the bed.

Kendra's lips formed into a pout. "Where are you going, Lucas?" she asked, rising on one elbow.

"I believe this is a good time for a glass of wine," he said, handing her a glass.

Slowly, she scooted to a sitting position and held the glass steady as he poured the wine. Already drunk with happiness, she watched him as he poured himself a glass and settled back down beside her on the bed.

"We shall drink to our happiness," he said, clinking her glass with his.

"To our happiness," she murmured. She tipped the glass to her lips and sipped slowly from it. Then her eyes widened. "Now I can show you," she said, eagerly climbing from the bed.

She set her glass down on a nightstand and went to a drawer where she had only this afternoon placed some of her nightclothes. She opened it and slipped a necklace from inside it. Carrying it behind her back, she crept back onto the bed beside Lucas. With mischief in her eyes, she slowly pulled the necklace out into the open and placed it about her neck and fastened it in place there.

"Well, I'll be damned," Lucas chuckled. "The squash blossom necklace. I had almost forgotten about it."

"Well, *I* hadn't," she said softly. "How could *you*, Lucas? It was your gift to me after we first met. You were even mysterious about it. You never did tell me its meaning."

"Ah, yes," he sighed. "The meaning."

"I will continue wearing it only if you tell me its meaning," she said stubbornly.

"Yes," he said, tracing the outline of the silver squash blossoms against her throat. "The meaning. I told you there would be a proper time to tell you."

"And? Is this the proper time?"

Lucas kissed her on the tip of the nose, then took a long sip of his wine as his eyes met hers and held. As he lowered the glass from his lips he set it down on the nightstand next to hers. He cupped her chin in his hand.

"The necklace?" he murmured. "The squash blossoms? They are a sign of fertility to the Indians. Whoever wears it will bear many proud children."

"Children?" Kendra whispered.

"Children."

"And from the first . . . when you gave me the necklace . . . you knew . . . ?"

"Yes. I knew for what purpose the necklace was worn," he said. "Yes. I knew. And I gave it to you."

"You had children in mind . . . when you gave me this necklace . . . ?"

"I knew that in time you would be mine," he said, smiling. "And, yes, I would love to have many children with you. I would like especially to see that a son is born from our union. I need that to carry on the name Hall."

"You are the last . . . ?"

"Yes."

Kendra lowered her eyes. "At first I had thought Quick Deer . . ."

He interrupted. "I know."

"And now I understand why Heart Speak was so angry when she saw your choice of gifts to me," she murmured.

"Yes. She had hoped I would marry her," he said. "But I never loved her. And I could never marry unless I truly loved."

Kendra crawled into Lucas's arms. "Darling, I'm so happy," she whispered. "I'm so glad you chose to marry me."

"Whom I even built this house for," he said.

Kendra cuddled next to him, peacefully, happily content. "Yes. My Garden of Eden," she whispered.

"Your what?" he chuckled.

"That first evening that I arrived here, for your dance?"

"Yes . . ."

"I fell in love with the area in which you chose to build the house," she said. "Everything is so plushly green and breathtaking. And the trees? Oh, so beautiful. I immediately thought of the Garden of Eden, as it's described in the Bible. But didn't I tell you this before?"

Lucas nuzzled her neck. "Maybe. Maybe not," he murmured.

"It is no longer my elusive Eden," she whispered. "Nor is it my elusive ecstasy. . . ."

"Your . . . what . . . ?" he queried with a raised eyebrow.

"Nothing," she laughed. "And, Lucas, why *are* we wasting so much time talking? I thought you said that you desired many children. Darling, make love to me again. . . ."

Put a Little Romance in Your Life With
Janelle Taylor

Put a Little Romance in Your Life With
Constance O'Day-Flannery